ANN M. MARTIN

THE BABY-SITTERS CLUB®

STACEY'S MISTAKE

A GRAPHIC NOVEL BY
ELLEN T. CRENSHAW
WITH COLOR BY BRADEN LAMB AND HANK JONES

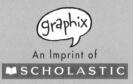

Graphix

An Imprint of
■SCHOLASTIC

Library of Congress Control Number: 2022948053

ISBN 978-1-338-61614-9 (hardcover)
ISBN 978-1-338-61613-2 (paperback)

10 9 8 7 6 5 4 3 2 1   23 24 25 26 27

Printed in China   62
First edition, October 2023

Edited by Cassandra Pelham Fulton and David Levithan
Book design by Shivana Sookdeo
Creative Director: Phil Falco
Publisher: David Saylor

This book is in honor of the birth of my
new godson, Andrew Cleveland Gordon

A. M. M.

For Chris and Erin, my first — and best — baby-sitters.
May our fledgling film series, *The Average Family,*
live forever in legend and infamy.

E. T. C.

KRISTY THOMAS
PRESIDENT

CLAUDIA KISHI
VICE PRESIDENT

MARY ANNE SPIER
SECRETARY

DAWN SCHAFER
TREASURER

JESSI RAMSEY
JUNIOR OFFICER

MALLORY PIKE
JUNIOR OFFICER

STACEY MCGILL
NEW YORK BRANCH

CHAPTER 1

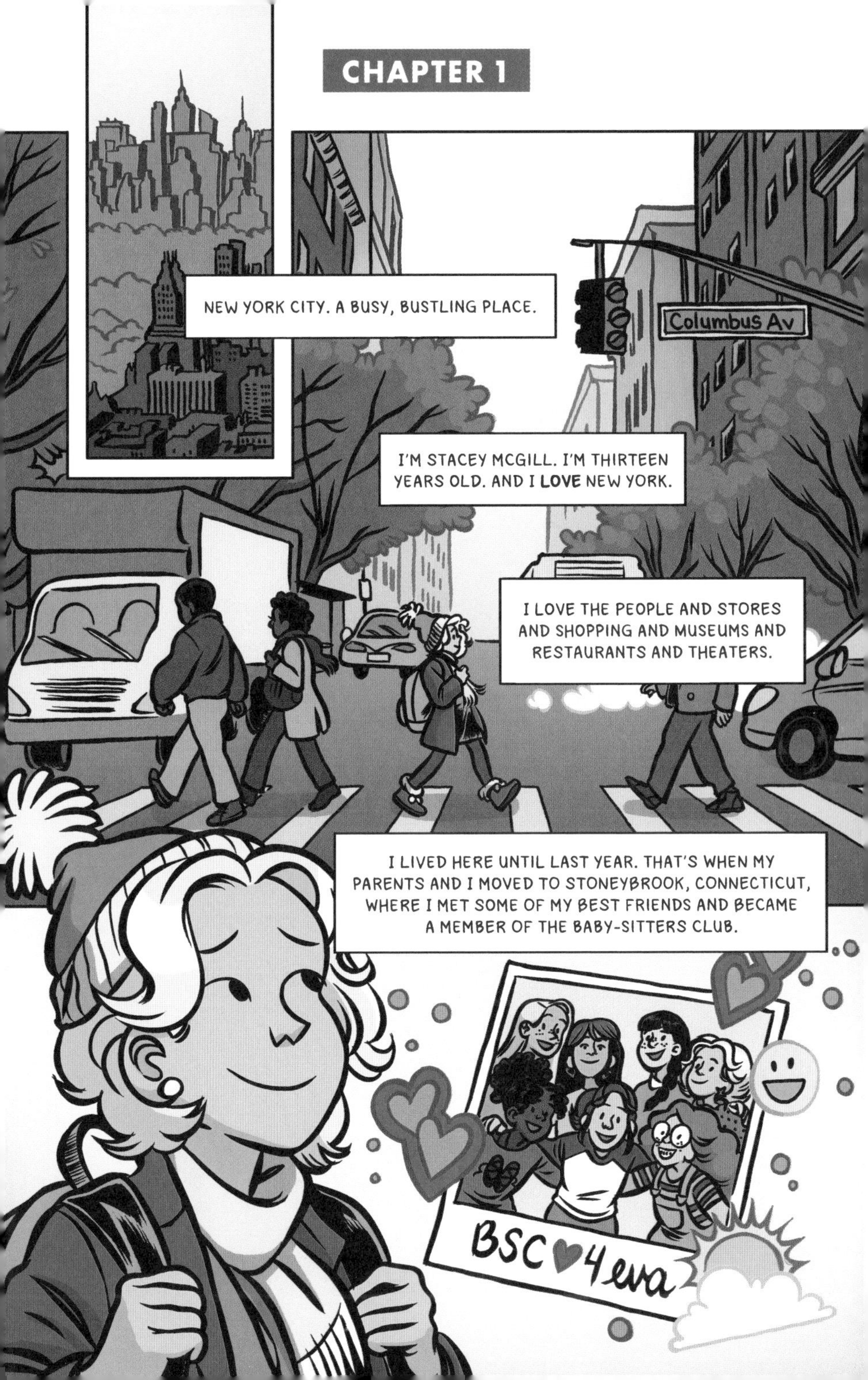
NEW YORK CITY. A BUSY, BUSTLING PLACE.
Columbus Av
I'M STACEY MCGILL. I'M THIRTEEN YEARS OLD. AND I **LOVE** NEW YORK.
I LOVE THE PEOPLE AND STORES AND SHOPPING AND MUSEUMS AND RESTAURANTS AND THEATERS.
I LIVED HERE UNTIL LAST YEAR. THAT'S WHEN MY PARENTS AND I MOVED TO STONEYBROOK, CONNECTICUT, WHERE I MET SOME OF MY BEST FRIENDS AND BECAME A MEMBER OF THE BABY-SITTERS CLUB.
BSC ♥ 4eva

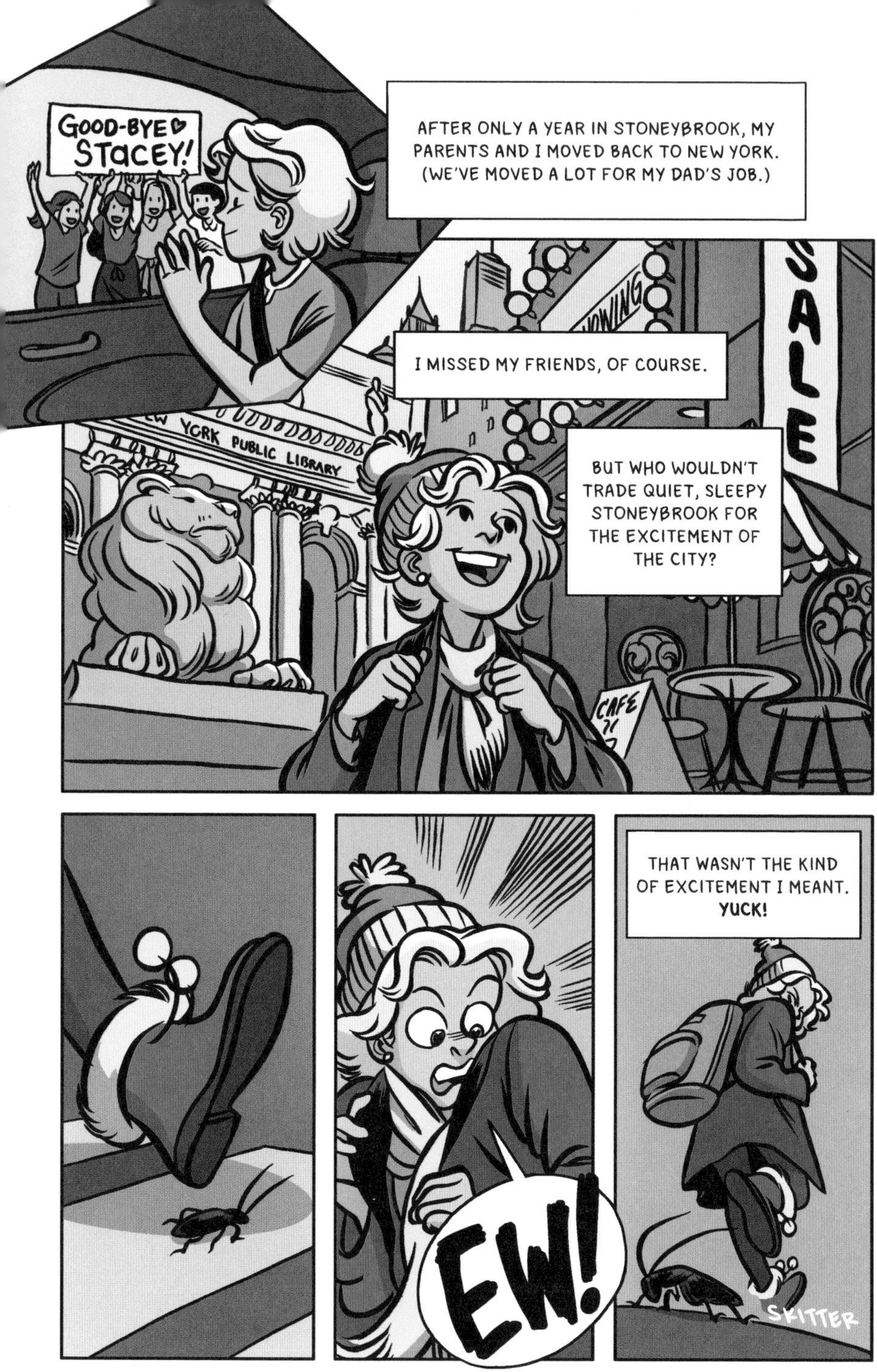
GOOD-BYE STACEY!
AFTER ONLY A YEAR IN STONEYBROOK, MY PARENTS AND I MOVED BACK TO NEW YORK. (WE'VE MOVED A LOT FOR MY DAD'S JOB.)
I MISSED MY FRIENDS, OF COURSE.
YORK PUBLIC LIBRARY
SALE
BUT WHO WOULDN'T TRADE QUIET, SLEEPY STONEYBROOK FOR THE EXCITEMENT OF THE CITY?
CAFE
EW!
THAT WASN'T THE KIND OF EXCITEMENT I MEANT. **YUCK!**
SKITTER

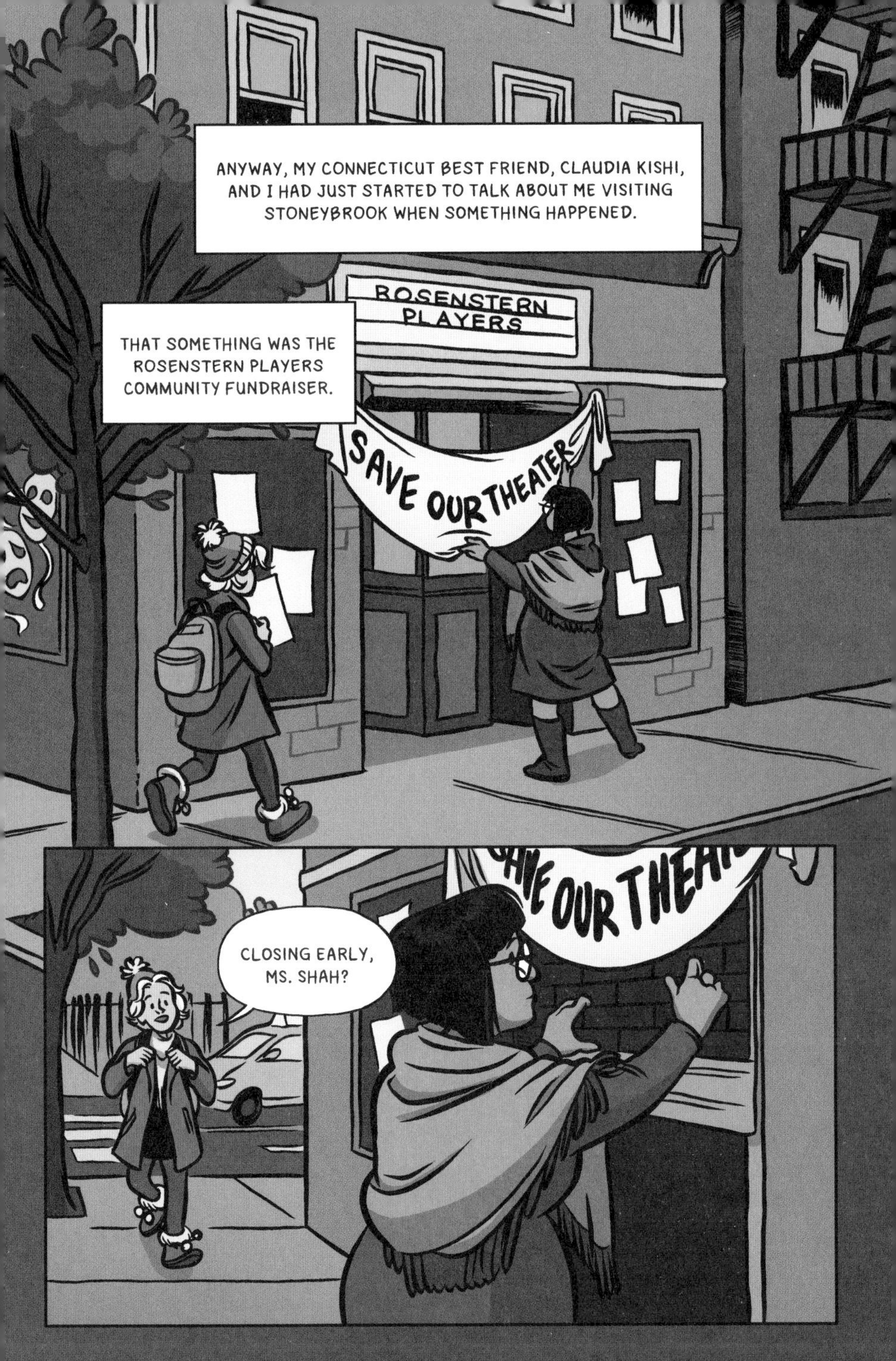
ANYWAY, MY CONNECTICUT BEST FRIEND, CLAUDIA KISHI, AND I HAD JUST STARTED TO TALK ABOUT ME VISITING STONEYBROOK WHEN SOMETHING HAPPENED.
ROSENSTERN PLAYERS
THAT SOMETHING WAS THE ROSENSTERN PLAYERS COMMUNITY FUNDRAISER.
SAVE OUR THEATER
CLOSING EARLY, MS. SHAH?

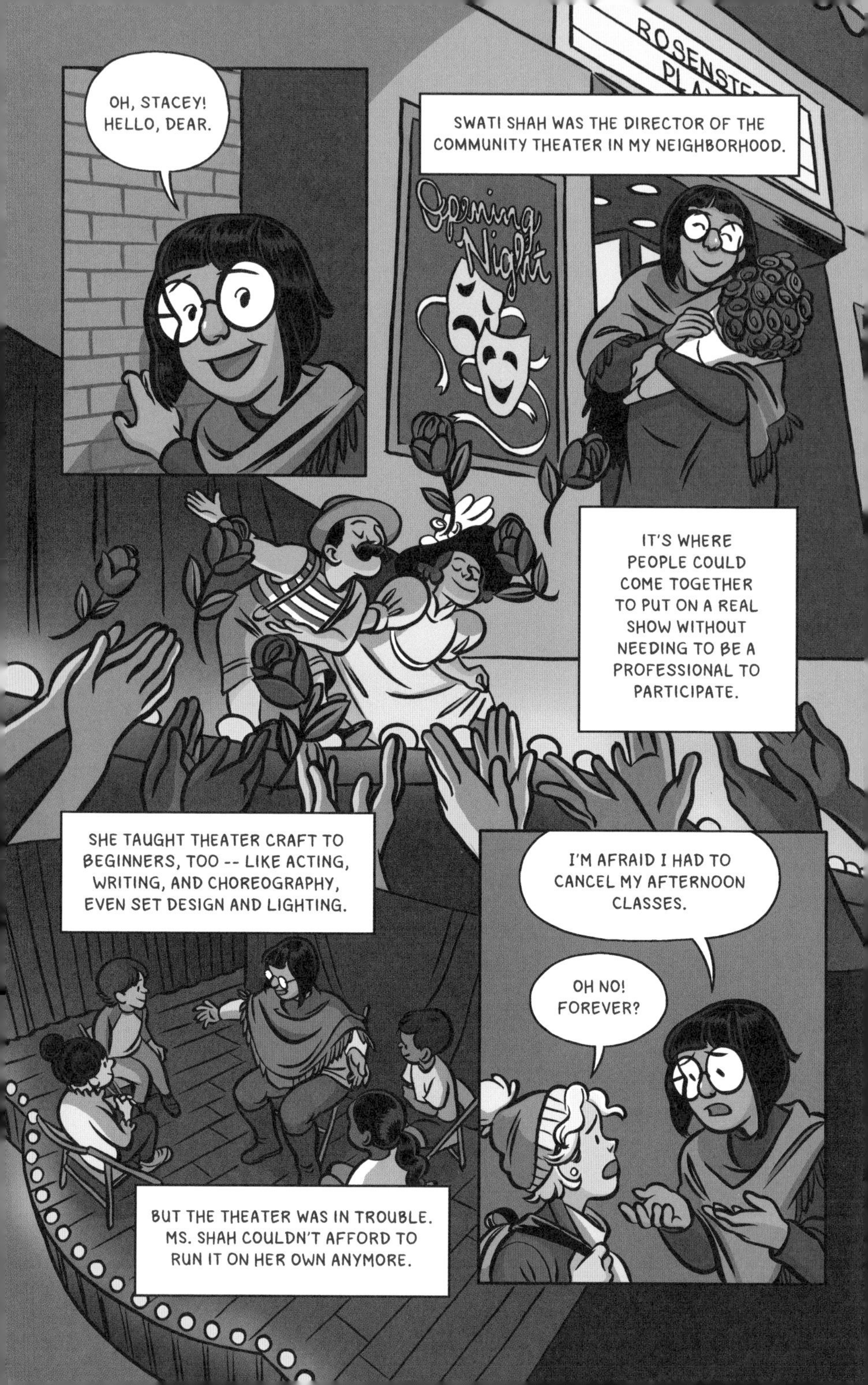
OH, STACEY! HELLO, DEAR.
SWATI SHAH WAS THE DIRECTOR OF THE COMMUNITY THEATER IN MY NEIGHBORHOOD.
Opening Night
IT'S WHERE PEOPLE COULD COME TOGETHER TO PUT ON A REAL SHOW WITHOUT NEEDING TO BE A PROFESSIONAL TO PARTICIPATE.
SHE TAUGHT THEATER CRAFT TO BEGINNERS, TOO -- LIKE ACTING, WRITING, AND CHOREOGRAPHY, EVEN SET DESIGN AND LIGHTING.
BUT THE THEATER WAS IN TROUBLE. MS. SHAH COULDN'T AFFORD TO RUN IT ON HER OWN ANYMORE.
I'M AFRAID I HAD TO CANCEL MY AFTERNOON CLASSES.
OH NO! FOREVER?

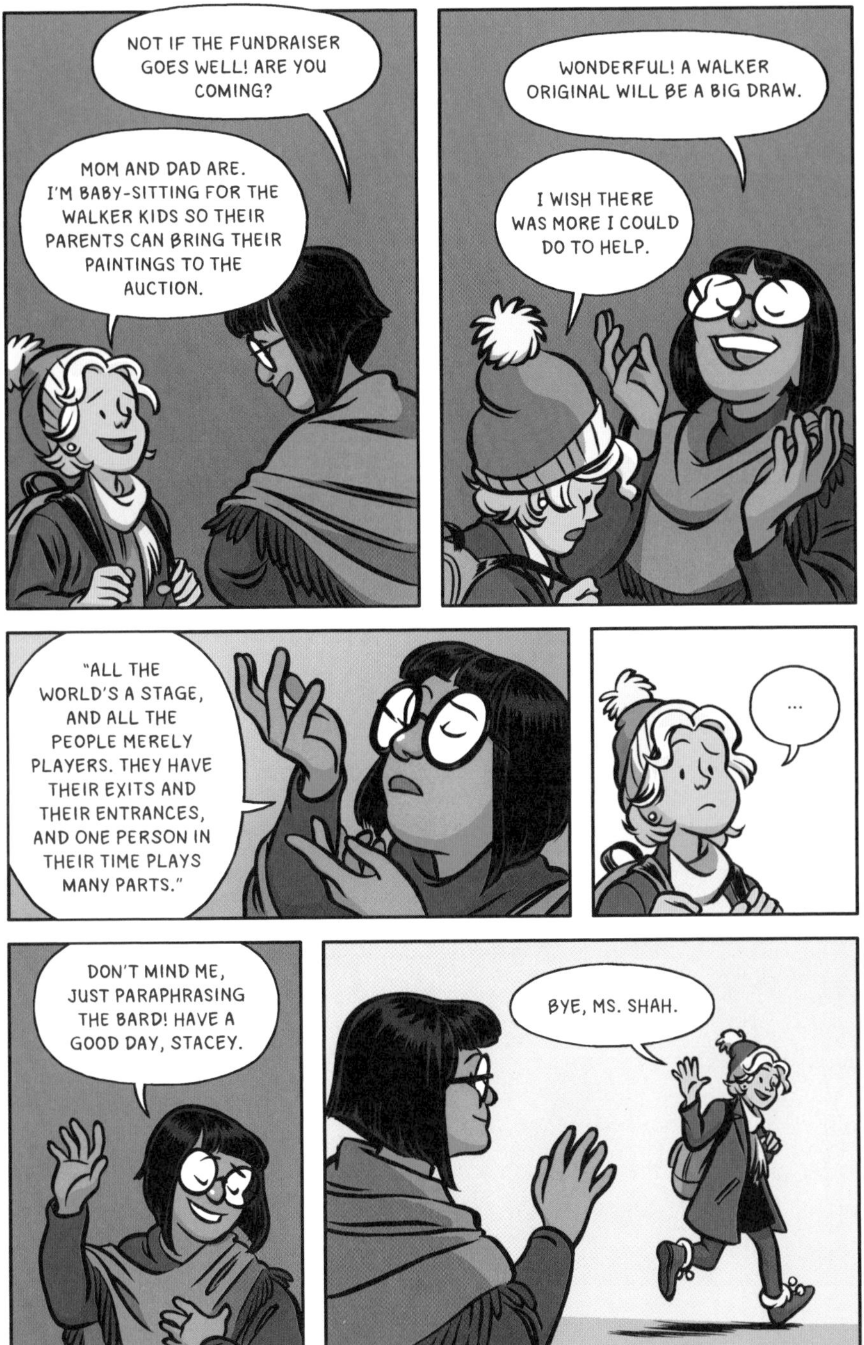
NOT IF THE FUNDRAISER GOES WELL! ARE YOU COMING?
MOM AND DAD ARE. I'M BABY-SITTING FOR THE WALKER KIDS SO THEIR PARENTS CAN BRING THEIR PAINTINGS TO THE AUCTION.
WONDERFUL! A WALKER ORIGINAL WILL BE A BIG DRAW.
I WISH THERE WAS MORE I COULD DO TO HELP.
"ALL THE WORLD'S A STAGE, AND ALL THE PEOPLE MERELY PLAYERS. THEY HAVE THEIR EXITS AND THEIR ENTRANCES, AND ONE PERSON IN THEIR TIME PLAYS MANY PARTS."
...
DON'T MIND ME, JUST PARAPHRASING THE BARD! HAVE A GOOD DAY, STACEY.
BYE, MS. SHAH.

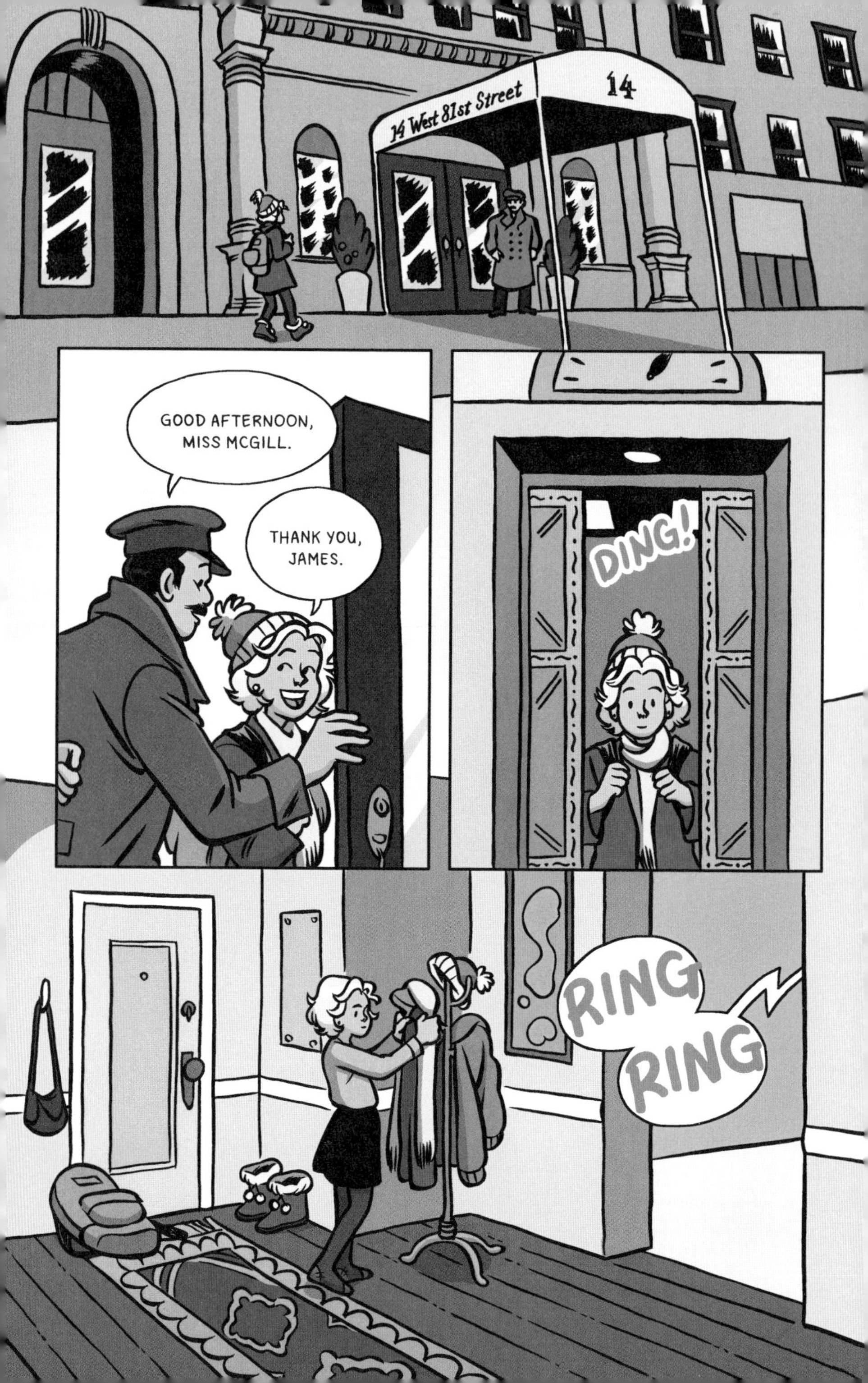
14 West 81st Street
14
GOOD AFTERNOON, MISS MCGILL.
THANK YOU, JAMES.
DING!
RING RING

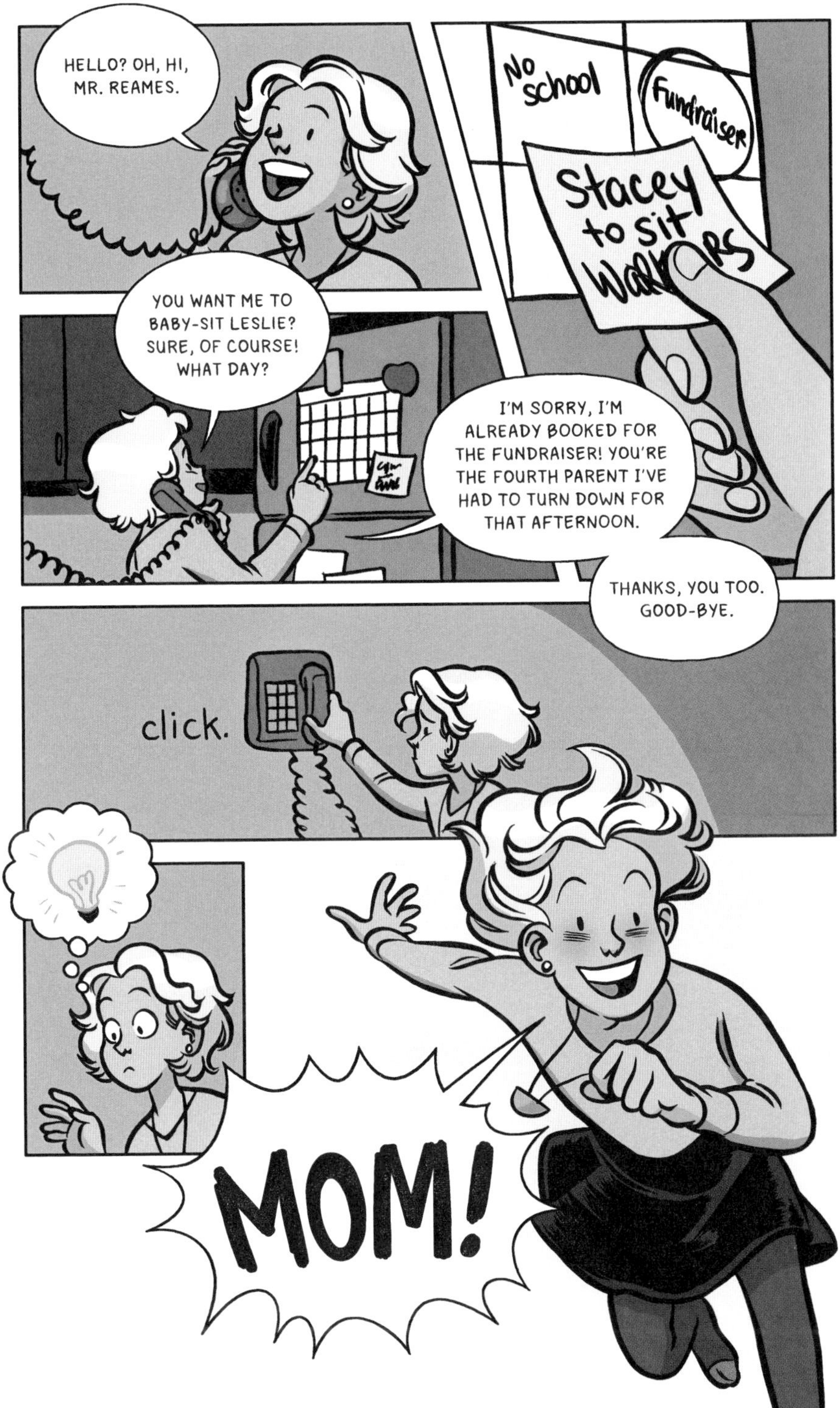
HELLO? OH, HI, MR. REAMES.
No school
Fundraiser
Stacey to sit
YOU WANT ME TO BABY-SIT LESLIE? SURE, OF COURSE! WHAT DAY?
I'M SORRY, I'M ALREADY BOOKED FOR THE FUNDRAISER! YOU'RE THE FOURTH PARENT I'VE HAD TO TURN DOWN FOR THAT AFTERNOON.
THANKS, YOU TOO. GOOD-BYE.
click.
MOM!

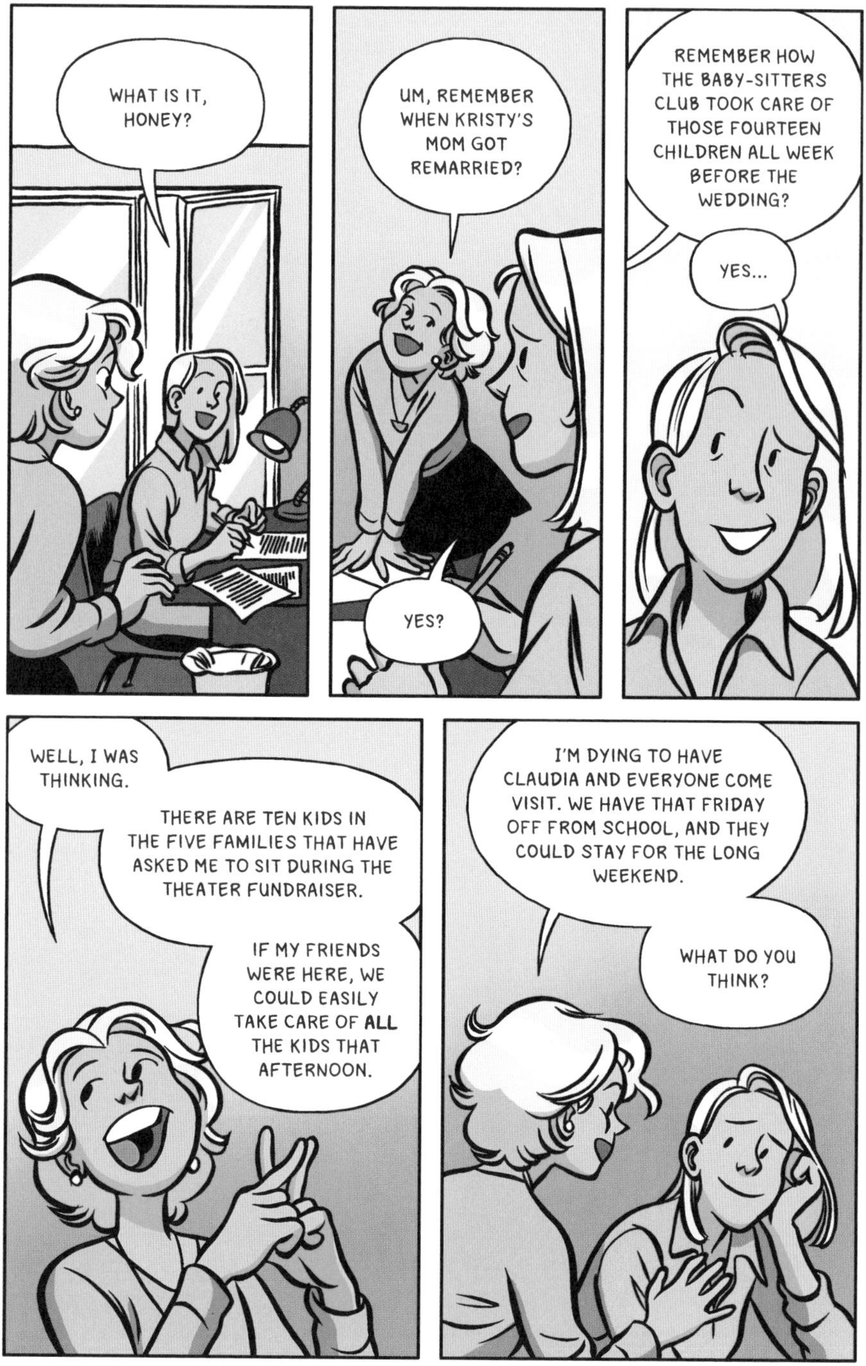

WHAT IS IT, HONEY?
UM, REMEMBER WHEN KRISTY'S MOM GOT REMARRIED?
YES?
REMEMBER HOW THE BABY-SITTERS CLUB TOOK CARE OF THOSE FOURTEEN CHILDREN ALL WEEK BEFORE THE WEDDING?
YES...
WELL, I WAS THINKING.
THERE ARE TEN KIDS IN THE FIVE FAMILIES THAT HAVE ASKED ME TO SIT DURING THE THEATER FUNDRAISER.
IF MY FRIENDS WERE HERE, WE COULD EASILY TAKE CARE OF **ALL** THE KIDS THAT AFTERNOON.
I'M DYING TO HAVE CLAUDIA AND EVERYONE COME VISIT. WE HAVE THAT FRIDAY OFF FROM SCHOOL, AND THEY COULD STAY FOR THE LONG WEEKEND.
WHAT DO YOU THINK?

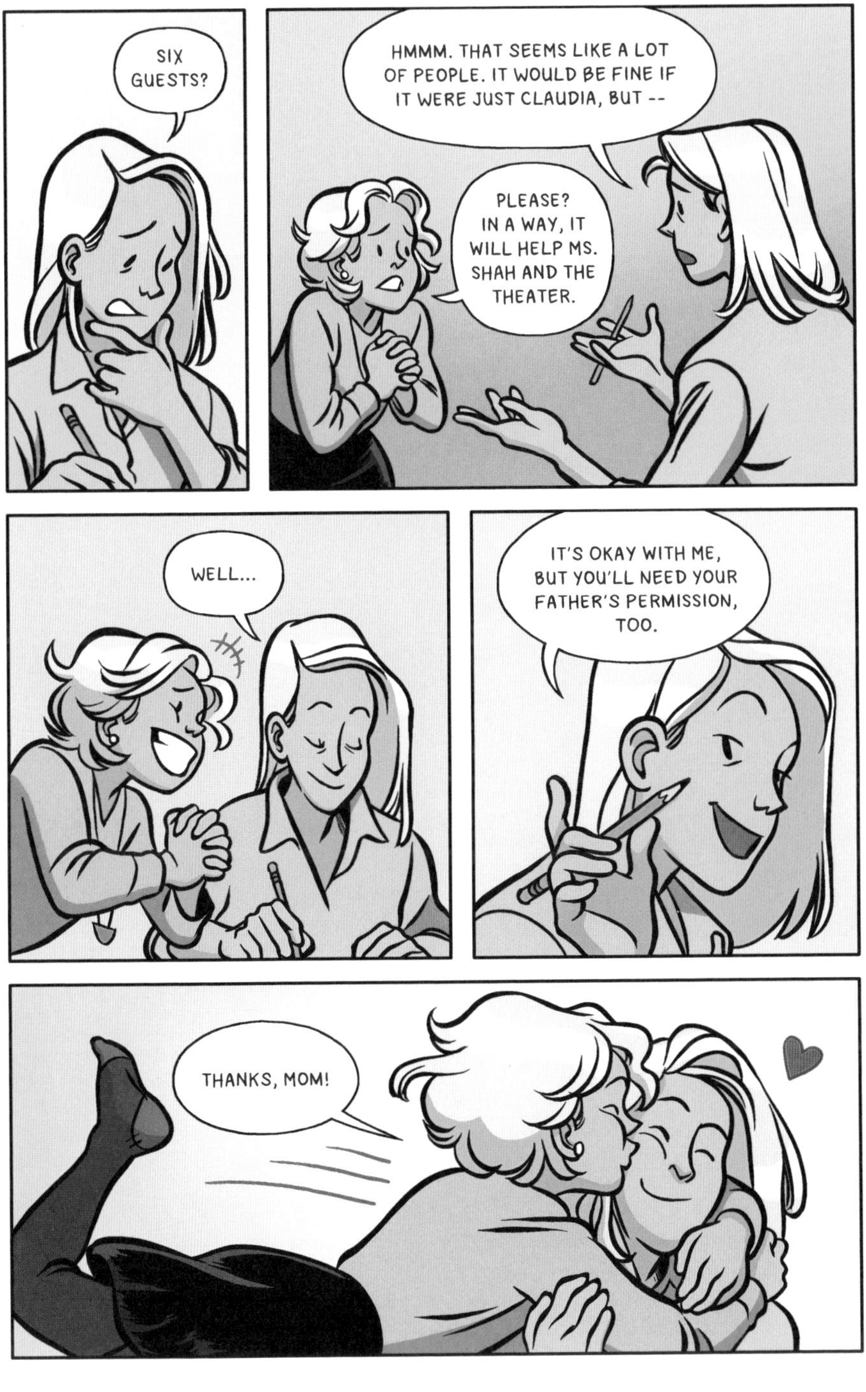
SIX GUESTS?
HMMM. THAT SEEMS LIKE A LOT OF PEOPLE. IT WOULD BE FINE IF IT WERE JUST CLAUDIA, BUT --
PLEASE? IN A WAY, IT WILL HELP MS. SHAH AND THE THEATER.
WELL...
IT'S OKAY WITH ME, BUT YOU'LL NEED YOUR FATHER'S PERMISSION, TOO.
THANKS, MOM!

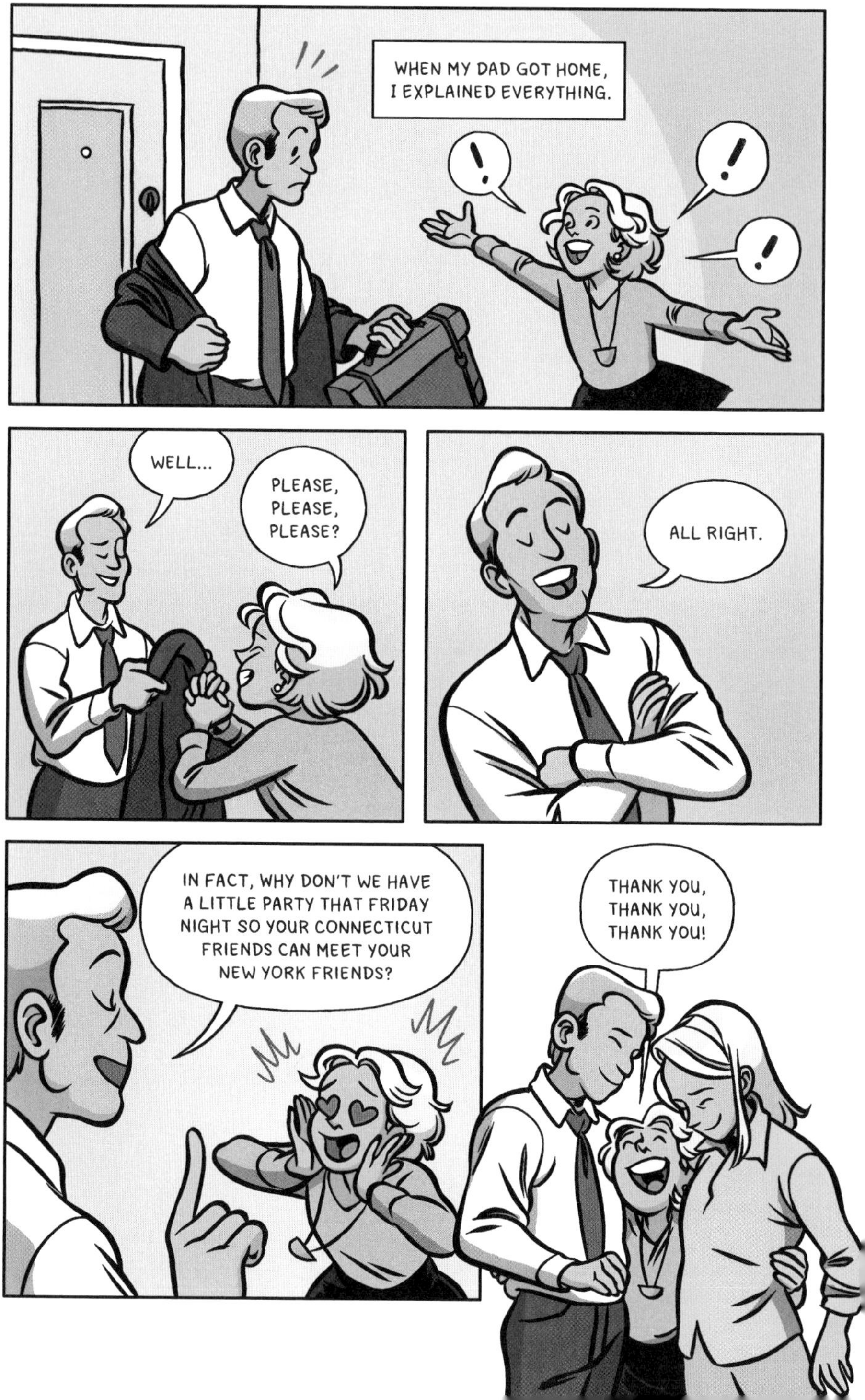
WHEN MY DAD GOT HOME, I EXPLAINED EVERYTHING.
!
!
!
WELL...
PLEASE, PLEASE, PLEASE?
ALL RIGHT.
IN FACT, WHY DON'T WE HAVE A LITTLE PARTY THAT FRIDAY NIGHT SO YOUR CONNECTICUT FRIENDS CAN MEET YOUR NEW YORK FRIENDS?
THANK YOU, THANK YOU, THANK YOU!

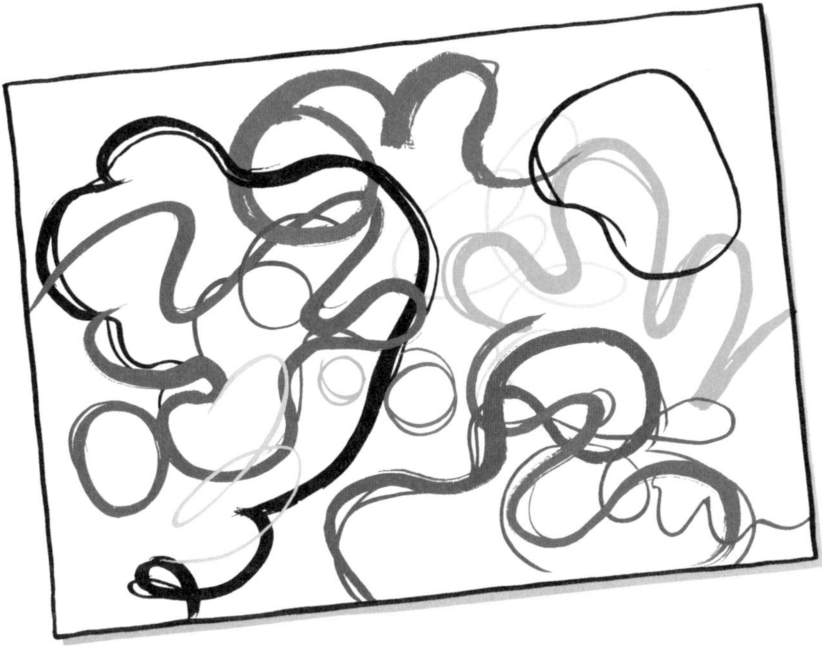
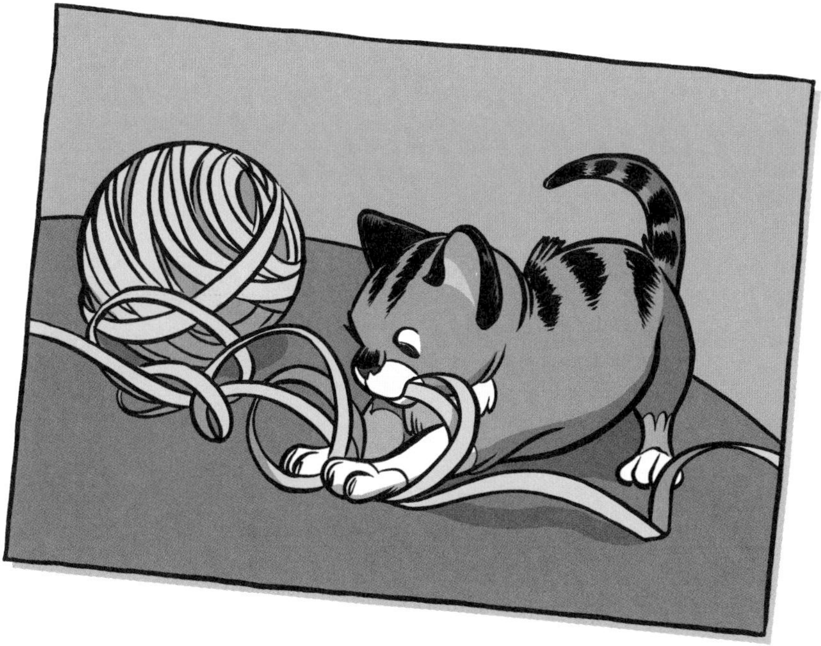

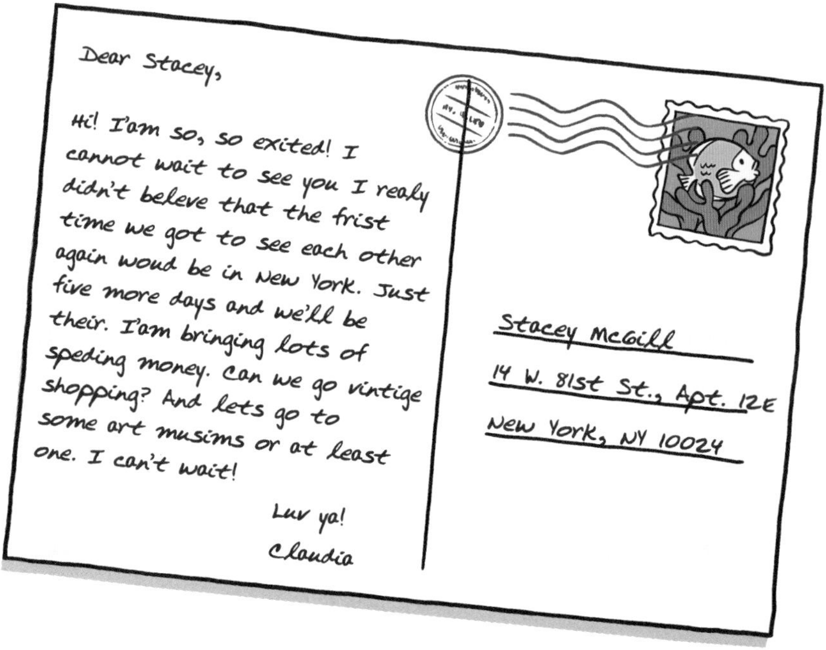
Dear Stacey,
Hi! I'am so, so exited! I cannot wait to see you I realy didn't beleve that the frist time we got to see each other again woud be in New York. Just five more days and we'll be their. I'am bringing lots of speding money. Can we go vintige shopping? And lets go to some art musims or at least one. I can't wait!
Luv ya!
Claudia
Stacey McGill
14 W. 81st St., Apt. 12E
New York, NY 10024

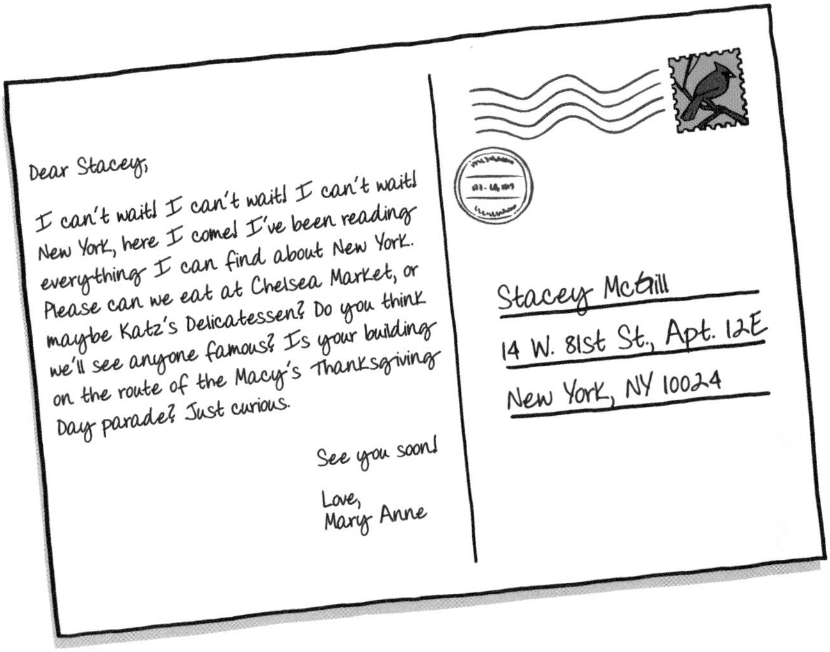
Dear Stacey,
I can't wait! I can't wait! I can't wait! New York, here I come! I've been reading everything I can find about New York. Please can we eat at Chelsea Market, or maybe Katz's Delicatessen? Do you think we'll see anyone famous? Is your building on the route of the Macy's Thanksgiving Day parade? Just curious.
See you soon!
Love,
Mary Anne
Stacey McGill
14 W. 81st St., Apt. 12E
New York, NY 10024

CHAPTER 2

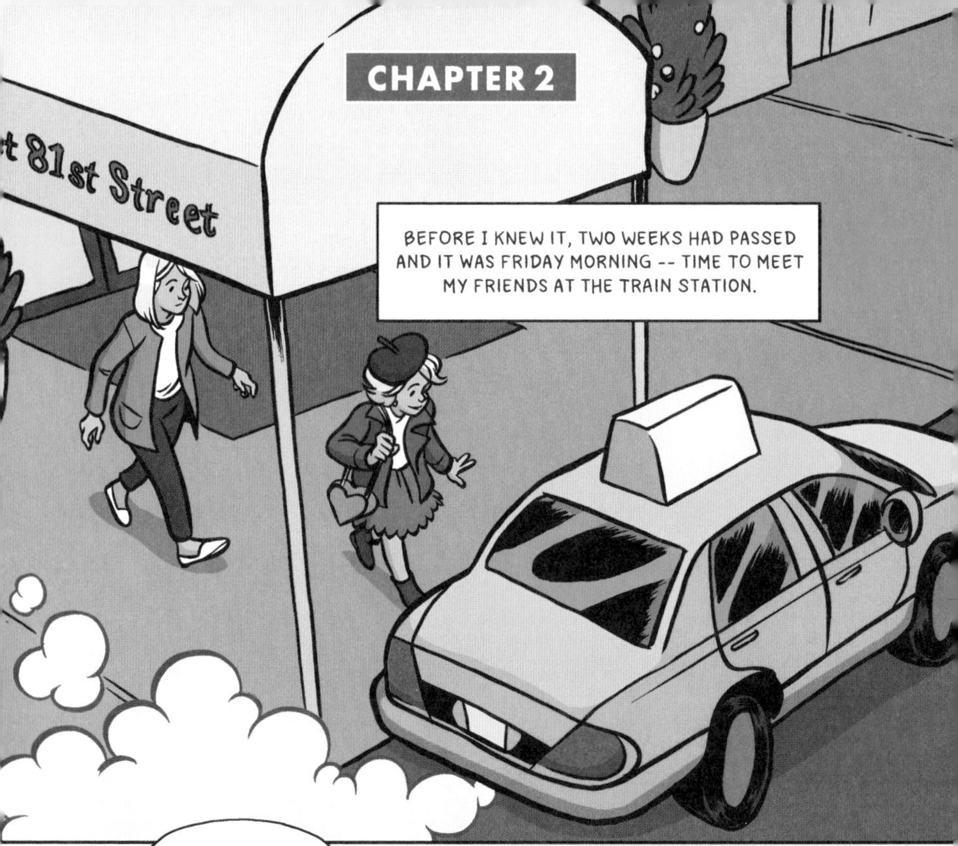
81st Street
BEFORE I KNEW IT, TWO WEEKS HAD PASSED AND IT WAS FRIDAY MORNING -- TIME TO MEET MY FRIENDS AT THE TRAIN STATION.

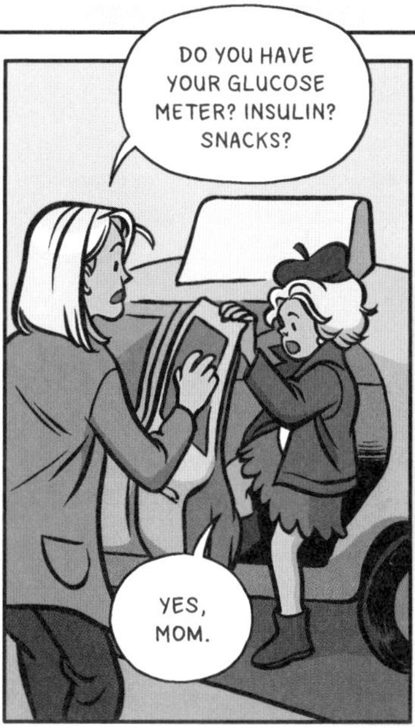
DO YOU HAVE YOUR GLUCOSE METER? INSULIN? SNACKS?
YES, MOM.

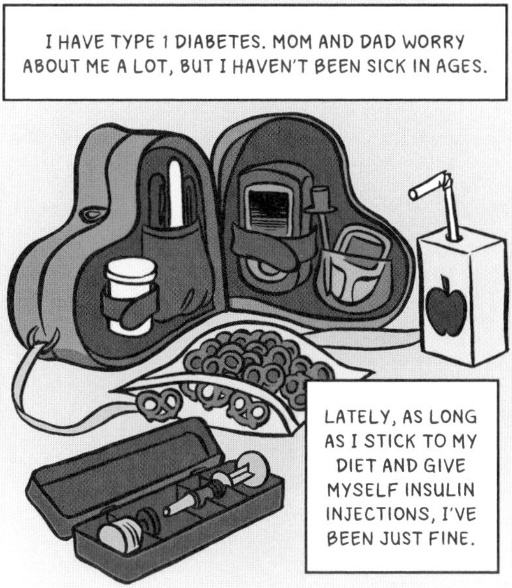
I HAVE TYPE 1 DIABETES. MOM AND DAD WORRY ABOUT ME A LOT, BUT I HAVEN'T BEEN SICK IN AGES.
LATELY, AS LONG AS I STICK TO MY DIET AND GIVE MYSELF INSULIN INJECTIONS, I'VE BEEN JUST FINE.

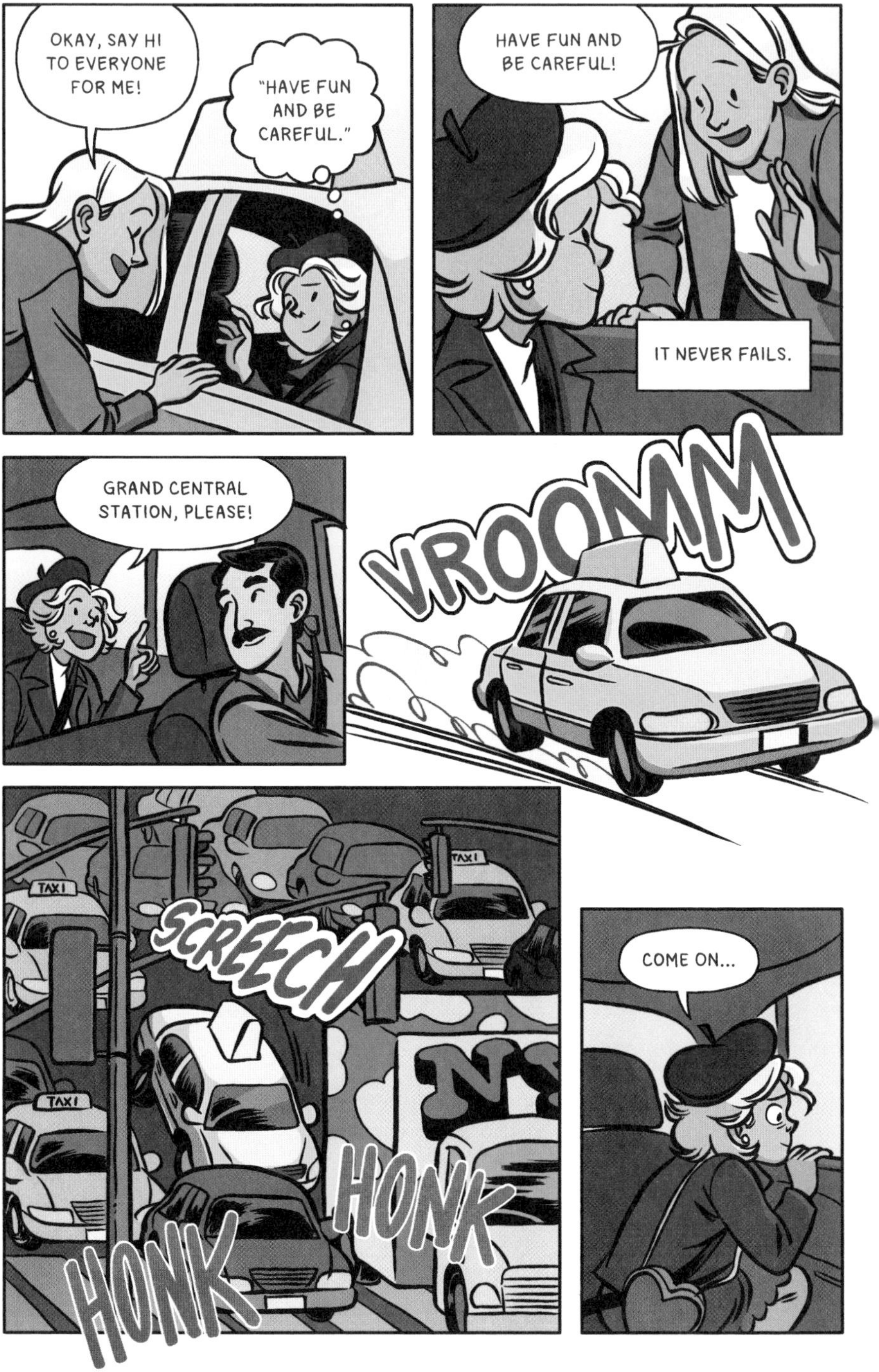
OKAY, SAY HI TO EVERYONE FOR ME!
"HAVE FUN AND BE CAREFUL."
HAVE FUN AND BE CAREFUL!
IT NEVER FAILS.
GRAND CENTRAL STATION, PLEASE!
VROOMM
SCREECH
NY
HONK
HONK
COME ON...

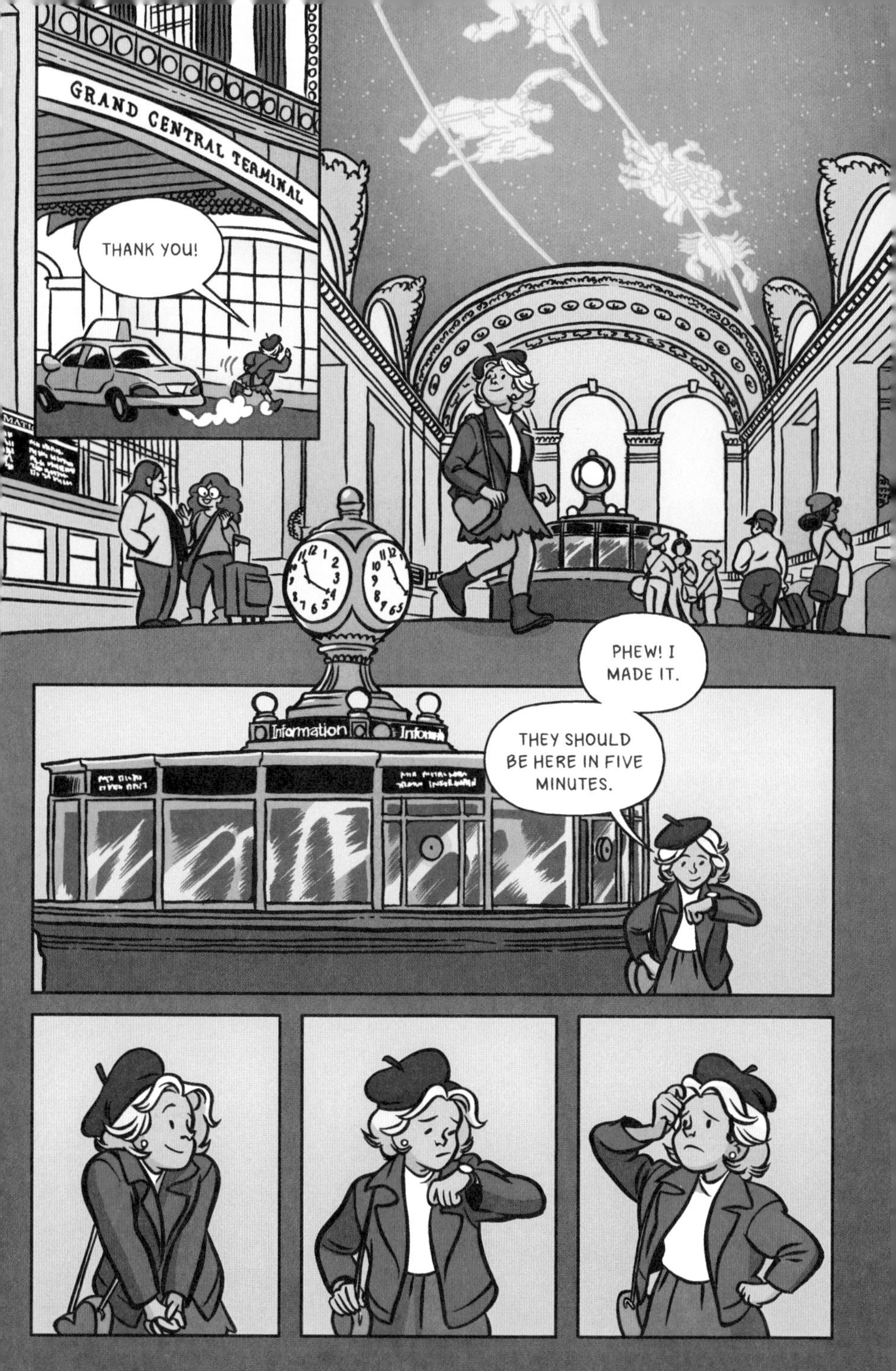
GRAND CENTRAL TERMINAL
THANK YOU!
Information
PHEW! I MADE IT.
THEY SHOULD BE HERE IN FIVE MINUTES.

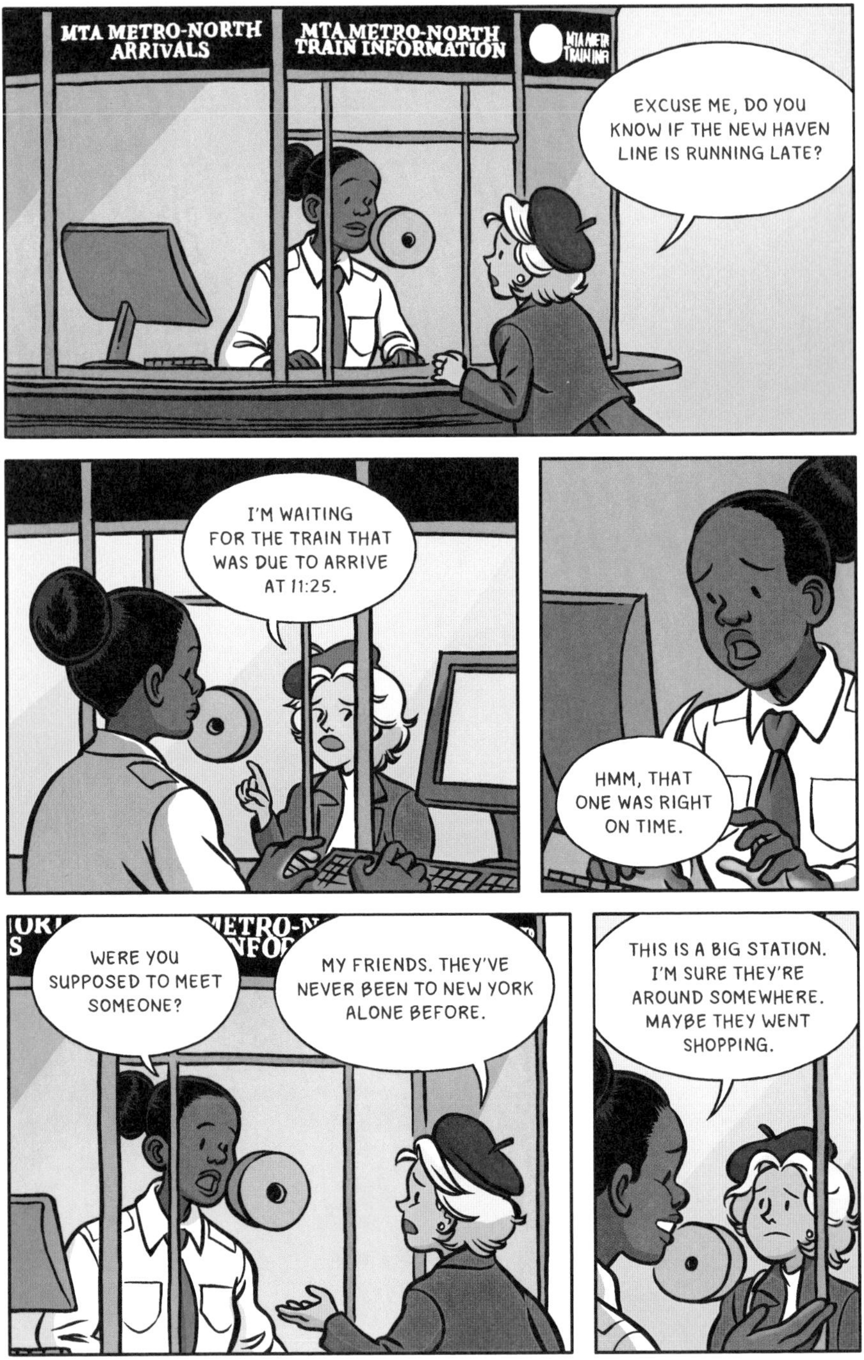
MTA METRO-NORTH ARRIVALS
MTA METRO-NORTH TRAIN INFORMATION
EXCUSE ME, DO YOU KNOW IF THE NEW HAVEN LINE IS RUNNING LATE?
I'M WAITING FOR THE TRAIN THAT WAS DUE TO ARRIVE AT 11:25.
HMM, THAT ONE WAS RIGHT ON TIME.
WERE YOU SUPPOSED TO MEET SOMEONE?
MY FRIENDS. THEY'VE NEVER BEEN TO NEW YORK ALONE BEFORE.
THIS IS A BIG STATION. I'M SURE THEY'RE AROUND SOMEWHERE. MAYBE THEY WENT SHOPPING.

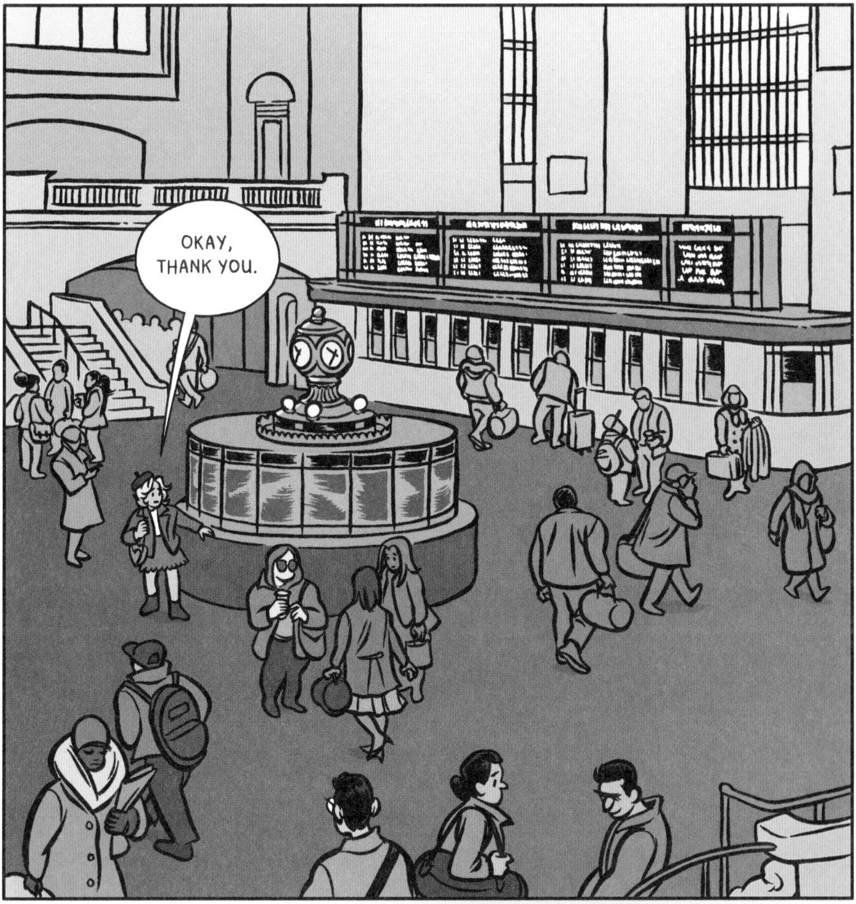
OKAY, THANK YOU.

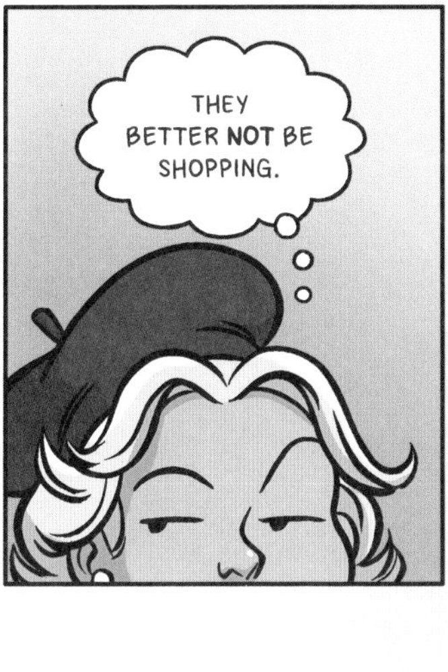
THEY BETTER **NOT** BE SHOPPING.

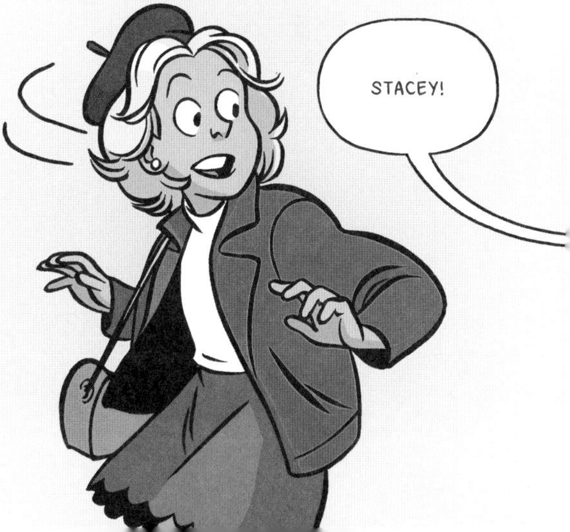
STACEY!

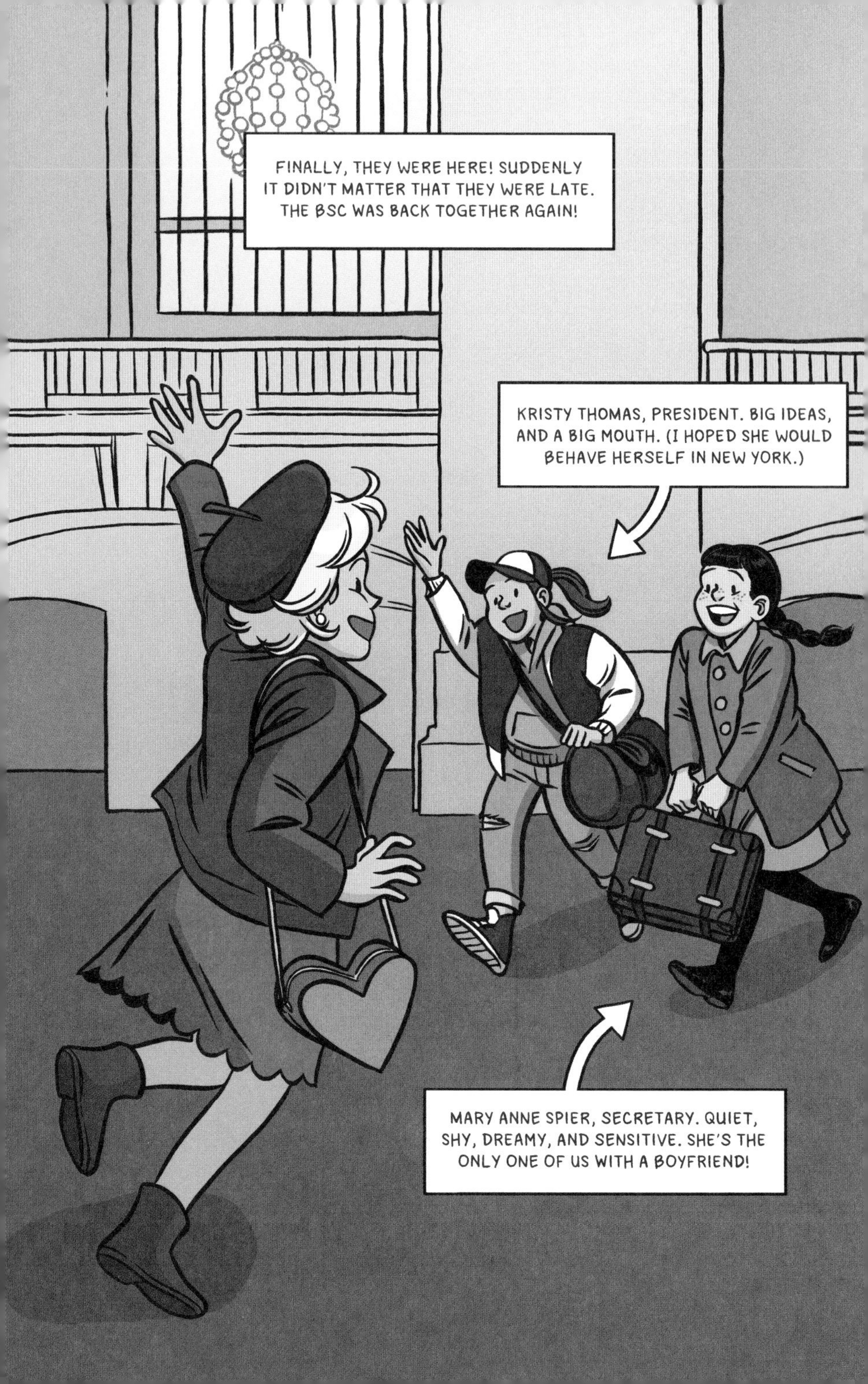
FINALLY, THEY WERE HERE! SUDDENLY IT DIDN'T MATTER THAT THEY WERE LATE. THE BSC WAS BACK TOGETHER AGAIN!
KRISTY THOMAS, PRESIDENT. BIG IDEAS, AND A BIG MOUTH. (I HOPED SHE WOULD BEHAVE HERSELF IN NEW YORK.)
MARY ANNE SPIER, SECRETARY. QUIET, SHY, DREAMY, AND SENSITIVE. SHE'S THE ONLY ONE OF US WITH A BOYFRIEND!

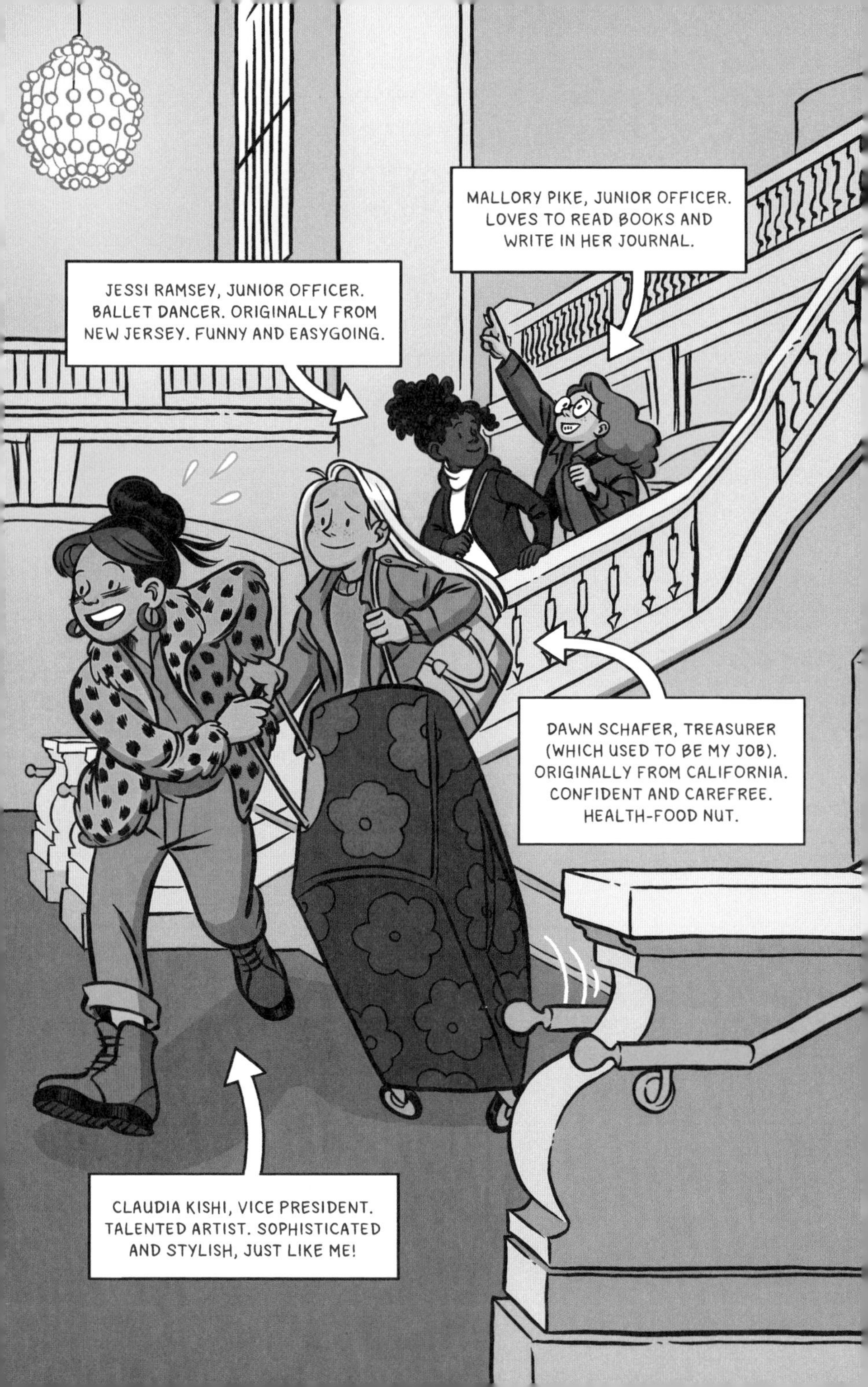
MALLORY PIKE, JUNIOR OFFICER. LOVES TO READ BOOKS AND WRITE IN HER JOURNAL.
JESSI RAMSEY, JUNIOR OFFICER. BALLET DANCER. ORIGINALLY FROM NEW JERSEY. FUNNY AND EASYGOING.
DAWN SCHAFER, TREASURER (WHICH USED TO BE MY JOB). ORIGINALLY FROM CALIFORNIA. CONFIDENT AND CAREFREE. HEALTH-FOOD NUT.
CLAUDIA KISHI, VICE PRESIDENT. TALENTED ARTIST. SOPHISTICATED AND STYLISH, JUST LIKE ME!

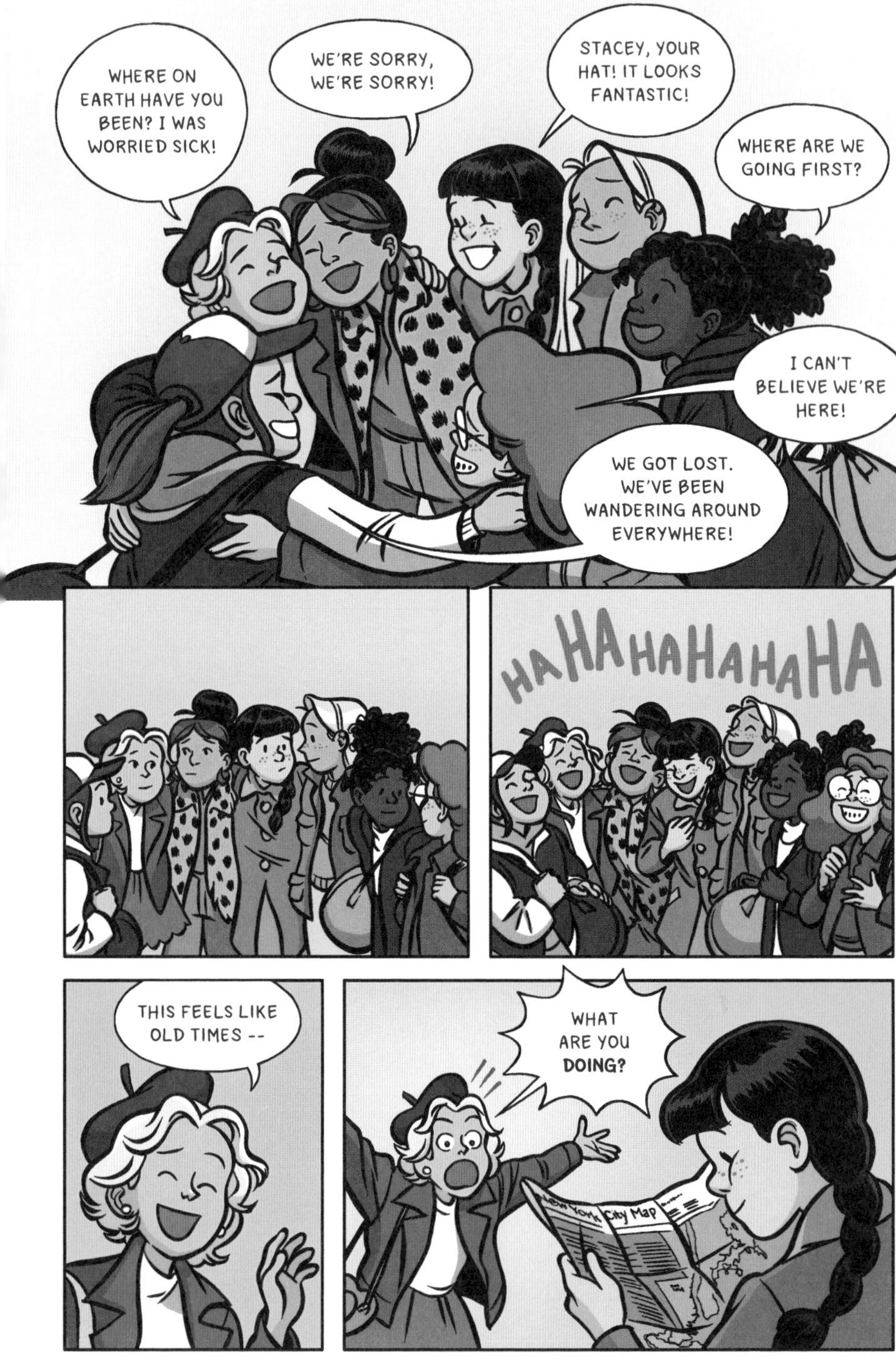
WHERE ON EARTH HAVE YOU BEEN? I WAS WORRIED SICK!
WE'RE SORRY, WE'RE SORRY!
STACEY, YOUR HAT! IT LOOKS FANTASTIC!
WHERE ARE WE GOING FIRST?
I CAN'T BELIEVE WE'RE HERE!
WE GOT LOST. WE'VE BEEN WANDERING AROUND EVERYWHERE!
HAHAHAHAHAHAHA
THIS FEELS LIKE OLD TIMES --
WHAT ARE YOU **DOING?**
New York City Map

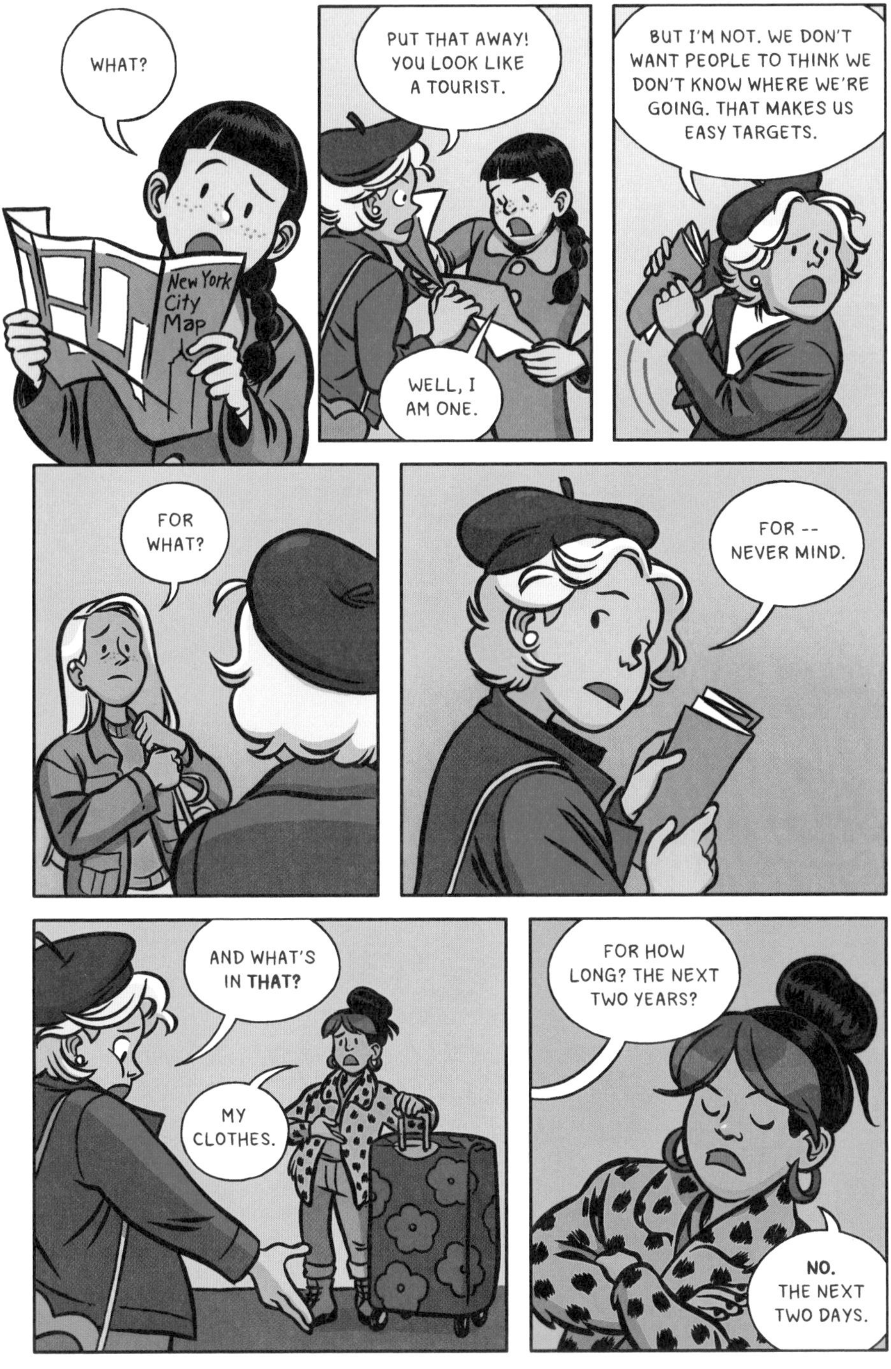
WHAT?
PUT THAT AWAY! YOU LOOK LIKE A TOURIST.
WELL, I AM ONE.
BUT I'M NOT. WE DON'T WANT PEOPLE TO THINK WE DON'T KNOW WHERE WE'RE GOING. THAT MAKES US EASY TARGETS.
New York City Map
FOR WHAT?
FOR -- NEVER MIND.
AND WHAT'S IN **THAT?**
MY CLOTHES.
FOR HOW LONG? THE NEXT TWO YEARS?
NO. THE NEXT TWO DAYS.

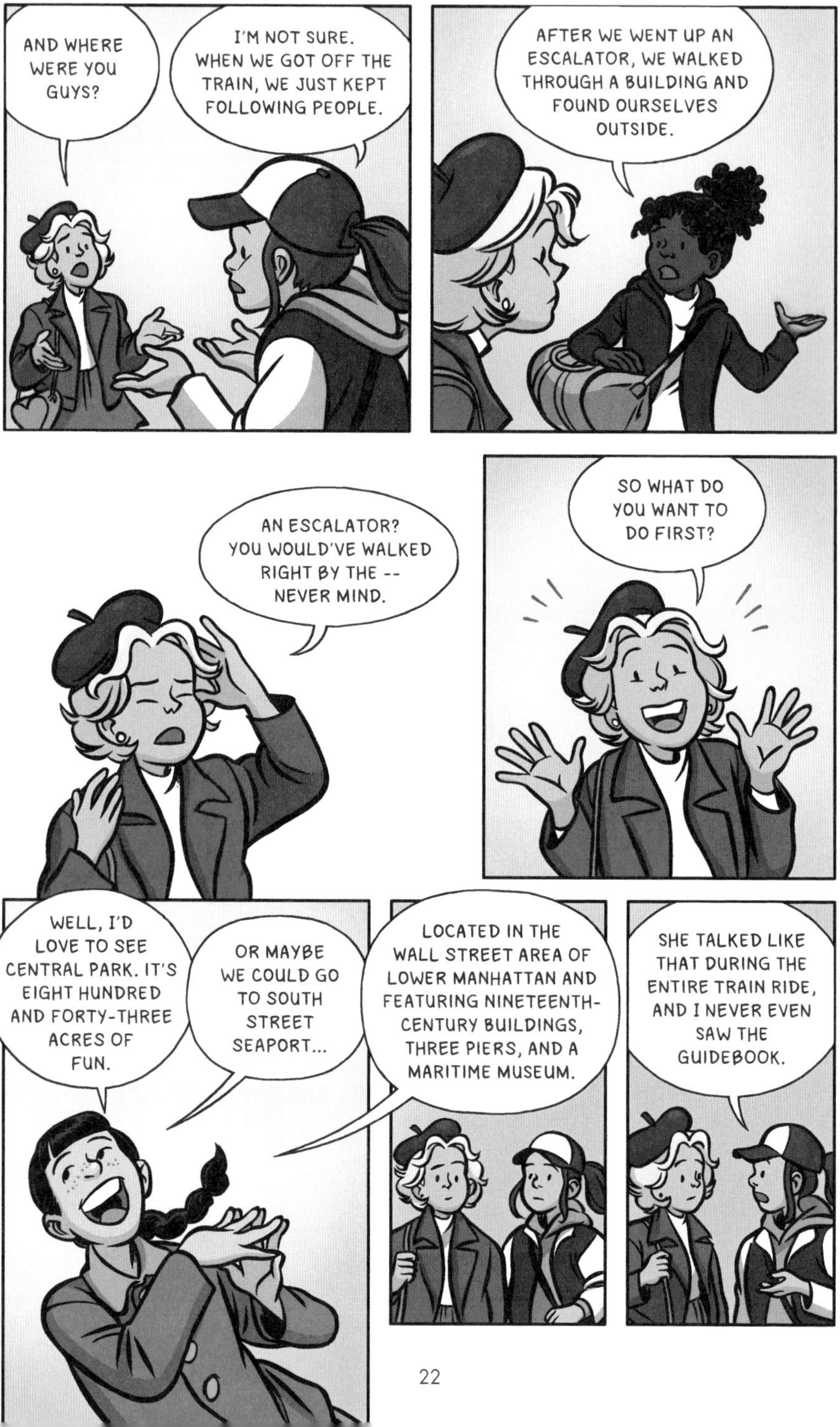
AND WHERE WERE YOU GUYS?
I'M NOT SURE. WHEN WE GOT OFF THE TRAIN, WE JUST KEPT FOLLOWING PEOPLE.
AFTER WE WENT UP AN ESCALATOR, WE WALKED THROUGH A BUILDING AND FOUND OURSELVES OUTSIDE.
AN ESCALATOR? YOU WOULD'VE WALKED RIGHT BY THE -- NEVER MIND.
SO WHAT DO YOU WANT TO DO FIRST?
WELL, I'D LOVE TO SEE CENTRAL PARK. IT'S EIGHT HUNDRED AND FORTY-THREE ACRES OF FUN.
OR MAYBE WE COULD GO TO SOUTH STREET SEAPORT...
LOCATED IN THE WALL STREET AREA OF LOWER MANHATTAN AND FEATURING NINETEENTH-CENTURY BUILDINGS, THREE PIERS, AND A MARITIME MUSEUM.
SHE TALKED LIKE THAT DURING THE ENTIRE TRAIN RIDE, AND I NEVER EVEN SAW THE GUIDEBOOK.

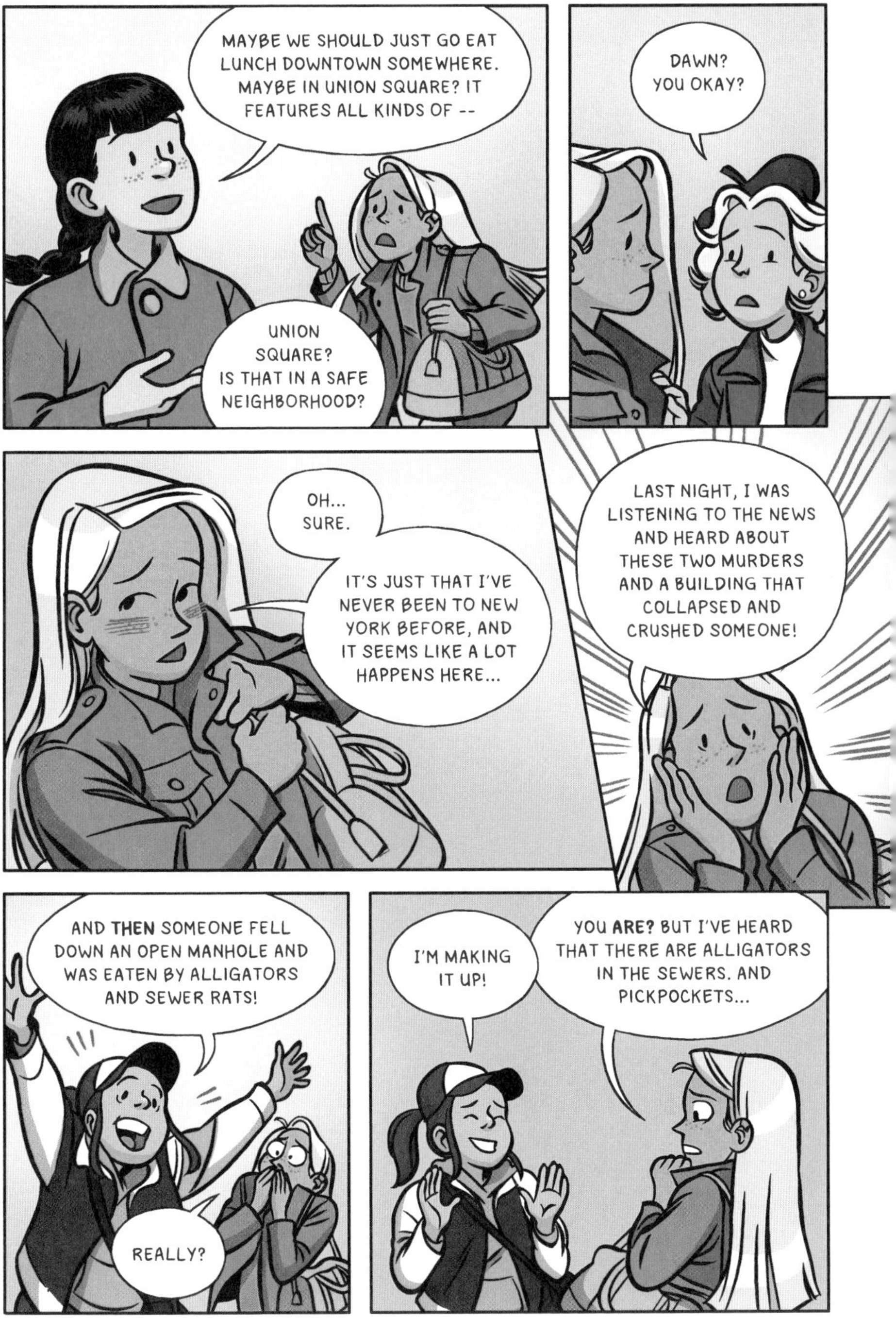
MAYBE WE SHOULD JUST GO EAT LUNCH DOWNTOWN SOMEWHERE. MAYBE IN UNION SQUARE? IT FEATURES ALL KINDS OF --
UNION SQUARE? IS THAT IN A SAFE NEIGHBORHOOD?
DAWN? YOU OKAY?
OH... SURE.
IT'S JUST THAT I'VE NEVER BEEN TO NEW YORK BEFORE, AND IT SEEMS LIKE A LOT HAPPENS HERE...
LAST NIGHT, I WAS LISTENING TO THE NEWS AND HEARD ABOUT THESE TWO MURDERS AND A BUILDING THAT COLLAPSED AND CRUSHED SOMEONE!
AND **THEN** SOMEONE FELL DOWN AN OPEN MANHOLE AND WAS EATEN BY ALLIGATORS AND SEWER RATS!
REALLY?
I'M MAKING IT UP!
YOU **ARE?** BUT I'VE HEARD THAT THERE ARE ALLIGATORS IN THE SEWERS. AND PICKPOCKETS...

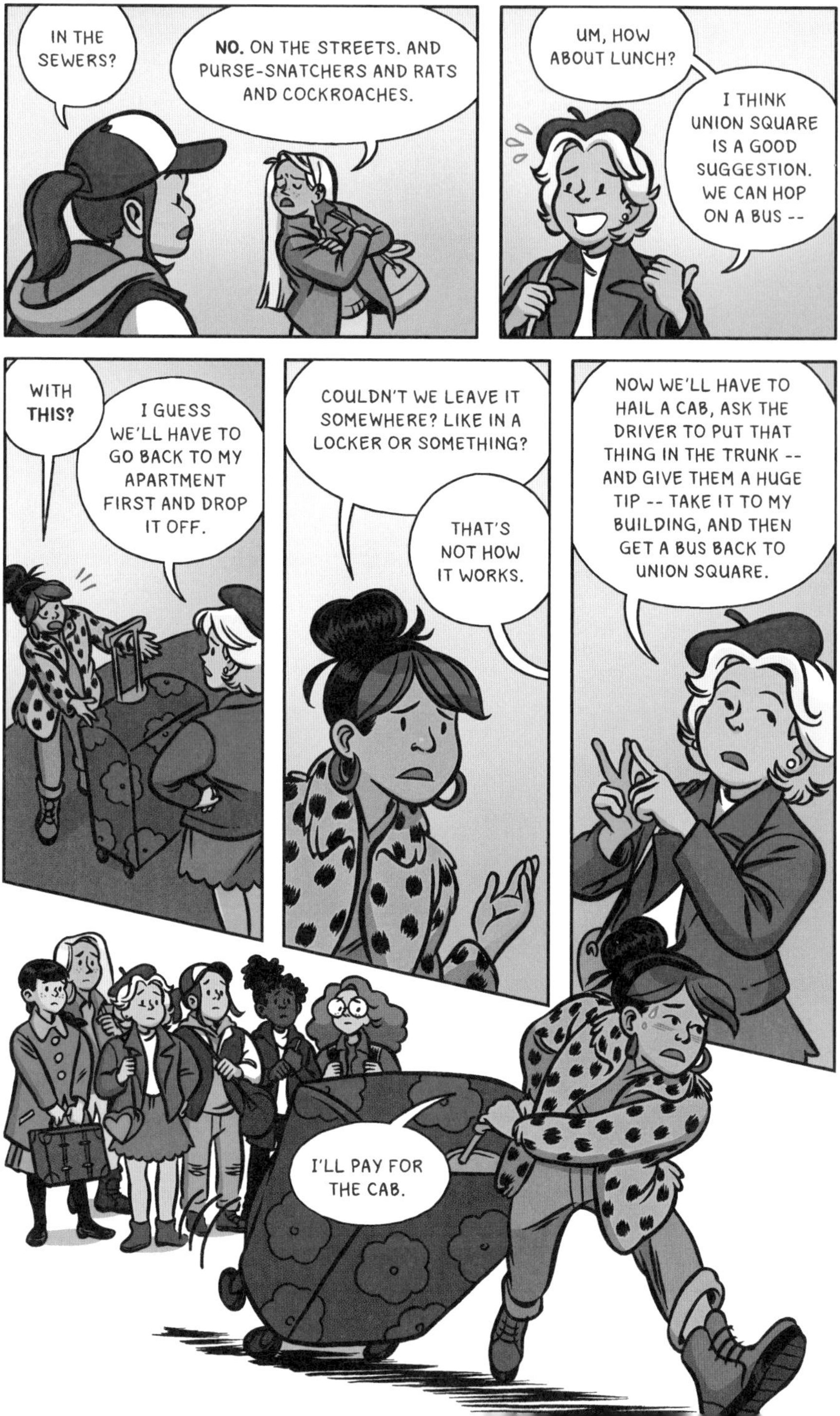
IN THE SEWERS?
NO. ON THE STREETS. AND PURSE-SNATCHERS AND RATS AND COCKROACHES.
UM, HOW ABOUT LUNCH?
I THINK UNION SQUARE IS A GOOD SUGGESTION. WE CAN HOP ON A BUS --
WITH THIS?
I GUESS WE'LL HAVE TO GO BACK TO MY APARTMENT FIRST AND DROP IT OFF.
COULDN'T WE LEAVE IT SOMEWHERE? LIKE IN A LOCKER OR SOMETHING?
THAT'S NOT HOW IT WORKS.
NOW WE'LL HAVE TO HAIL A CAB, ASK THE DRIVER TO PUT THAT THING IN THE TRUNK -- AND GIVE THEM A HUGE TIP -- TAKE IT TO MY BUILDING, AND THEN GET A BUS BACK TO UNION SQUARE.
I'LL PAY FOR THE CAB.

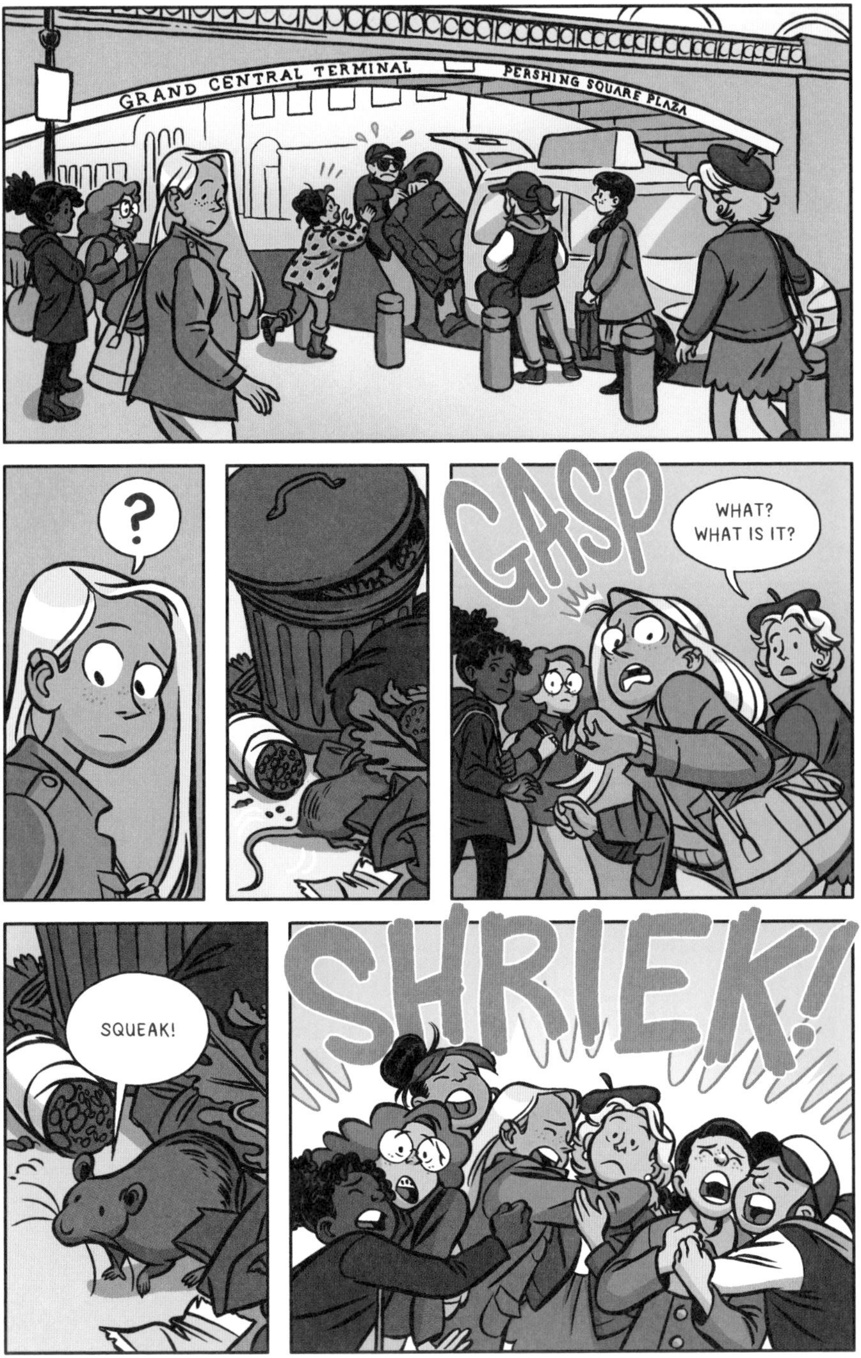
GRAND CENTRAL TERMINAL
PERSHING SQUARE PLAZA
?
GASP
WHAT? WHAT IS IT?
SQUEAK!
SHRIEK!

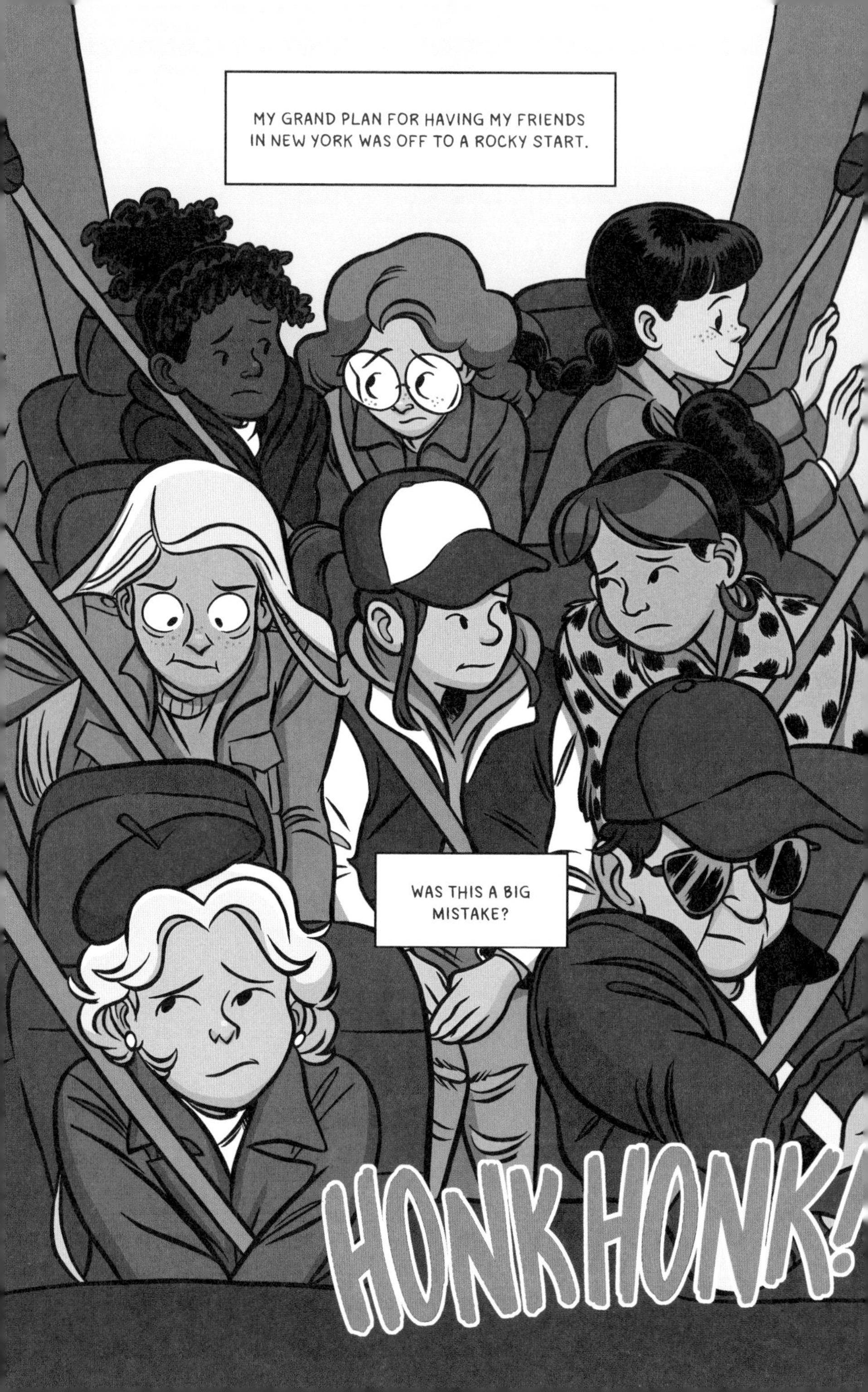
MY GRAND PLAN FOR HAVING MY FRIENDS IN NEW YORK WAS OFF TO A ROCKY START.
WAS THIS A BIG MISTAKE?
HONK HONK!

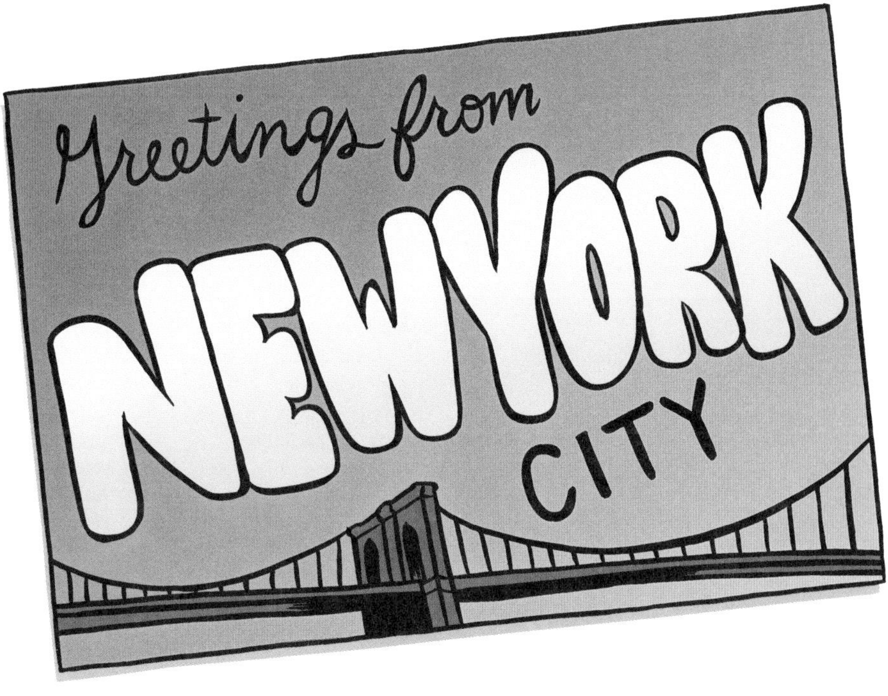
Greetings from
NEW YORK
CITY

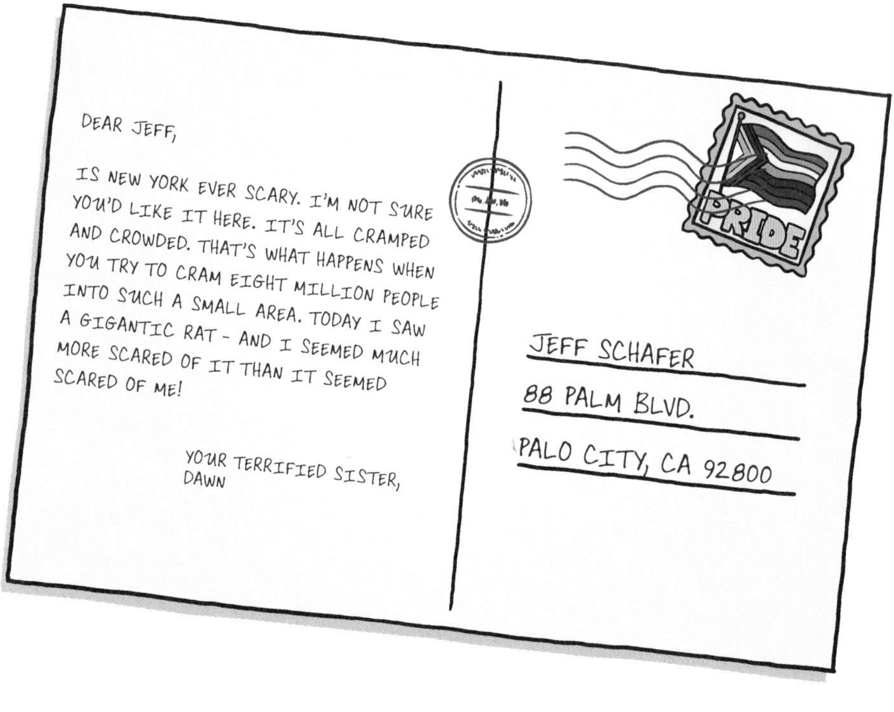
DEAR JEFF,
IS NEW YORK EVER SCARY. I'M NOT SURE YOU'D LIKE IT HERE. IT'S ALL CRAMPED AND CROWDED. THAT'S WHAT HAPPENS WHEN YOU TRY TO CRAM EIGHT MILLION PEOPLE INTO SUCH A SMALL AREA. TODAY I SAW A GIGANTIC RAT - AND I SEEMED MUCH MORE SCARED OF IT THAN IT SEEMED SCARED OF ME!
YOUR TERRIFIED SISTER,
DAWN
PRIDE
JEFF SCHAFER
88 PALM BLVD.
PALO CITY, CA 92800

CHAPTER 3

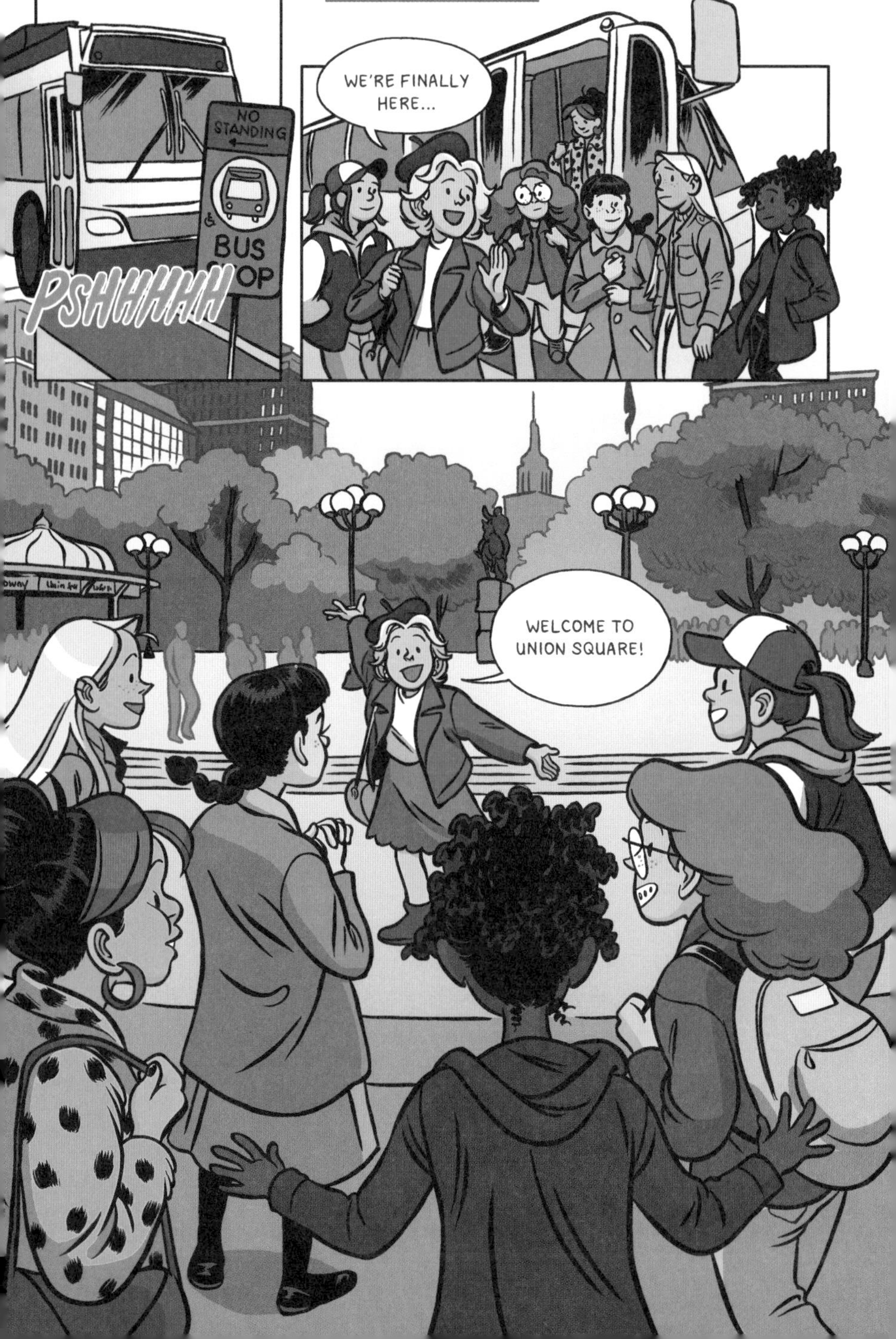
NO STANDING
BUS
PSHHHHH
WE'RE FINALLY HERE...
WELCOME TO UNION SQUARE!

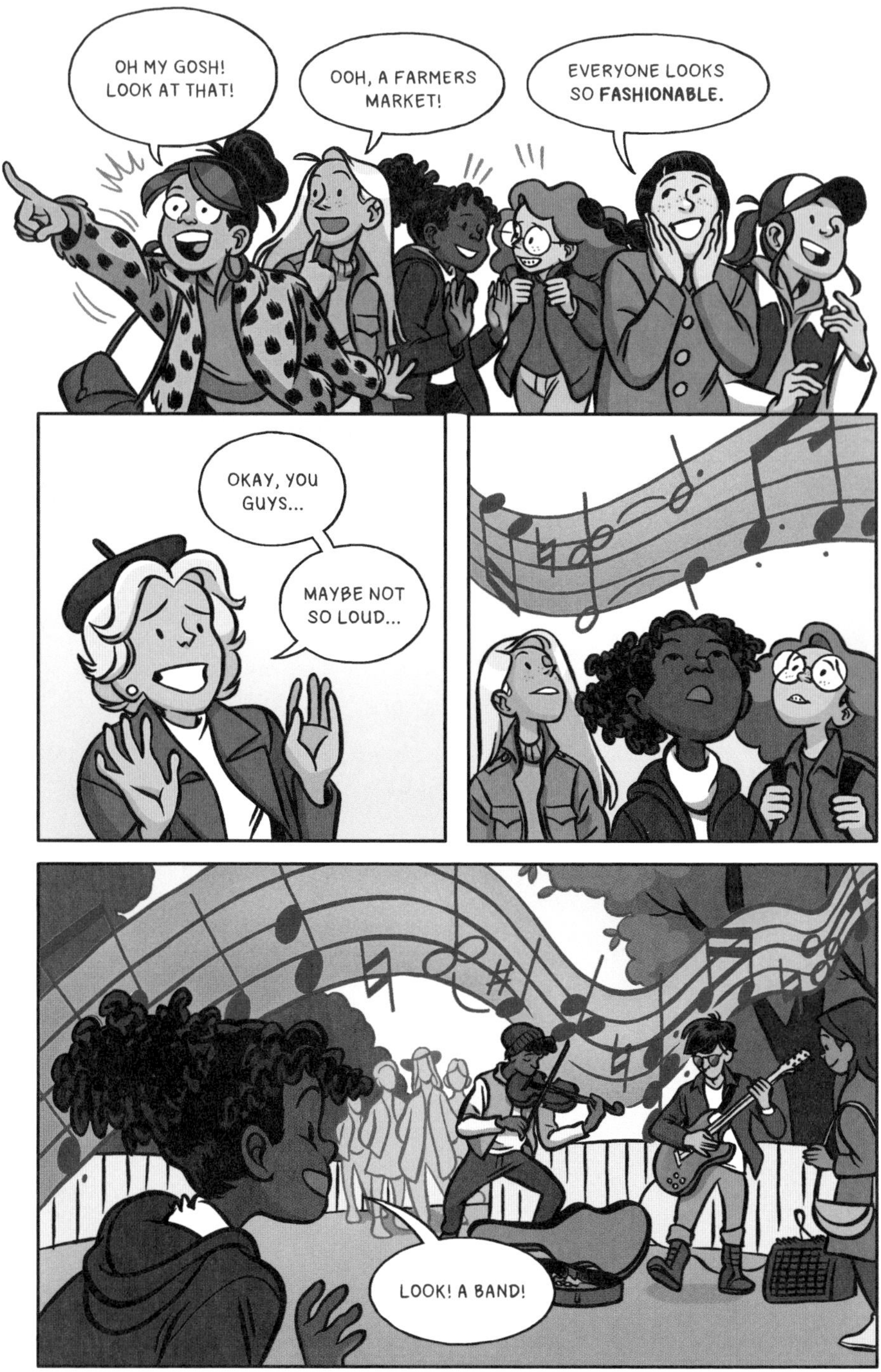
OH MY GOSH! LOOK AT THAT!
OOH, A FARMERS MARKET!
EVERYONE LOOKS SO **FASHIONABLE.**
OKAY, YOU GUYS...
MAYBE NOT SO LOUD...
LOOK! A BAND!

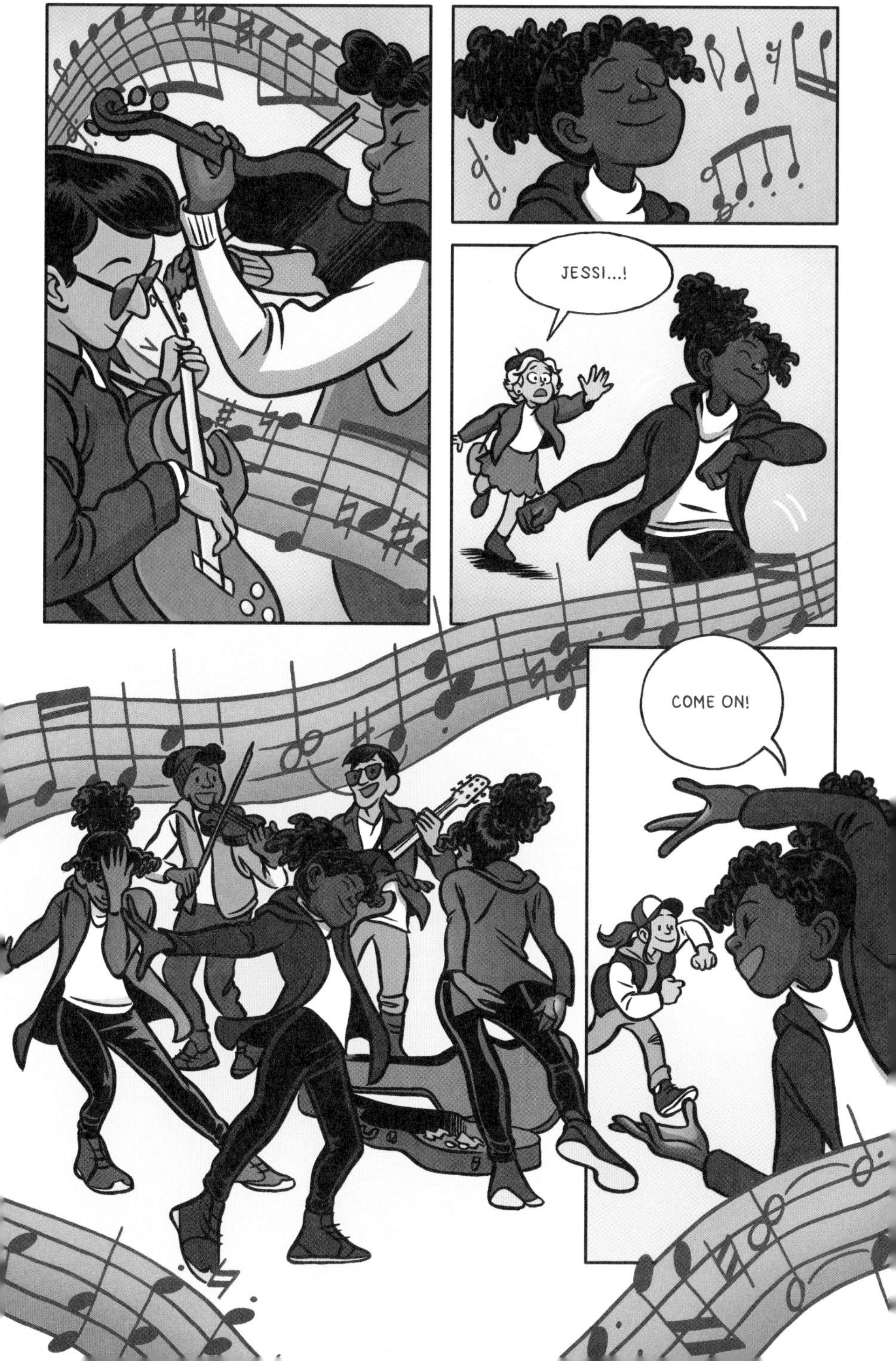
JESSI...!
COME ON!

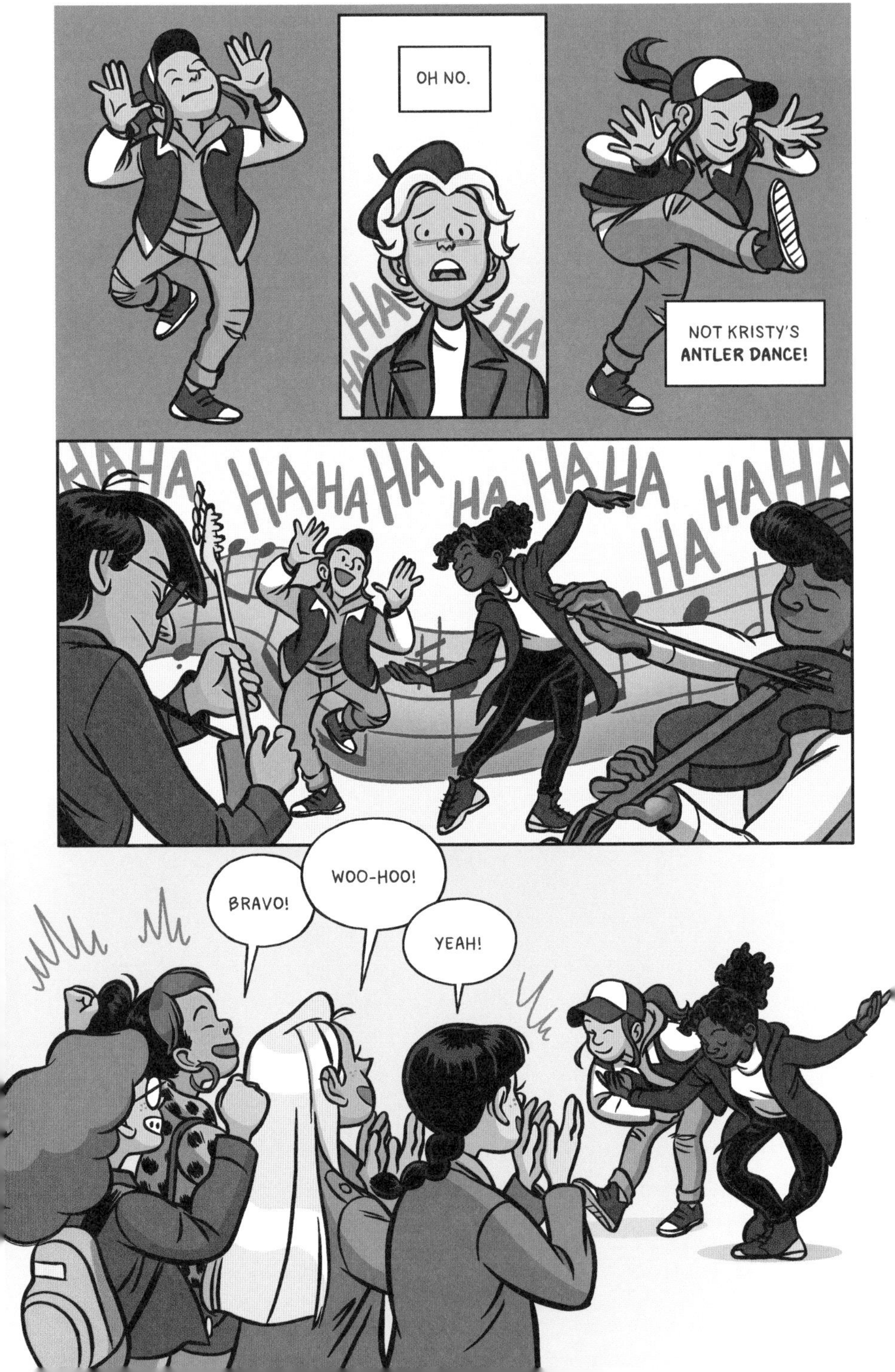
OH NO.
HA HA HA
NOT KRISTY'S ANTLER DANCE!
HAHA HAHAHA HA HAHA HAHA HA
BRAVO!
WOO-HOO!
YEAH!

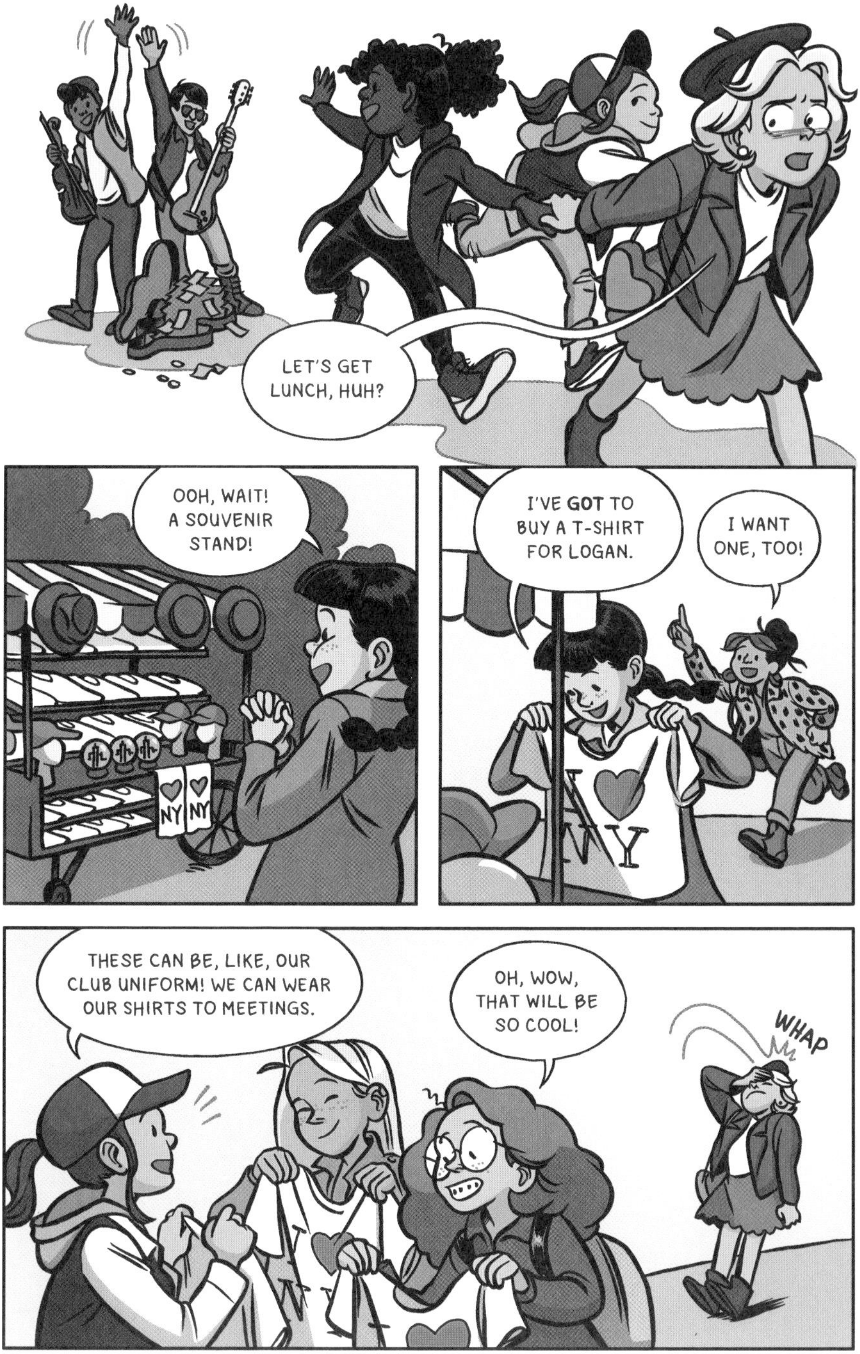
LET'S GET LUNCH, HUH?
OOH, WAIT! A SOUVENIR STAND!
NY
NY
I'VE **GOT** TO BUY A T-SHIRT FOR LOGAN.
I WANT ONE, TOO!
THESE CAN BE, LIKE, OUR CLUB UNIFORM! WE CAN WEAR OUR SHIRTS TO MEETINGS.
OH, WOW, THAT WILL BE SO COOL!
WHAP

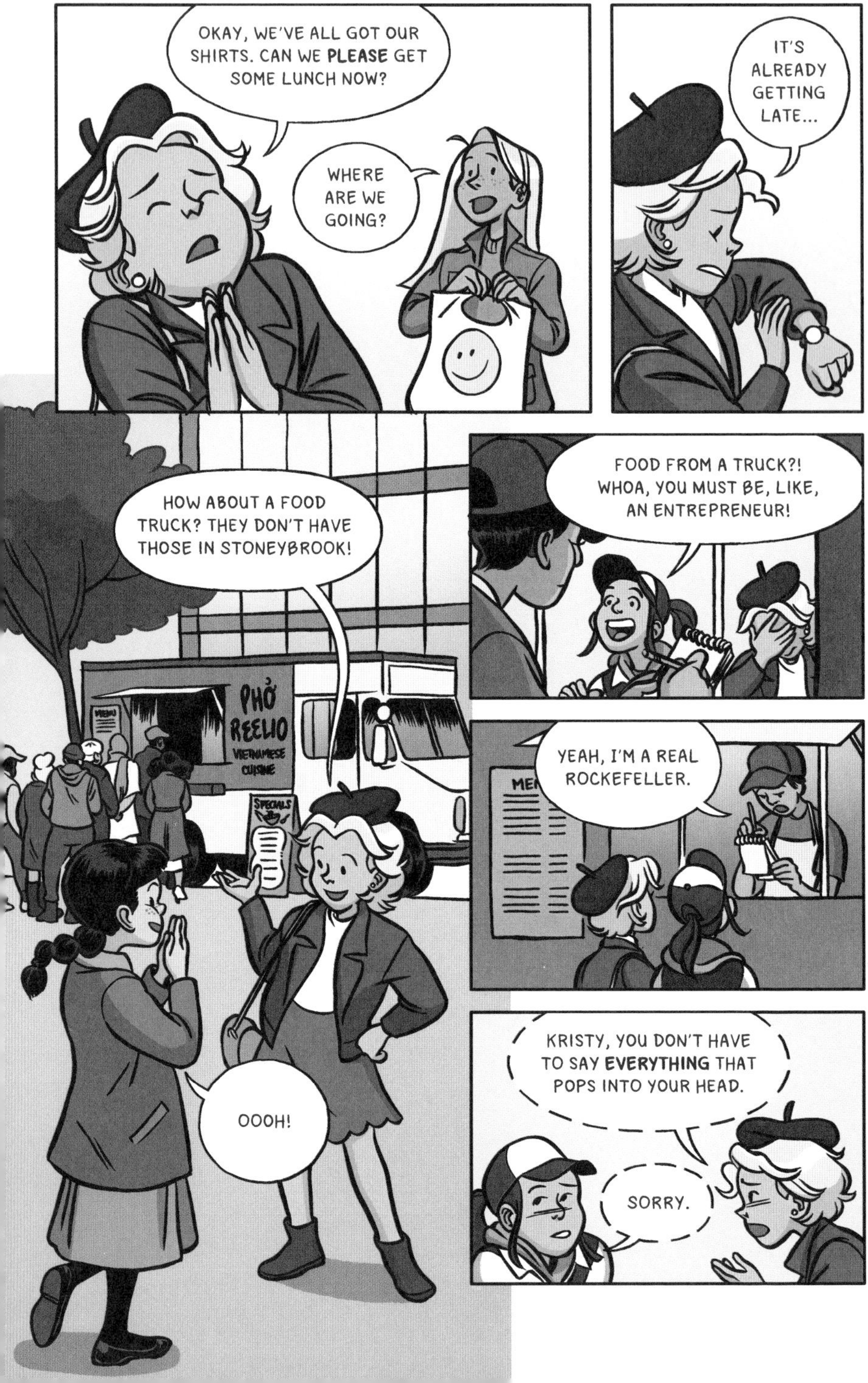

OKAY, WE'VE ALL GOT OUR SHIRTS. CAN WE **PLEASE** GET SOME LUNCH NOW?
WHERE ARE WE GOING?
IT'S ALREADY GETTING LATE...
HOW ABOUT A FOOD TRUCK? THEY DON'T HAVE THOSE IN STONEYBROOK!
PHỞ REELIO
VIETNAMESE CUISINE
SPECIALS
OOOH!
FOOD FROM A TRUCK?! WHOA, YOU MUST BE, LIKE, AN ENTREPRENEUR!
YEAH, I'M A REAL ROCKEFELLER.
KRISTY, YOU DON'T HAVE TO SAY **EVERYTHING** THAT POPS INTO YOUR HEAD.
SORRY.

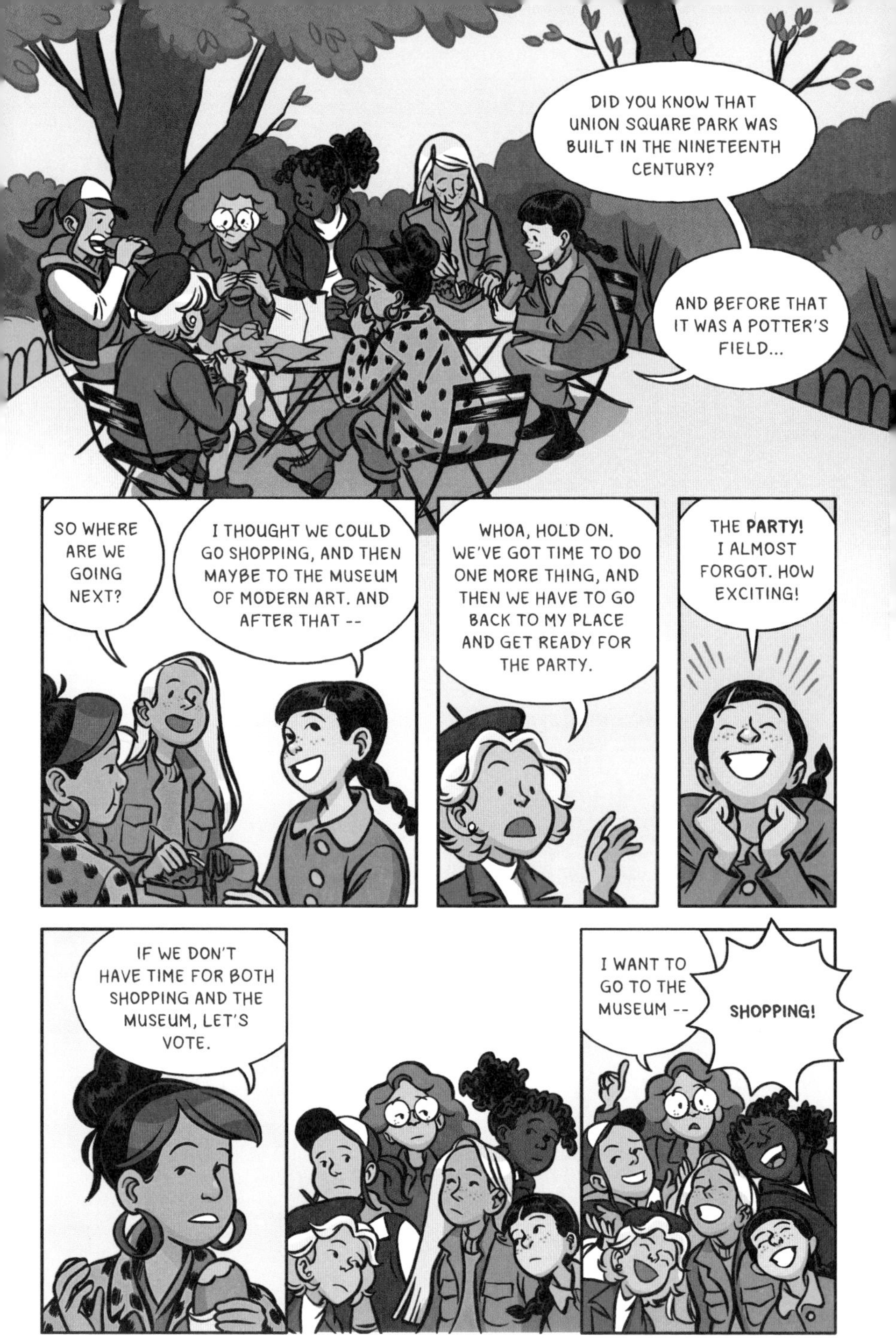
DID YOU KNOW THAT UNION SQUARE PARK WAS BUILT IN THE NINETEENTH CENTURY?
AND BEFORE THAT IT WAS A POTTER'S FIELD...
SO WHERE ARE WE GOING NEXT?
I THOUGHT WE COULD GO SHOPPING, AND THEN MAYBE TO THE MUSEUM OF MODERN ART. AND AFTER THAT --
WHOA, HOLD ON. WE'VE GOT TIME TO DO ONE MORE THING, AND THEN WE HAVE TO GO BACK TO MY PLACE AND GET READY FOR THE PARTY.
THE **PARTY!** I ALMOST FORGOT. HOW EXCITING!
IF WE DON'T HAVE TIME FOR BOTH SHOPPING AND THE MUSEUM, LET'S VOTE.
I WANT TO GO TO THE MUSEUM --
SHOPPING!

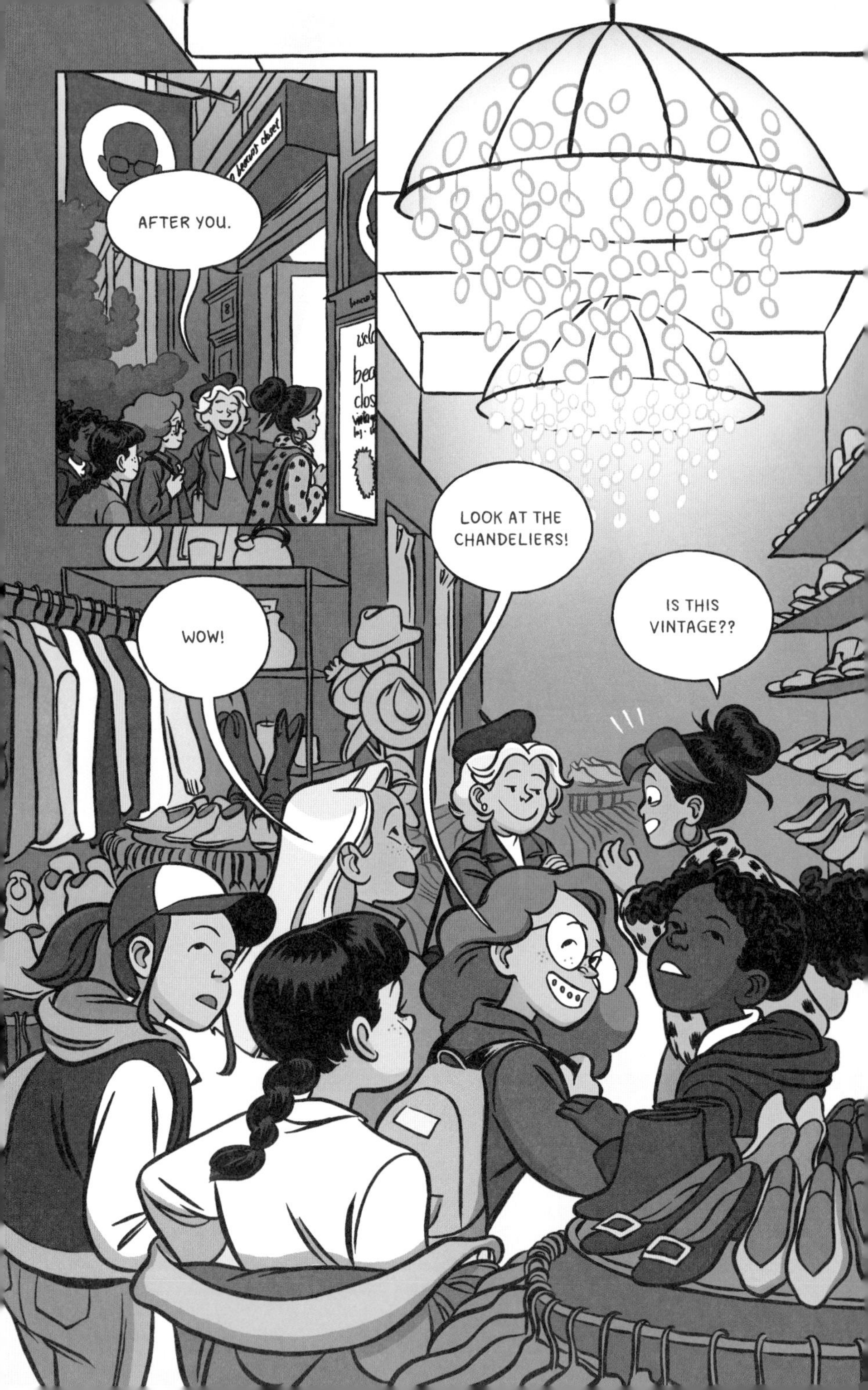
AFTER YOU.
WOW!
LOOK AT THE CHANDELIERS!
IS THIS VINTAGE??

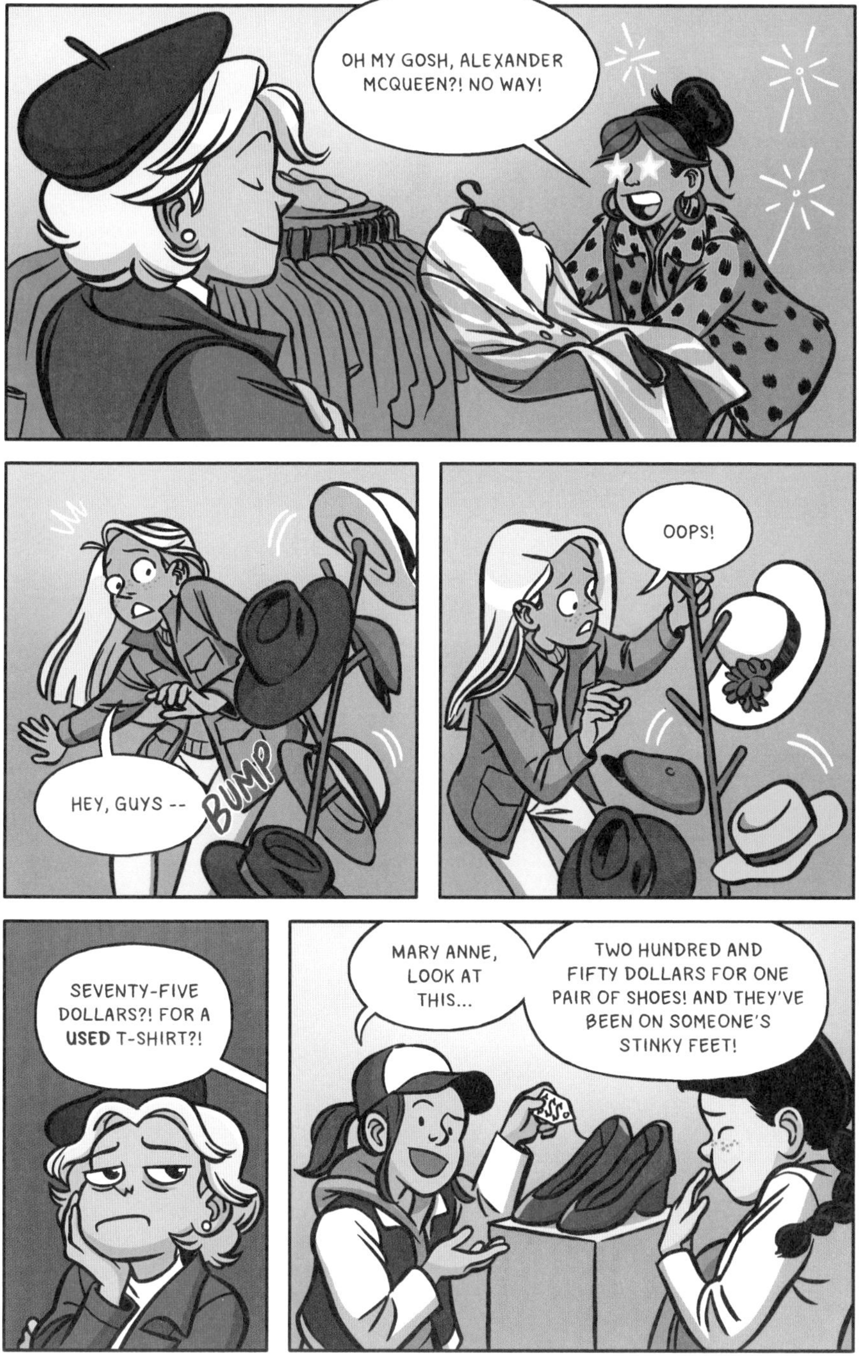
OH MY GOSH, ALEXANDER MCQUEEN?! NO WAY!
HEY, GUYS --
BUMP
OOPS!
SEVENTY-FIVE DOLLARS?! FOR A **USED** T-SHIRT?!
MARY ANNE, LOOK AT THIS...
TWO HUNDRED AND FIFTY DOLLARS FOR ONE PAIR OF SHOES! AND THEY'VE BEEN ON SOMEONE'S STINKY FEET!

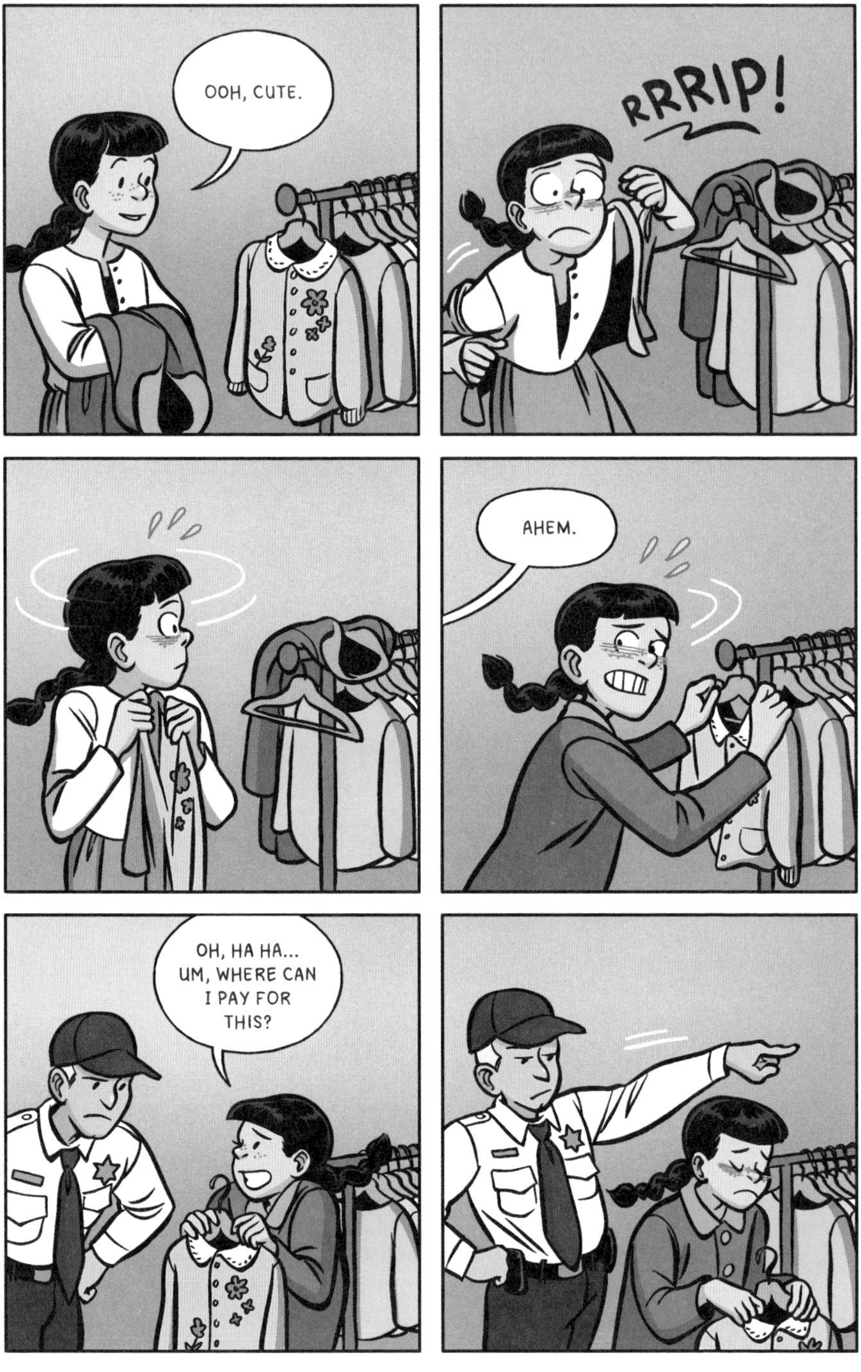
OOH, CUTE.
RRRIP!
AHEM.
OH, HA HA... UM, WHERE CAN I PAY FOR THIS?

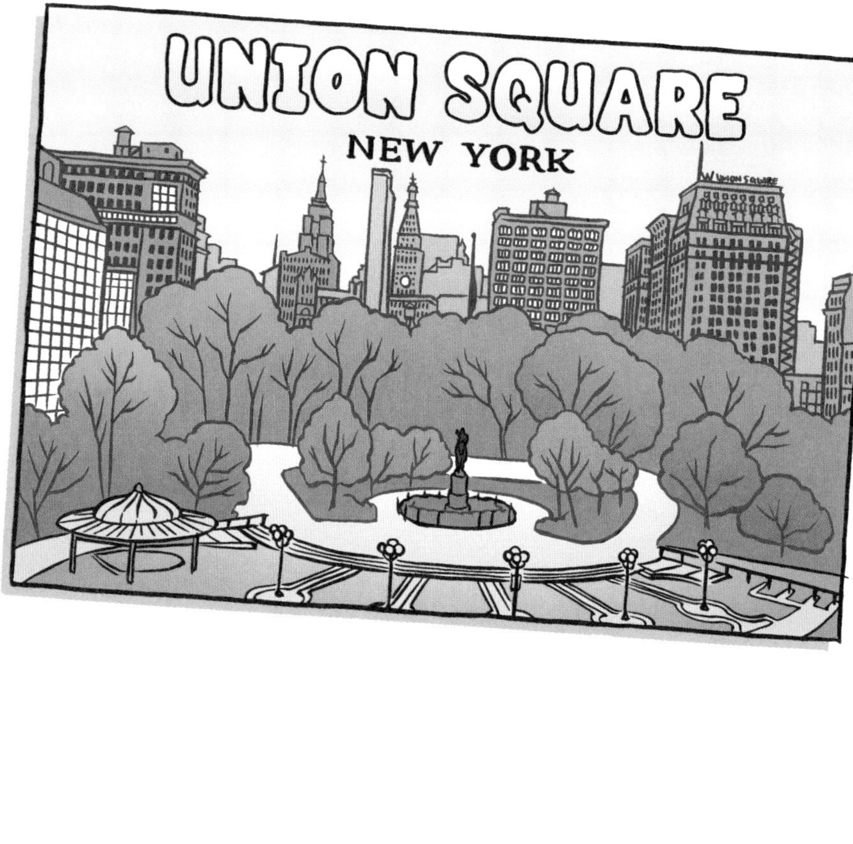
UNION SQUARE
NEW YORK
W UNION SQUARE

Dear Mom, Dad, Mimi, and Janine –

New York is so so cool. We whent to Union Square and ate Vietnamese food from a truck and whent vintige shopping. I bought a coat and Mary Ann allmost got arested but don't tell her father. We also met the kids we'll be siting for tomorrow. Tonight Stacey is having a party for us at her apartment.

Love ya,
Claudia

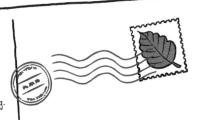

The Kishi Family
58 Bradford Ct.
Stoneybrook, CT 06800

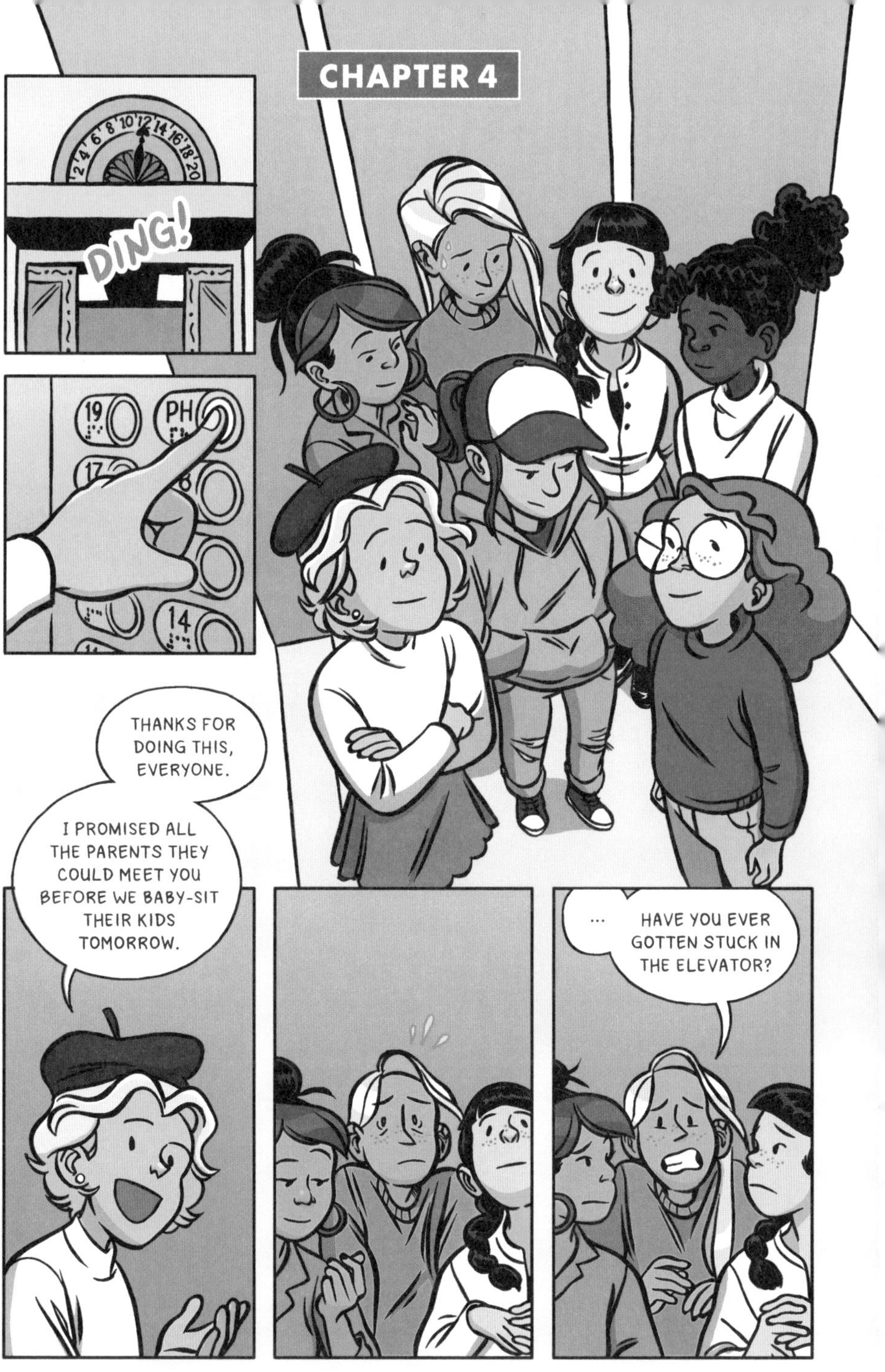
CHAPTER 4
DING!
THANKS FOR DOING THIS, EVERYONE.
I PROMISED ALL THE PARENTS THEY COULD MEET YOU BEFORE WE BABY-SIT THEIR KIDS TOMORROW.
...
HAVE YOU EVER GOTTEN STUCK IN THE ELEVATOR?

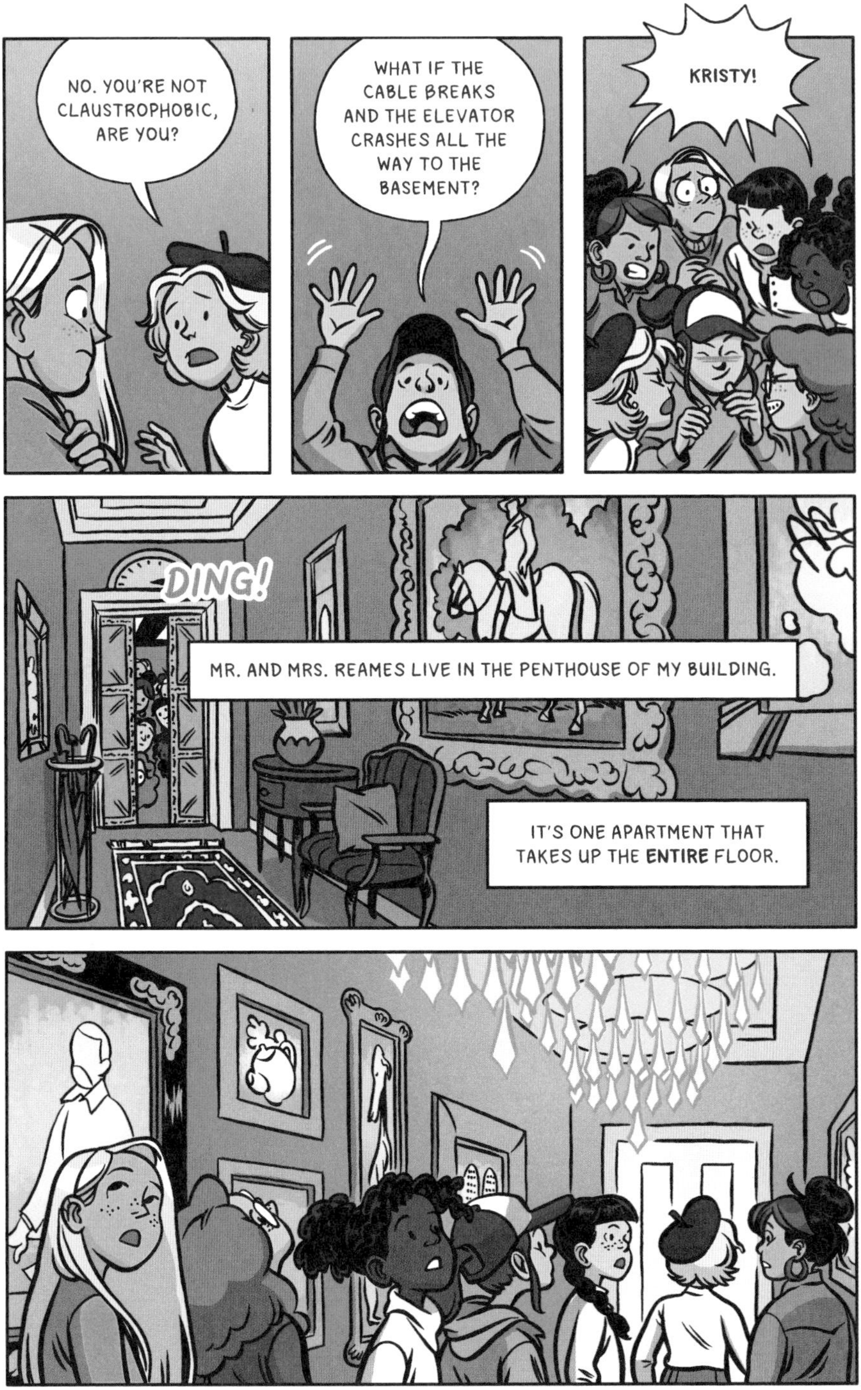
NO. YOU'RE NOT CLAUSTROPHOBIC, ARE YOU?
WHAT IF THE CABLE BREAKS AND THE ELEVATOR CRASHES ALL THE WAY TO THE BASEMENT?
KRISTY!
DING!
MR. AND MRS. REAMES LIVE IN THE PENTHOUSE OF MY BUILDING.
IT'S ONE APARTMENT THAT TAKES UP THE ENTIRE FLOOR.

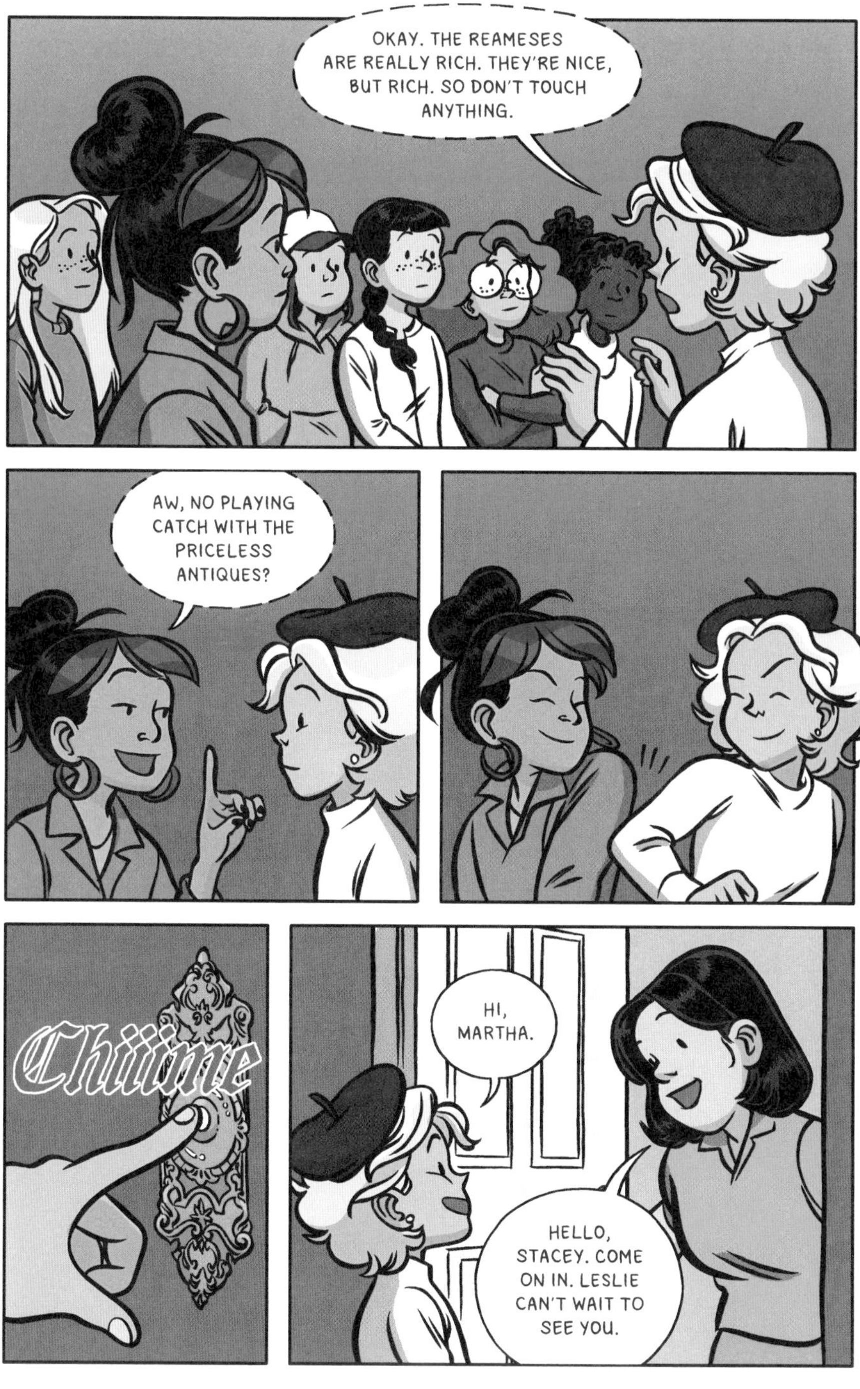
OKAY. THE REAMESES ARE REALLY RICH. THEY'RE NICE, BUT RICH. SO DON'T TOUCH ANYTHING.
AW, NO PLAYING CATCH WITH THE PRICELESS ANTIQUES?
Chiiime
HI, MARTHA.
HELLO, STACEY. COME ON IN. LESLIE CAN'T WAIT TO SEE YOU.

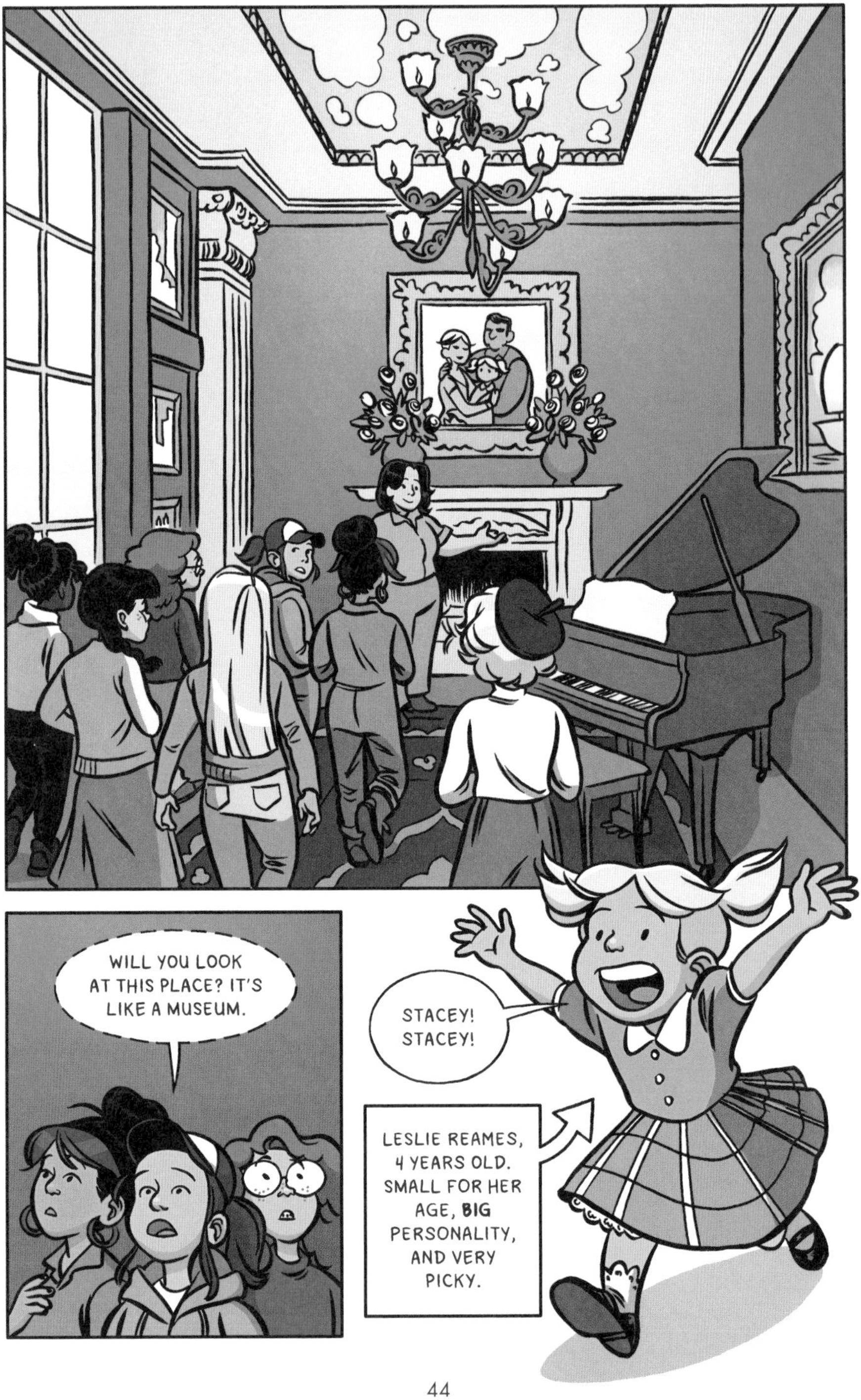
WILL YOU LOOK AT THIS PLACE? IT'S LIKE A MUSEUM.
STACEY! STACEY!
LESLIE REAMES, 4 YEARS OLD. SMALL FOR HER AGE, **BIG** PERSONALITY, AND VERY PICKY.

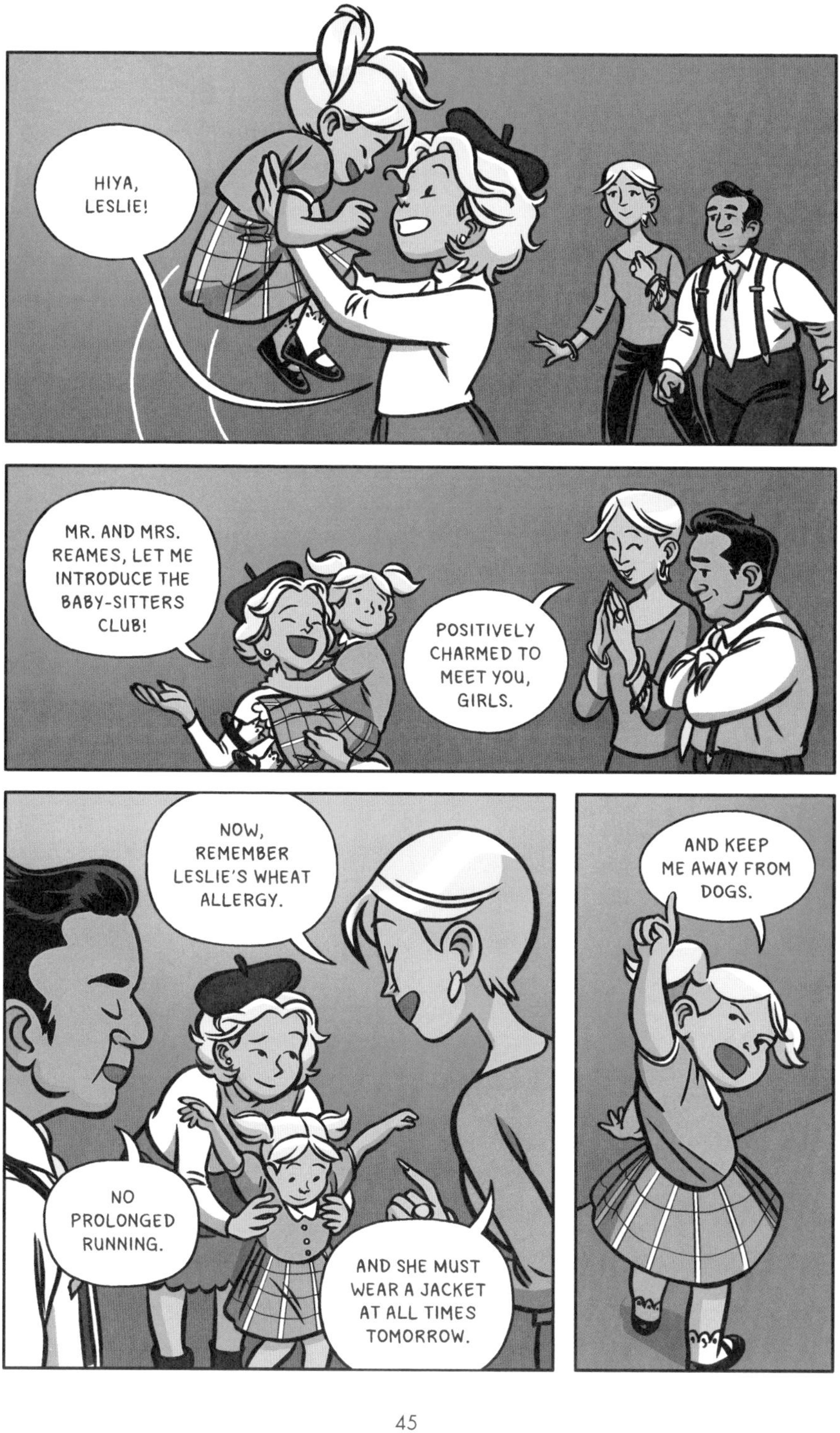
HIYA, LESLIE!
MR. AND MRS. REAMES, LET ME INTRODUCE THE BABY-SITTERS CLUB!
POSITIVELY CHARMED TO MEET YOU, GIRLS.
NOW, REMEMBER LESLIE'S WHEAT ALLERGY.
NO PROLONGED RUNNING.
AND SHE MUST WEAR A JACKET AT ALL TIMES TOMORROW.
AND KEEP ME AWAY FROM DOGS.

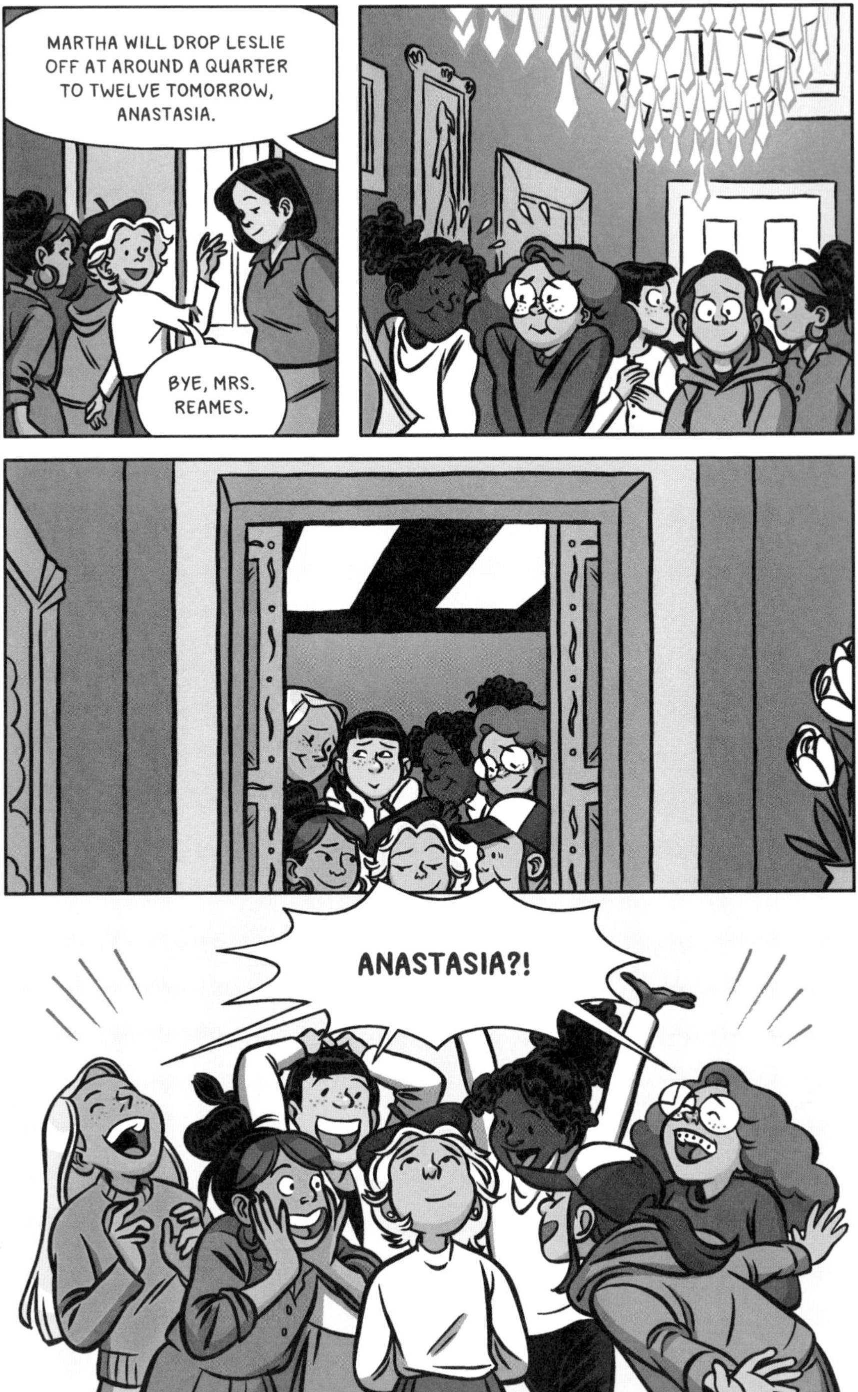
MARTHA WILL DROP LESLIE OFF AT AROUND A QUARTER TO TWELVE TOMORROW, ANASTASIA.
BYE, MRS. REAMES.
ANASTASIA?!

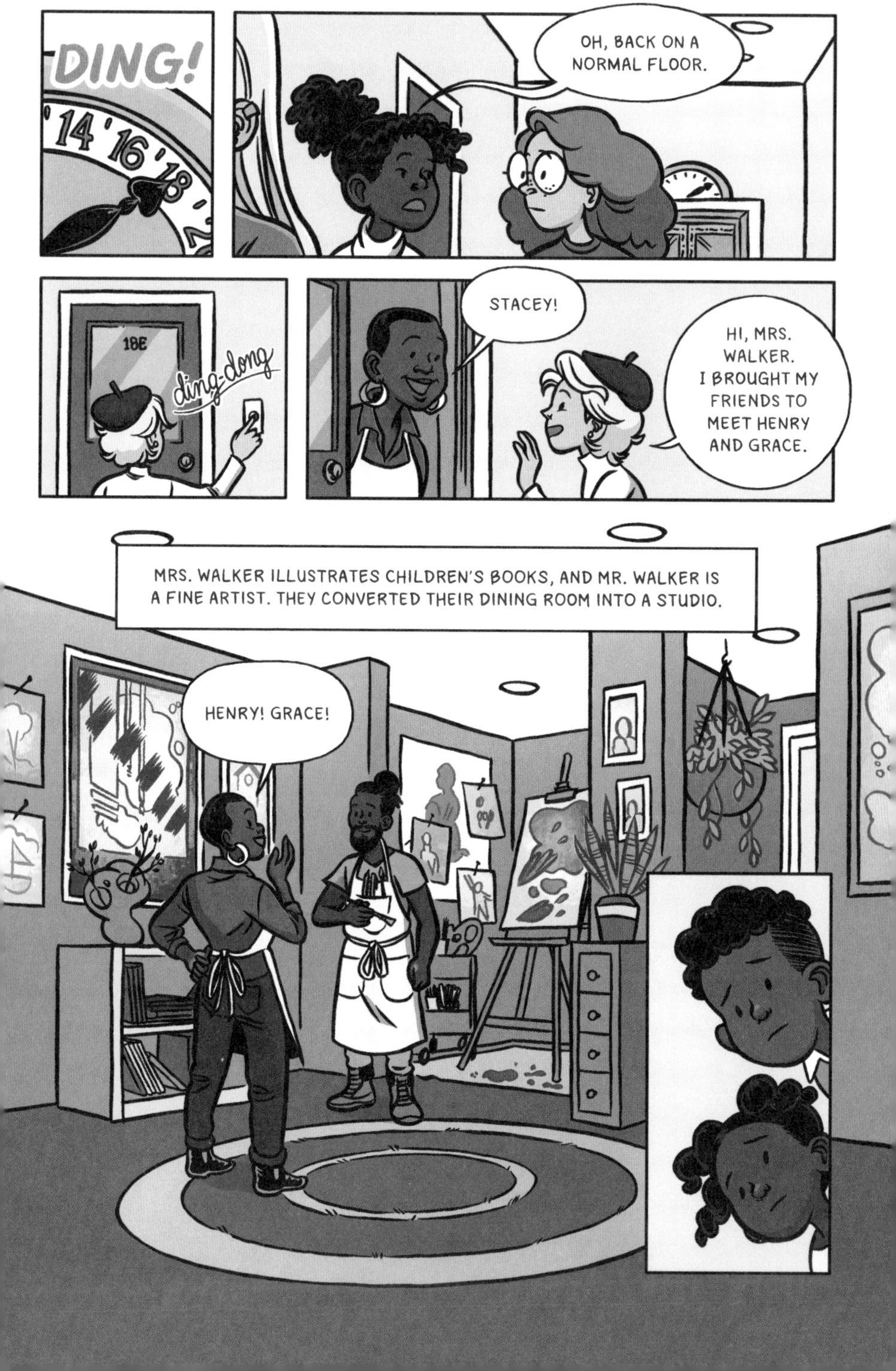
DING!
OH, BACK ON A NORMAL FLOOR.
18E
ding-dong
STACEY!
HI, MRS. WALKER. I BROUGHT MY FRIENDS TO MEET HENRY AND GRACE.
MRS. WALKER ILLUSTRATES CHILDREN'S BOOKS, AND MR. WALKER IS A FINE ARTIST. THEY CONVERTED THEIR DINING ROOM INTO A STUDIO.
HENRY! GRACE!

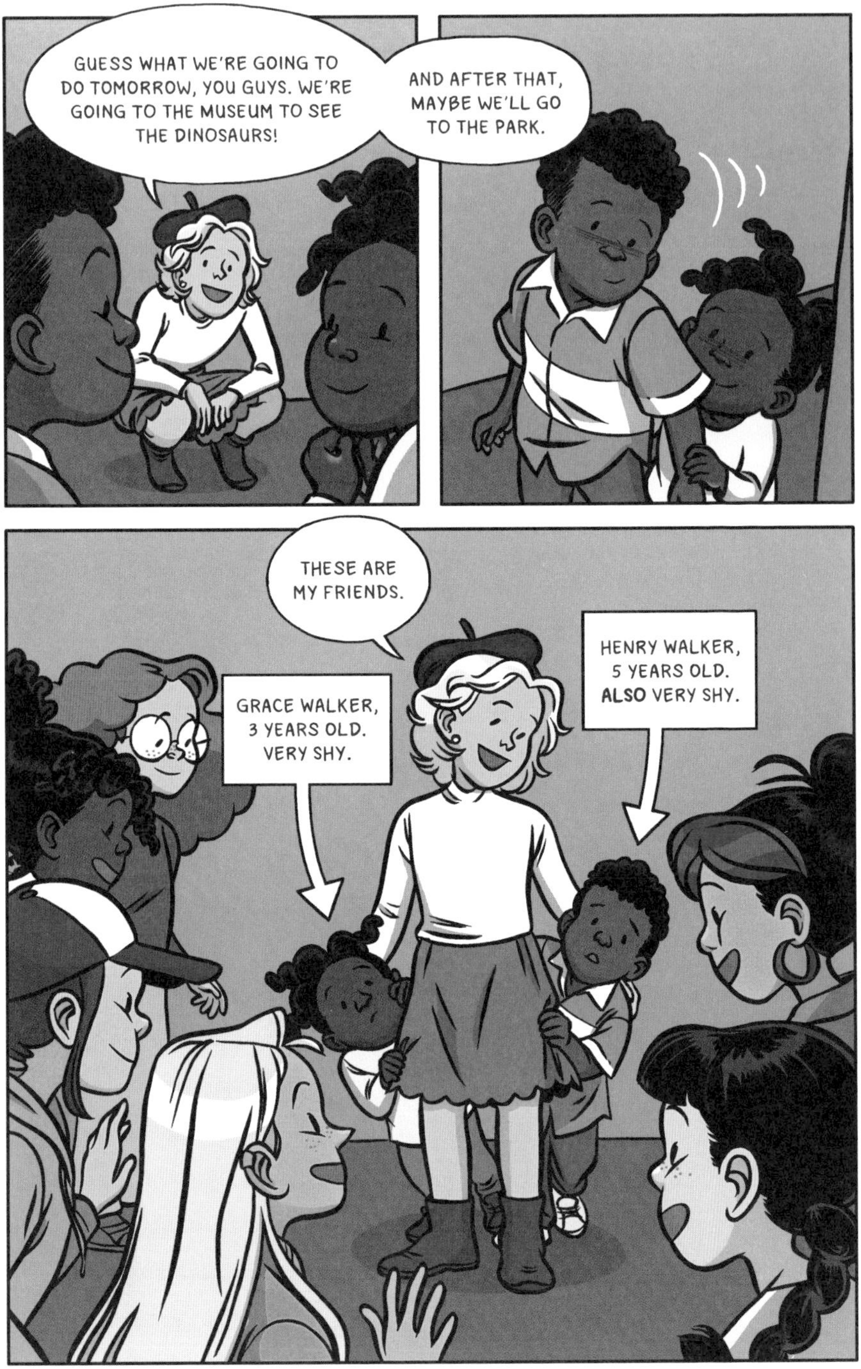
GUESS WHAT WE'RE GOING TO DO TOMORROW, YOU GUYS. WE'RE GOING TO THE MUSEUM TO SEE THE DINOSAURS!
AND AFTER THAT, MAYBE WE'LL GO TO THE PARK.
THESE ARE MY FRIENDS.
GRACE WALKER, 3 YEARS OLD. VERY SHY.
HENRY WALKER, 5 YEARS OLD. **ALSO** VERY SHY.

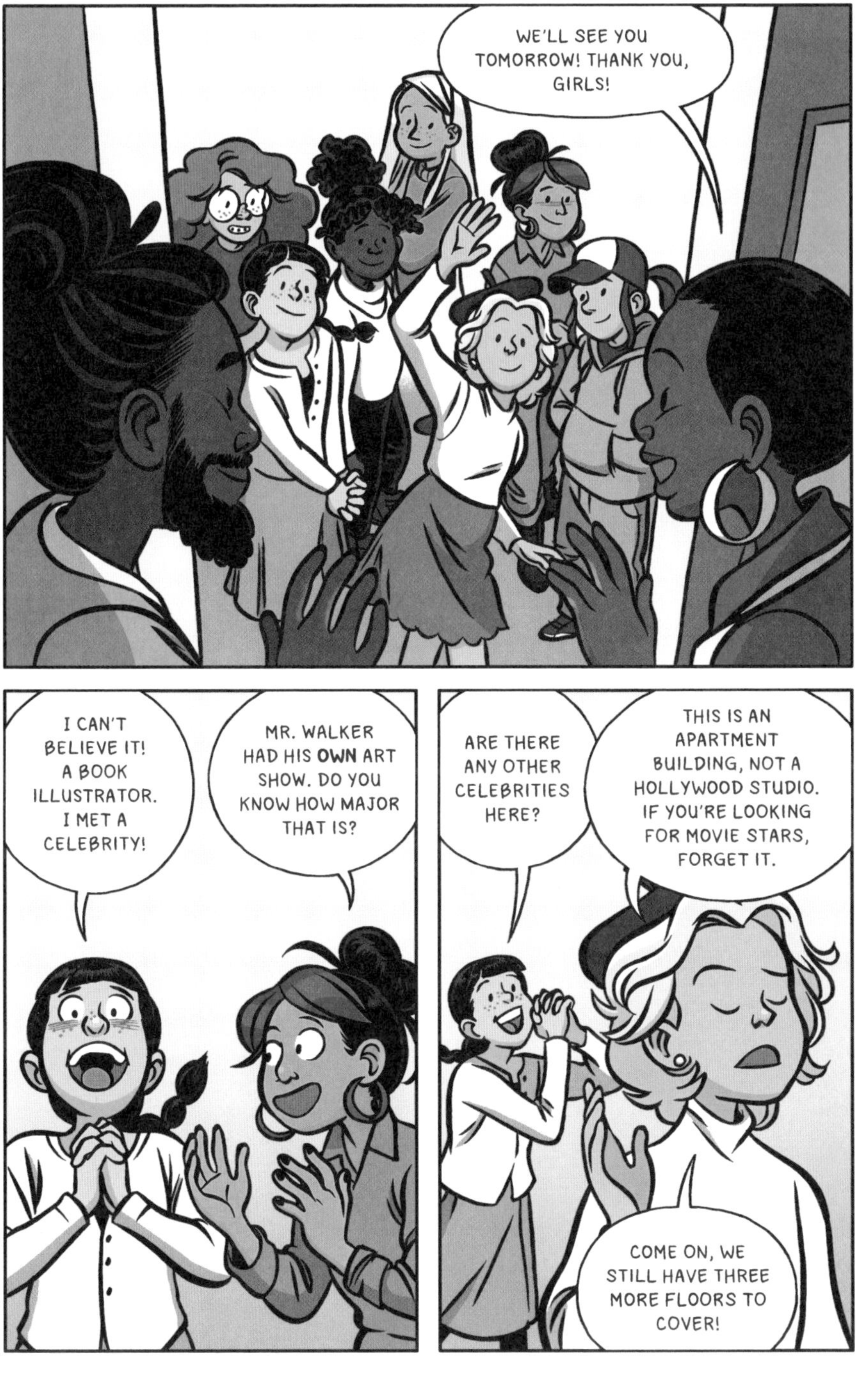
WE'LL SEE YOU TOMORROW! THANK YOU, GIRLS!
I CAN'T BELIEVE IT! A BOOK ILLUSTRATOR. I MET A CELEBRITY!
MR. WALKER HAD HIS **OWN** ART SHOW. DO YOU KNOW HOW MAJOR THAT IS?
ARE THERE ANY OTHER CELEBRITIES HERE?
THIS IS AN APARTMENT BUILDING, NOT A HOLLYWOOD STUDIO. IF YOU'RE LOOKING FOR MOVIE STARS, FORGET IT.
COME ON, WE STILL HAVE THREE MORE FLOORS TO COVER!

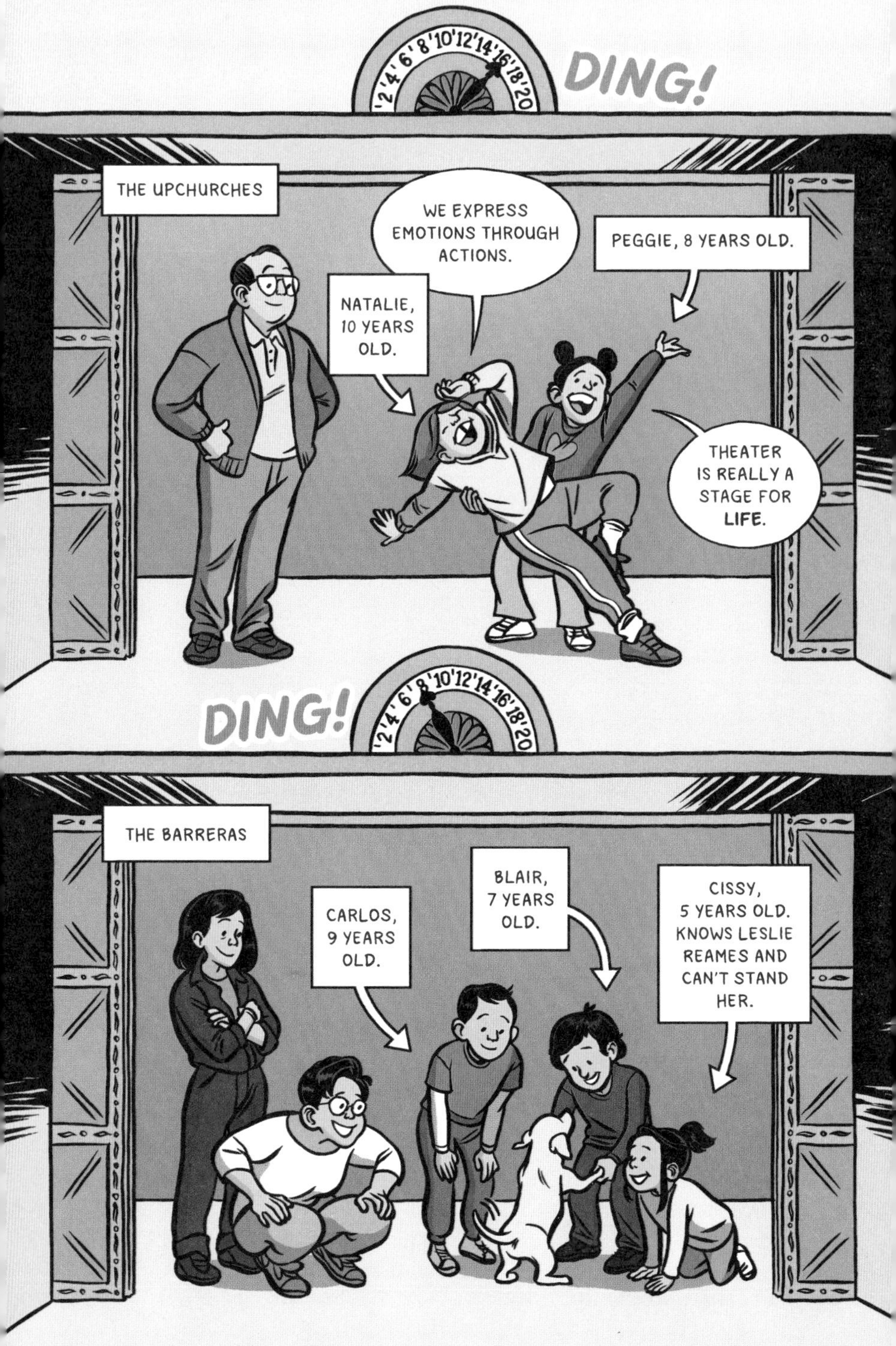
'2 '4 '6 '8 '10 '12 '14 '16 '18 '20
DING!
THE UPCHURCHES
WE EXPRESS EMOTIONS THROUGH ACTIONS.
NATALIE, 10 YEARS OLD.
PEGGIE, 8 YEARS OLD.
THEATER IS REALLY A STAGE FOR **LIFE.**
DING!
'2 '4 '6 '8 '10 '12 '14 '16 '18 '20
THE BARRERAS
CARLOS, 9 YEARS OLD.
BLAIR, 7 YEARS OLD.
CISSY, 5 YEARS OLD. KNOWS LESLIE REAMES AND CAN'T STAND HER.

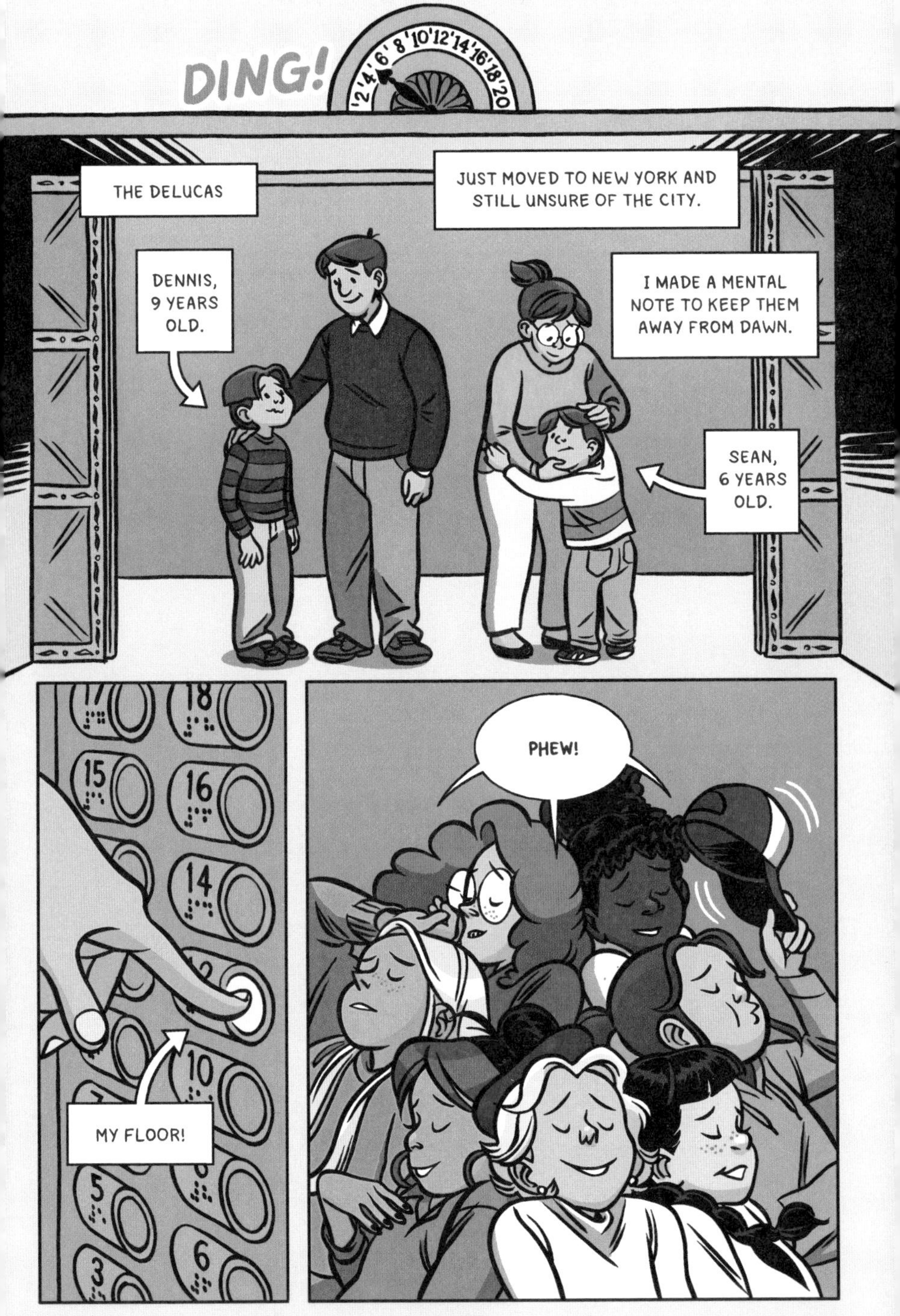
DING!
'2 '4 '6 '8 '10 '12 '14 '16 '18 '20
THE DELUCAS
JUST MOVED TO NEW YORK AND STILL UNSURE OF THE CITY.
DENNIS, 9 YEARS OLD.
I MADE A MENTAL NOTE TO KEEP THEM AWAY FROM DAWN.
SEAN, 6 YEARS OLD.
MY FLOOR!
PHEW!

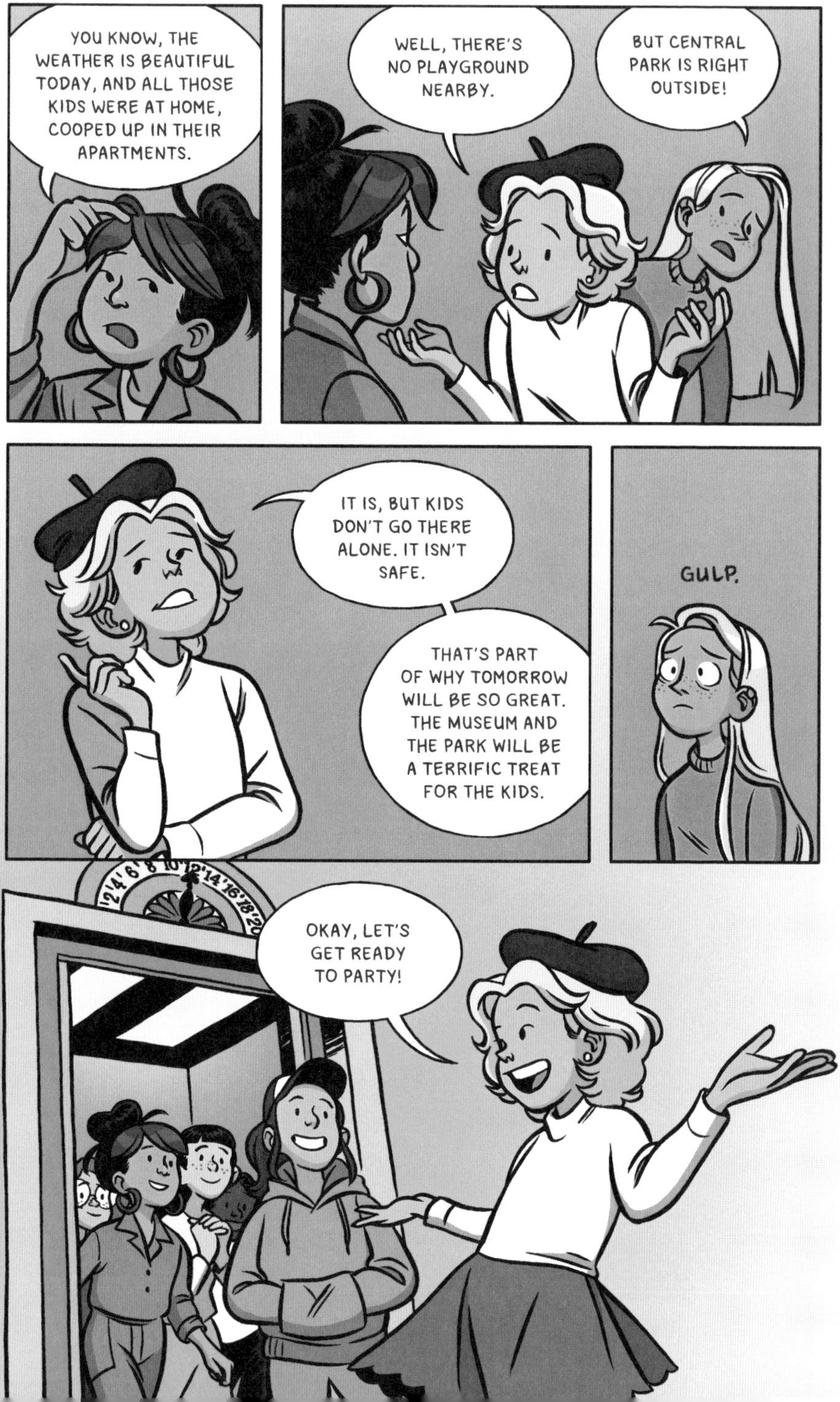
YOU KNOW, THE WEATHER IS BEAUTIFUL TODAY, AND ALL THOSE KIDS WERE AT HOME, COOPED UP IN THEIR APARTMENTS.
WELL, THERE'S NO PLAYGROUND NEARBY.
BUT CENTRAL PARK IS RIGHT OUTSIDE!
IT IS, BUT KIDS DON'T GO THERE ALONE. IT ISN'T SAFE.
THAT'S PART OF WHY TOMORROW WILL BE SO GREAT. THE MUSEUM AND THE PARK WILL BE A TERRIFIC TREAT FOR THE KIDS.
GULP.
OKAY, LET'S GET READY TO PARTY!

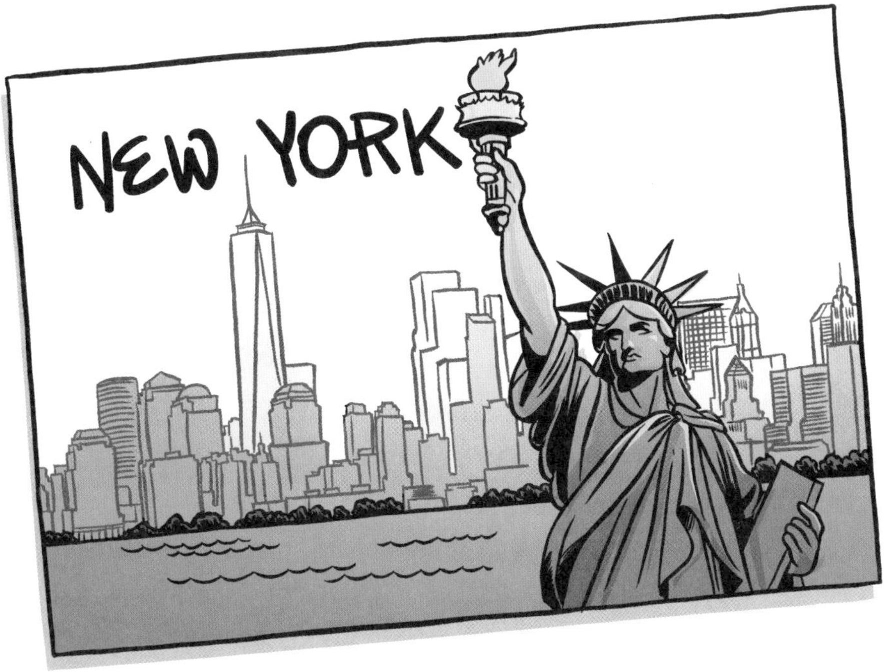
NEW YORK

Dear Dad and Tigger,

New York is fabulous. We met a true and honest celebrity - two of them actually: Mr. and Mrs. Walker. They're artists. I'm looking forward to Stacey's party, which is tonight. Don't worry, Mr. and Mrs. McGill will both be at home. Then, tomorrow we take the kids to the American Museum of Natural History and Central Park!

Love,
Mary Anne

Mr. Richard Spier (and Tigger)
78 Bradford Ct.
Stoneybrook, CT 06800

CHAPTER 5

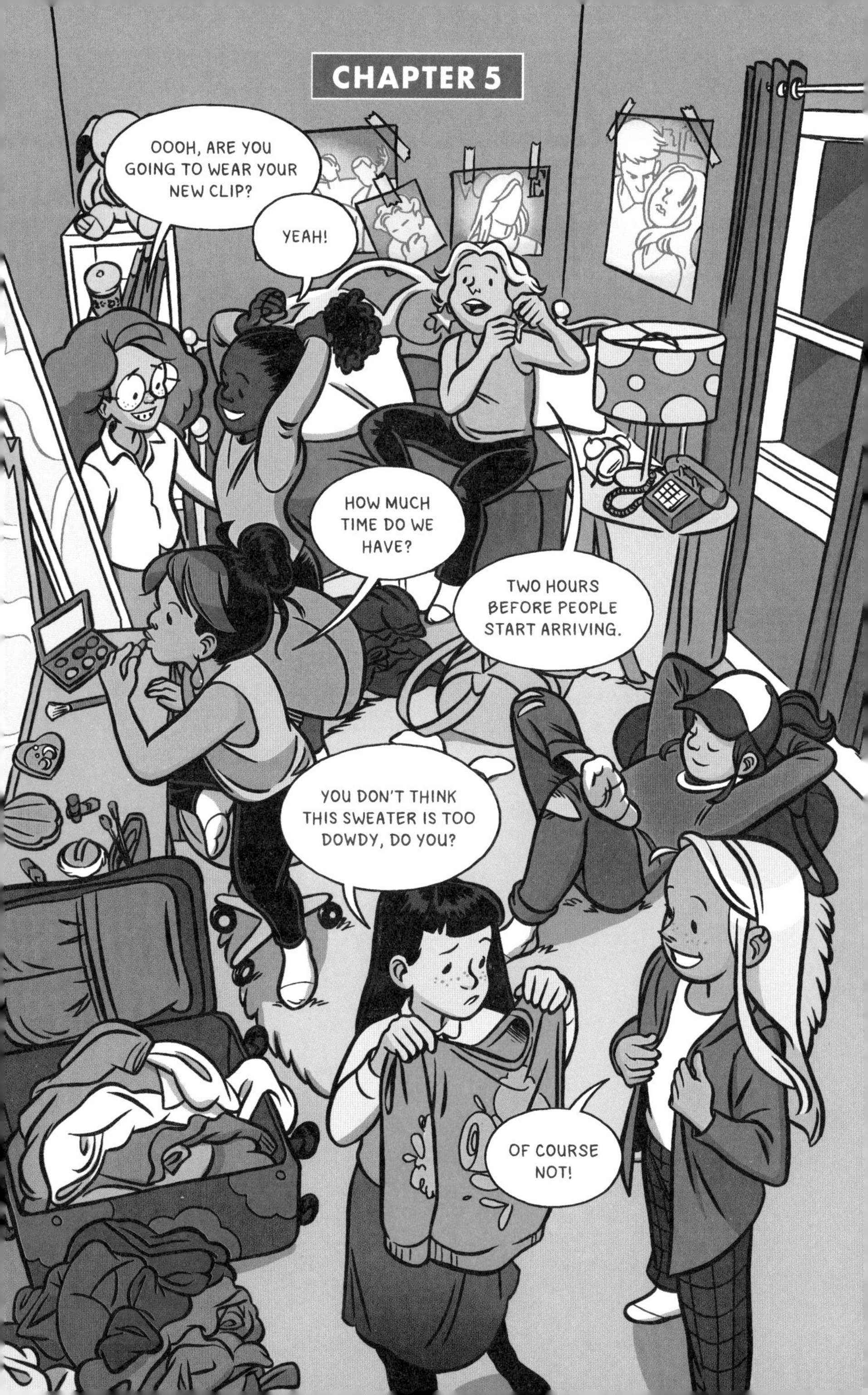
OOOH, ARE YOU GOING TO WEAR YOUR NEW CLIP?
YEAH!
HOW MUCH TIME DO WE HAVE?
TWO HOURS BEFORE PEOPLE START ARRIVING.
YOU DON'T THINK THIS SWEATER IS TOO DOWDY, DO YOU?
OF COURSE NOT!

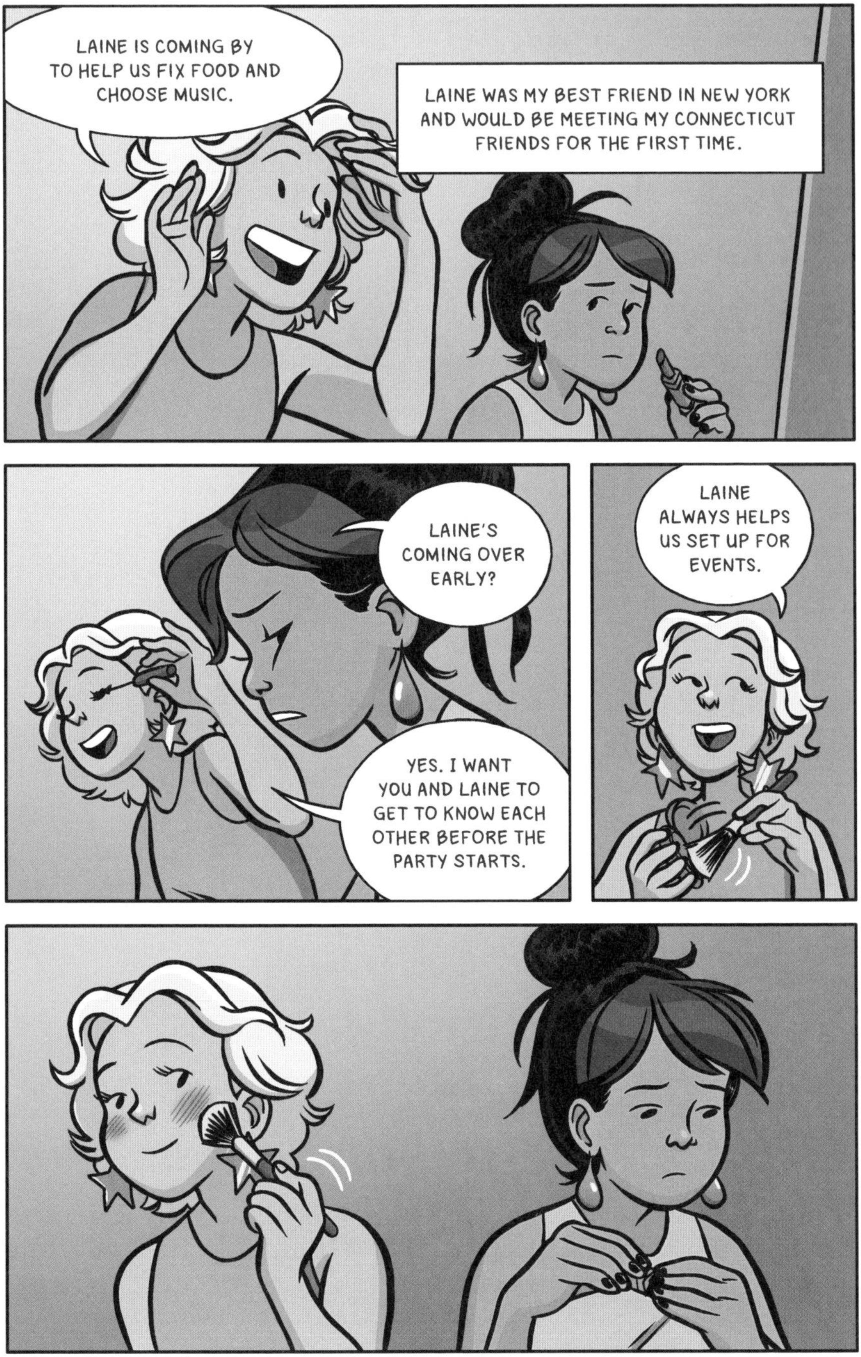
LAINE IS COMING BY TO HELP US FIX FOOD AND CHOOSE MUSIC.
LAINE WAS MY BEST FRIEND IN NEW YORK AND WOULD BE MEETING MY CONNECTICUT FRIENDS FOR THE FIRST TIME.
LAINE'S COMING OVER EARLY?
YES. I WANT YOU AND LAINE TO GET TO KNOW EACH OTHER BEFORE THE PARTY STARTS.
LAINE ALWAYS HELPS US SET UP FOR EVENTS.

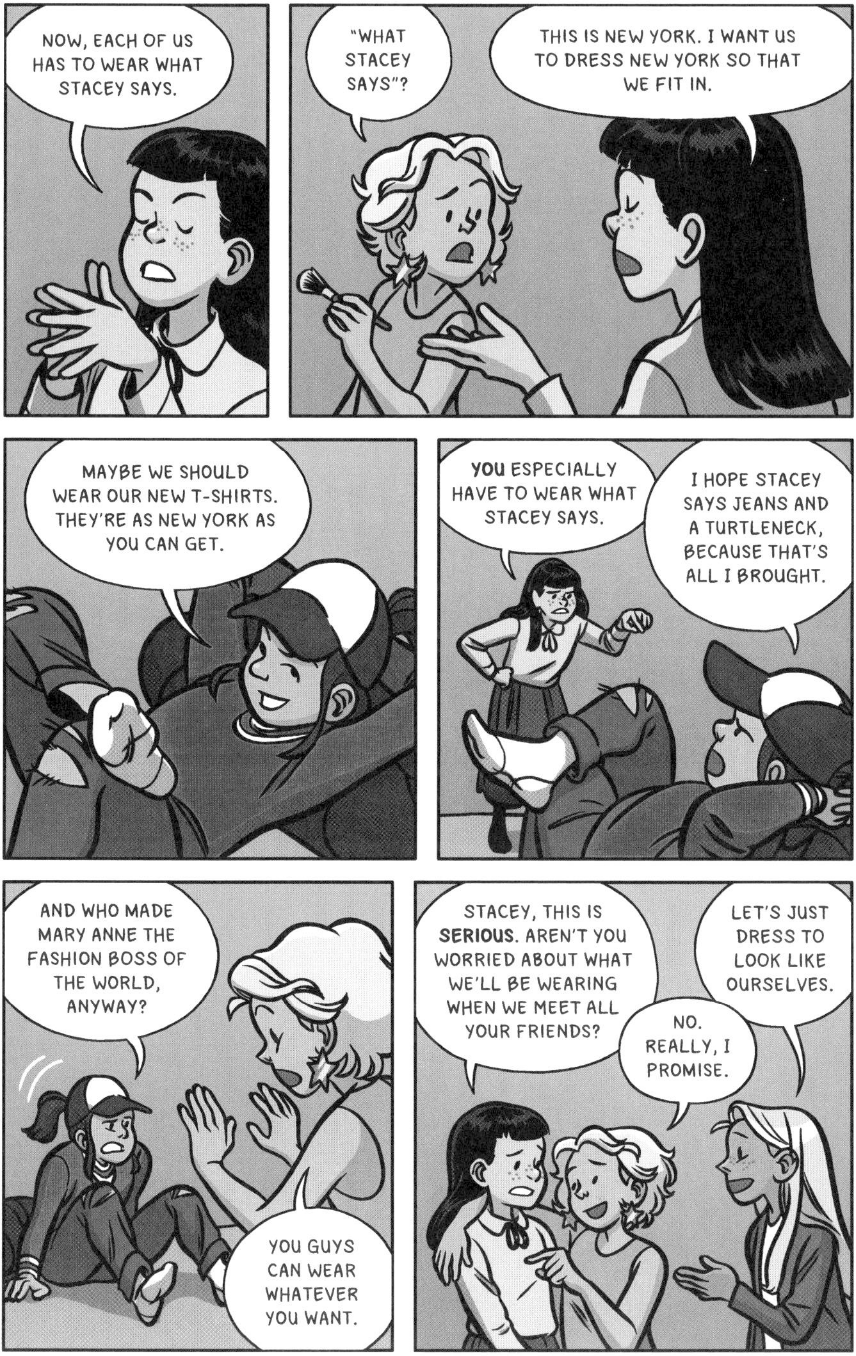
NOW, EACH OF US HAS TO WEAR WHAT STACEY SAYS.
"WHAT STACEY SAYS"?
THIS IS NEW YORK. I WANT US TO DRESS NEW YORK SO THAT WE FIT IN.
MAYBE WE SHOULD WEAR OUR NEW T-SHIRTS. THEY'RE AS NEW YORK AS YOU CAN GET.
YOU ESPECIALLY HAVE TO WEAR WHAT STACEY SAYS.
I HOPE STACEY SAYS JEANS AND A TURTLENECK, BECAUSE THAT'S ALL I BROUGHT.
AND WHO MADE MARY ANNE THE FASHION BOSS OF THE WORLD, ANYWAY?
YOU GUYS CAN WEAR WHATEVER YOU WANT.
STACEY, THIS IS **SERIOUS**. AREN'T YOU WORRIED ABOUT WHAT WE'LL BE WEARING WHEN WE MEET ALL YOUR FRIENDS?
NO. REALLY, I PROMISE.
LET'S JUST DRESS TO LOOK LIKE OURSELVES.

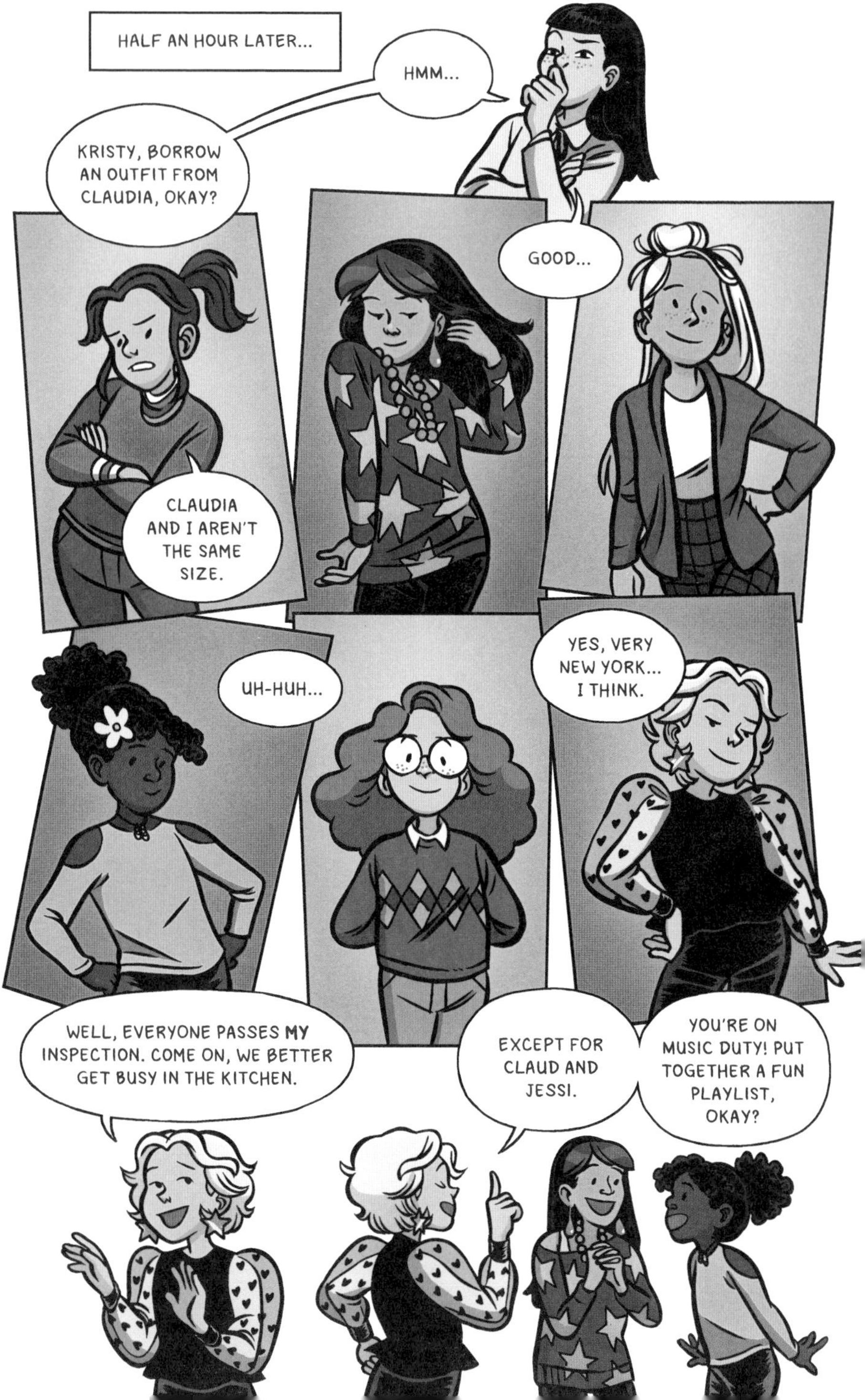
HALF AN HOUR LATER...
HMM...
KRISTY, BORROW AN OUTFIT FROM CLAUDIA, OKAY?
CLAUDIA AND I AREN'T THE SAME SIZE.
GOOD...
UH-HUH...
YES, VERY NEW YORK... I THINK.
WELL, EVERYONE PASSES MY INSPECTION. COME ON, WE BETTER GET BUSY IN THE KITCHEN.
EXCEPT FOR CLAUD AND JESSI.
YOU'RE ON MUSIC DUTY! PUT TOGETHER A FUN PLAYLIST, OKAY?

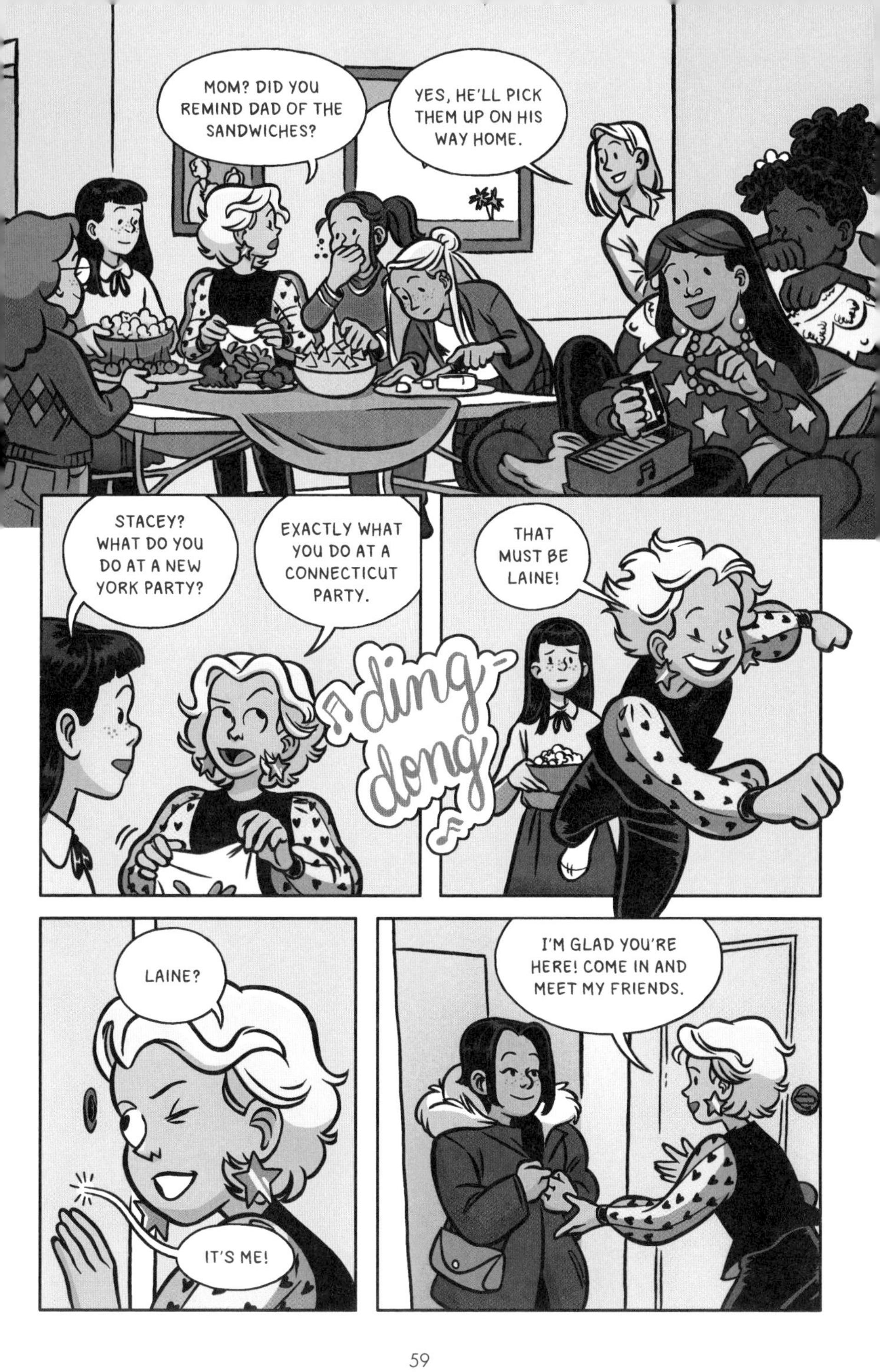
MOM? DID YOU REMIND DAD OF THE SANDWICHES?
YES, HE'LL PICK THEM UP ON HIS WAY HOME.
STACEY? WHAT DO YOU DO AT A NEW YORK PARTY?
EXACTLY WHAT YOU DO AT A CONNECTICUT PARTY.
ding dong
THAT MUST BE LAINE!
LAINE?
IT'S ME!
I'M GLAD YOU'RE HERE! COME IN AND MEET MY FRIENDS.

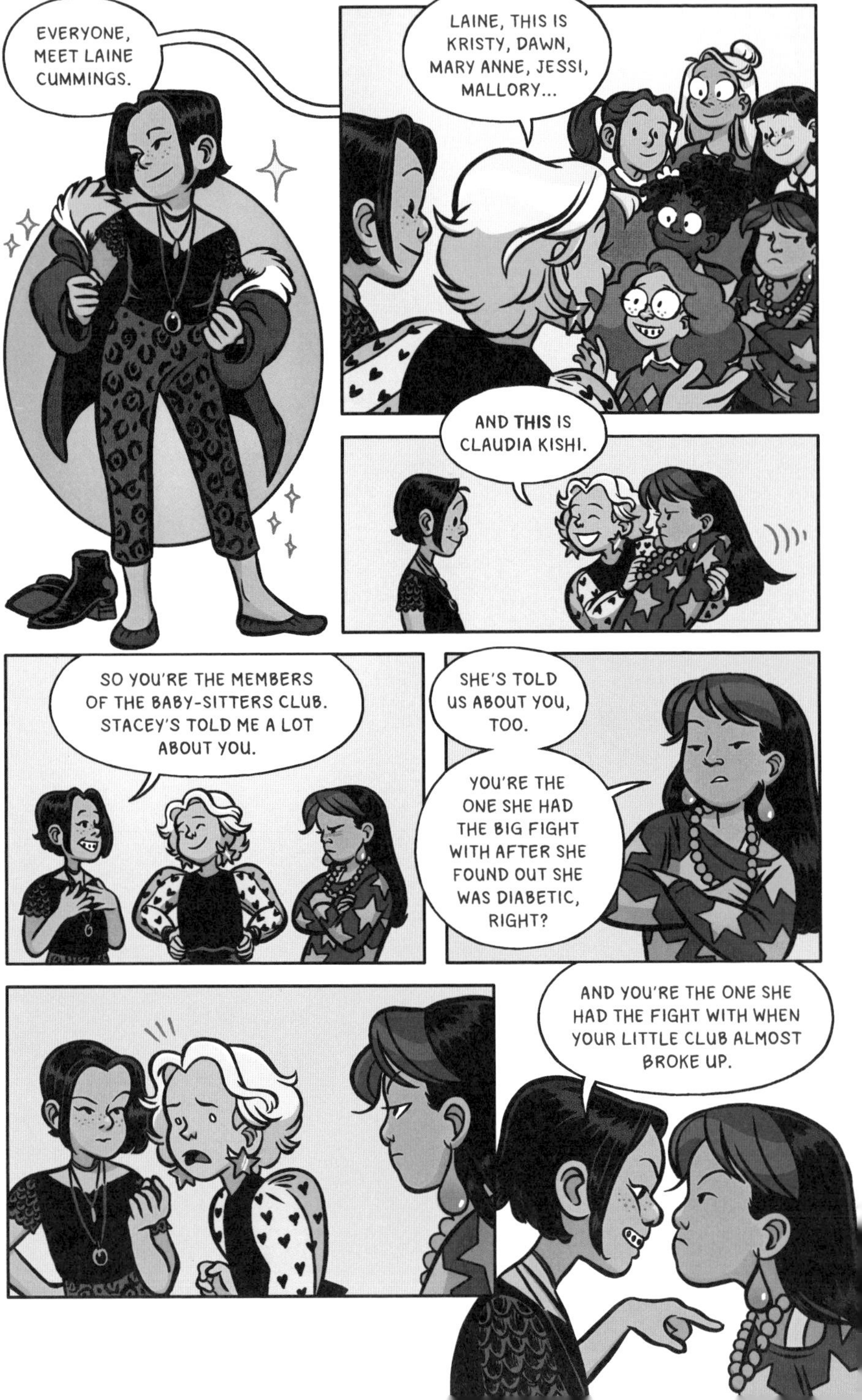
EVERYONE, MEET LAINE CUMMINGS.
LAINE, THIS IS KRISTY, DAWN, MARY ANNE, JESSI, MALLORY...
AND **THIS** IS CLAUDIA KISHI.
SO YOU'RE THE MEMBERS OF THE BABY-SITTERS CLUB. STACEY'S TOLD ME A LOT ABOUT YOU.
SHE'S TOLD US ABOUT YOU, TOO.
YOU'RE THE ONE SHE HAD THE BIG FIGHT WITH AFTER SHE FOUND OUT SHE WAS DIABETIC, RIGHT?
AND YOU'RE THE ONE SHE HAD THE FIGHT WITH WHEN YOUR LITTLE CLUB ALMOST BROKE UP.

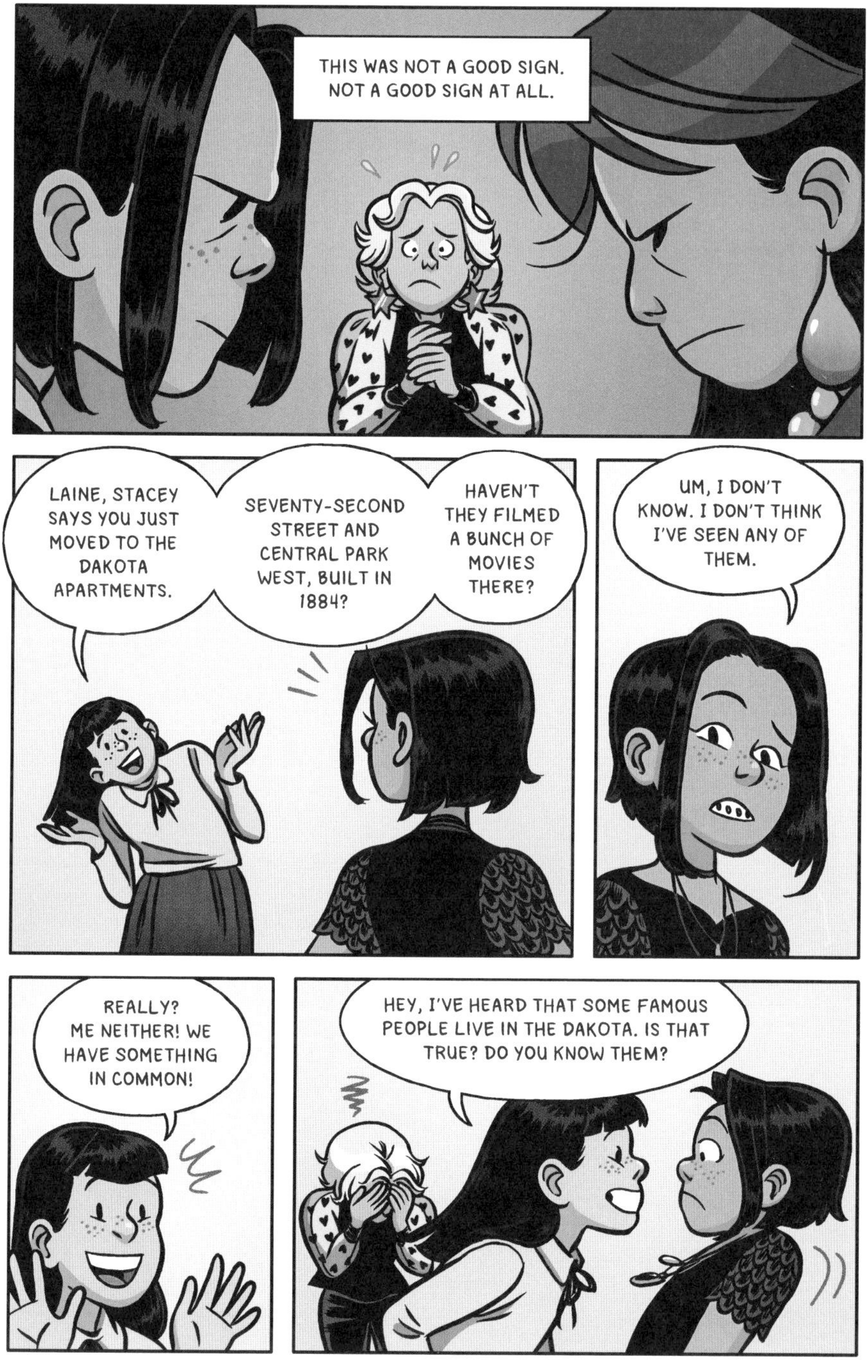
THIS WAS NOT A GOOD SIGN. NOT A GOOD SIGN AT ALL.
LAINE, STACEY SAYS YOU JUST MOVED TO THE DAKOTA APARTMENTS.
SEVENTY-SECOND STREET AND CENTRAL PARK WEST, BUILT IN 1884?
HAVEN'T THEY FILMED A BUNCH OF MOVIES THERE?
UM, I DON'T KNOW. I DON'T THINK I'VE SEEN ANY OF THEM.
REALLY? ME NEITHER! WE HAVE SOMETHING IN COMMON!
HEY, I'VE HEARD THAT SOME FAMOUS PEOPLE LIVE IN THE DAKOTA. IS THAT TRUE? DO YOU KNOW THEM?

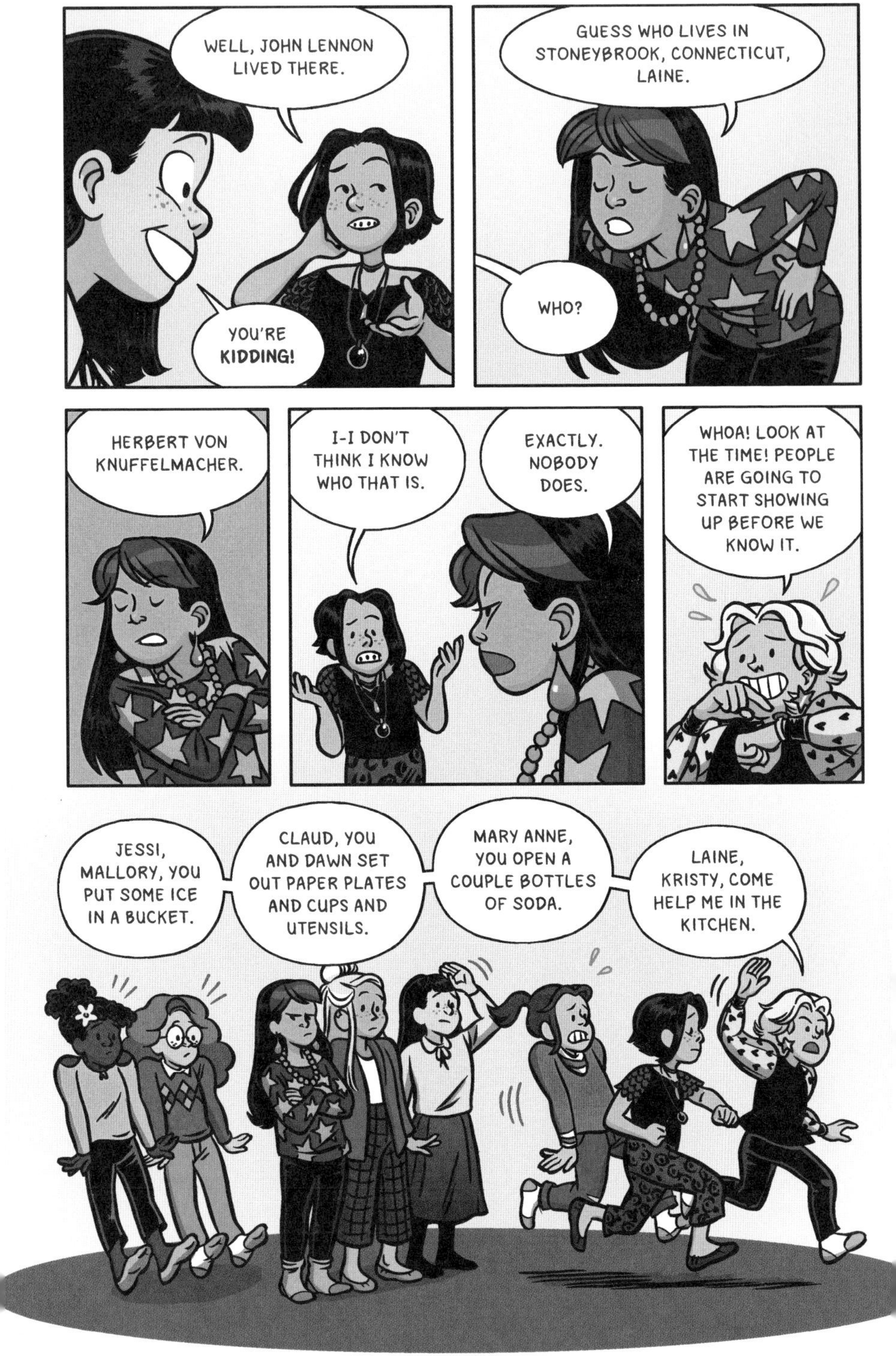
WELL, JOHN LENNON LIVED THERE.
YOU'RE **KIDDING!**
GUESS WHO LIVES IN STONEYBROOK, CONNECTICUT, LAINE.
WHO?
HERBERT VON KNUFFELMACHER.
I-I DON'T THINK I KNOW WHO THAT IS.
EXACTLY. NOBODY DOES.
WHOA! LOOK AT THE TIME! PEOPLE ARE GOING TO START SHOWING UP BEFORE WE KNOW IT.
JESSI, MALLORY, YOU PUT SOME ICE IN A BUCKET.
CLAUD, YOU AND DAWN SET OUT PAPER PLATES AND CUPS AND UTENSILS.
MARY ANNE, YOU OPEN A COUPLE BOTTLES OF SODA.
LAINE, KRISTY, COME HELP ME IN THE KITCHEN.

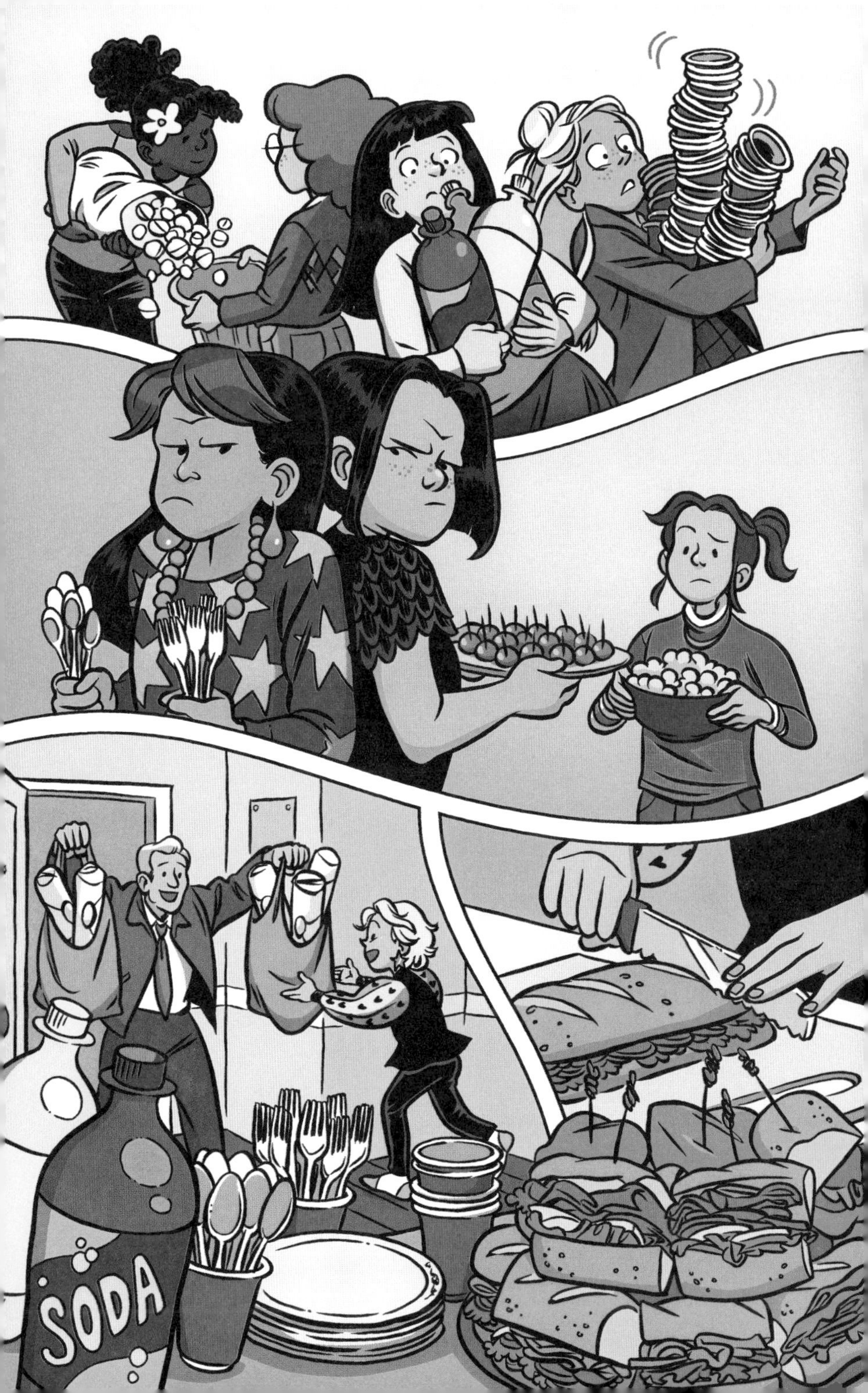
SODA

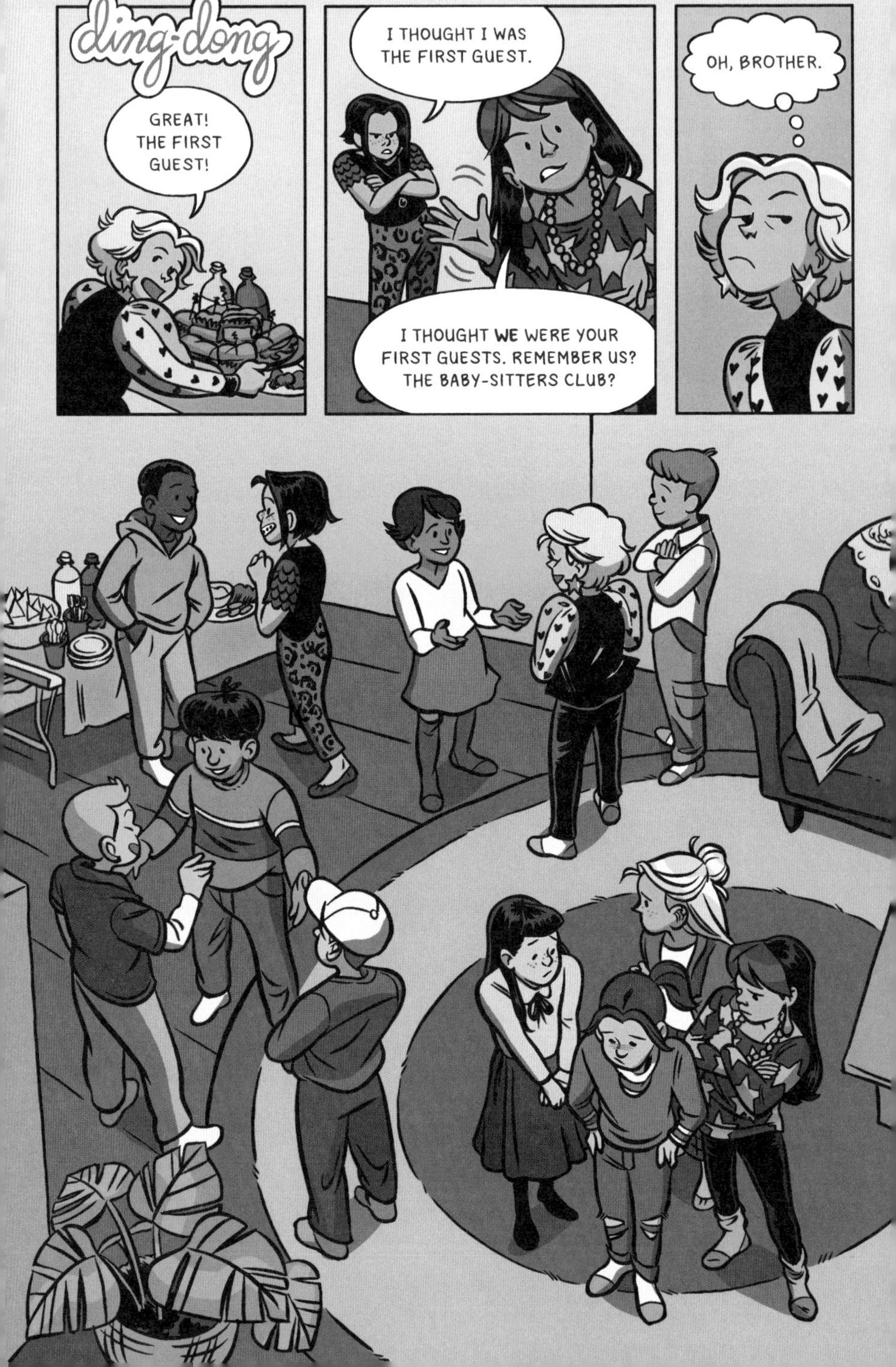
ding-dong
GREAT! THE FIRST GUEST!
I THOUGHT I WAS THE FIRST GUEST.
I THOUGHT **WE** WERE YOUR FIRST GUESTS. REMEMBER US? THE BABY-SITTERS CLUB?
OH, BROTHER.

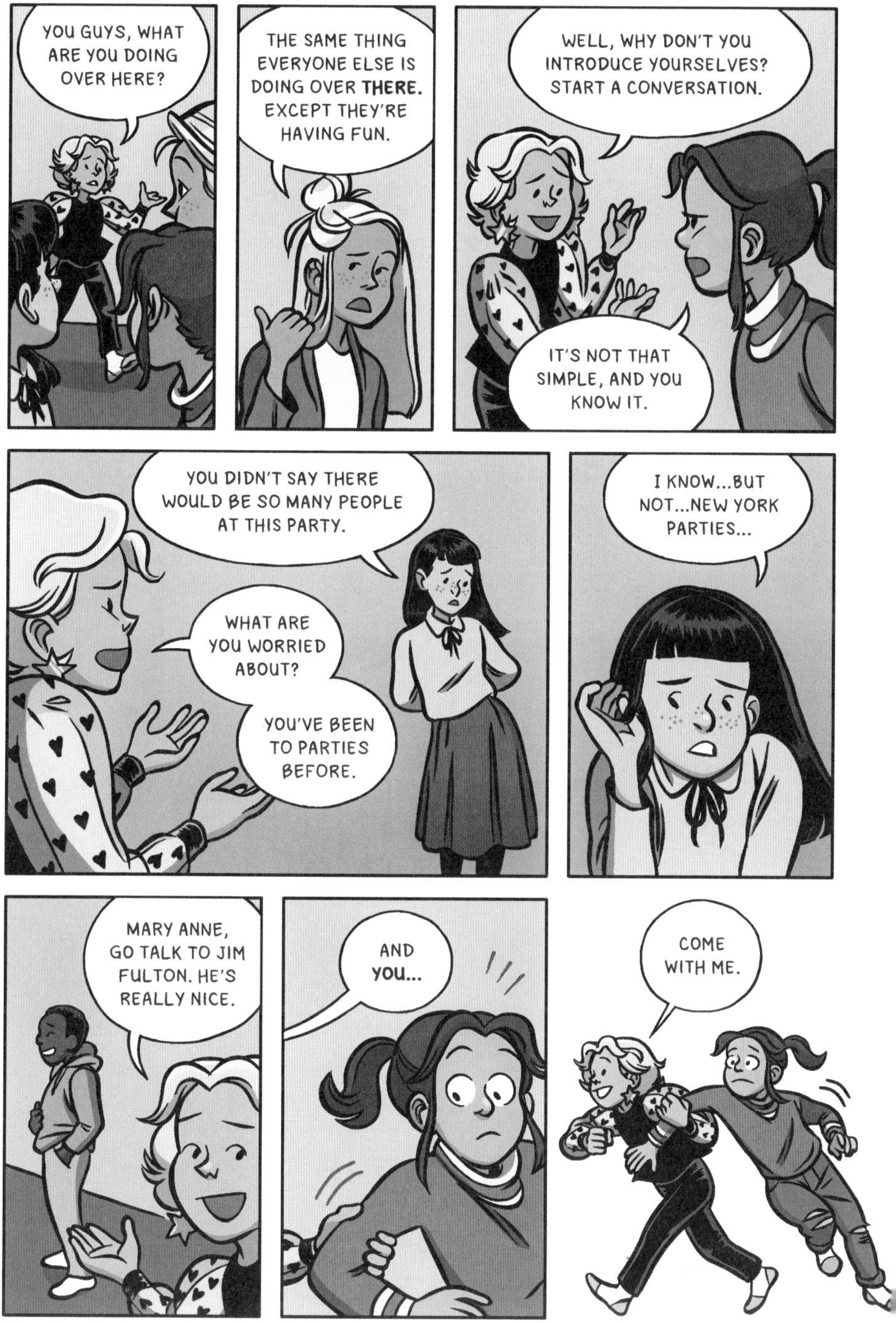
YOU GUYS, WHAT ARE YOU DOING OVER HERE?
THE SAME THING EVERYONE ELSE IS DOING OVER **THERE.** EXCEPT THEY'RE HAVING FUN.
WELL, WHY DON'T YOU INTRODUCE YOURSELVES? START A CONVERSATION.
IT'S NOT THAT SIMPLE, AND YOU KNOW IT.
YOU DIDN'T SAY THERE WOULD BE SO MANY PEOPLE AT THIS PARTY.
WHAT ARE YOU WORRIED ABOUT?
YOU'VE BEEN TO PARTIES BEFORE.
I KNOW...BUT NOT...NEW YORK PARTIES...
MARY ANNE, GO TALK TO JIM FULTON. HE'S REALLY NICE.
AND **YOU...**
COME WITH ME.

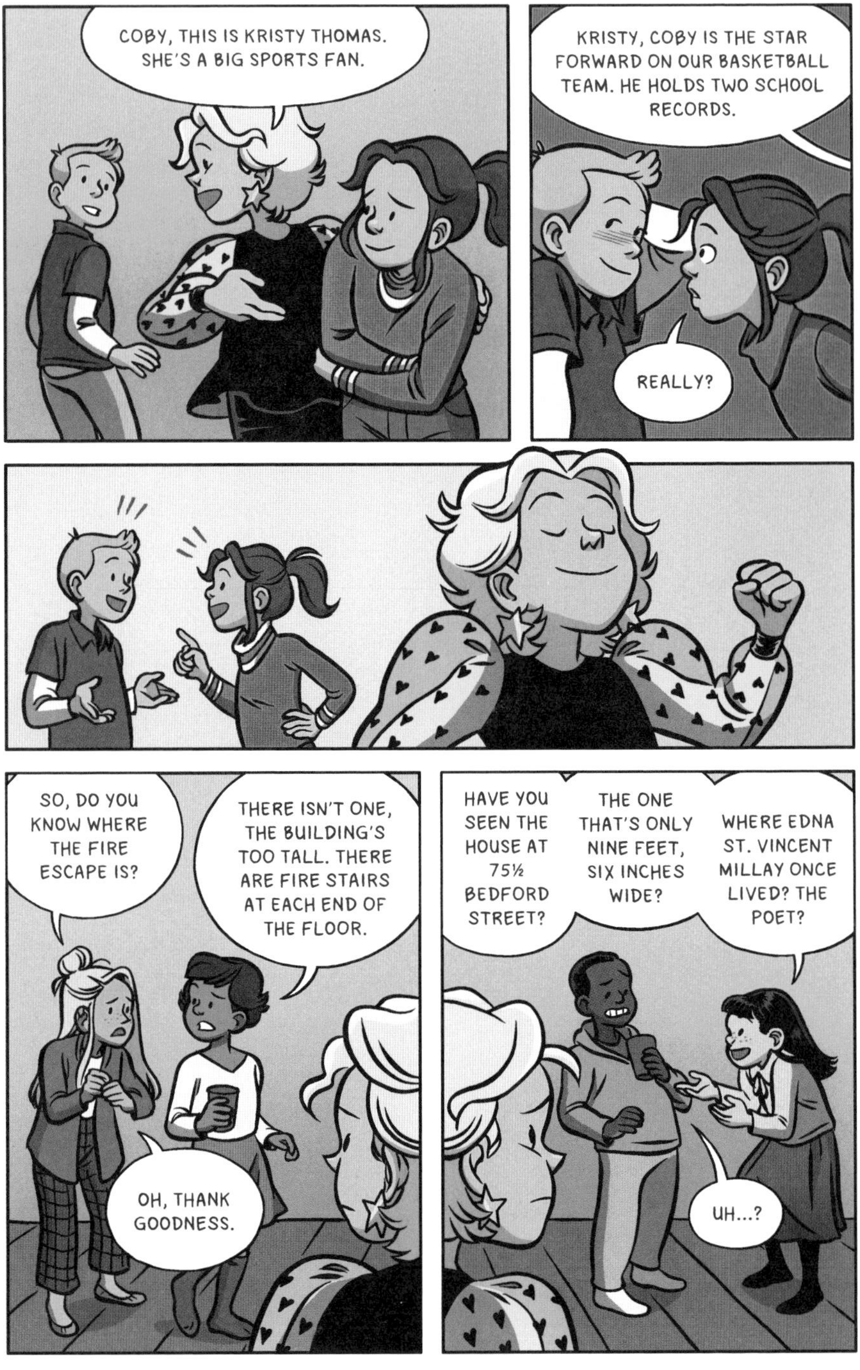
COBY, THIS IS KRISTY THOMAS. SHE'S A BIG SPORTS FAN.
KRISTY, COBY IS THE STAR FORWARD ON OUR BASKETBALL TEAM. HE HOLDS TWO SCHOOL RECORDS.
REALLY?
SO, DO YOU KNOW WHERE THE FIRE ESCAPE IS?
THERE ISN'T ONE, THE BUILDING'S TOO TALL. THERE ARE FIRE STAIRS AT EACH END OF THE FLOOR.
OH, THANK GOODNESS.
HAVE YOU SEEN THE HOUSE AT 75½ BEDFORD STREET?
THE ONE THAT'S ONLY NINE FEET, SIX INCHES WIDE?
WHERE EDNA ST. VINCENT MILLAY ONCE LIVED? THE POET?
UH...?

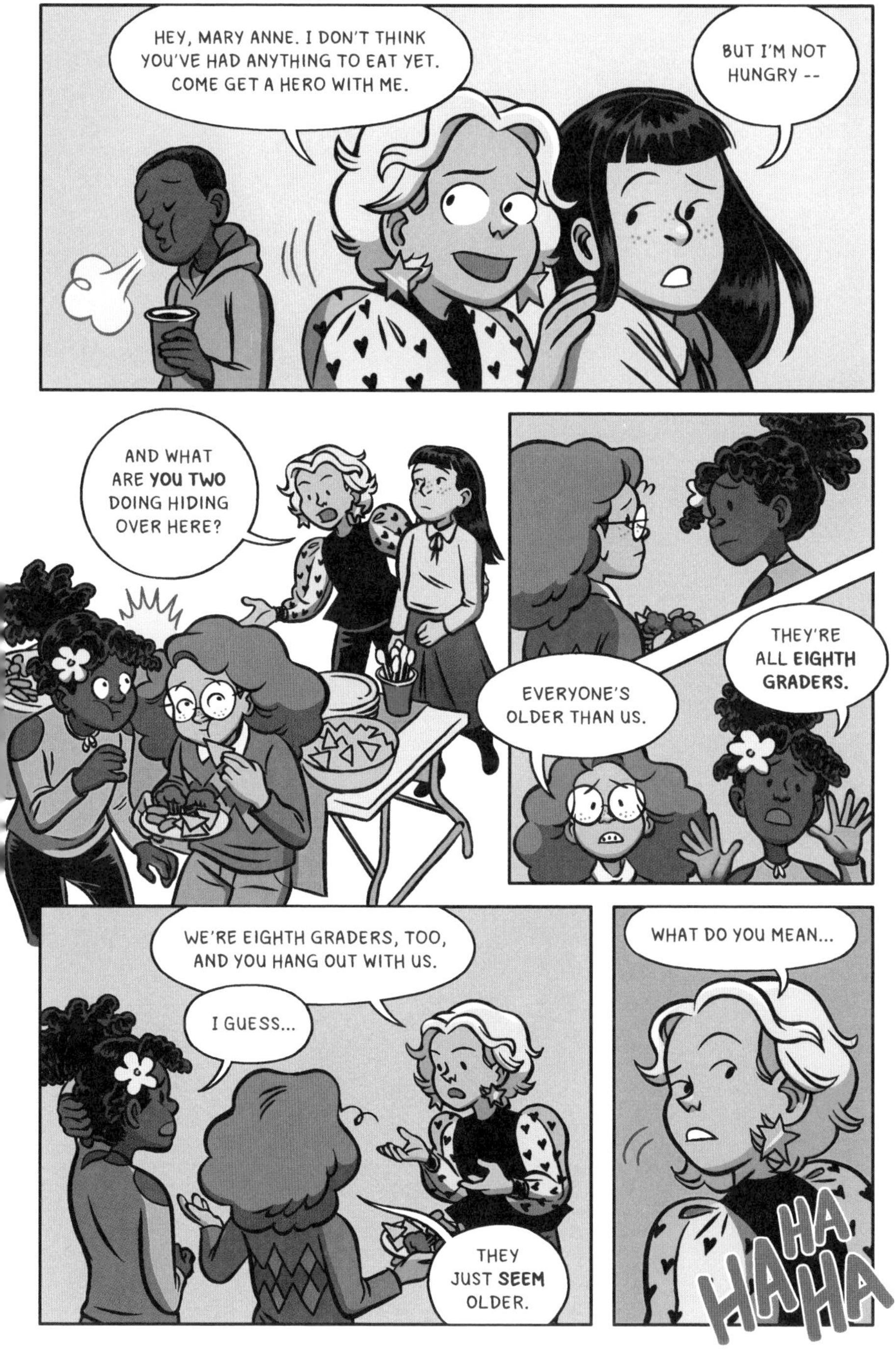
HEY, MARY ANNE. I DON'T THINK YOU'VE HAD ANYTHING TO EAT YET. COME GET A HERO WITH ME.
BUT I'M NOT HUNGRY --
AND WHAT ARE **YOU TWO** DOING HIDING OVER HERE?
EVERYONE'S OLDER THAN US.
THEY'RE ALL **EIGHTH GRADERS.**
WE'RE EIGHTH GRADERS, TOO, AND YOU HANG OUT WITH US.
I GUESS...
THEY JUST **SEEM** OLDER.
WHAT DO YOU MEAN...
HA HA HA HA

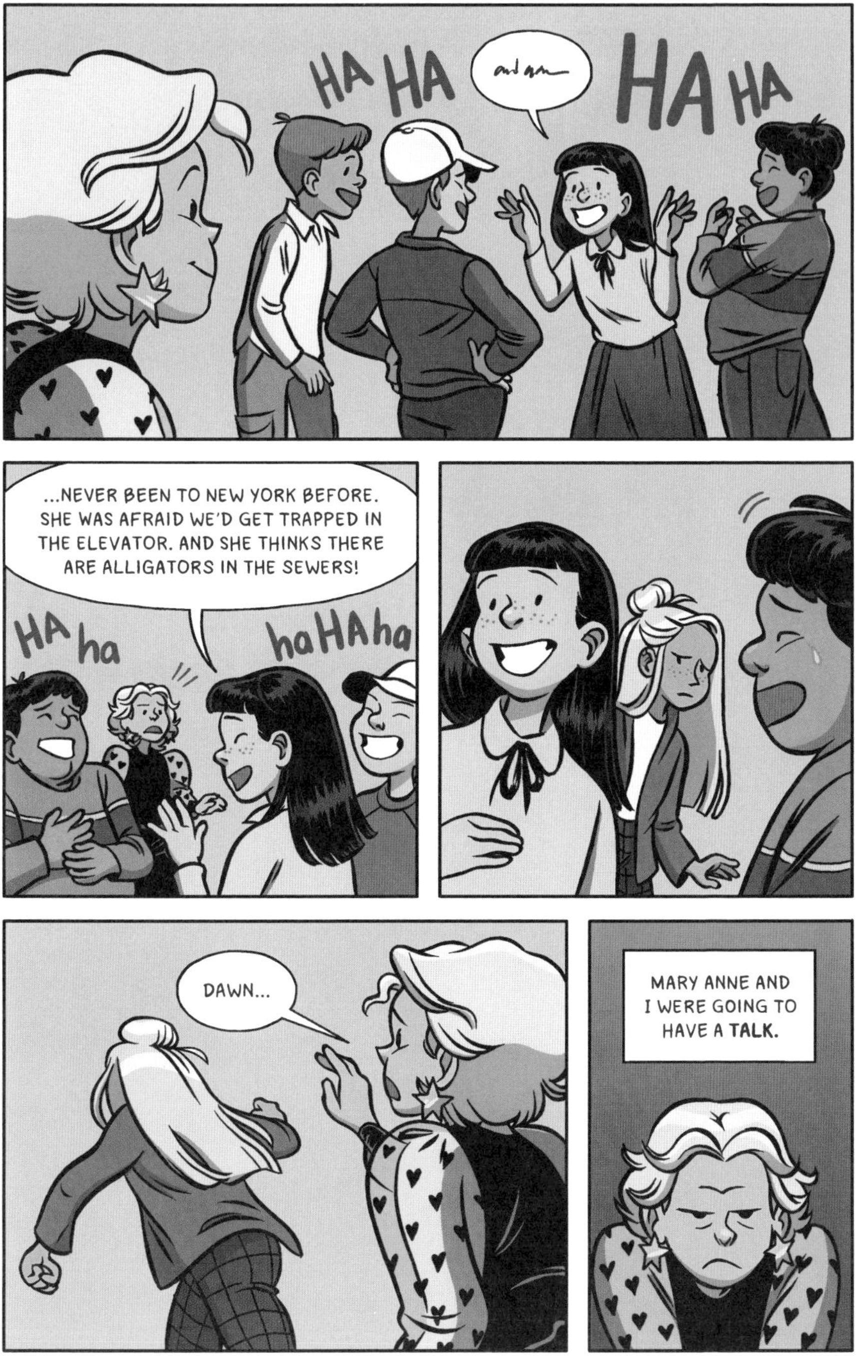
HA HA
HA HA
...NEVER BEEN TO NEW YORK BEFORE. SHE WAS AFRAID WE'D GET TRAPPED IN THE ELEVATOR. AND SHE THINKS THERE ARE ALLIGATORS IN THE SEWERS!
HA ha
haHAha
DAWN...
MARY ANNE AND I WERE GOING TO HAVE A **TALK.**

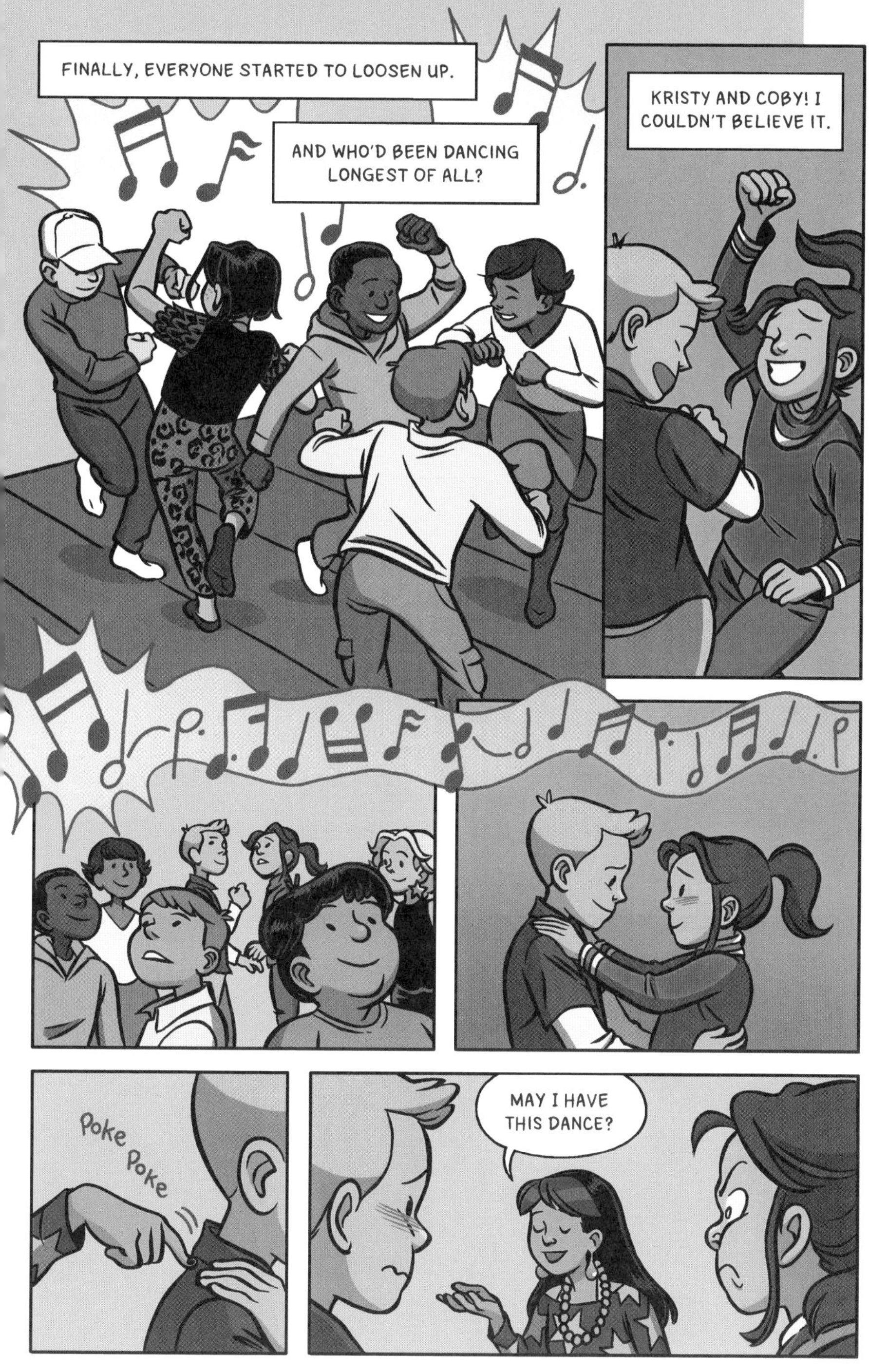
FINALLY, EVERYONE STARTED TO LOOSEN UP.
AND WHO'D BEEN DANCING LONGEST OF ALL?
KRISTY AND COBY! I COULDN'T BELIEVE IT.
POKE POKE
MAY I HAVE THIS DANCE?

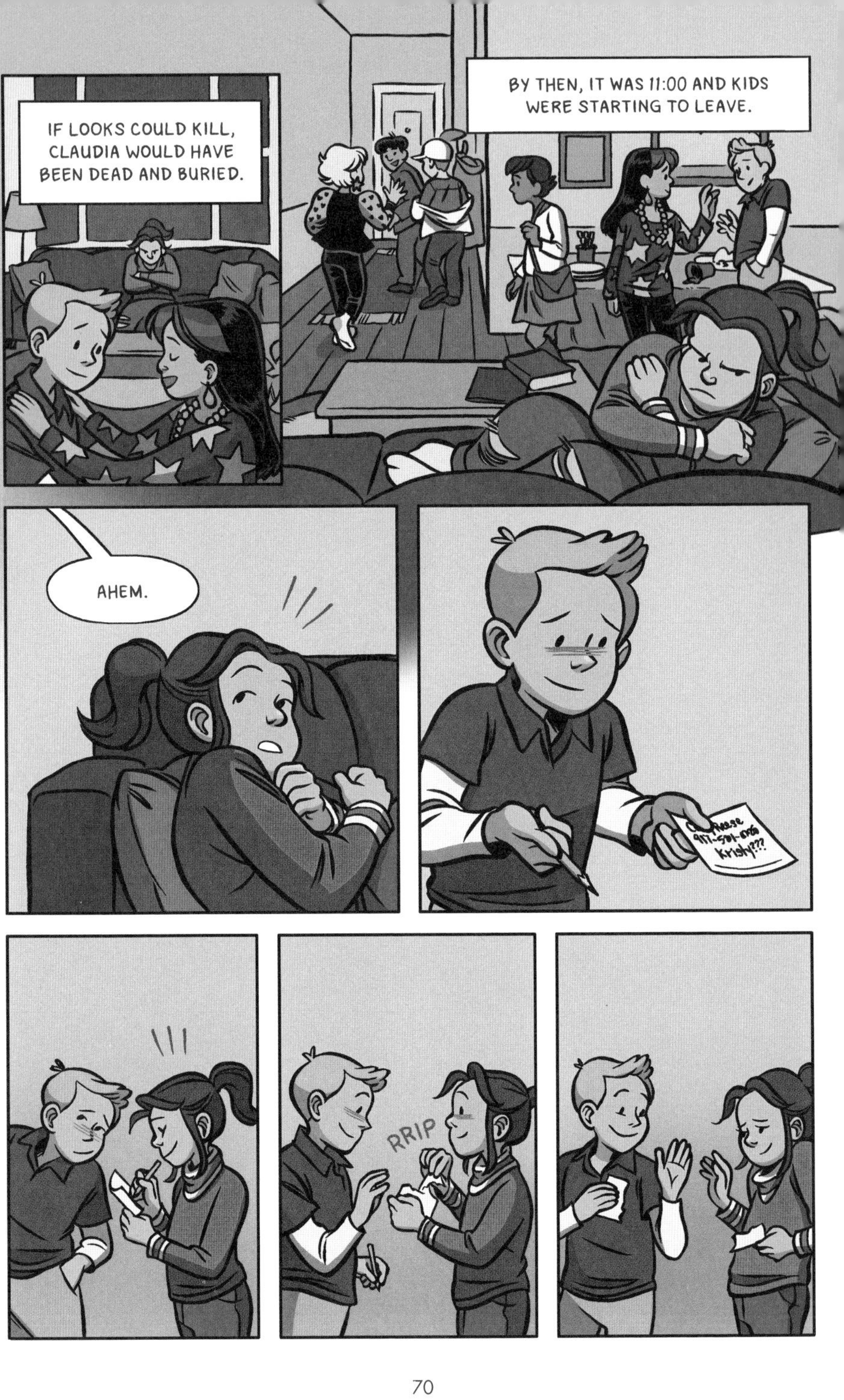
IF LOOKS COULD KILL, CLAUDIA WOULD HAVE BEEN DEAD AND BURIED.
BY THEN, IT WAS 11:00 AND KIDS WERE STARTING TO LEAVE.
AHEM.
Kristy???
RRIP

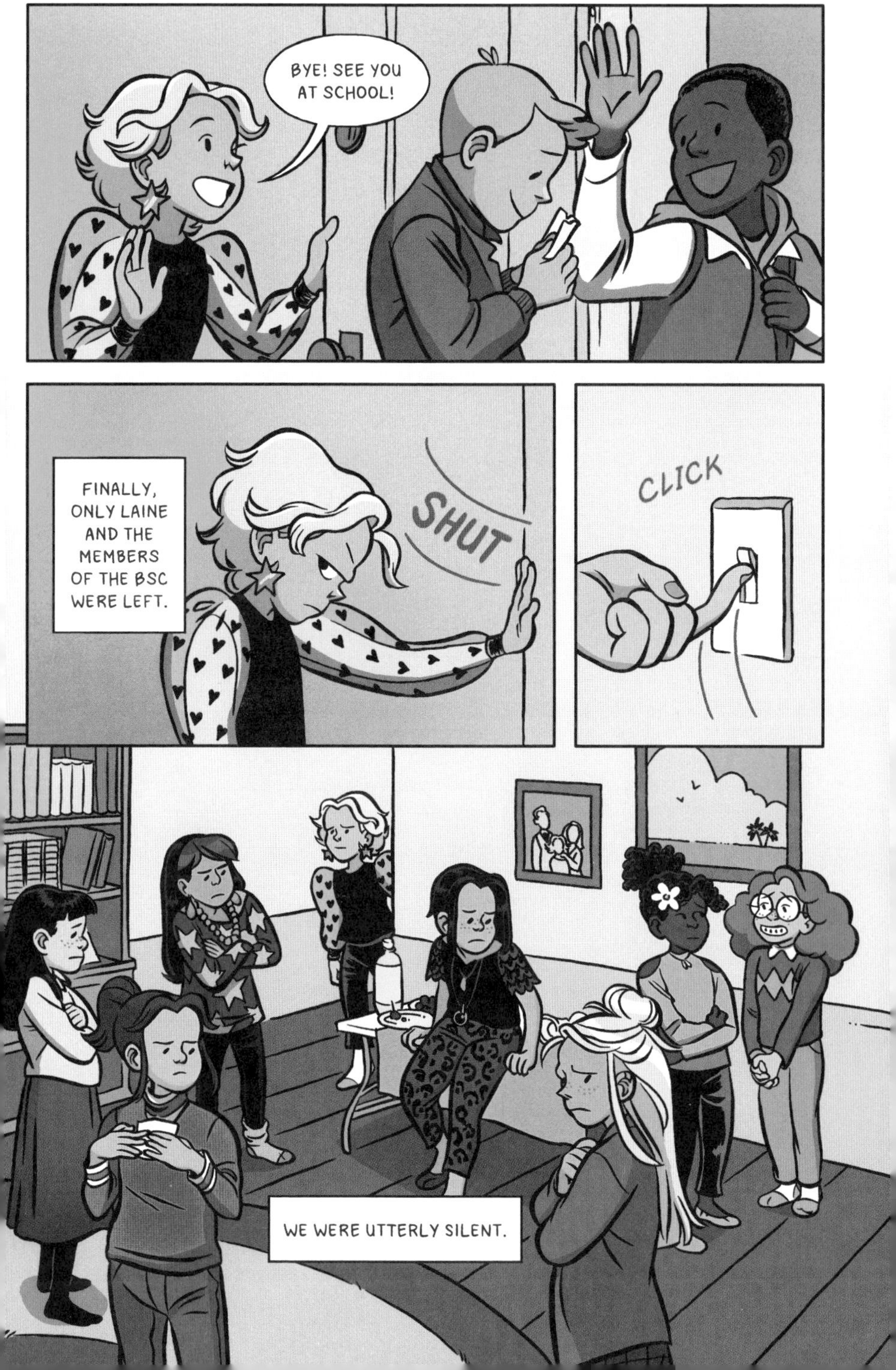
BYE! SEE YOU AT SCHOOL!
FINALLY, ONLY LAINE AND THE MEMBERS OF THE BSC WERE LEFT.
SHUT
CLICK
WE WERE UTTERLY SILENT.

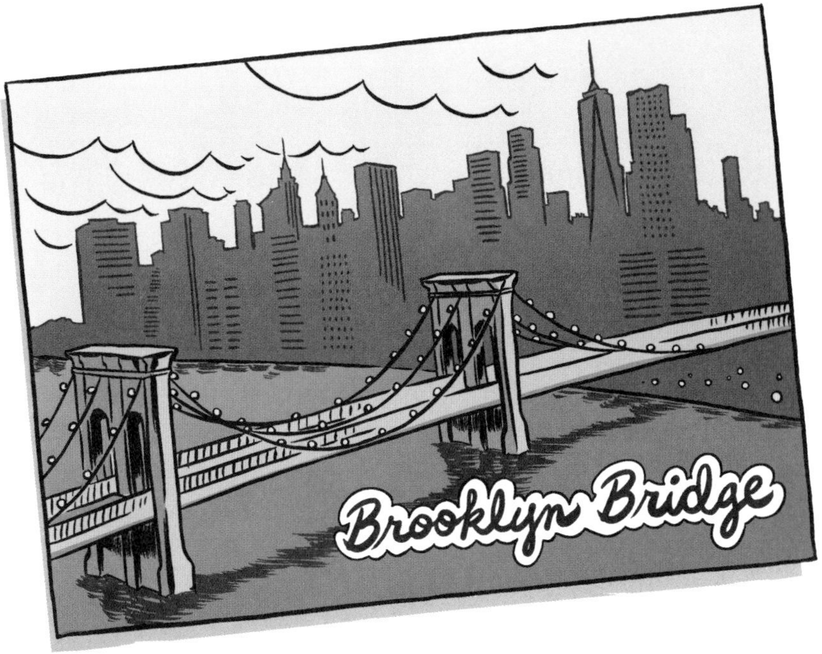
Brooklyn Bridge

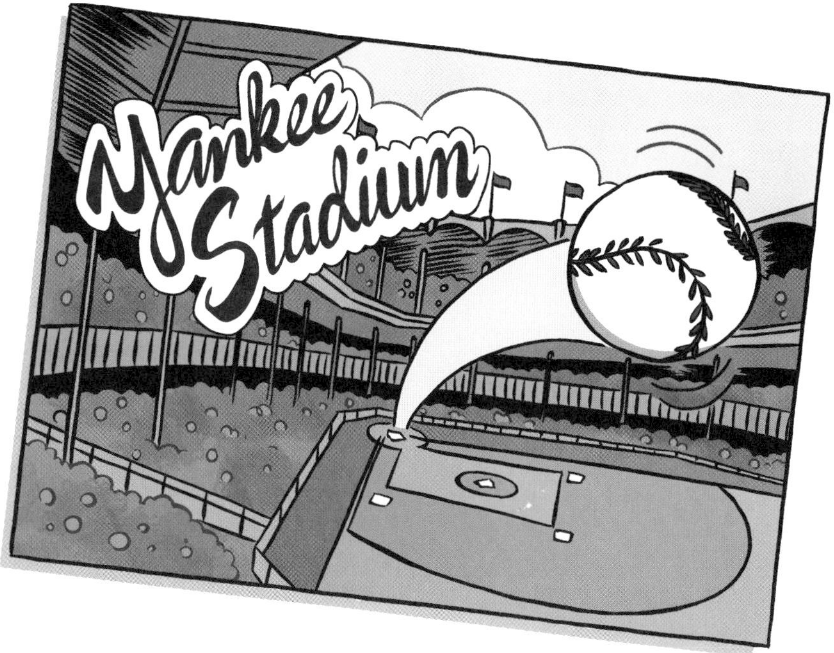
Yankee Stadium

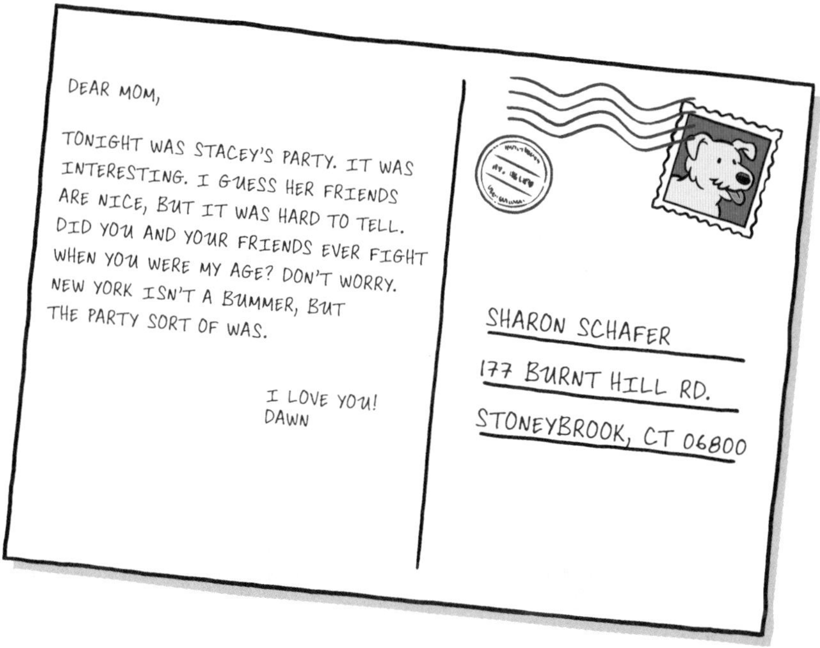
DEAR MOM,
TONIGHT WAS STACEY'S PARTY. IT WAS INTERESTING. I GUESS HER FRIENDS ARE NICE, BUT IT WAS HARD TO TELL. DID YOU AND YOUR FRIENDS EVER FIGHT WHEN YOU WERE MY AGE? DON'T WORRY. NEW YORK ISN'T A BUMMER, BUT THE PARTY SORT OF WAS.
I LOVE YOU!
DAWN
SHARON SCHAFER
177 BURNT HILL RD.
STONEYBROOK, CT 06800

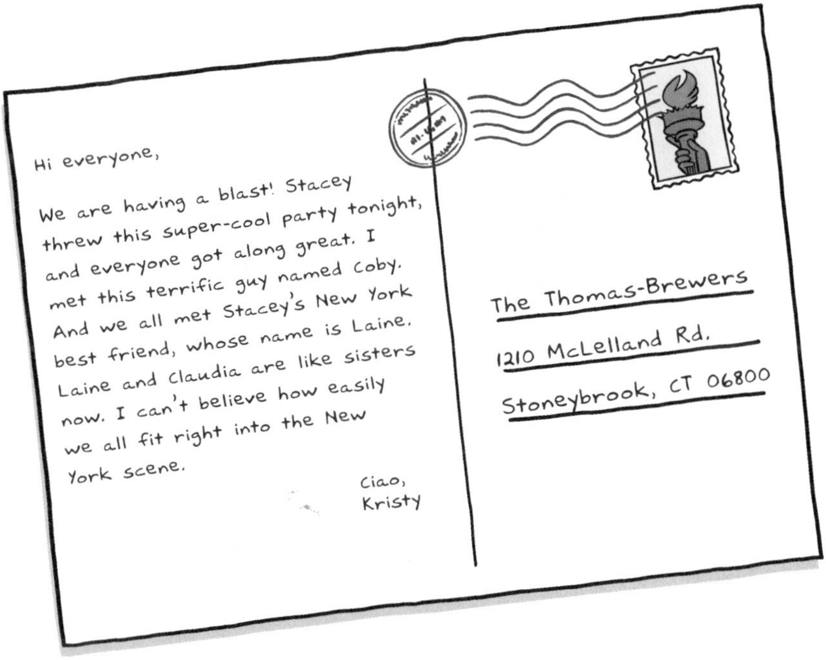
Hi everyone,
We are having a blast! Stacey threw this super-cool party tonight, and everyone got along great. I met this terrific guy named Coby. And we all met Stacey's New York best friend, whose name is Laine. Laine and Claudia are like sisters now. I can't believe how easily we all fit right into the New York scene.
Ciao,
Kristy
The Thomas-Brewers
1210 McLelland Rd.
Stoneybrook, CT 06800

CHAPTER 6

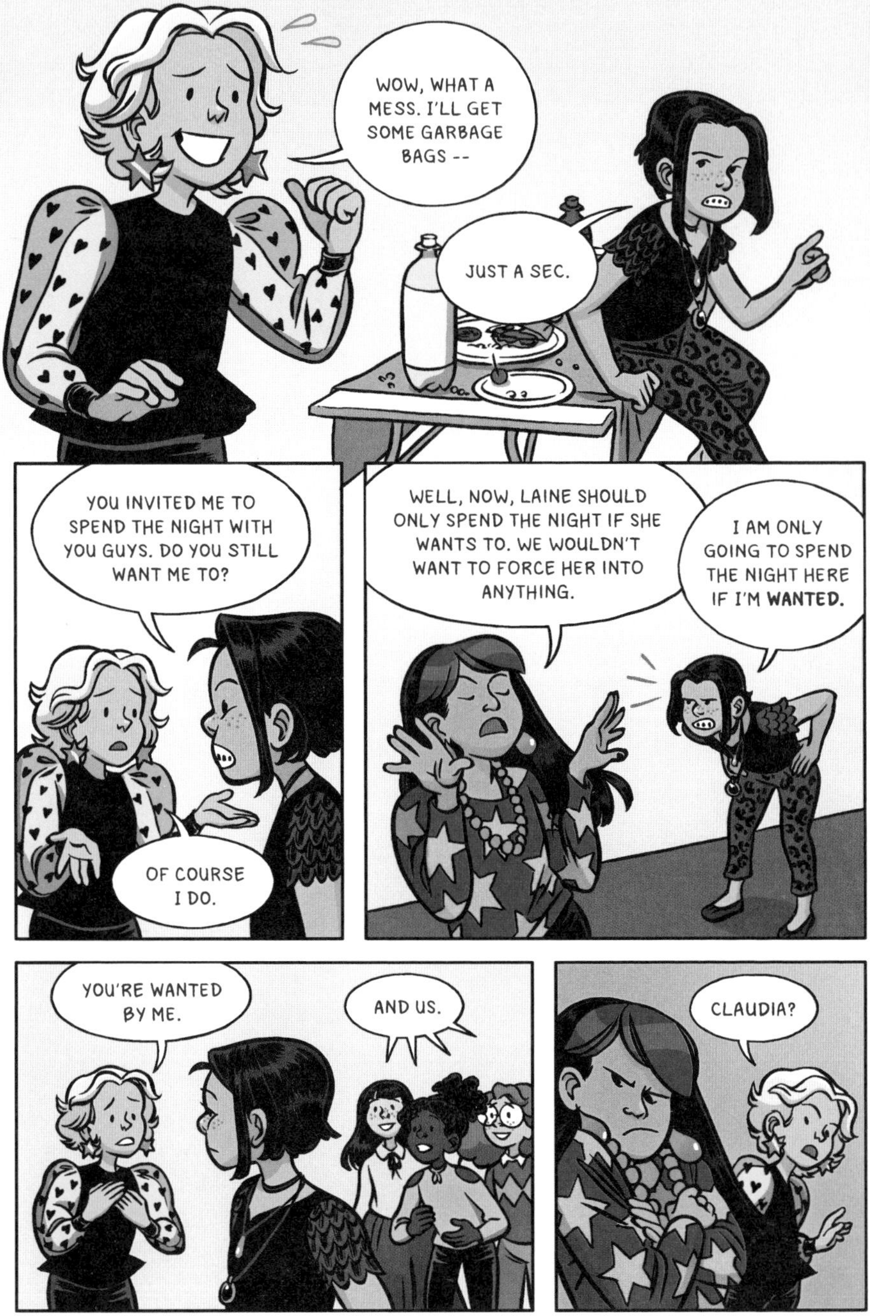
WOW, WHAT A MESS. I'LL GET SOME GARBAGE BAGS --
JUST A SEC.
YOU INVITED ME TO SPEND THE NIGHT WITH YOU GUYS. DO YOU STILL WANT ME TO?
OF COURSE I DO.
WELL, NOW, LAINE SHOULD ONLY SPEND THE NIGHT IF SHE WANTS TO. WE WOULDN'T WANT TO FORCE HER INTO ANYTHING.
I AM ONLY GOING TO SPEND THE NIGHT HERE IF I'M **WANTED.**
YOU'RE WANTED BY ME.
AND US.
CLAUDIA?

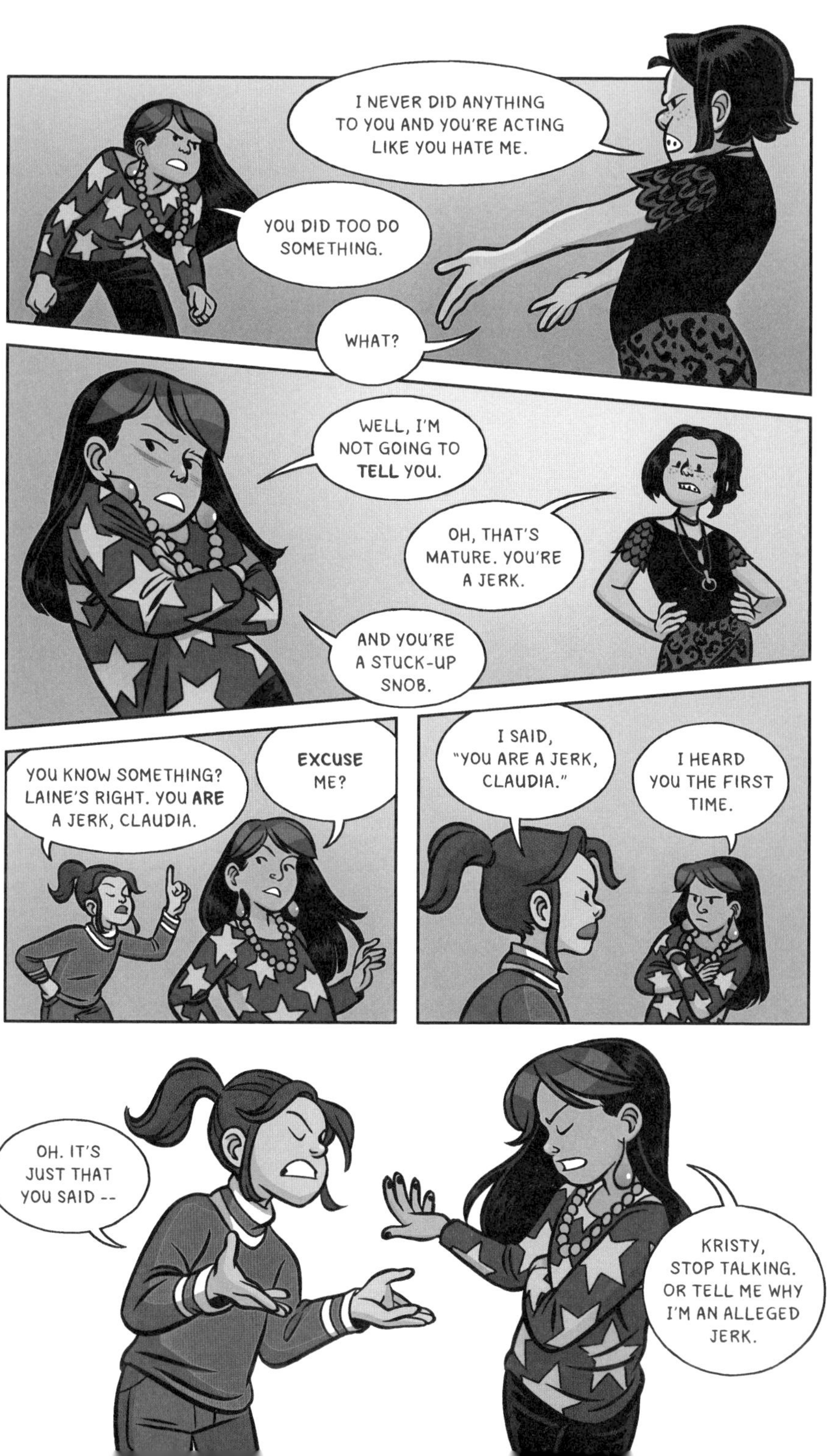
I NEVER DID ANYTHING TO YOU AND YOU'RE ACTING LIKE YOU HATE ME.
YOU DID TOO DO SOMETHING.
WHAT?
WELL, I'M NOT GOING TO **TELL** YOU.
OH, THAT'S MATURE. YOU'RE A JERK.
AND YOU'RE A STUCK-UP SNOB.
YOU KNOW SOMETHING? LAINE'S RIGHT. YOU **ARE** A JERK, CLAUDIA.
EXCUSE ME?
I SAID, "YOU ARE A JERK, CLAUDIA."
I HEARD YOU THE FIRST TIME.
OH. IT'S JUST THAT YOU SAID --
KRISTY, STOP TALKING. OR TELL ME WHY I'M AN ALLEGED JERK.

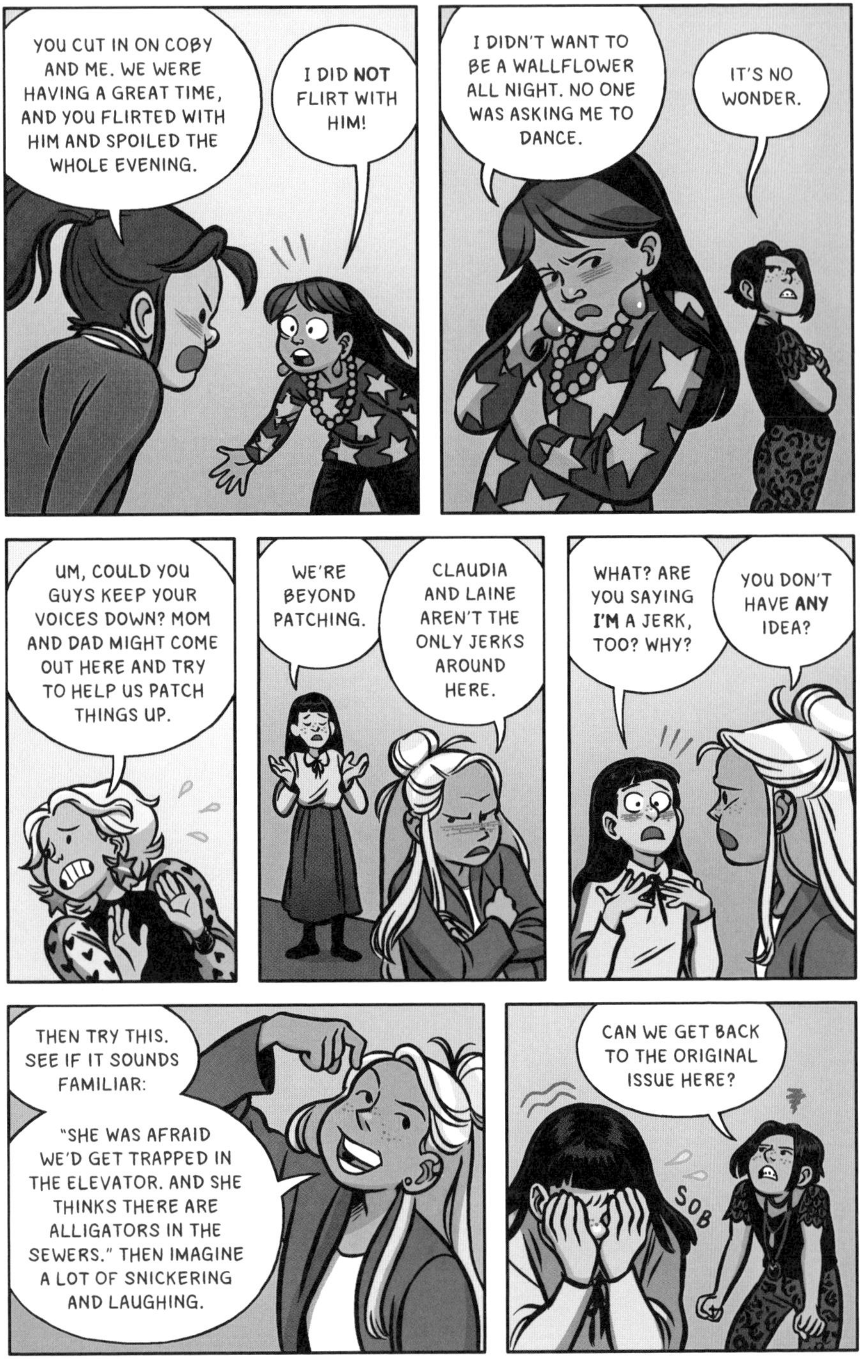
YOU CUT IN ON COBY AND ME. WE WERE HAVING A GREAT TIME, AND YOU FLIRTED WITH HIM AND SPOILED THE WHOLE EVENING.
I DID **NOT** FLIRT WITH HIM!
I DIDN'T WANT TO BE A WALLFLOWER ALL NIGHT. NO ONE WAS ASKING ME TO DANCE.
IT'S NO WONDER.
UM, COULD YOU GUYS KEEP YOUR VOICES DOWN? MOM AND DAD MIGHT COME OUT HERE AND TRY TO HELP US PATCH THINGS UP.
WE'RE BEYOND PATCHING.
CLAUDIA AND LAINE AREN'T THE ONLY JERKS AROUND HERE.
WHAT? ARE YOU SAYING **I'M** A JERK, TOO? WHY?
YOU DON'T HAVE **ANY** IDEA?
THEN TRY THIS. SEE IF IT SOUNDS FAMILIAR:
"SHE WAS AFRAID WE'D GET TRAPPED IN THE ELEVATOR. AND SHE THINKS THERE ARE ALLIGATORS IN THE SEWERS." THEN IMAGINE A LOT OF SNICKERING AND LAUGHING.
CAN WE GET BACK TO THE ORIGINAL ISSUE HERE?
SOB

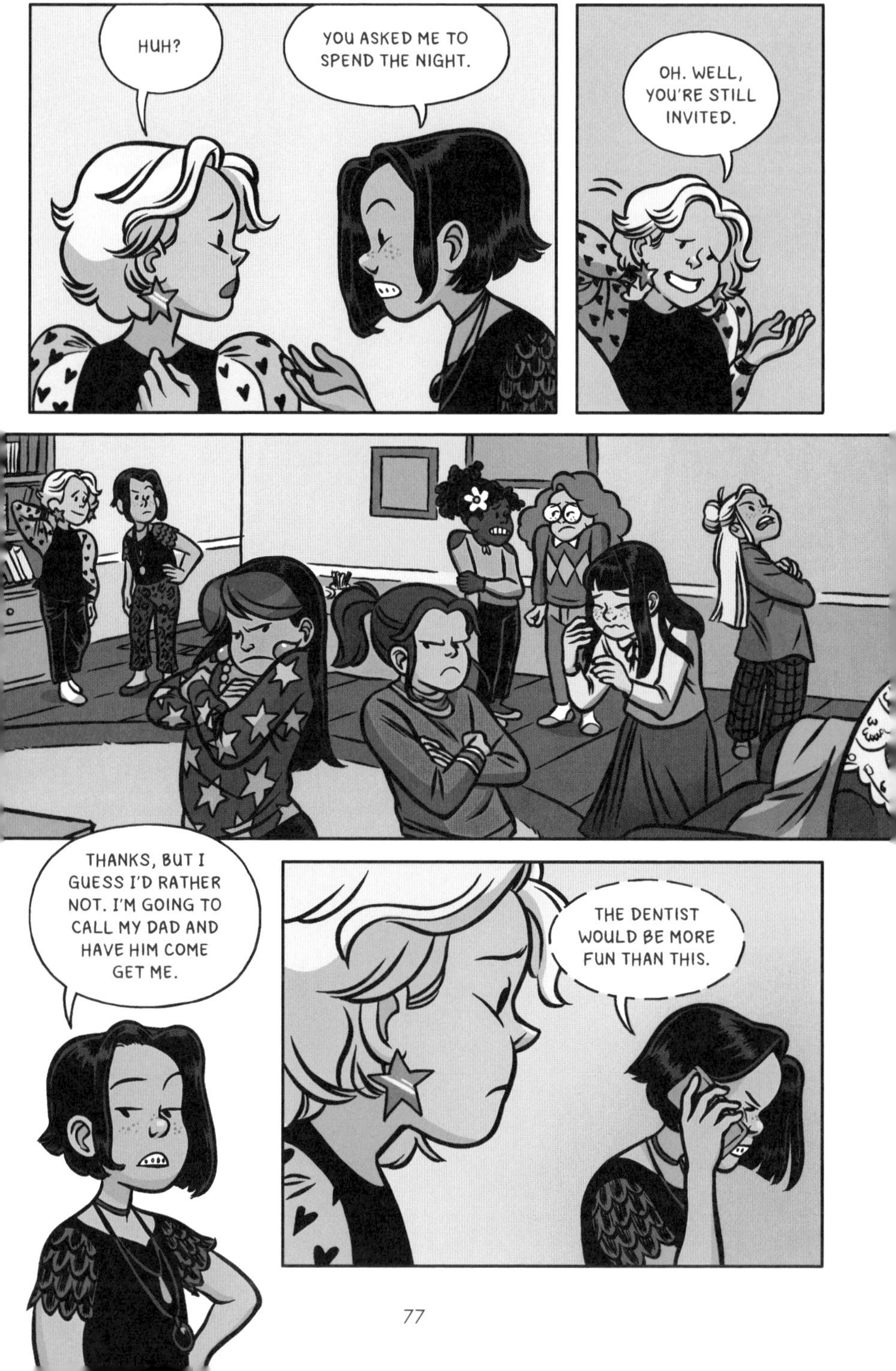
HUH?
YOU ASKED ME TO SPEND THE NIGHT.
OH. WELL, YOU'RE STILL INVITED.
THANKS, BUT I GUESS I'D RATHER NOT. I'M GOING TO CALL MY DAD AND HAVE HIM COME GET ME.
THE DENTIST WOULD BE MORE FUN THAN THIS.

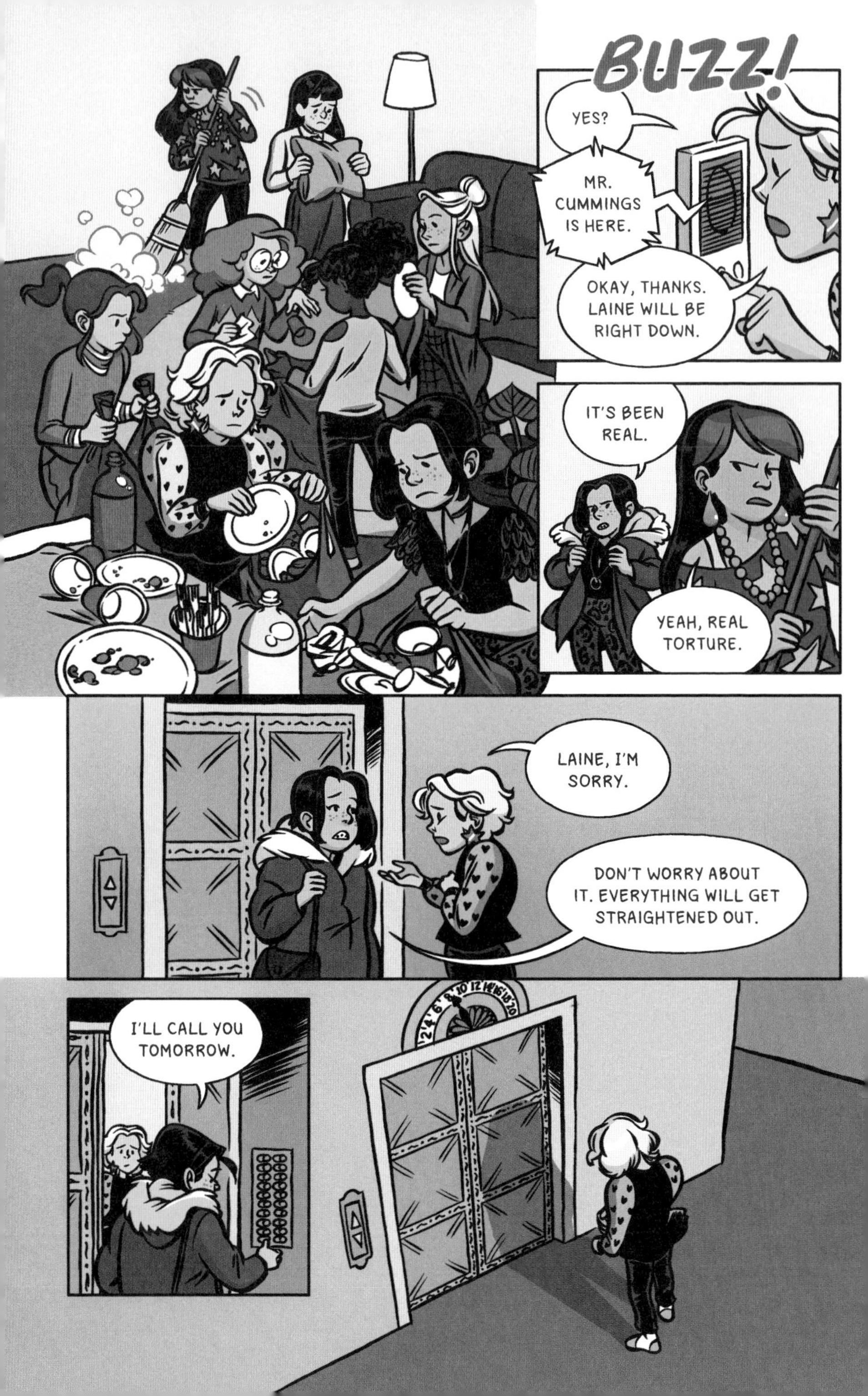
BUZZ!
YES?
MR. CUMMINGS IS HERE.
OKAY, THANKS. LAINE WILL BE RIGHT DOWN.
IT'S BEEN REAL.
YEAH, REAL TORTURE.
LAINE, I'M SORRY.
DON'T WORRY ABOUT IT. EVERYTHING WILL GET STRAIGHTENED OUT.
I'LL CALL YOU TOMORROW.

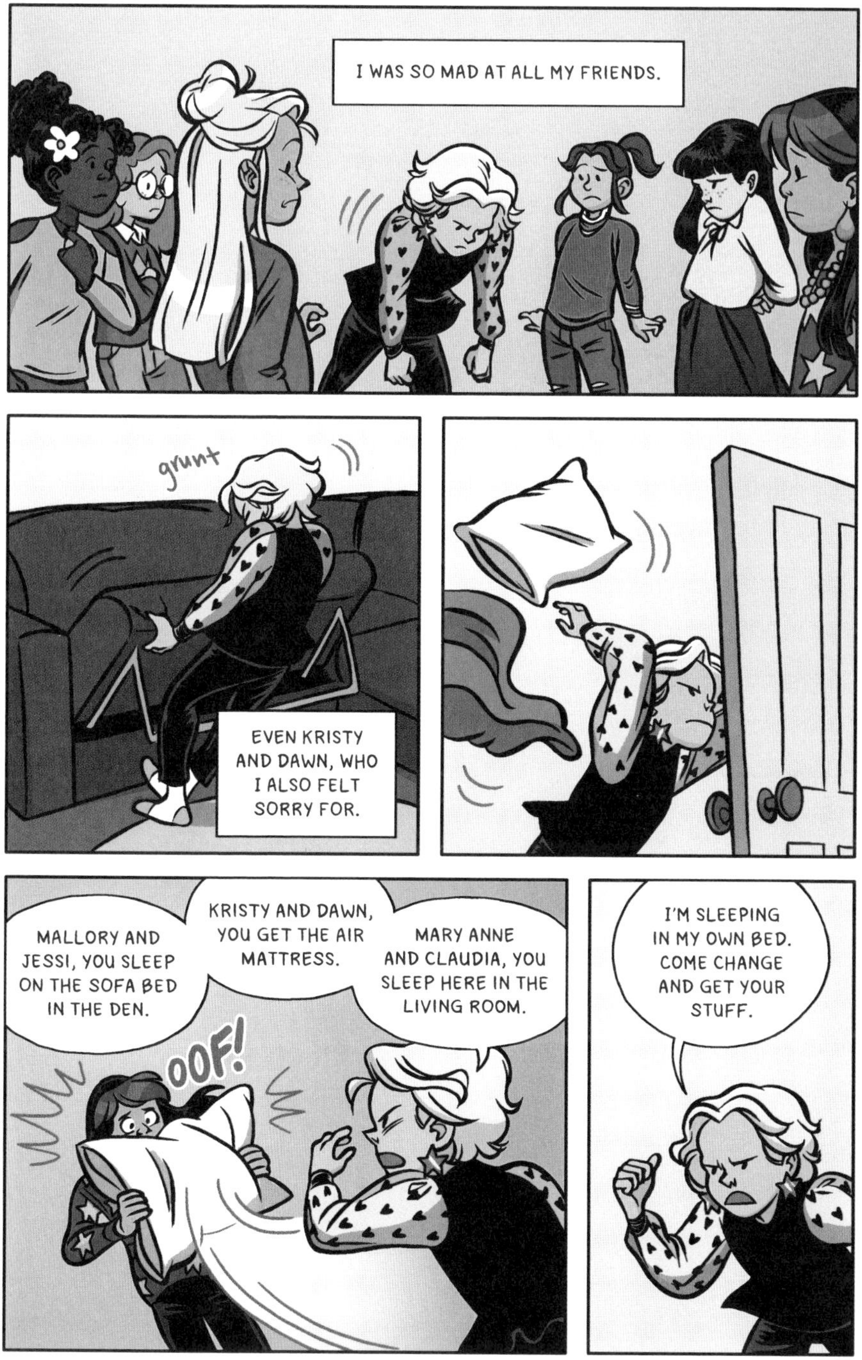
I WAS SO MAD AT ALL MY FRIENDS.
grunt
EVEN KRISTY AND DAWN, WHO I ALSO FELT SORRY FOR.
MALLORY AND JESSI, YOU SLEEP ON THE SOFA BED IN THE DEN.
KRISTY AND DAWN, YOU GET THE AIR MATTRESS.
MARY ANNE AND CLAUDIA, YOU SLEEP HERE IN THE LIVING ROOM.
OOF!
I'M SLEEPING IN MY OWN BED. COME CHANGE AND GET YOUR STUFF.

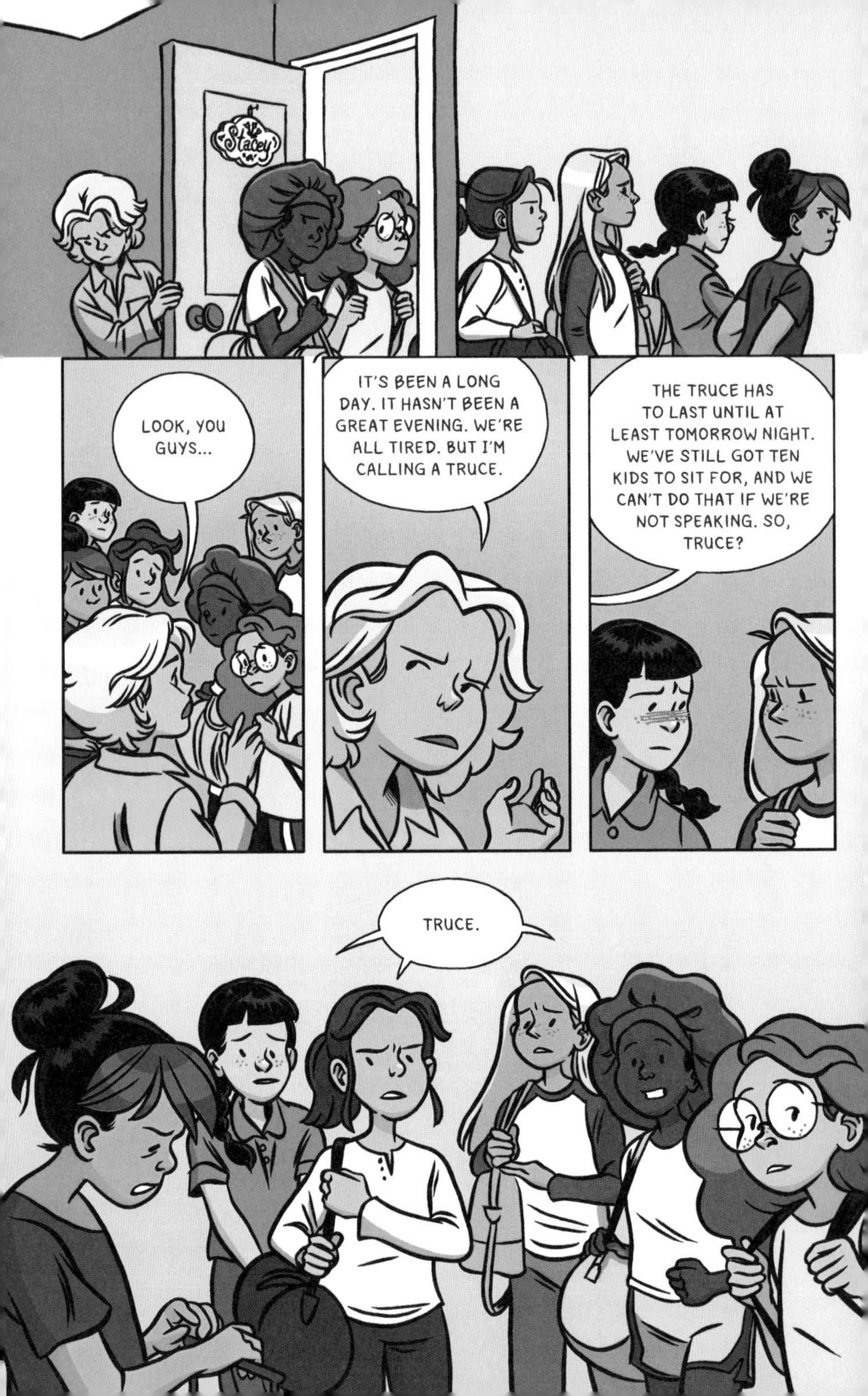
Stacey
LOOK, YOU GUYS...
IT'S BEEN A LONG DAY. IT HASN'T BEEN A GREAT EVENING. WE'RE ALL TIRED. BUT I'M CALLING A TRUCE.
THE TRUCE HAS TO LAST UNTIL AT LEAST TOMORROW NIGHT. WE'VE STILL GOT TEN KIDS TO SIT FOR, AND WE CAN'T DO THAT IF WE'RE NOT SPEAKING. SO, TRUCE?
TRUCE.

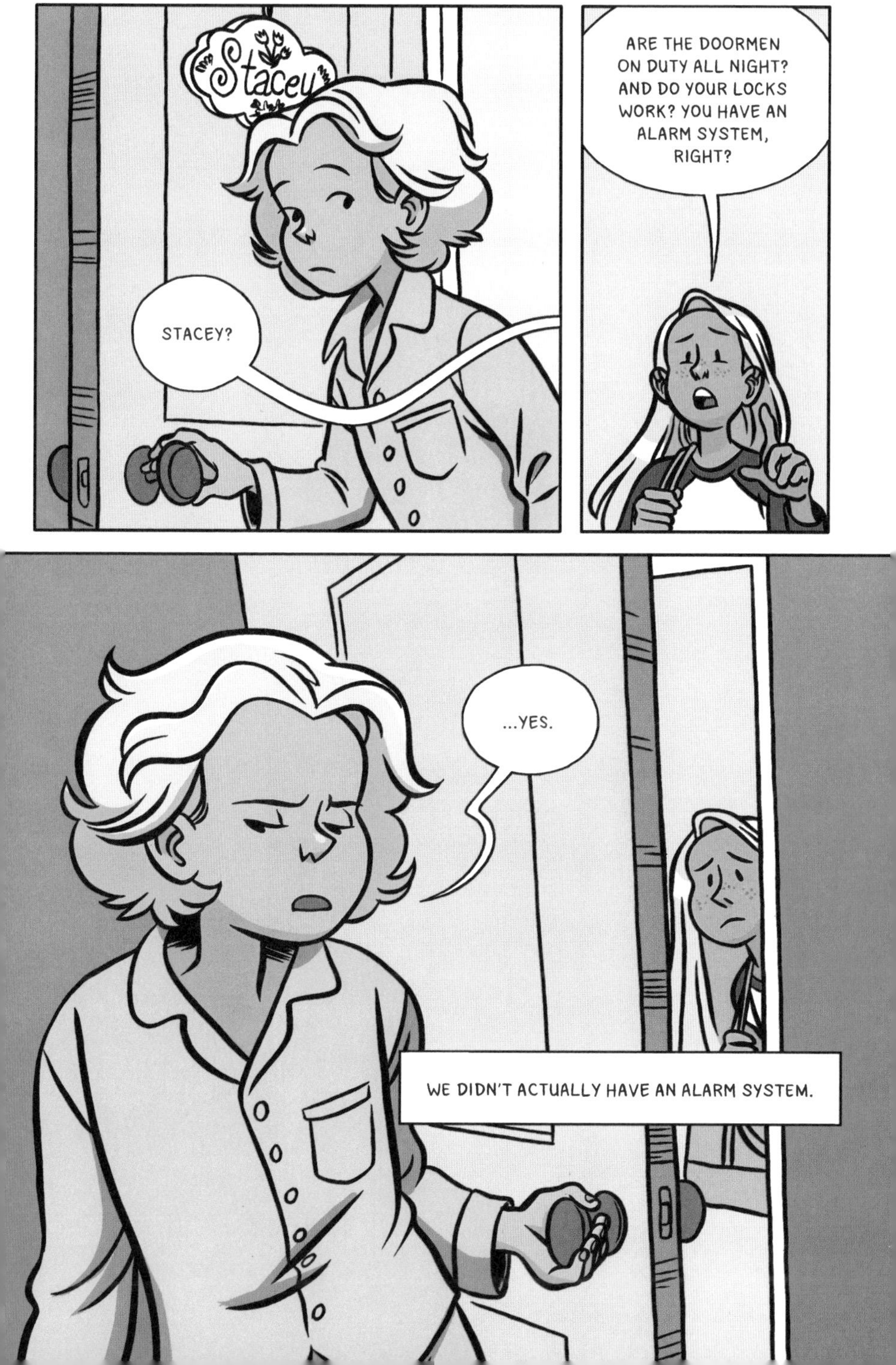
Stacey
STACEY?
ARE THE DOORMEN ON DUTY ALL NIGHT? AND DO YOUR LOCKS WORK? YOU HAVE AN ALARM SYSTEM, RIGHT?
...YES.
WE DIDN'T ACTUALLY HAVE AN ALARM SYSTEM.

CHAPTER 7

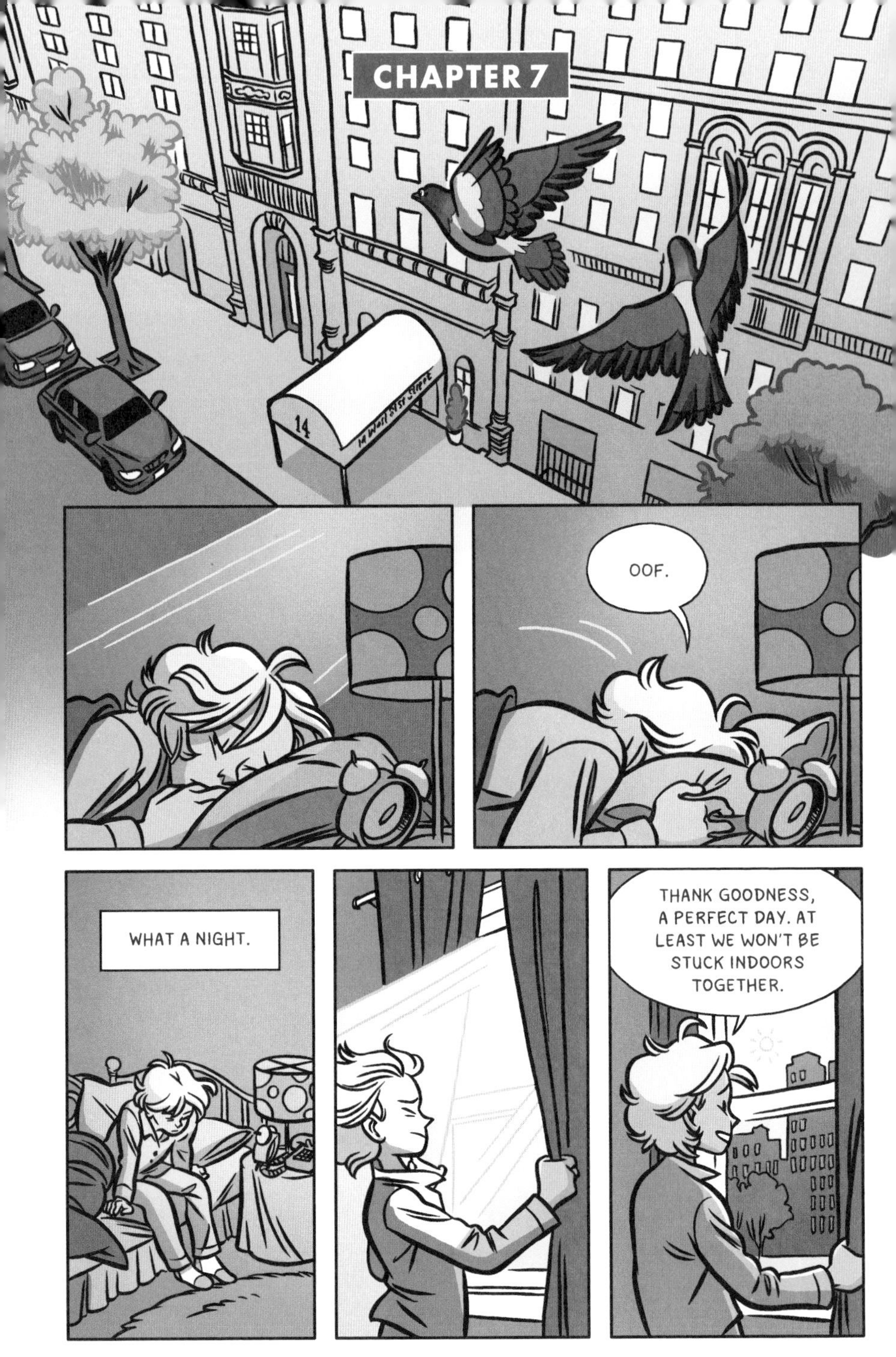
14
OOF.
WHAT A NIGHT.
THANK GOODNESS, A PERFECT DAY. AT LEAST WE WON'T BE STUCK INDOORS TOGETHER.

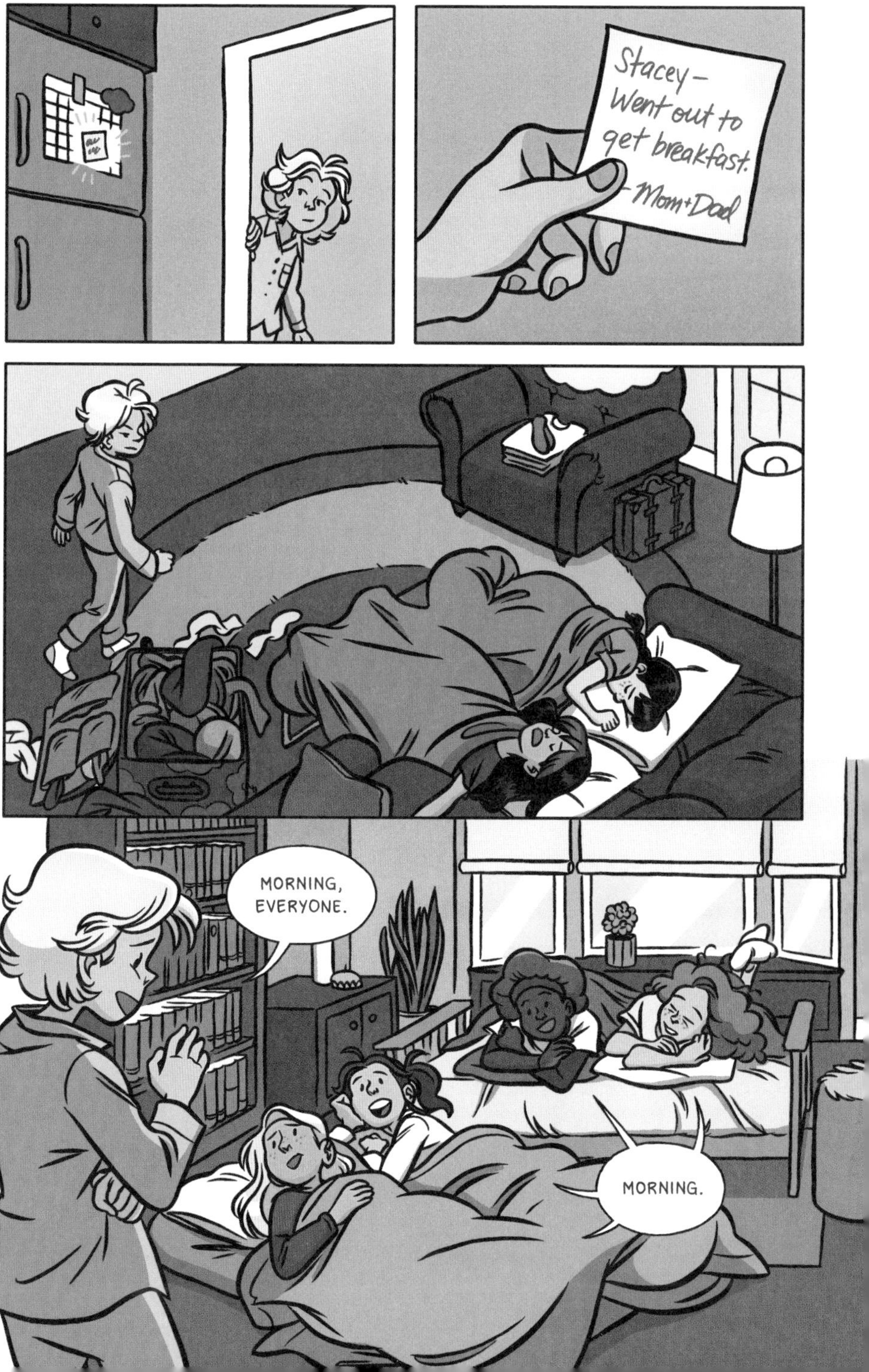
Stacey—
Went out to
get breakfast.
—Mom+Dad
MORNING, EVERYONE.
MORNING.

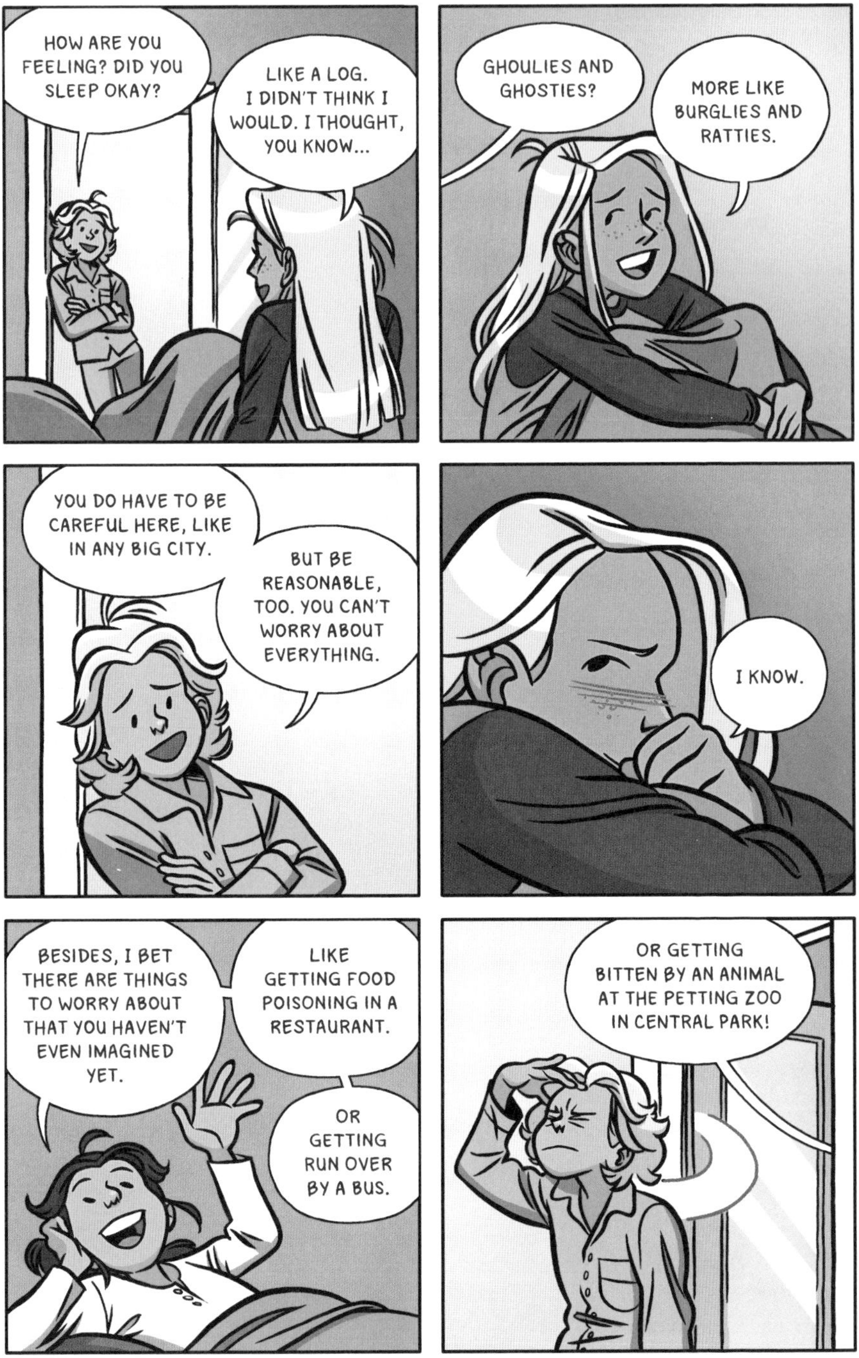
HOW ARE YOU FEELING? DID YOU SLEEP OKAY?
LIKE A LOG. I DIDN'T THINK I WOULD. I THOUGHT, YOU KNOW...
GHOULIES AND GHOSTIES?
MORE LIKE BURGLIES AND RATTIES.
YOU DO HAVE TO BE CAREFUL HERE, LIKE IN ANY BIG CITY.
BUT BE REASONABLE, TOO. YOU CAN'T WORRY ABOUT EVERYTHING.
I KNOW.
BESIDES, I BET THERE ARE THINGS TO WORRY ABOUT THAT YOU HAVEN'T EVEN IMAGINED YET.
LIKE GETTING FOOD POISONING IN A RESTAURANT.
OR GETTING RUN OVER BY A BUS.
OR GETTING BITTEN BY AN ANIMAL AT THE PETTING ZOO IN CENTRAL PARK!

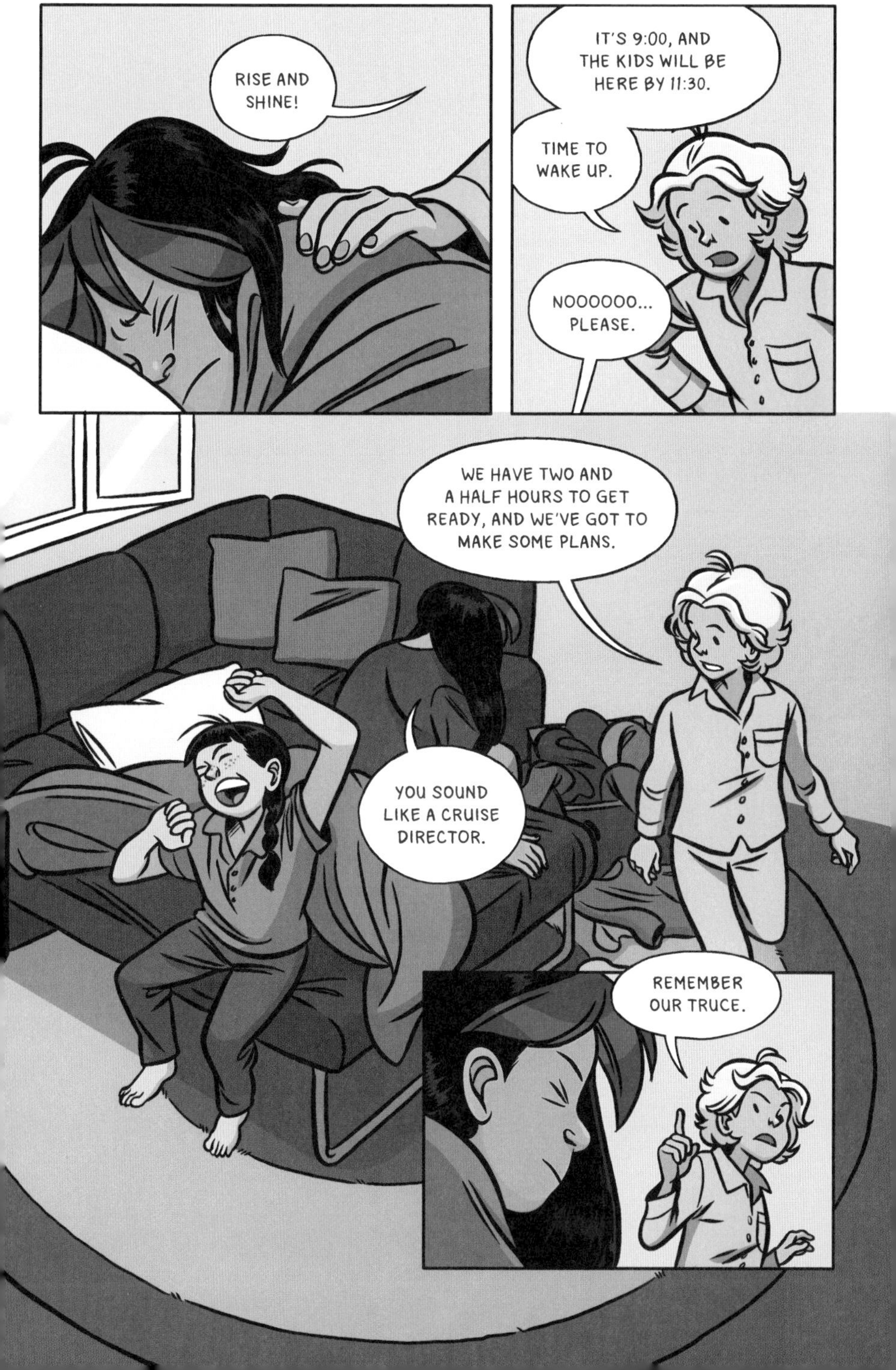
RISE AND SHINE!
IT'S 9:00, AND THE KIDS WILL BE HERE BY 11:30.
TIME TO WAKE UP.
NOOOOOO... PLEASE.
WE HAVE TWO AND A HALF HOURS TO GET READY, AND WE'VE GOT TO MAKE SOME PLANS.
YOU SOUND LIKE A CRUISE DIRECTOR.
REMEMBER OUR TRUCE.

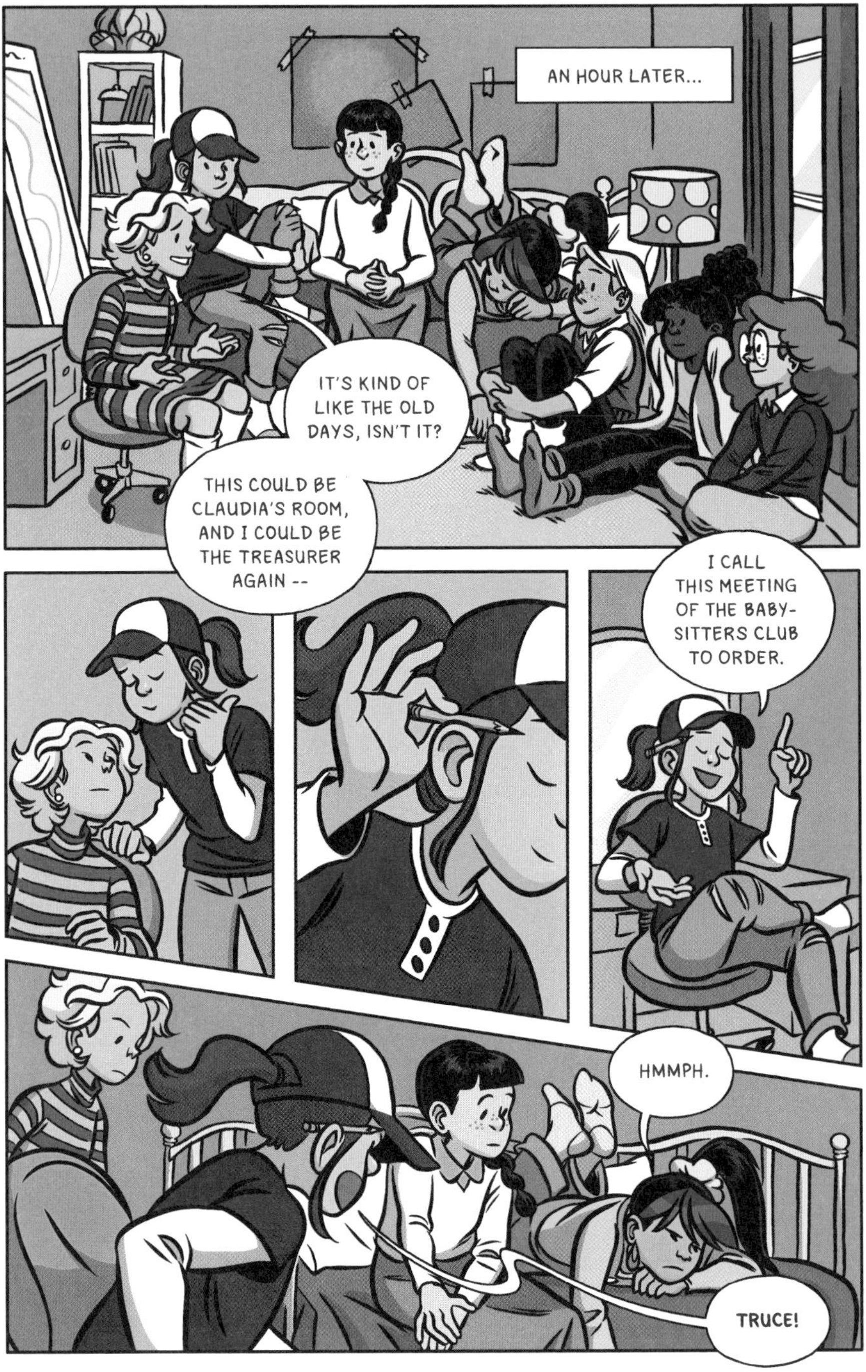
AN HOUR LATER...
IT'S KIND OF LIKE THE OLD DAYS, ISN'T IT?
THIS COULD BE CLAUDIA'S ROOM, AND I COULD BE THE TREASURER AGAIN --
I CALL THIS MEETING OF THE BABY-SITTERS CLUB TO ORDER.
HMMPH.
TRUCE!

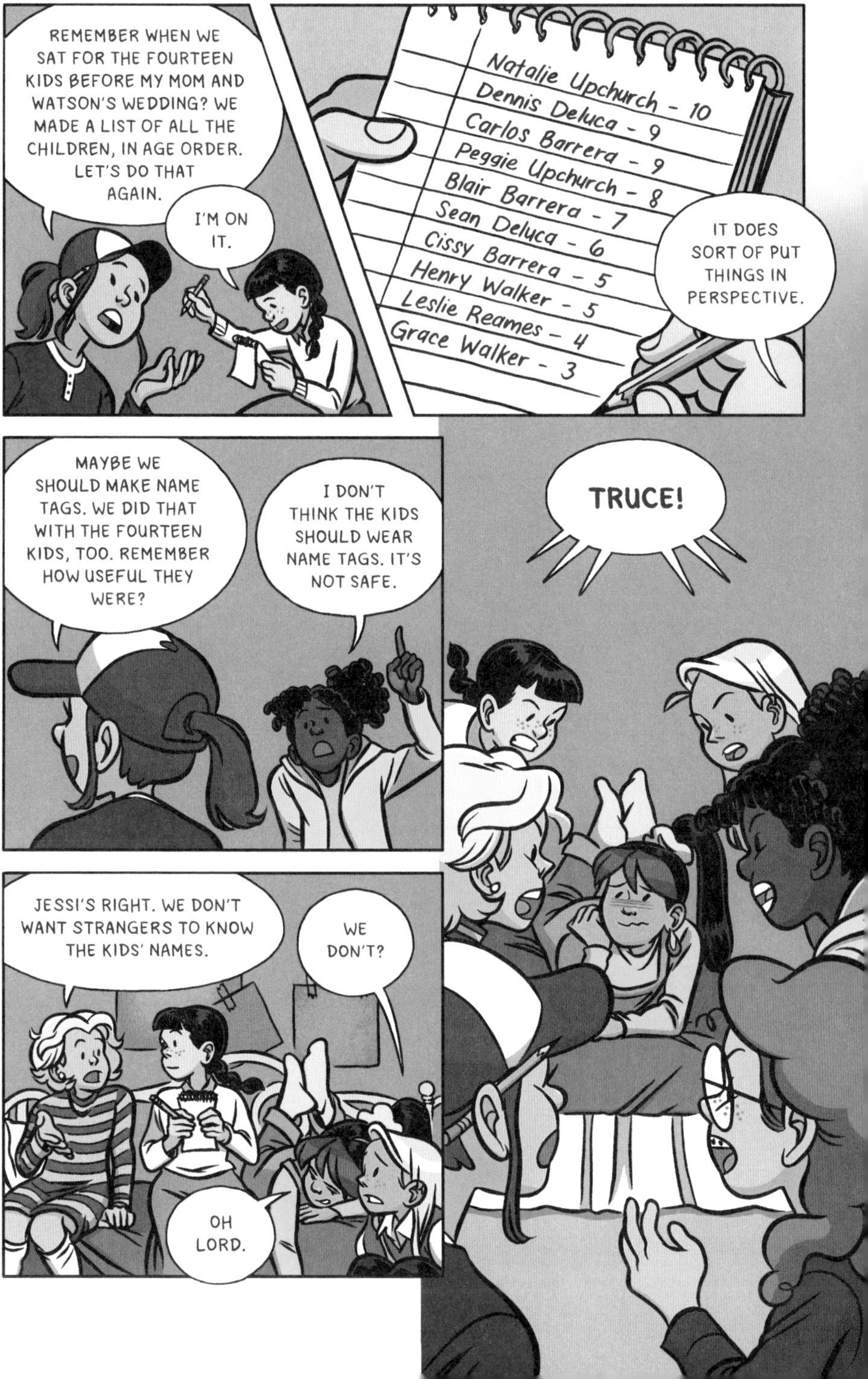
REMEMBER WHEN WE SAT FOR THE FOURTEEN KIDS BEFORE MY MOM AND WATSON'S WEDDING? WE MADE A LIST OF ALL THE CHILDREN, IN AGE ORDER. LET'S DO THAT AGAIN.
I'M ON IT.
Natalie Upchurch - 10
Dennis Deluca - 9
Carlos Barrera - 9
Peggie Upchurch - 8
Blair Barrera - 7
Sean Deluca - 6
Cissy Barrera - 5
Henry Walker - 5
Leslie Reames - 4
Grace Walker - 3
IT DOES SORT OF PUT THINGS IN PERSPECTIVE.
MAYBE WE SHOULD MAKE NAME TAGS. WE DID THAT WITH THE FOURTEEN KIDS, TOO. REMEMBER HOW USEFUL THEY WERE?
I DON'T THINK THE KIDS SHOULD WEAR NAME TAGS. IT'S NOT SAFE.
JESSI'S RIGHT. WE DON'T WANT STRANGERS TO KNOW THE KIDS' NAMES.
WE DON'T?
OH LORD.
TRUCE!

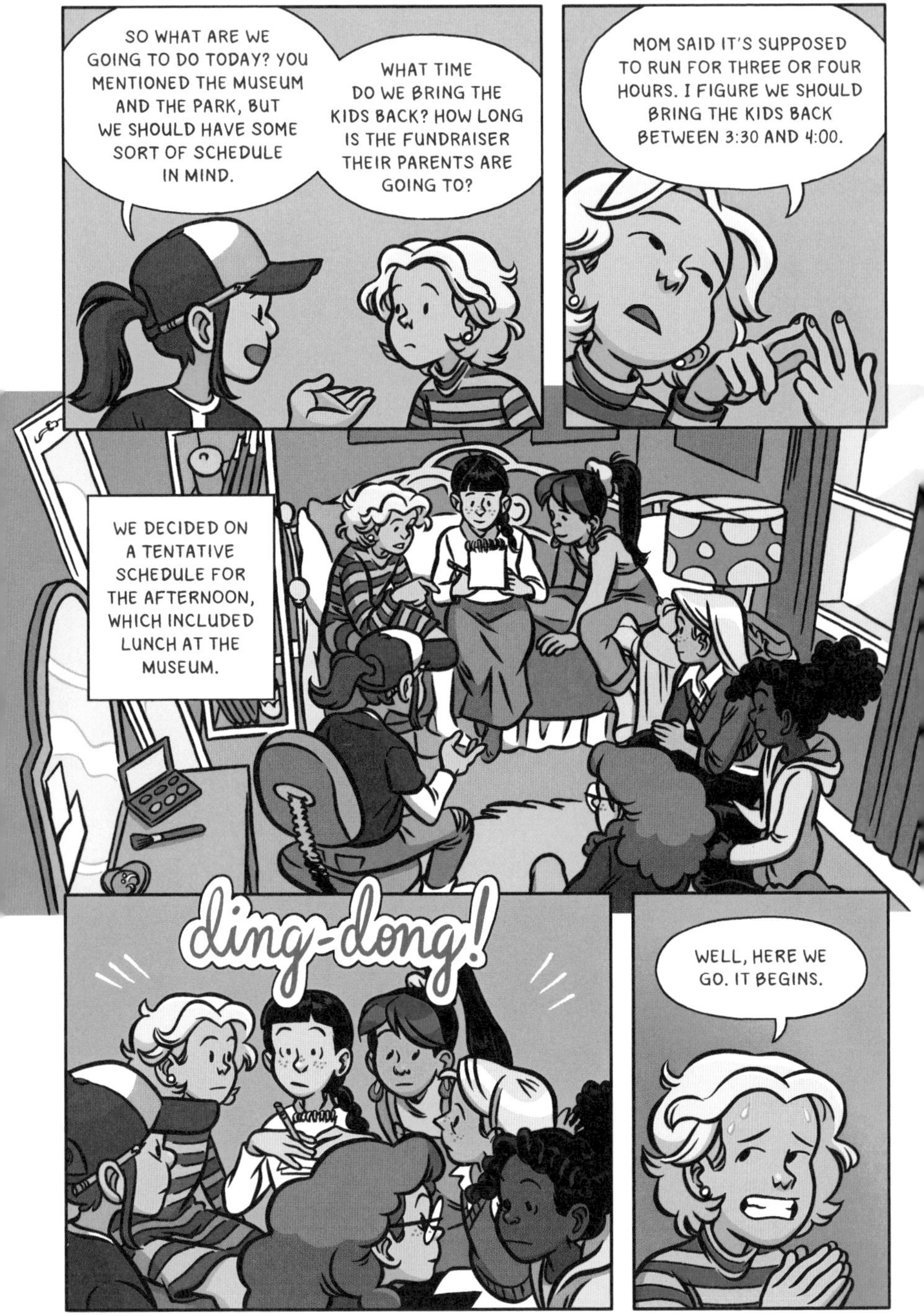
SO WHAT ARE WE GOING TO DO TODAY? YOU MENTIONED THE MUSEUM AND THE PARK, BUT WE SHOULD HAVE SOME SORT OF SCHEDULE IN MIND.
WHAT TIME DO WE BRING THE KIDS BACK? HOW LONG IS THE FUNDRAISER THEIR PARENTS ARE GOING TO?
MOM SAID IT'S SUPPOSED TO RUN FOR THREE OR FOUR HOURS. I FIGURE WE SHOULD BRING THE KIDS BACK BETWEEN 3:30 AND 4:00.
WE DECIDED ON A TENTATIVE SCHEDULE FOR THE AFTERNOON, WHICH INCLUDED LUNCH AT THE MUSEUM.
ding-dong!
WELL, HERE WE GO. IT BEGINS.

Hi everyone,

Today we went to the American Museum of Natural History. It was so cool. Dinosaur skeletons everywhere, and big cases showing animals in their habitats. You would have loved it. But boy, did we have a scare! We lost one of the kids we were sitting for, but everything turned out fine.

Love,
Mallory

The Pike Family

134 Slate St.

Stoneybrook, CT 06800

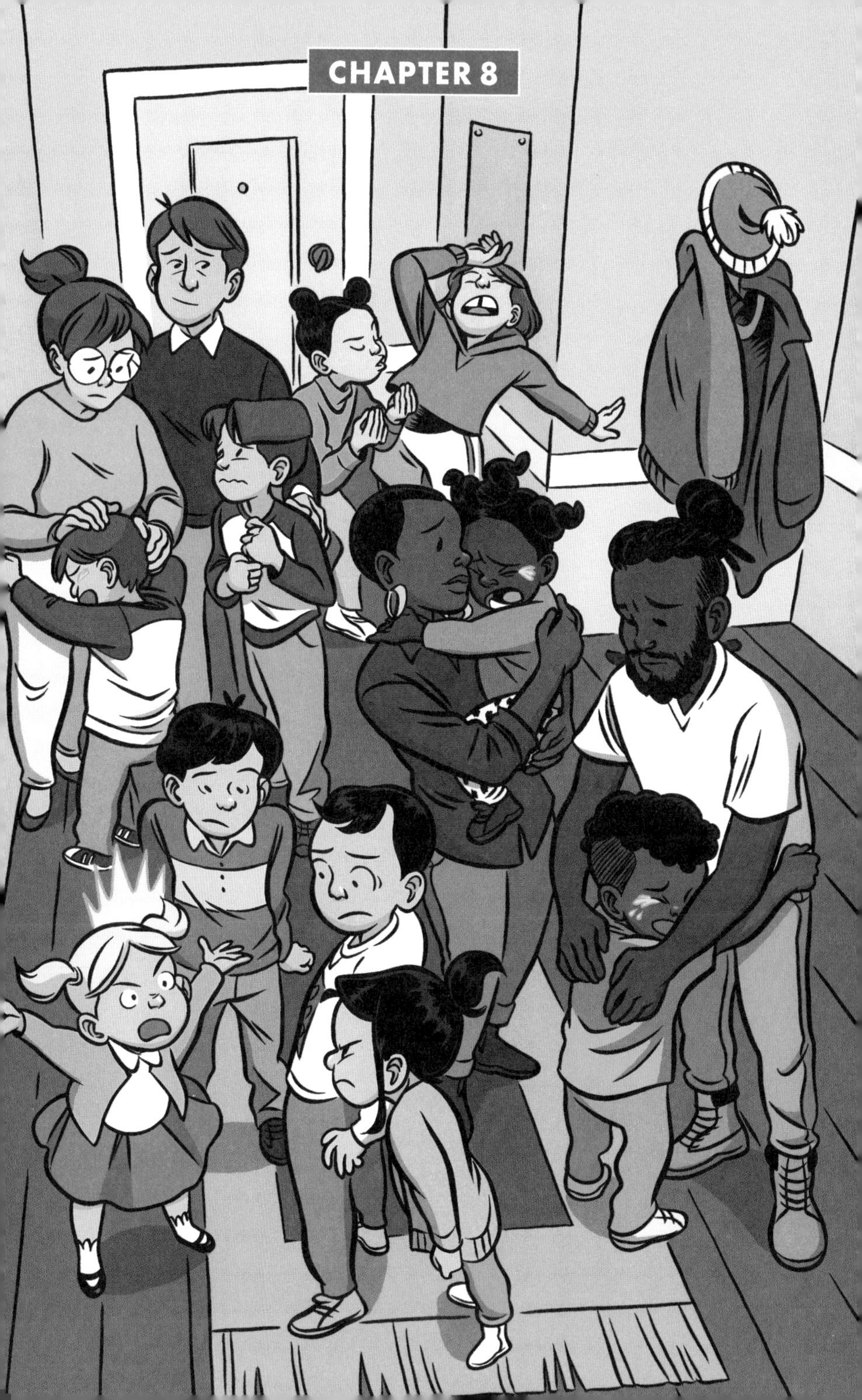
CHAPTER 8

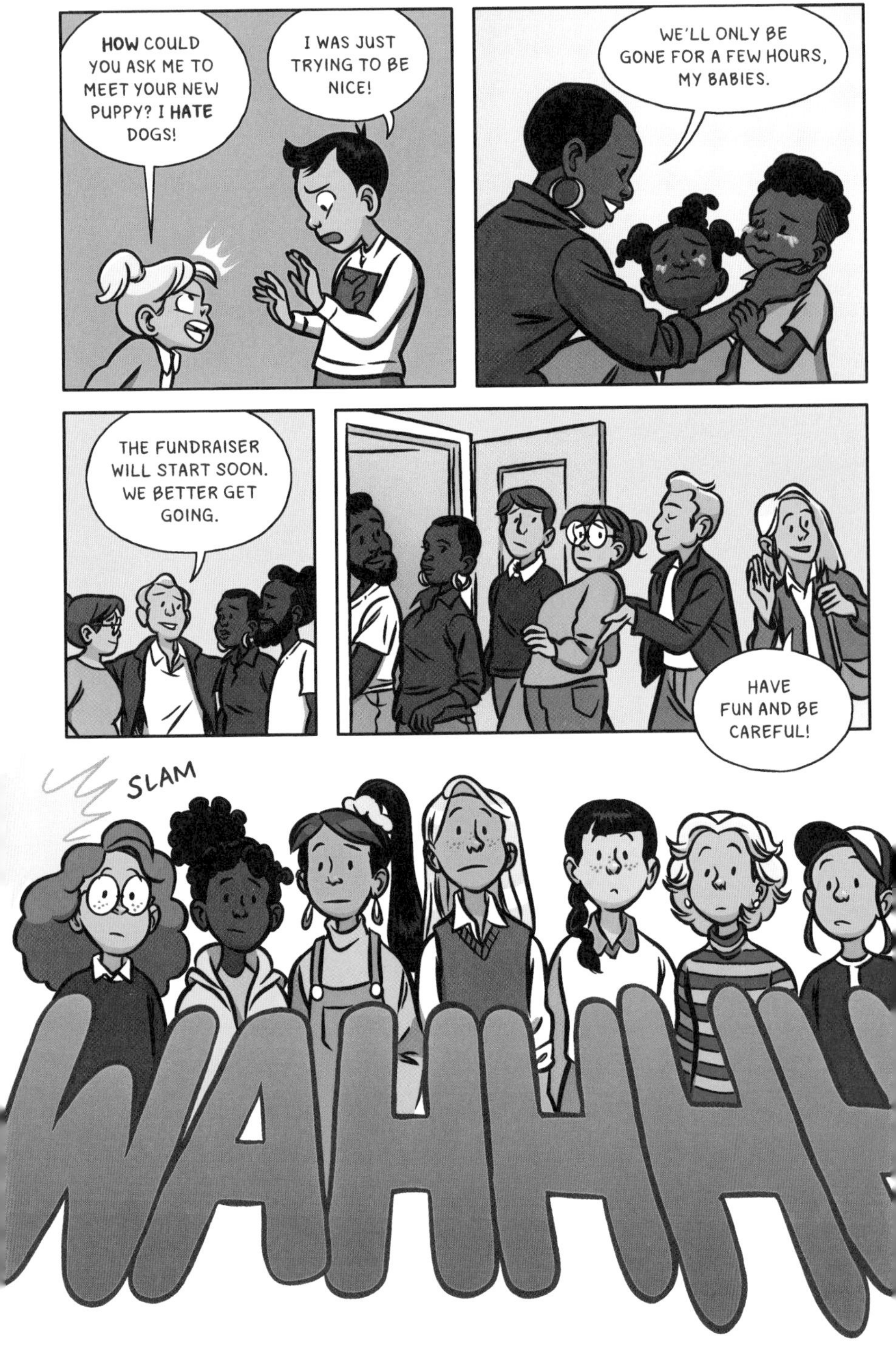

HOW COULD YOU ASK ME TO MEET YOUR NEW PUPPY? I HATE DOGS!
I WAS JUST TRYING TO BE NICE!
WE'LL ONLY BE GONE FOR A FEW HOURS, MY BABIES.
THE FUNDRAISER WILL START SOON. WE BETTER GET GOING.
HAVE FUN AND BE CAREFUL!
SLAM
WAHHH

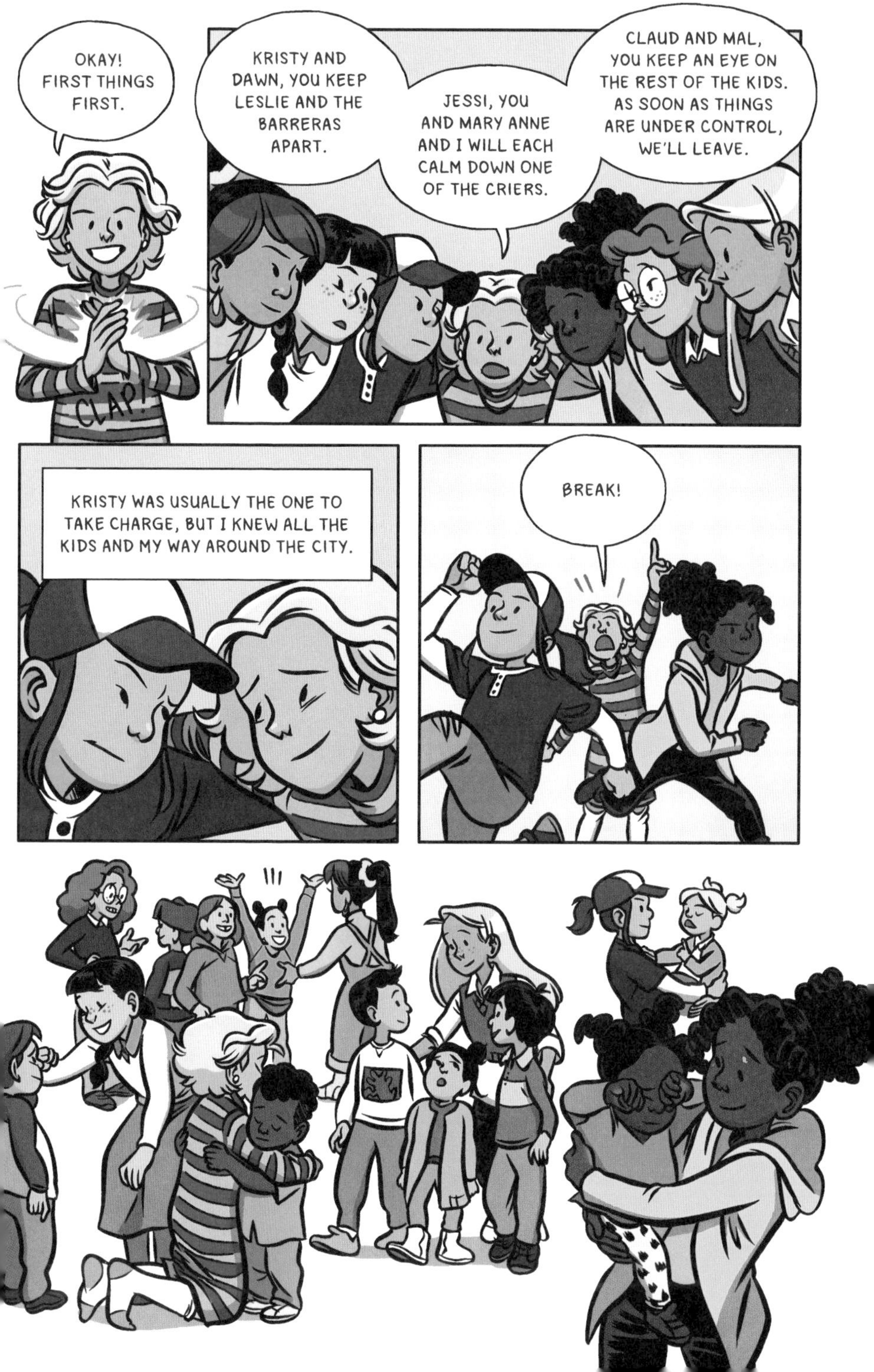
OKAY! FIRST THINGS FIRST.
CLAP!
KRISTY AND DAWN, YOU KEEP LESLIE AND THE BARRERAS APART.
JESSI, YOU AND MARY ANNE AND I WILL EACH CALM DOWN ONE OF THE CRIERS.
CLAUD AND MAL, YOU KEEP AN EYE ON THE REST OF THE KIDS. AS SOON AS THINGS ARE UNDER CONTROL, WE'LL LEAVE.
KRISTY WAS USUALLY THE ONE TO TAKE CHARGE, BUT I KNEW ALL THE KIDS AND MY WAY AROUND THE CITY.
BREAK!

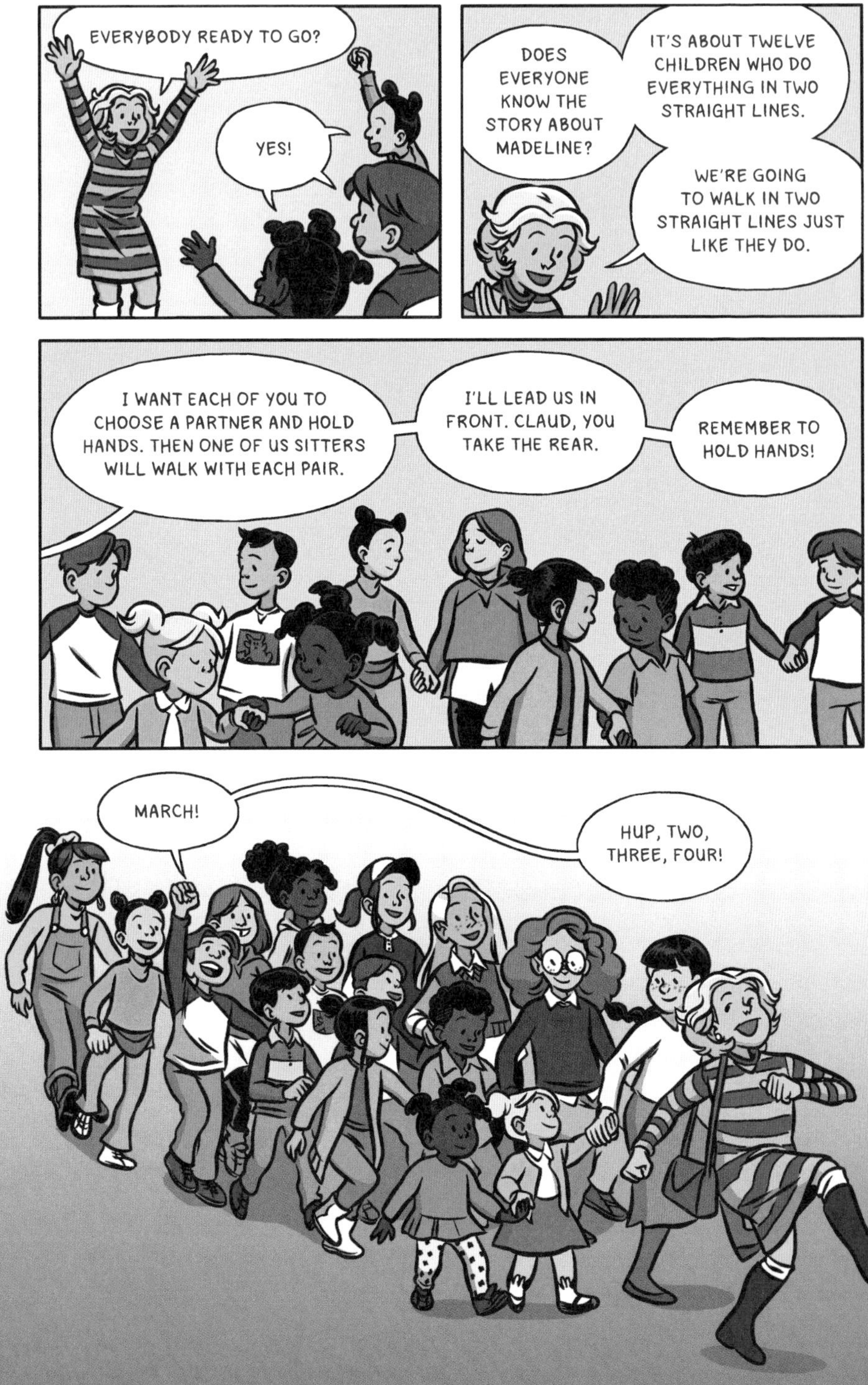
EVERYBODY READY TO GO?
YES!
DOES EVERYONE KNOW THE STORY ABOUT MADELINE?
IT'S ABOUT TWELVE CHILDREN WHO DO EVERYTHING IN TWO STRAIGHT LINES.
WE'RE GOING TO WALK IN TWO STRAIGHT LINES JUST LIKE THEY DO.
I WANT EACH OF YOU TO CHOOSE A PARTNER AND HOLD HANDS. THEN ONE OF US SITTERS WILL WALK WITH EACH PAIR.
I'LL LEAD US IN FRONT. CLAUD, YOU TAKE THE REAR.
REMEMBER TO HOLD HANDS!
MARCH!
HUP, TWO, THREE, FOUR!

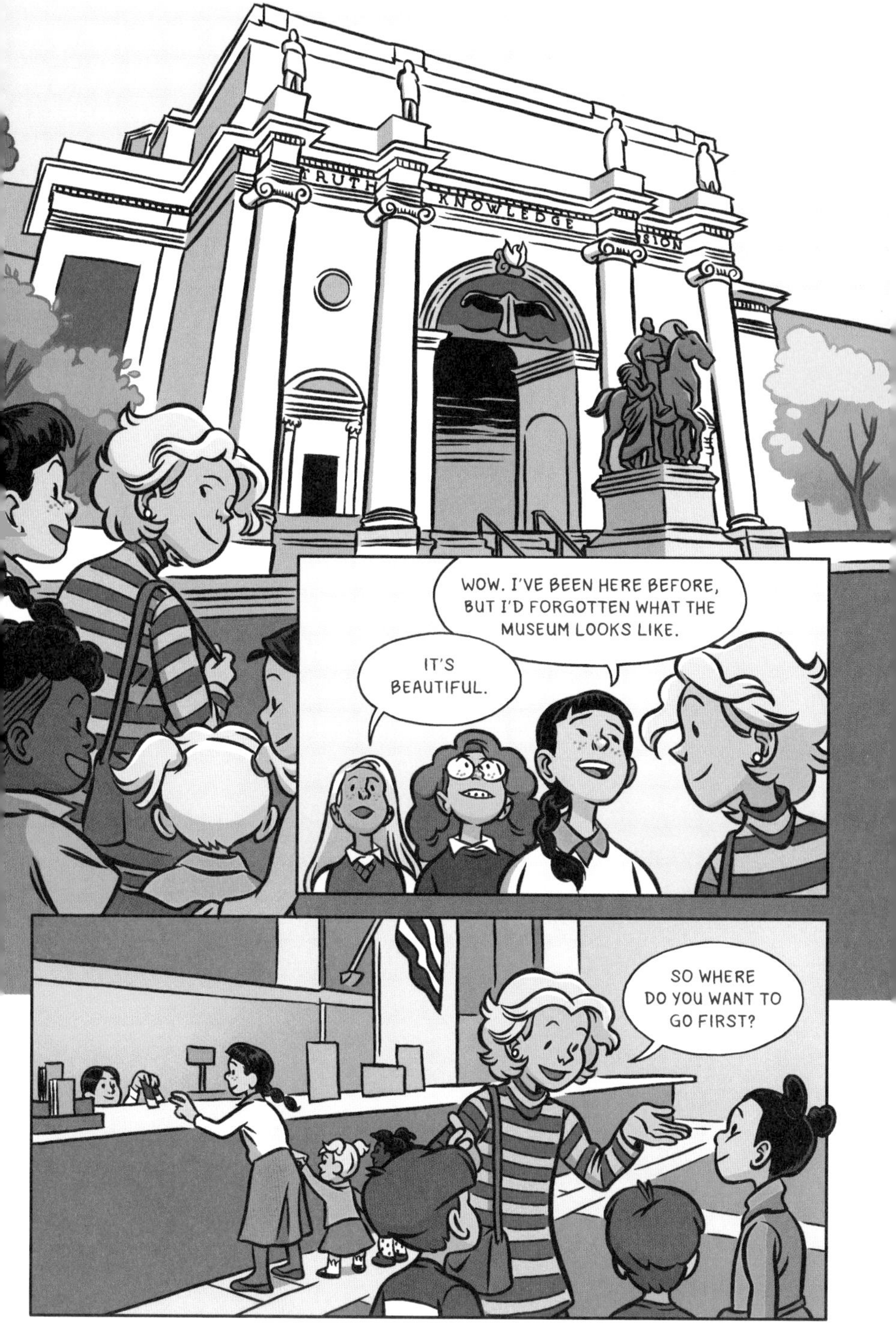
TRUTH
KNOWLEDGE
SION
WOW. I'VE BEEN HERE BEFORE, BUT I'D FORGOTTEN WHAT THE MUSEUM LOOKS LIKE.
IT'S BEAUTIFUL.
SO WHERE DO YOU WANT TO GO FIRST?

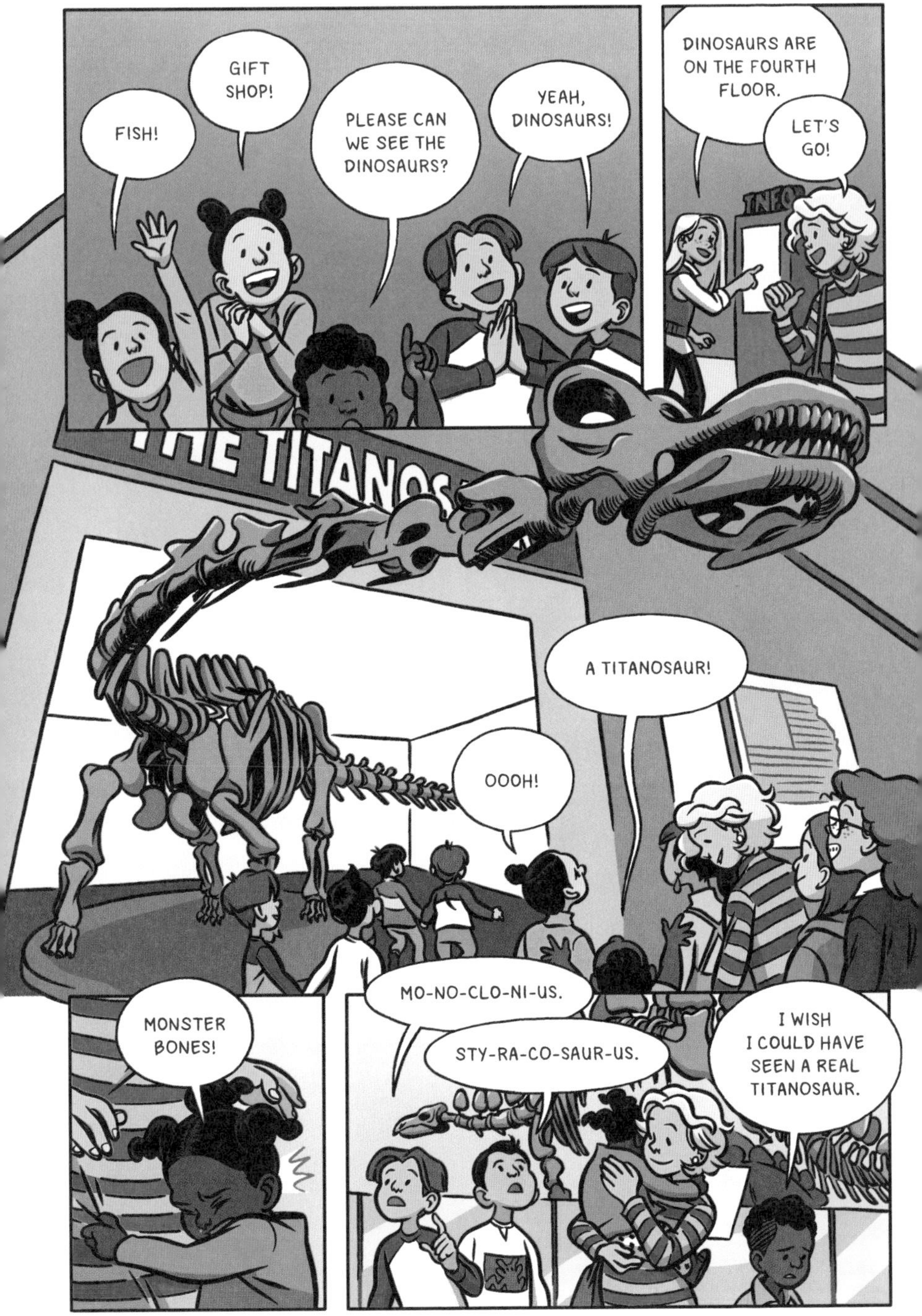
FISH!
GIFT SHOP!
PLEASE CAN WE SEE THE DINOSAURS?
YEAH, DINOSAURS!
DINOSAURS ARE ON THE FOURTH FLOOR.
LET'S GO!
INFO
THE TITANOS
A TITANOSAUR!
OOOH!
MONSTER BONES!
MO-NO-CLO-NI-US.
STY-RA-CO-SAUR-US.
I WISH I COULD HAVE SEEN A REAL TITANOSAUR.

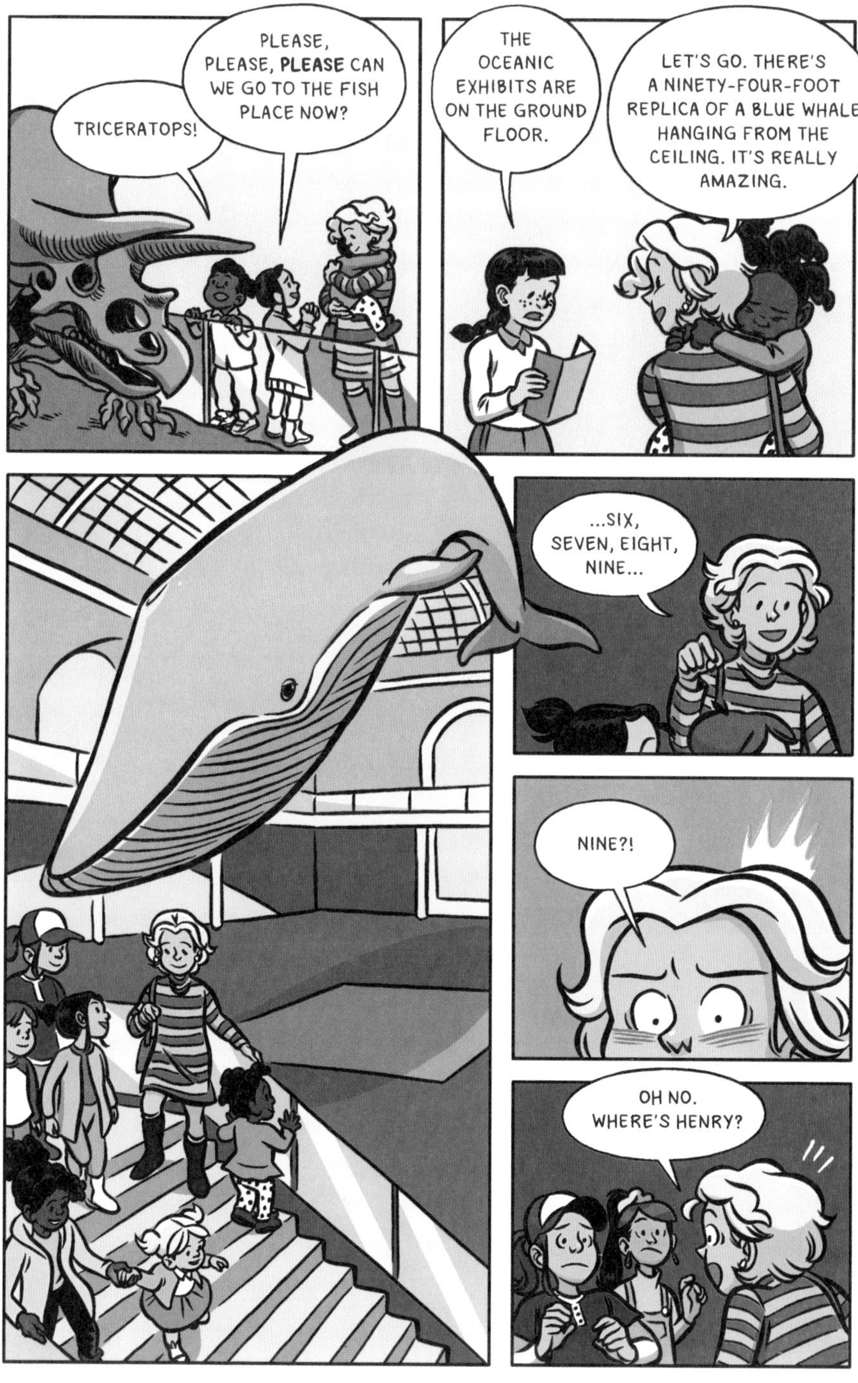
TRICERATOPS!
PLEASE, PLEASE, **PLEASE** CAN WE GO TO THE FISH PLACE NOW?
THE OCEANIC EXHIBITS ARE ON THE GROUND FLOOR.
LET'S GO. THERE'S A NINETY-FOUR-FOOT REPLICA OF A BLUE WHALE HANGING FROM THE CEILING. IT'S REALLY AMAZING.
...SIX, SEVEN, EIGHT, NINE...
NINE?!
OH NO. WHERE'S HENRY?

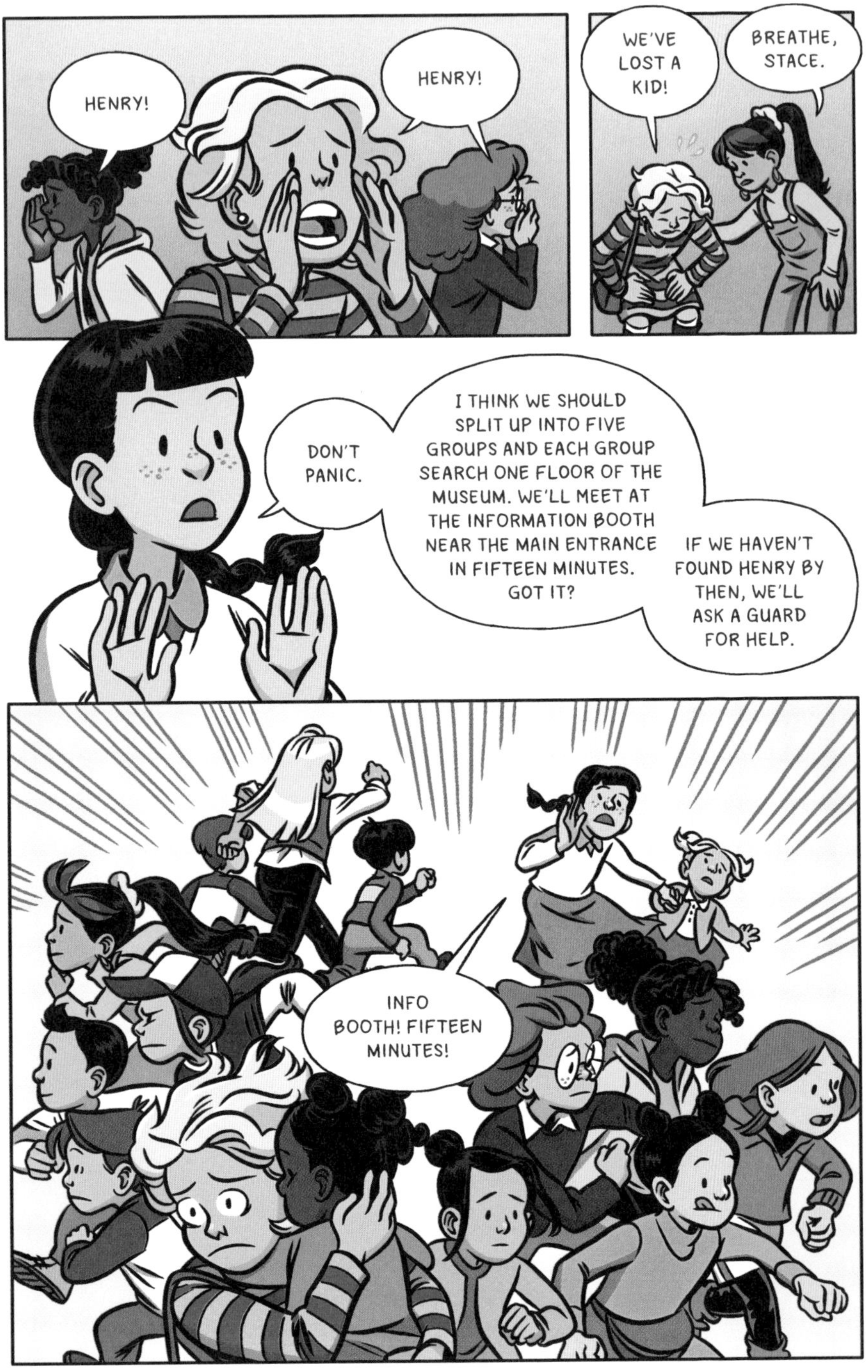
HENRY!
HENRY!
WE'VE LOST A KID!
BREATHE, STACE.
DON'T PANIC.
I THINK WE SHOULD SPLIT UP INTO FIVE GROUPS AND EACH GROUP SEARCH ONE FLOOR OF THE MUSEUM. WE'LL MEET AT THE INFORMATION BOOTH NEAR THE MAIN ENTRANCE IN FIFTEEN MINUTES. GOT IT?
IF WE HAVEN'T FOUND HENRY BY THEN, WE'LL ASK A GUARD FOR HELP.
INFO BOOTH! FIFTEEN MINUTES!

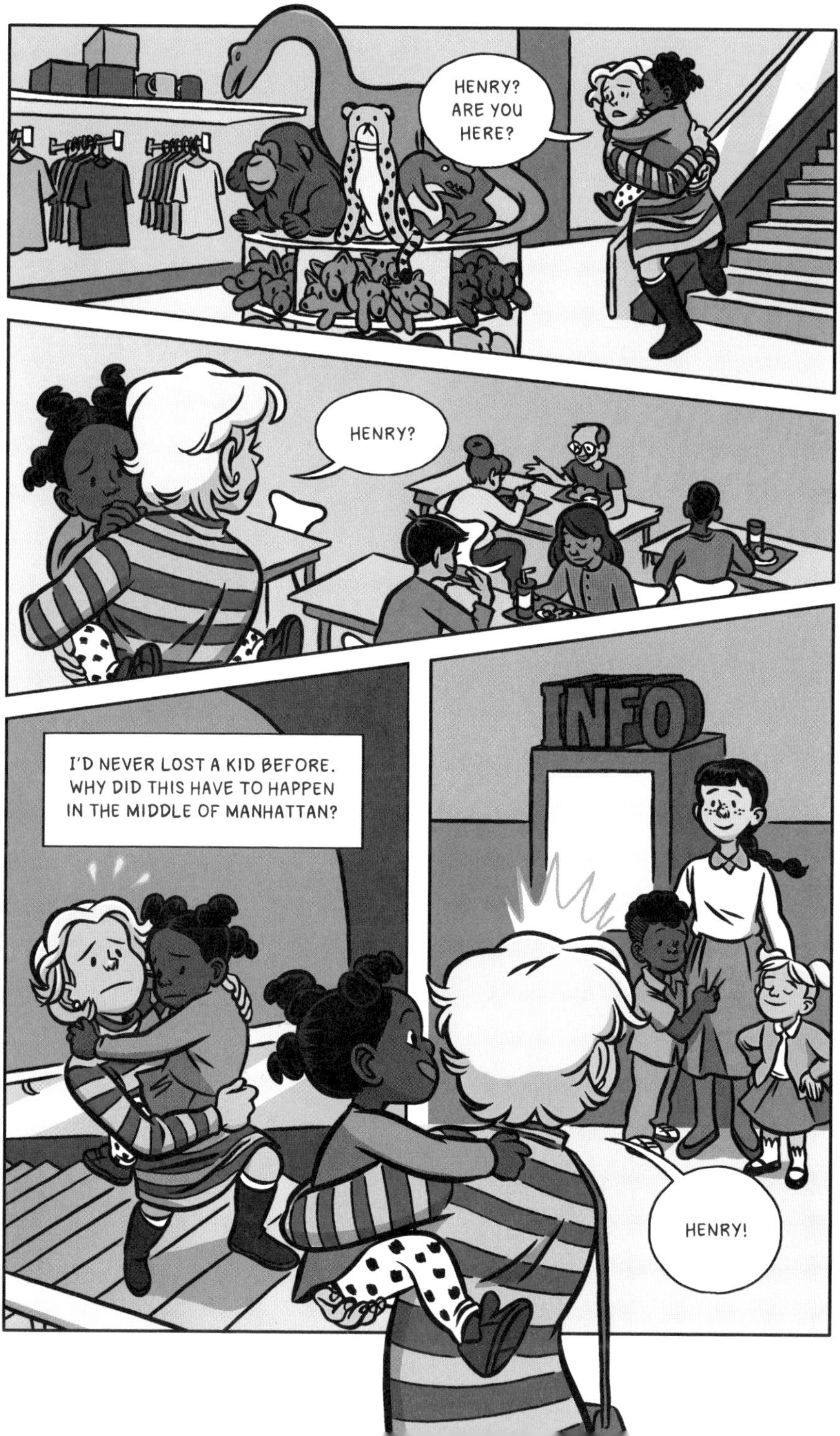
HENRY? ARE YOU HERE?
HENRY?
I'D NEVER LOST A KID BEFORE. WHY DID THIS HAVE TO HAPPEN IN THE MIDDLE OF MANHATTAN?
INFO
HENRY!

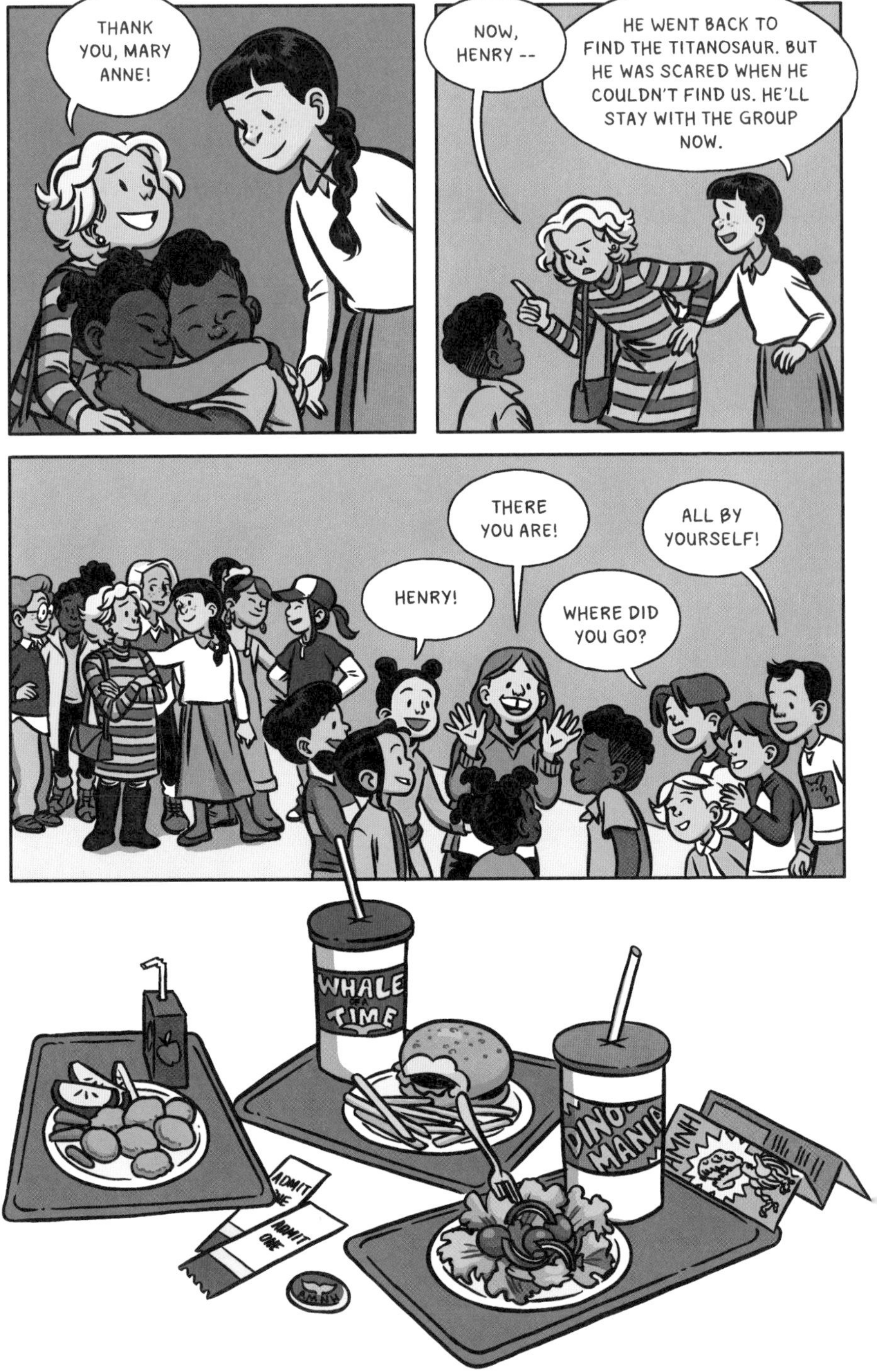
THANK YOU, MARY ANNE!
NOW, HENRY --
HE WENT BACK TO FIND THE TITANOSAUR. BUT HE WAS SCARED WHEN HE COULDN'T FIND US. HE'LL STAY WITH THE GROUP NOW.
HENRY!
THERE YOU ARE!
WHERE DID YOU GO?
ALL BY YOURSELF!
WHALE
TIME
DINO-MANIA
AMNH
ADMIT ONE
ADMIT ONE
AMNH

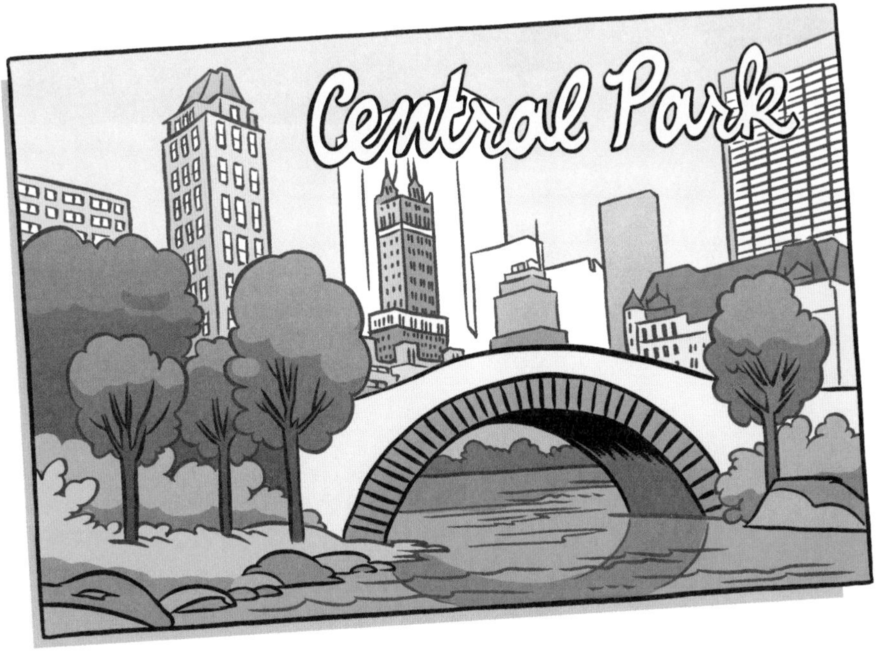
Central Park

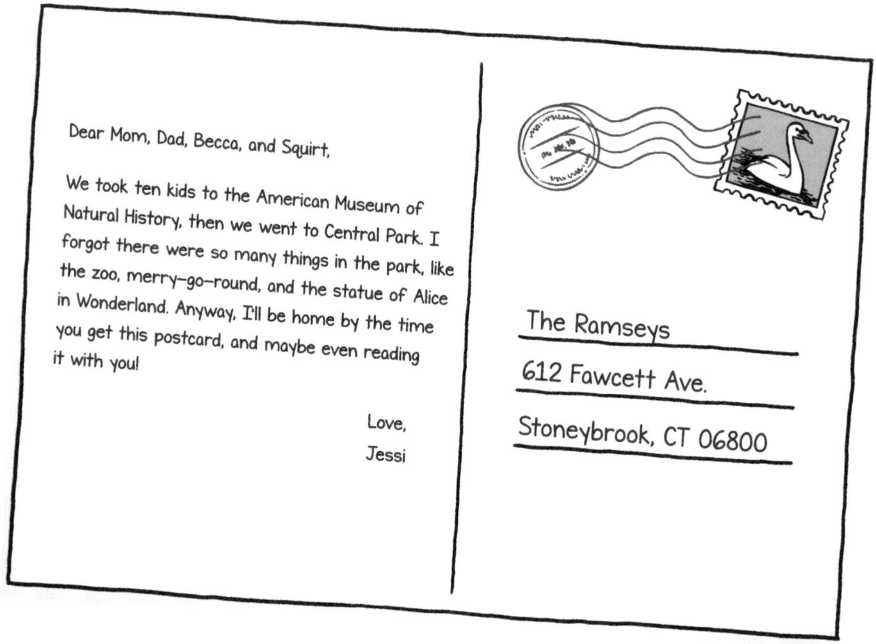

Dear Mom, Dad, Becca, and Squirt,

We took ten kids to the American Museum of Natural History, then we went to Central Park. I forgot there were so many things in the park, like the zoo, merry-go-round, and the statue of Alice in Wonderland. Anyway, I'll be home by the time you get this postcard, and maybe even reading it with you!

Love,
Jessi

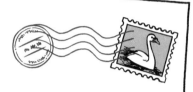

The Ramseys

612 Fawcett Ave.

Stoneybrook, CT 06800

CHAPTER 9

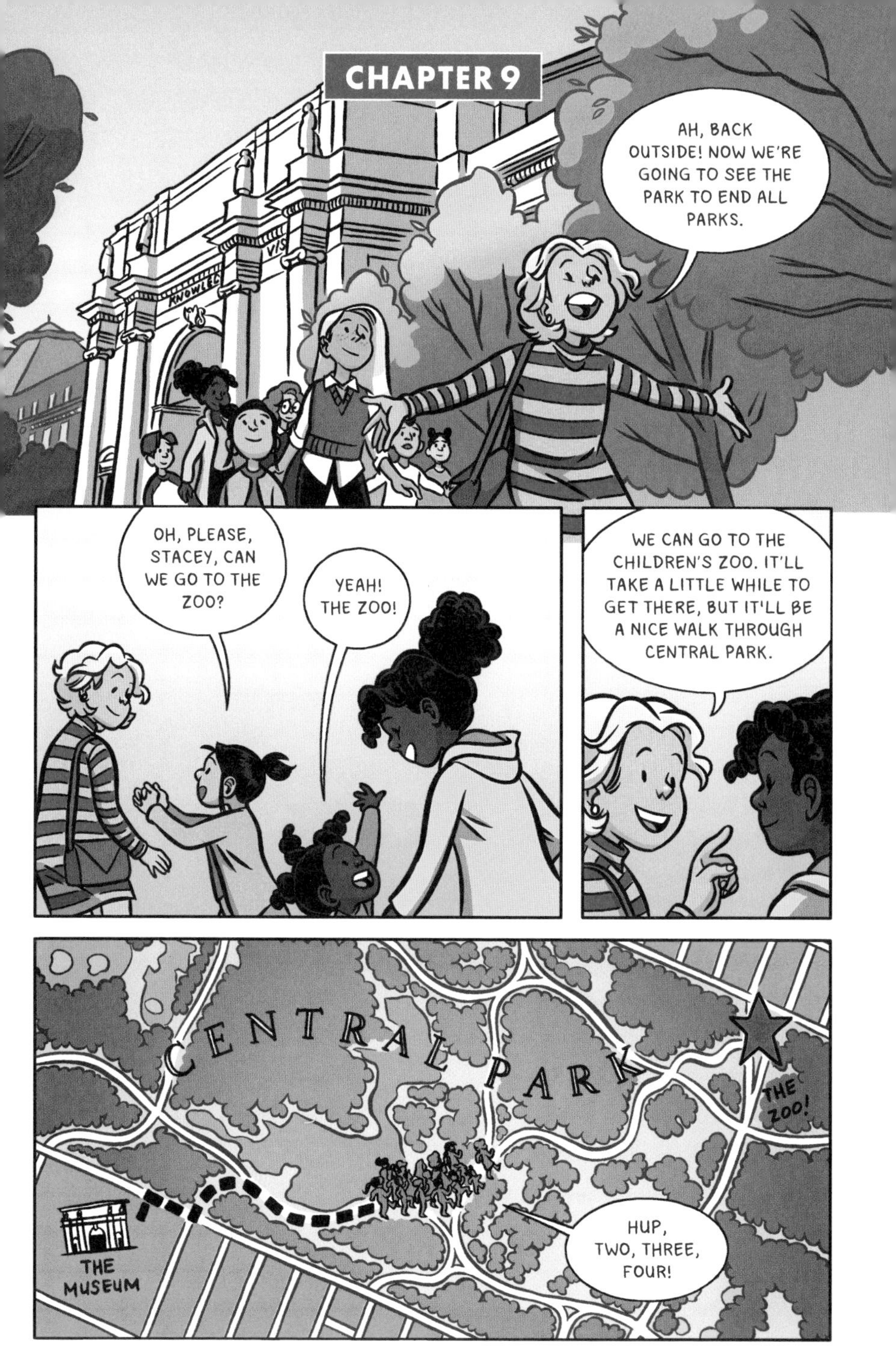
AH, BACK OUTSIDE! NOW WE'RE GOING TO SEE THE PARK TO END ALL PARKS.
OH, PLEASE, STACEY, CAN WE GO TO THE ZOO?
YEAH! THE ZOO!
WE CAN GO TO THE CHILDREN'S ZOO. IT'LL TAKE A LITTLE WHILE TO GET THERE, BUT IT'LL BE A NICE WALK THROUGH CENTRAL PARK.
CENTRAL PARK
THE ZOO!
THE MUSEUM
HUP, TWO, THREE, FOUR!

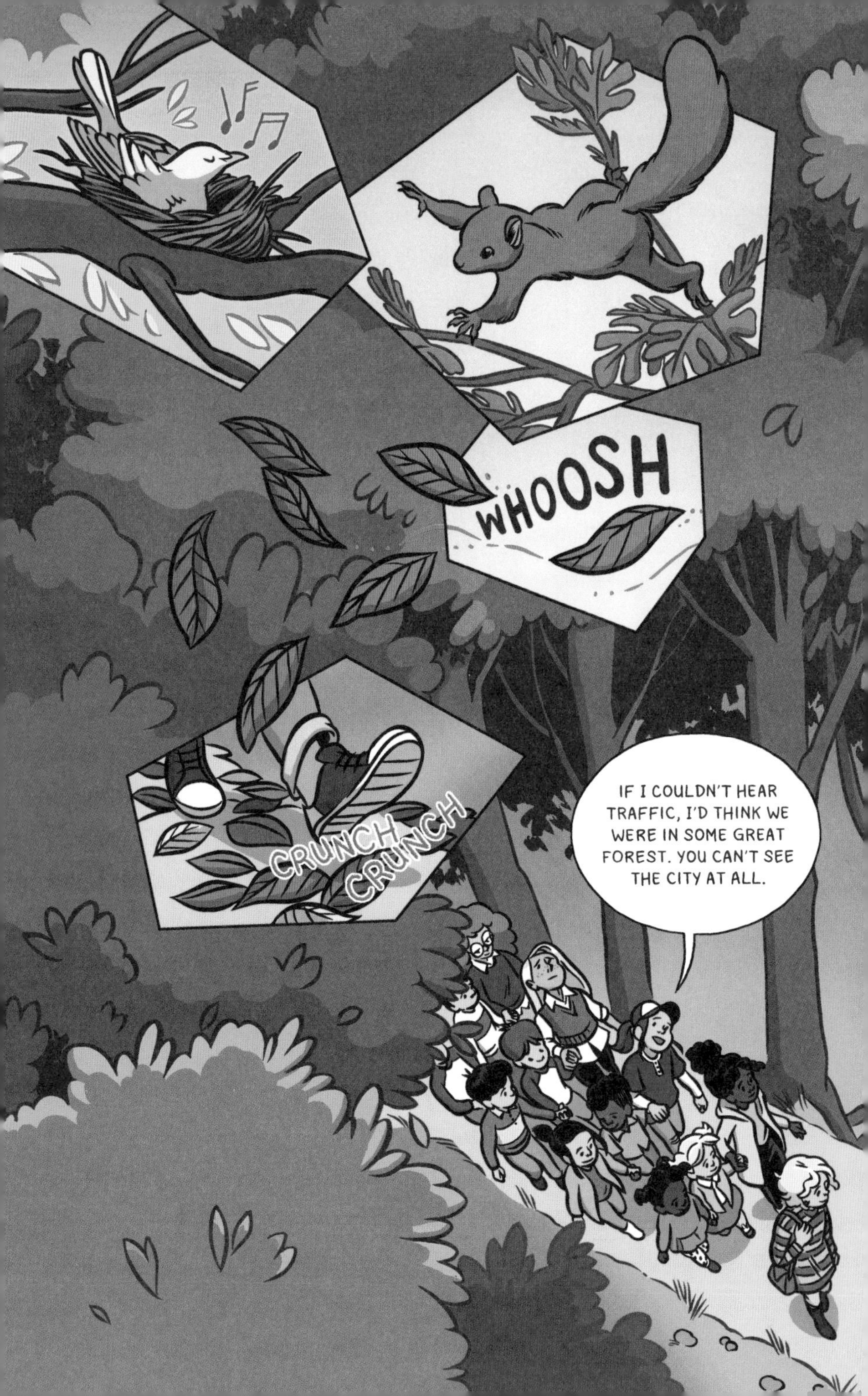
WHOOSH
CRUNCH
CRUNCH
IF I COULDN'T HEAR TRAFFIC, I'D THINK WE WERE IN SOME GREAT FOREST. YOU CAN'T SEE THE CITY AT ALL.

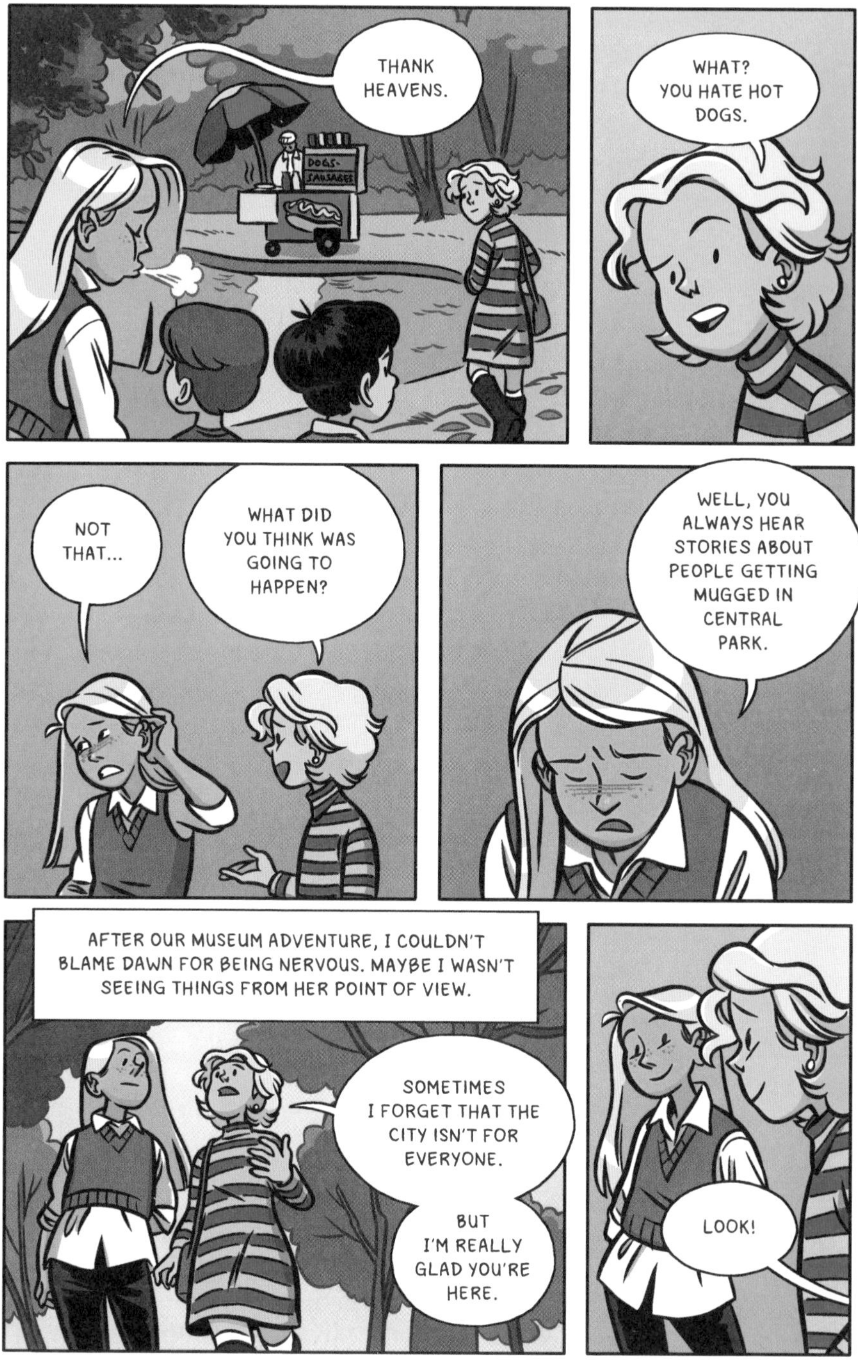
THANK HEAVENS.
WHAT? YOU HATE HOT DOGS.
DOGS- SAUSAGES
NOT THAT...
WHAT DID YOU THINK WAS GOING TO HAPPEN?
WELL, YOU ALWAYS HEAR STORIES ABOUT PEOPLE GETTING MUGGED IN CENTRAL PARK.
AFTER OUR MUSEUM ADVENTURE, I COULDN'T BLAME DAWN FOR BEING NERVOUS. MAYBE I WASN'T SEEING THINGS FROM HER POINT OF VIEW.
SOMETIMES I FORGET THAT THE CITY ISN'T FOR EVERYONE.
BUT I'M REALLY GLAD YOU'RE HERE.
LOOK!

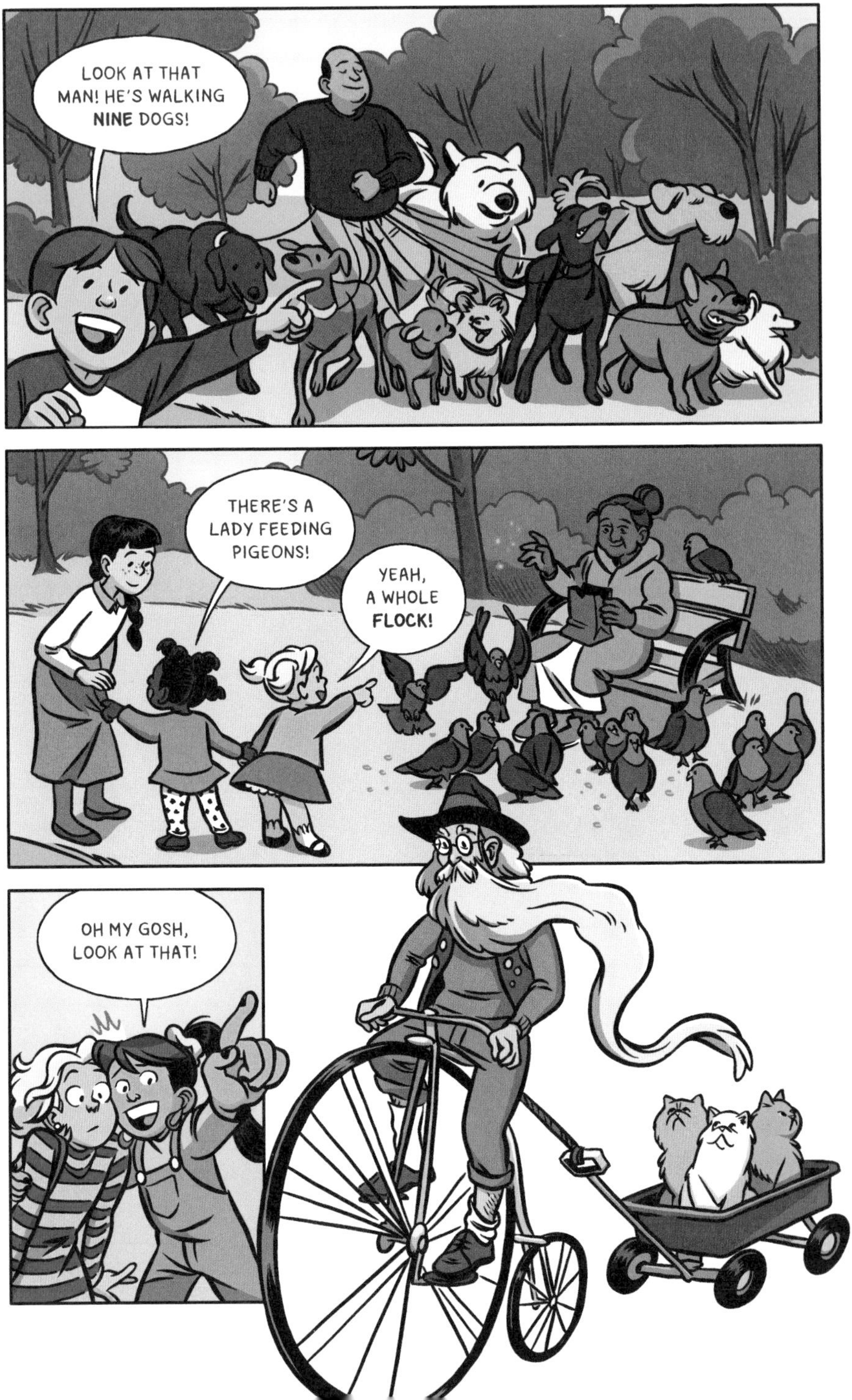
LOOK AT THAT MAN! HE'S WALKING **NINE** DOGS!
THERE'S A LADY FEEDING PIGEONS!
YEAH, A WHOLE **FLOCK**!
OH MY GOSH, LOOK AT THAT!

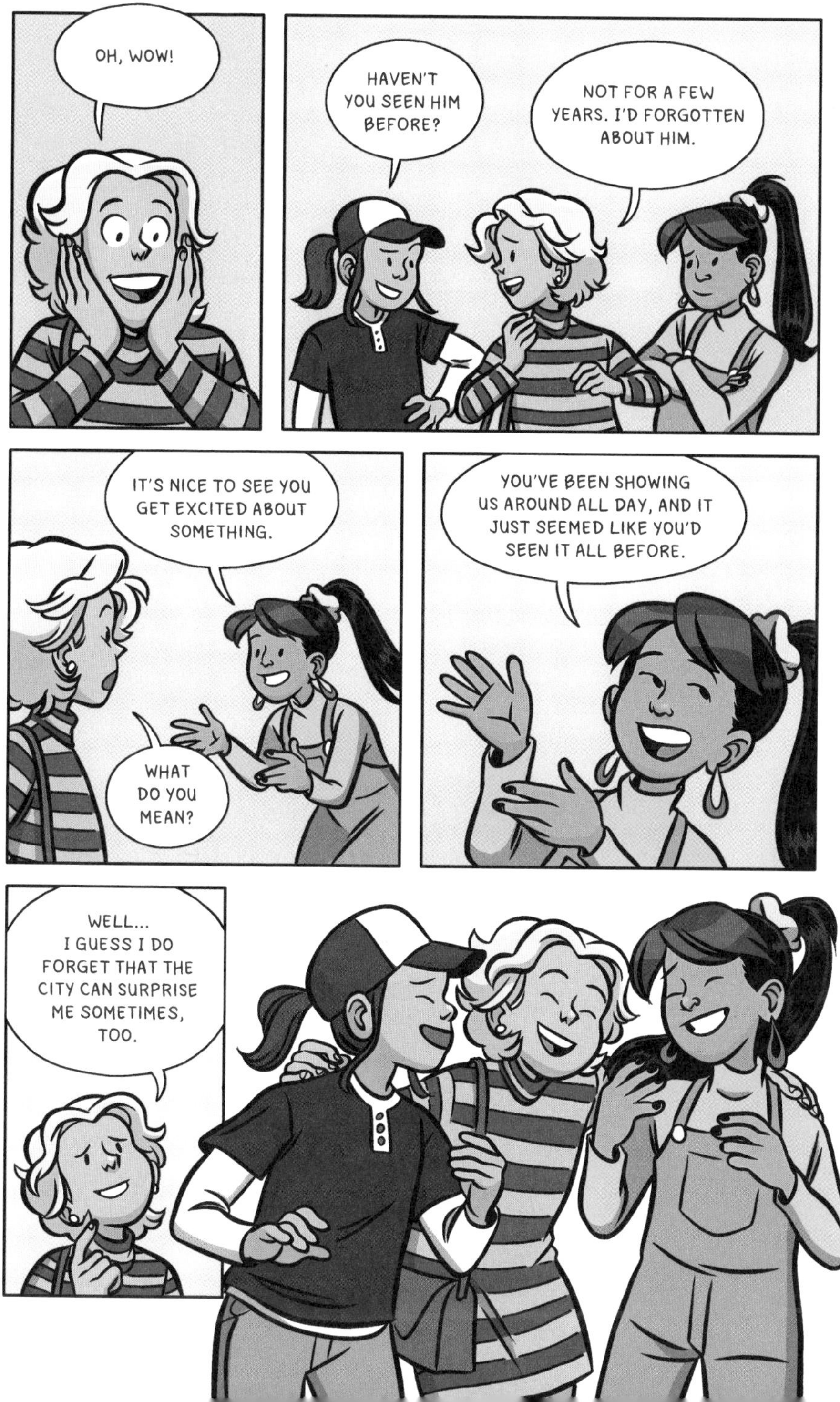
OH, WOW!
HAVEN'T YOU SEEN HIM BEFORE?
NOT FOR A FEW YEARS. I'D FORGOTTEN ABOUT HIM.
IT'S NICE TO SEE YOU GET EXCITED ABOUT SOMETHING.
WHAT DO YOU MEAN?
YOU'VE BEEN SHOWING US AROUND ALL DAY, AND IT JUST SEEMED LIKE YOU'D SEEN IT ALL BEFORE.
WELL... I GUESS I DO FORGET THAT THE CITY CAN SURPRISE ME SOMETIMES, TOO.

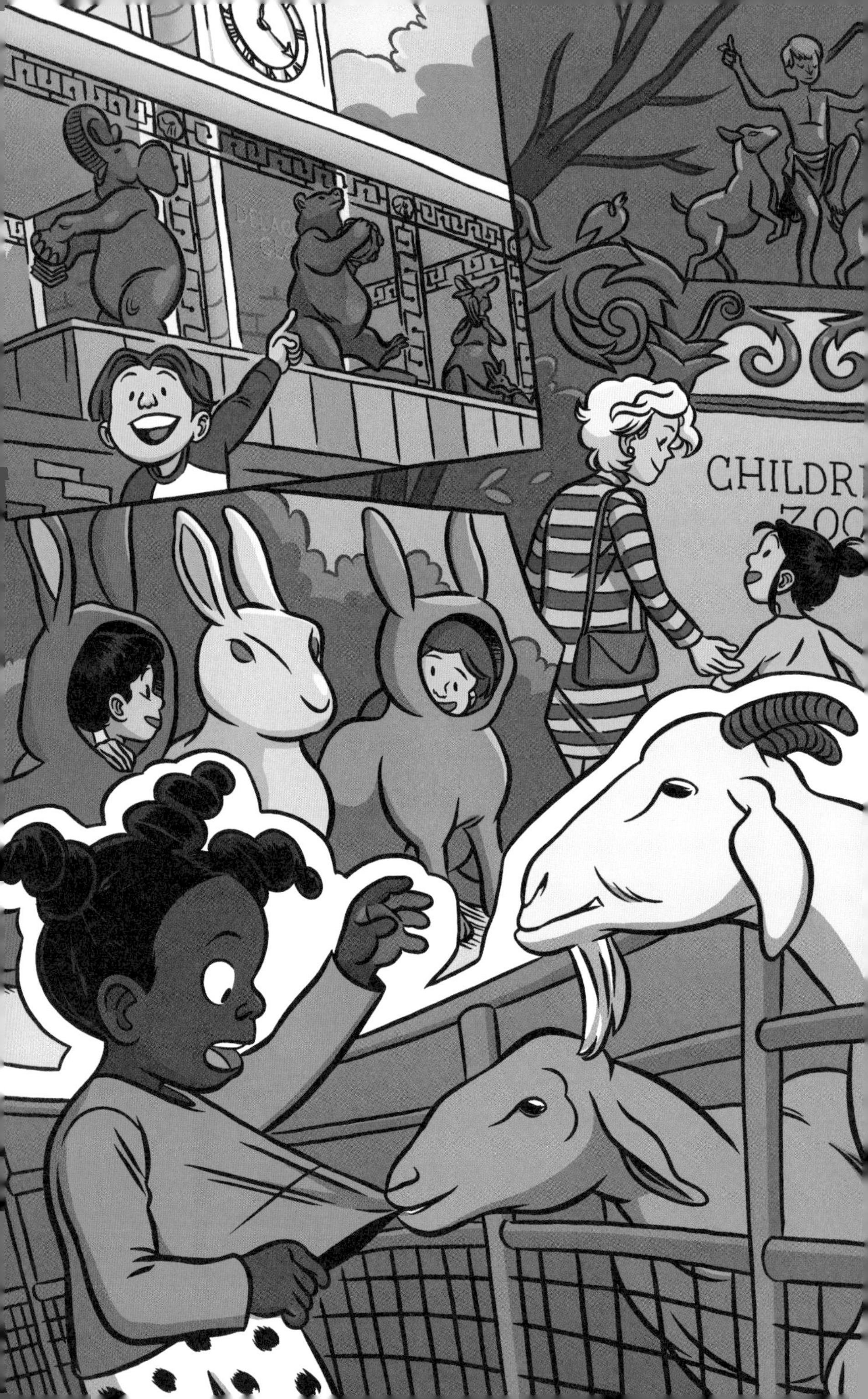

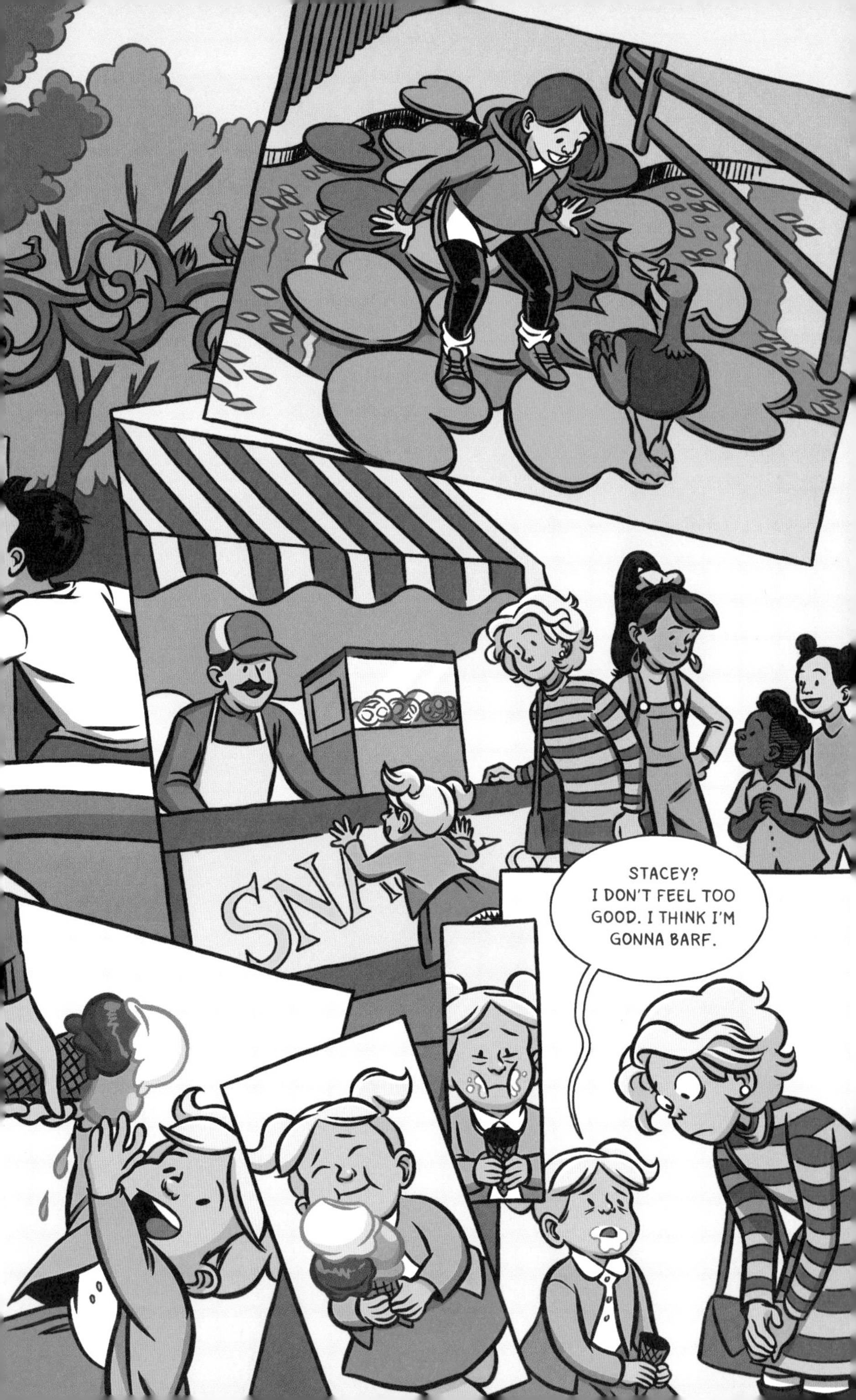
STACEY? I DON'T FEEL TOO GOOD. I THINK I'M GONNA BARF.

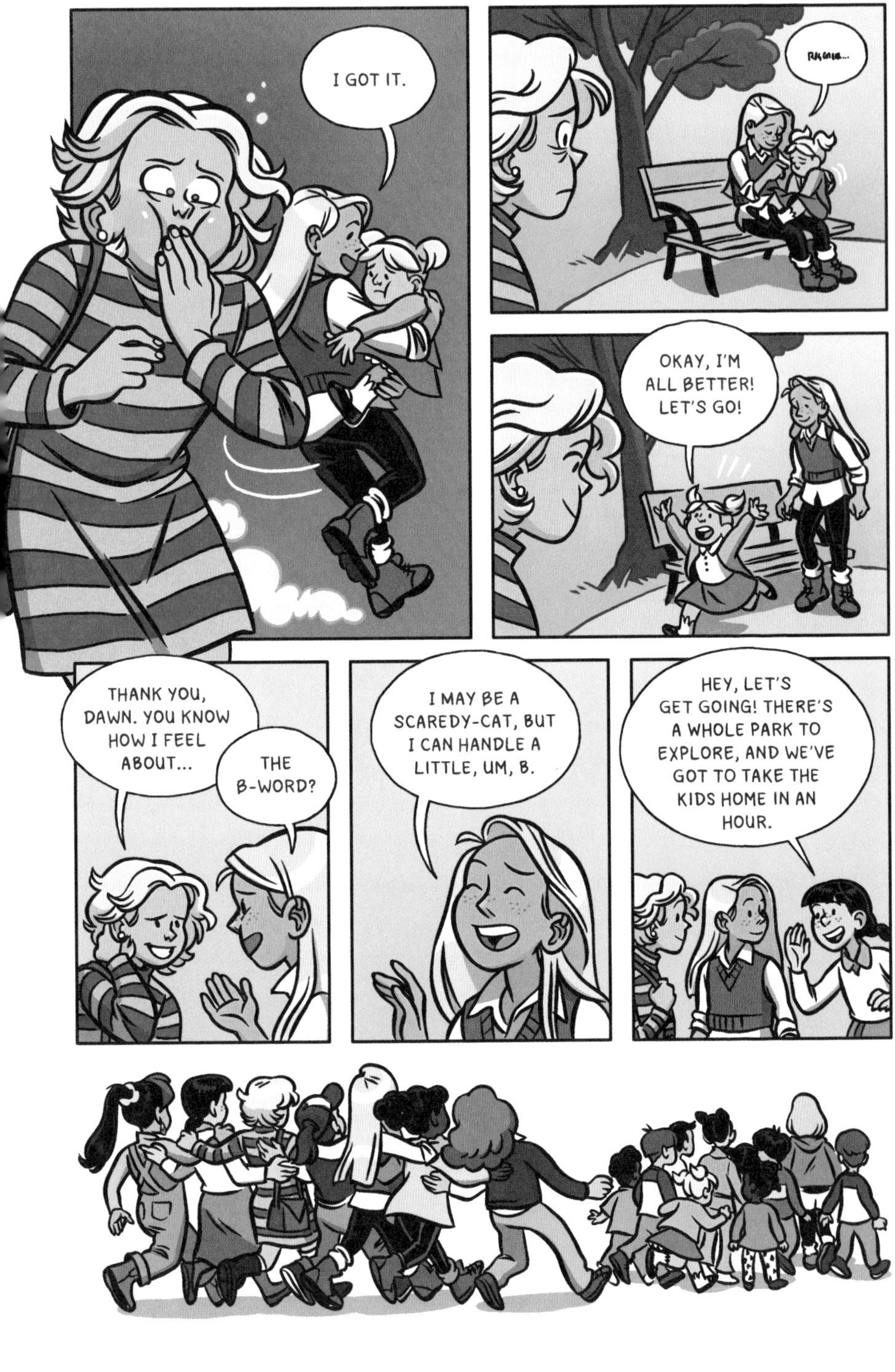
I GOT IT.
THANK YOU, DAWN. YOU KNOW HOW I FEEL ABOUT...
THE B-WORD?
I MAY BE A SCAREDY-CAT, BUT I CAN HANDLE A LITTLE, UM, B.
OKAY, I'M ALL BETTER! LET'S GO!
HEY, LET'S GET GOING! THERE'S A WHOLE PARK TO EXPLORE, AND WE'VE GOT TO TAKE THE KIDS HOME IN AN HOUR.

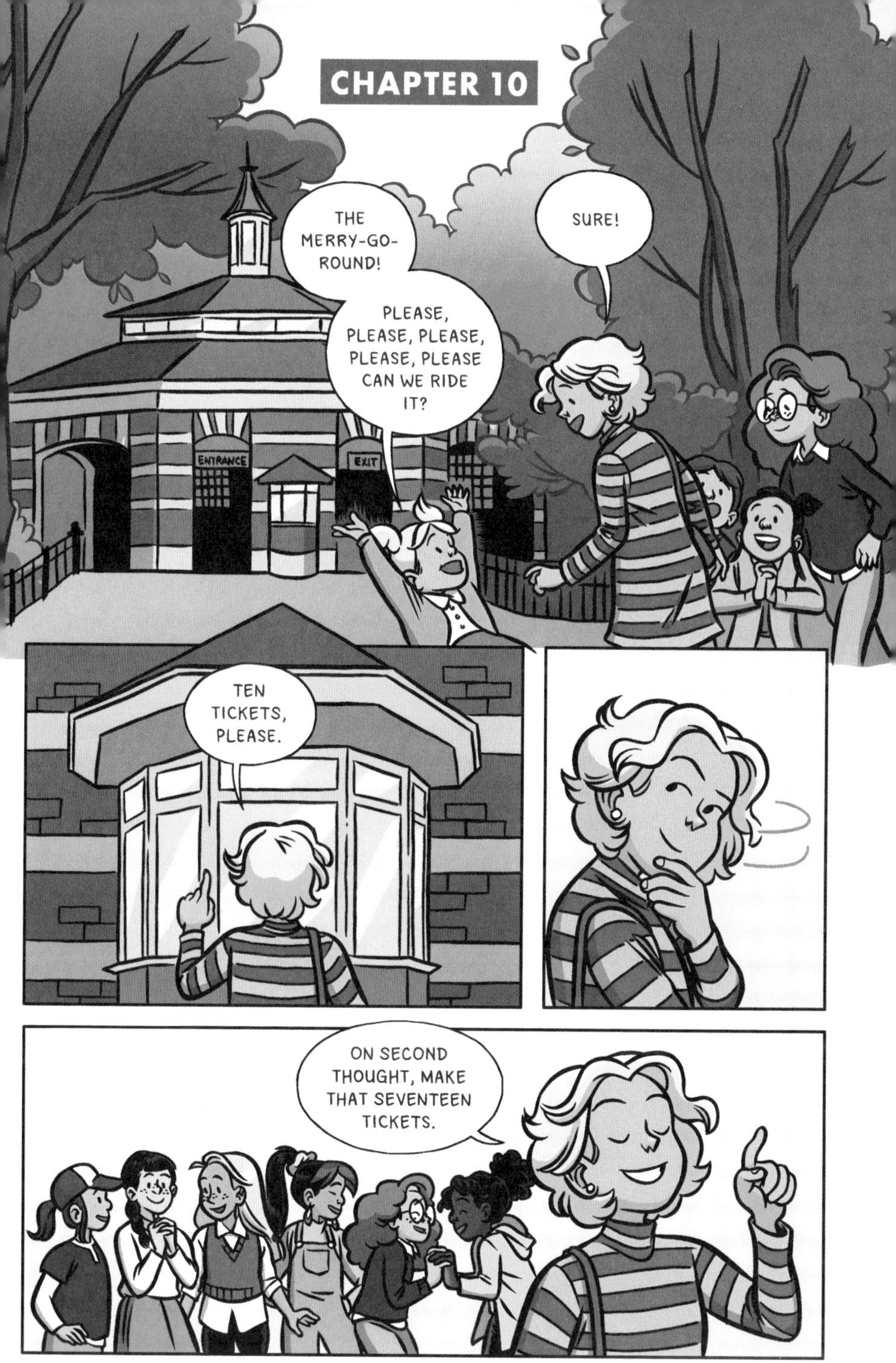
CHAPTER 10
THE MERRY-GO-ROUND!
PLEASE, PLEASE, PLEASE, PLEASE, PLEASE CAN WE RIDE IT?
SURE!
ENTRANCE
EXIT
TEN TICKETS, PLEASE.
ON SECOND THOUGHT, MAKE THAT SEVENTEEN TICKETS.

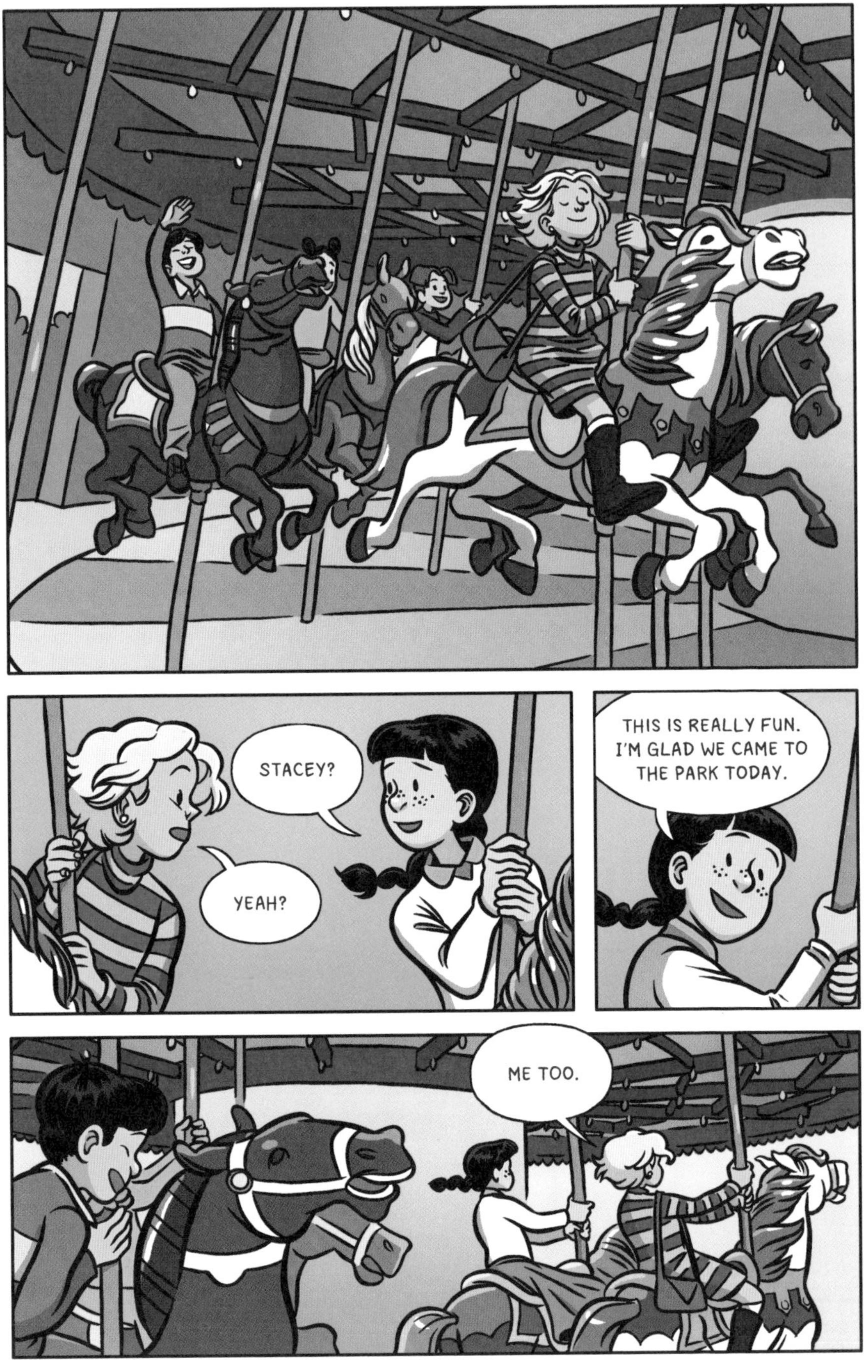
STACEY?
YEAH?
THIS IS REALLY FUN. I'M GLAD WE CAME TO THE PARK TODAY.
ME TOO.

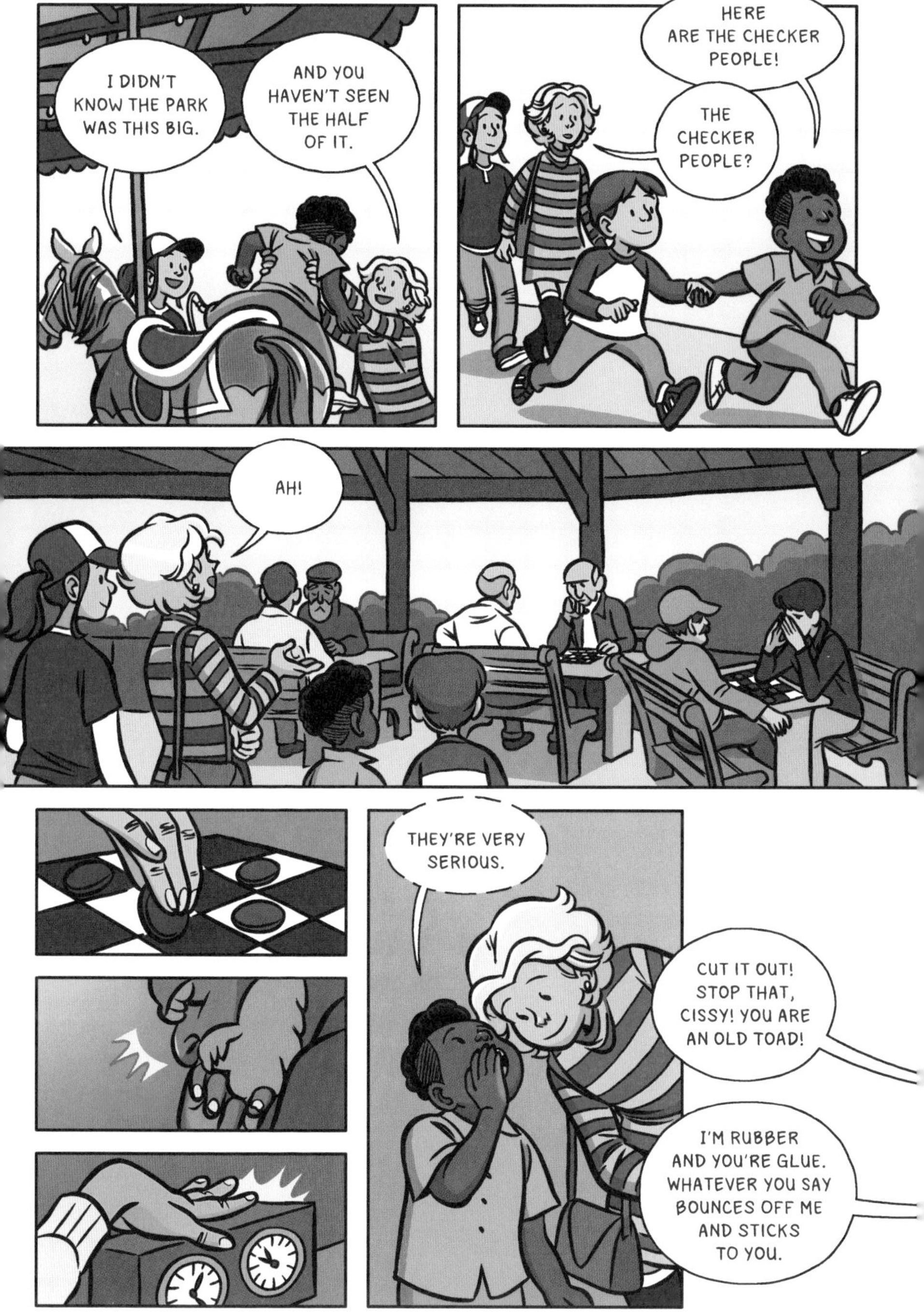
I DIDN'T KNOW THE PARK WAS THIS BIG.
AND YOU HAVEN'T SEEN THE HALF OF IT.
HERE ARE THE CHECKER PEOPLE!
THE CHECKER PEOPLE?
AH!
THEY'RE VERY SERIOUS.
CUT IT OUT! STOP THAT, CISSY! YOU ARE AN OLD TOAD!
I'M RUBBER AND YOU'RE GLUE. WHATEVER YOU SAY BOUNCES OFF ME AND STICKS TO YOU.

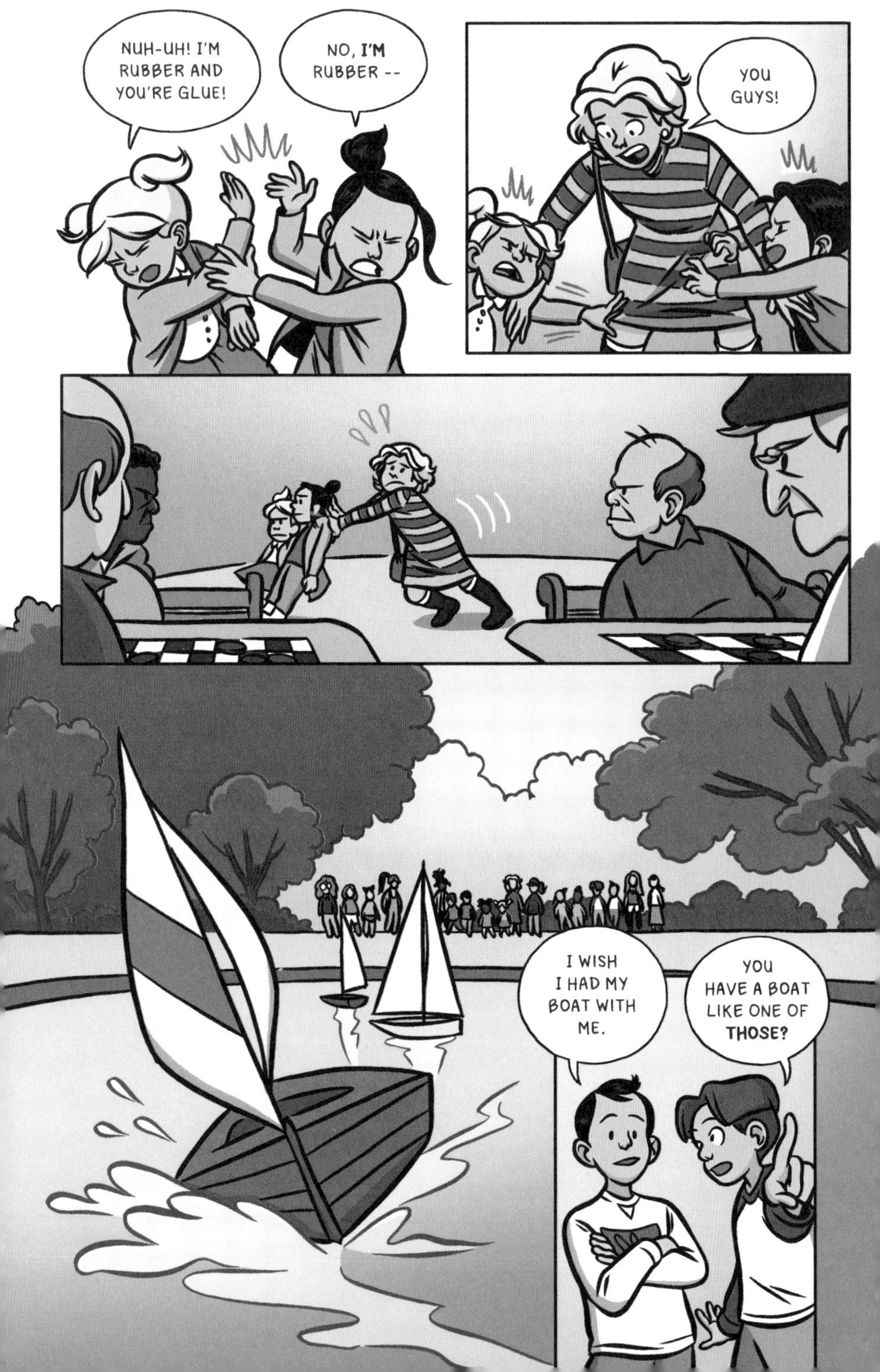
NUH-UH! I'M RUBBER AND YOU'RE GLUE!
NO, I'M RUBBER --
YOU GUYS!
I WISH I HAD MY BOAT WITH ME.
YOU HAVE A BOAT LIKE ONE OF THOSE?

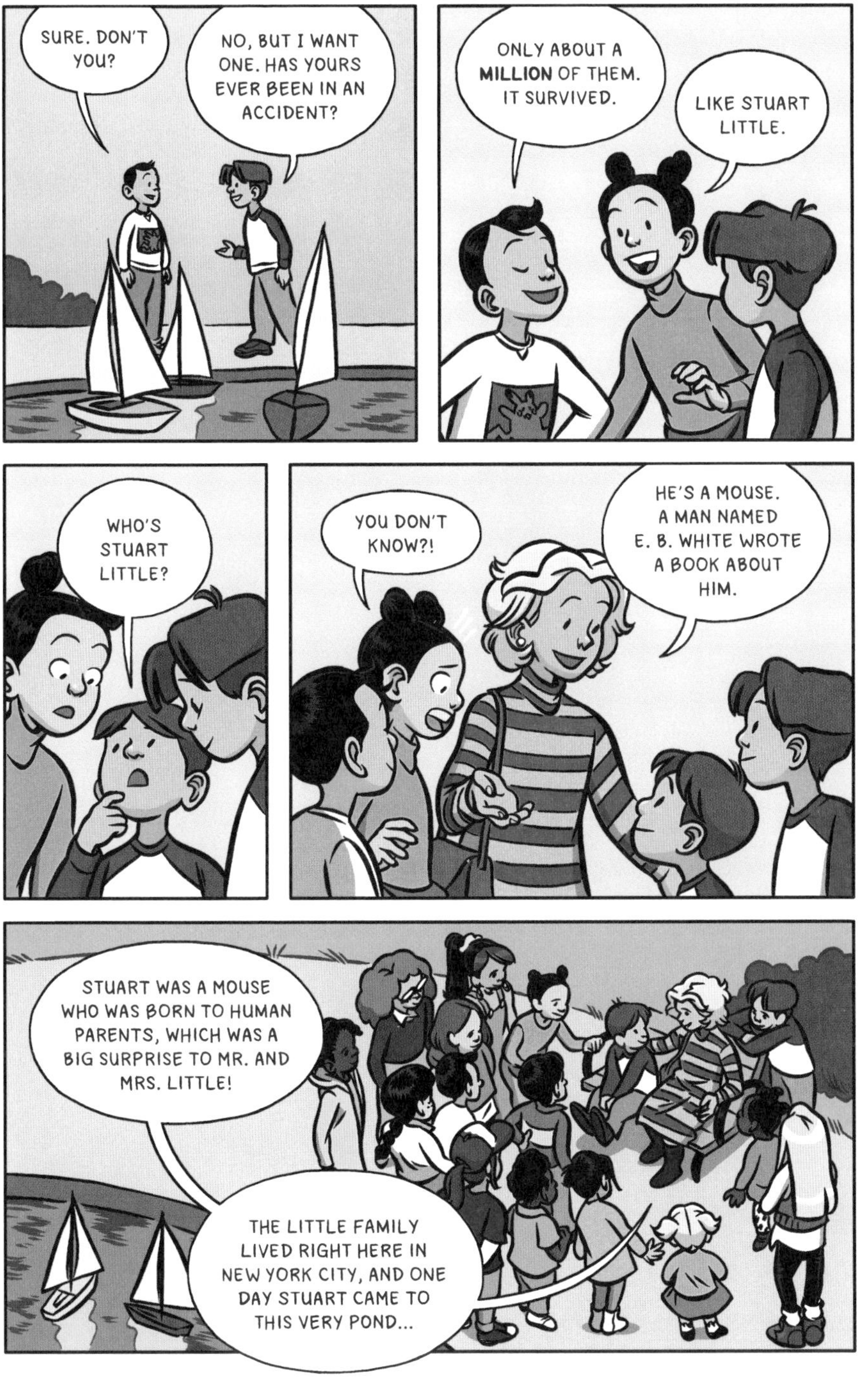
SURE. DON'T YOU?
NO, BUT I WANT ONE. HAS YOURS EVER BEEN IN AN ACCIDENT?
ONLY ABOUT A **MILLION** OF THEM. IT SURVIVED.
LIKE STUART LITTLE.
WHO'S STUART LITTLE?
YOU DON'T KNOW?!
HE'S A MOUSE. A MAN NAMED E. B. WHITE WROTE A BOOK ABOUT HIM.
STUART WAS A MOUSE WHO WAS BORN TO HUMAN PARENTS, WHICH WAS A BIG SURPRISE TO MR. AND MRS. LITTLE!
THE LITTLE FAMILY LIVED RIGHT HERE IN NEW YORK CITY, AND ONE DAY STUART CAME TO THIS VERY POND...

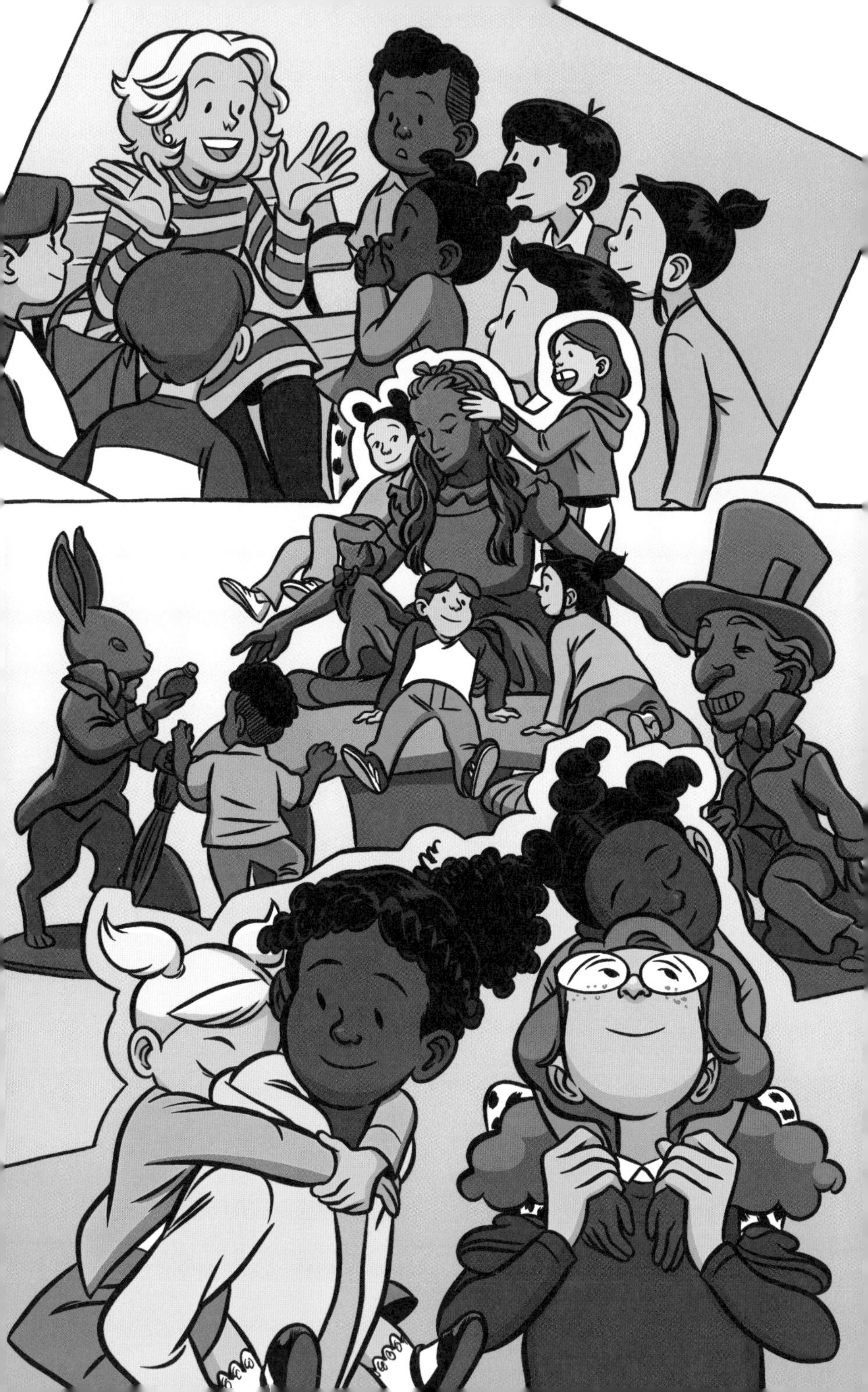

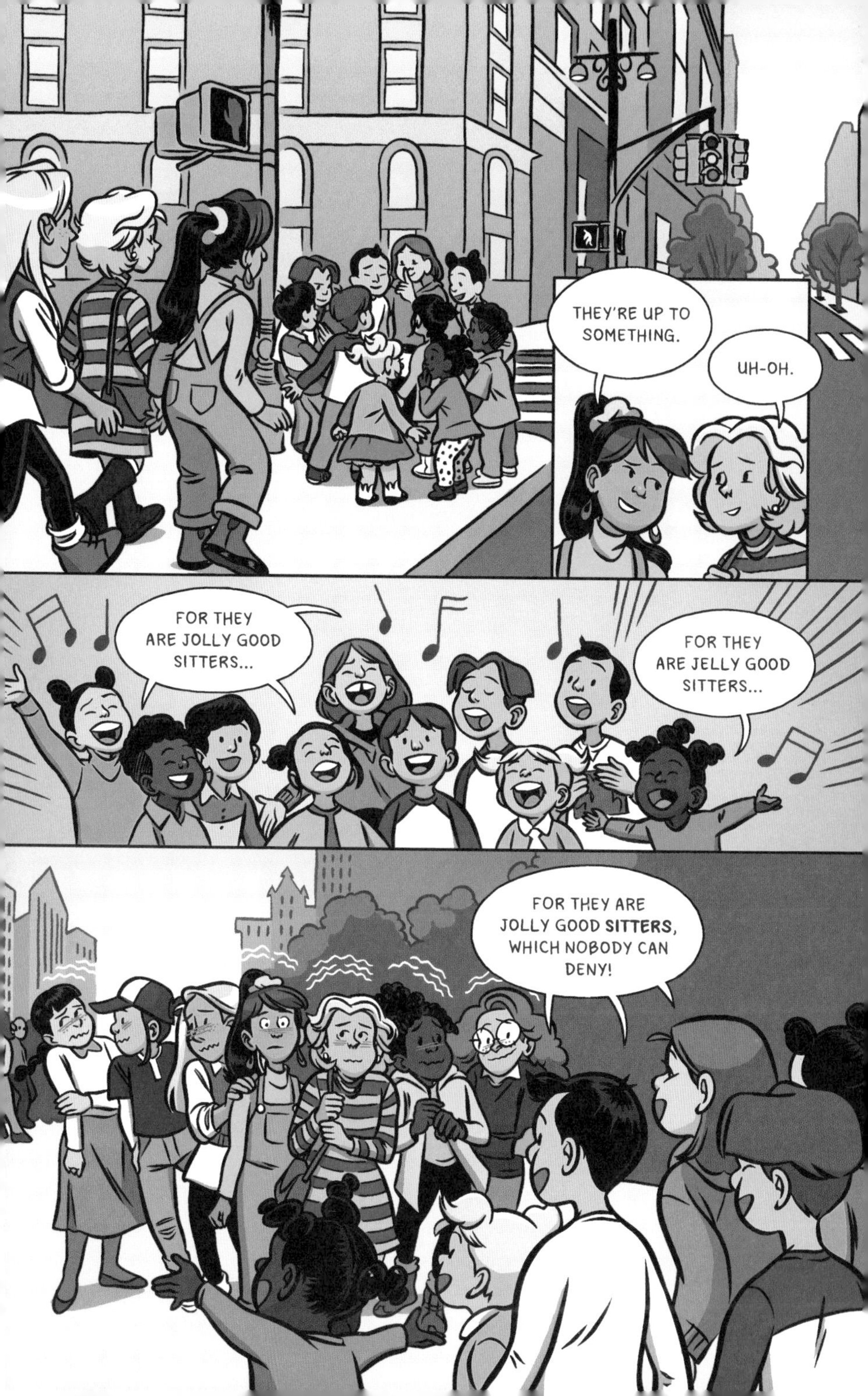
THEY'RE UP TO SOMETHING.
UH-OH.
FOR THEY ARE JOLLY GOOD SITTERS...
FOR THEY ARE JELLY GOOD SITTERS...
FOR THEY ARE JOLLY GOOD **SITTERS**, WHICH NOBODY CAN DENY!

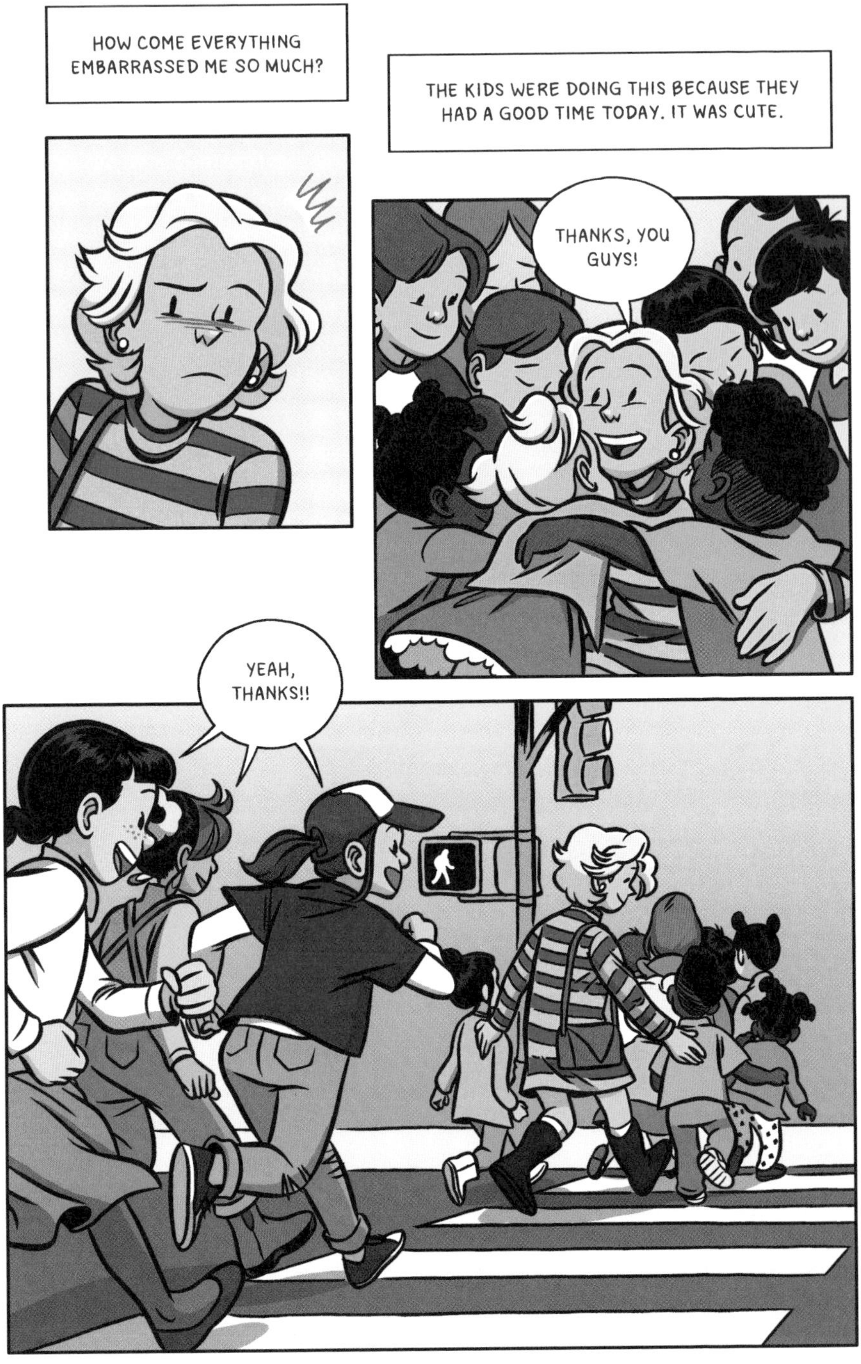
HOW COME EVERYTHING EMBARRASSED ME SO MUCH?
THE KIDS WERE DOING THIS BECAUSE THEY HAD A GOOD TIME TODAY. IT WAS CUTE.
THANKS, YOU GUYS!
YEAH, THANKS!!

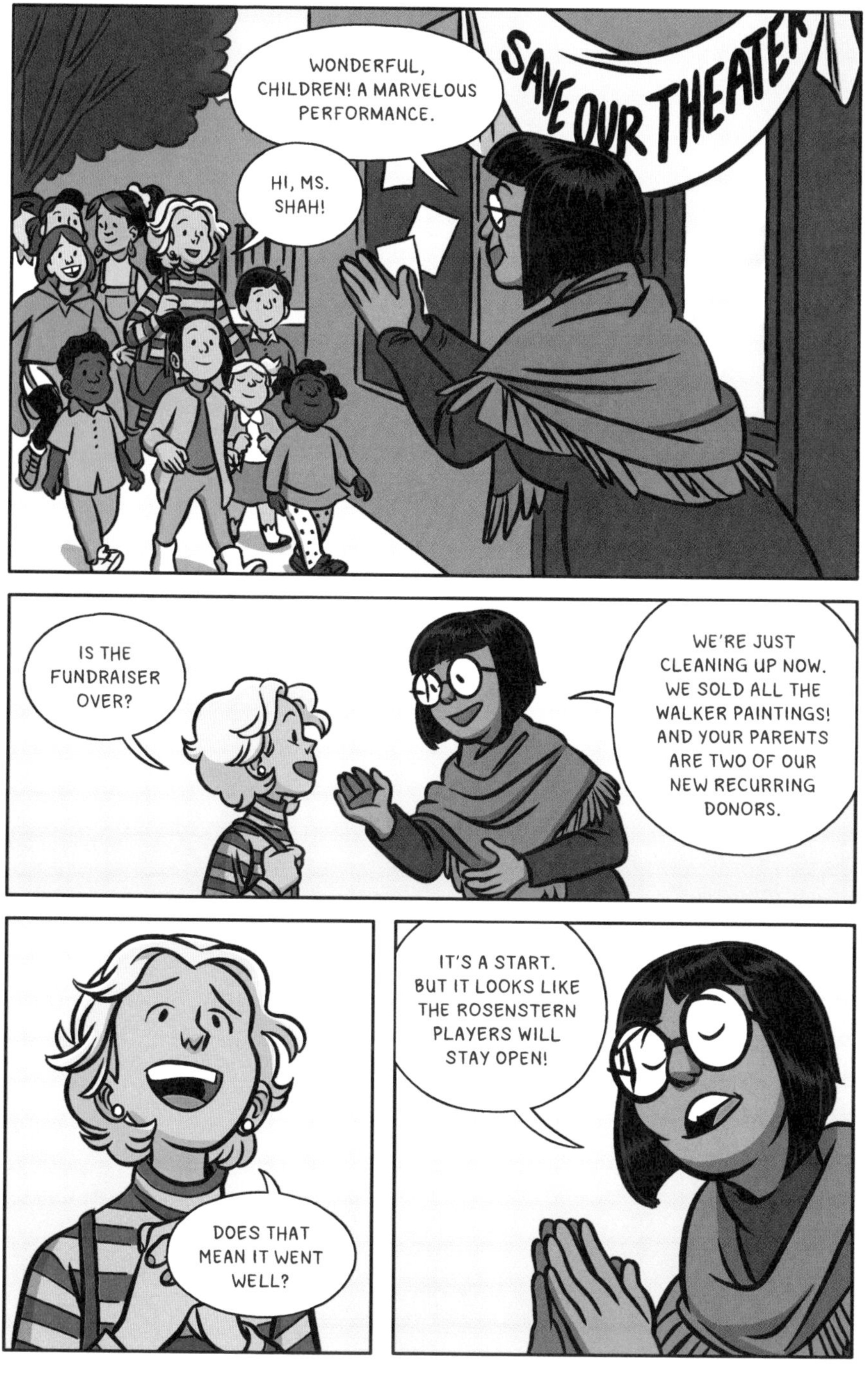

SAVE OUR THEATER
WONDERFUL, CHILDREN! A MARVELOUS PERFORMANCE.
HI, MS. SHAH!
IS THE FUNDRAISER OVER?
WE'RE JUST CLEANING UP NOW. WE SOLD ALL THE WALKER PAINTINGS! AND YOUR PARENTS ARE TWO OF OUR NEW RECURRING DONORS.
DOES THAT MEAN IT WENT WELL?
IT'S A START. BUT IT LOOKS LIKE THE ROSENSTERN PLAYERS WILL STAY OPEN!

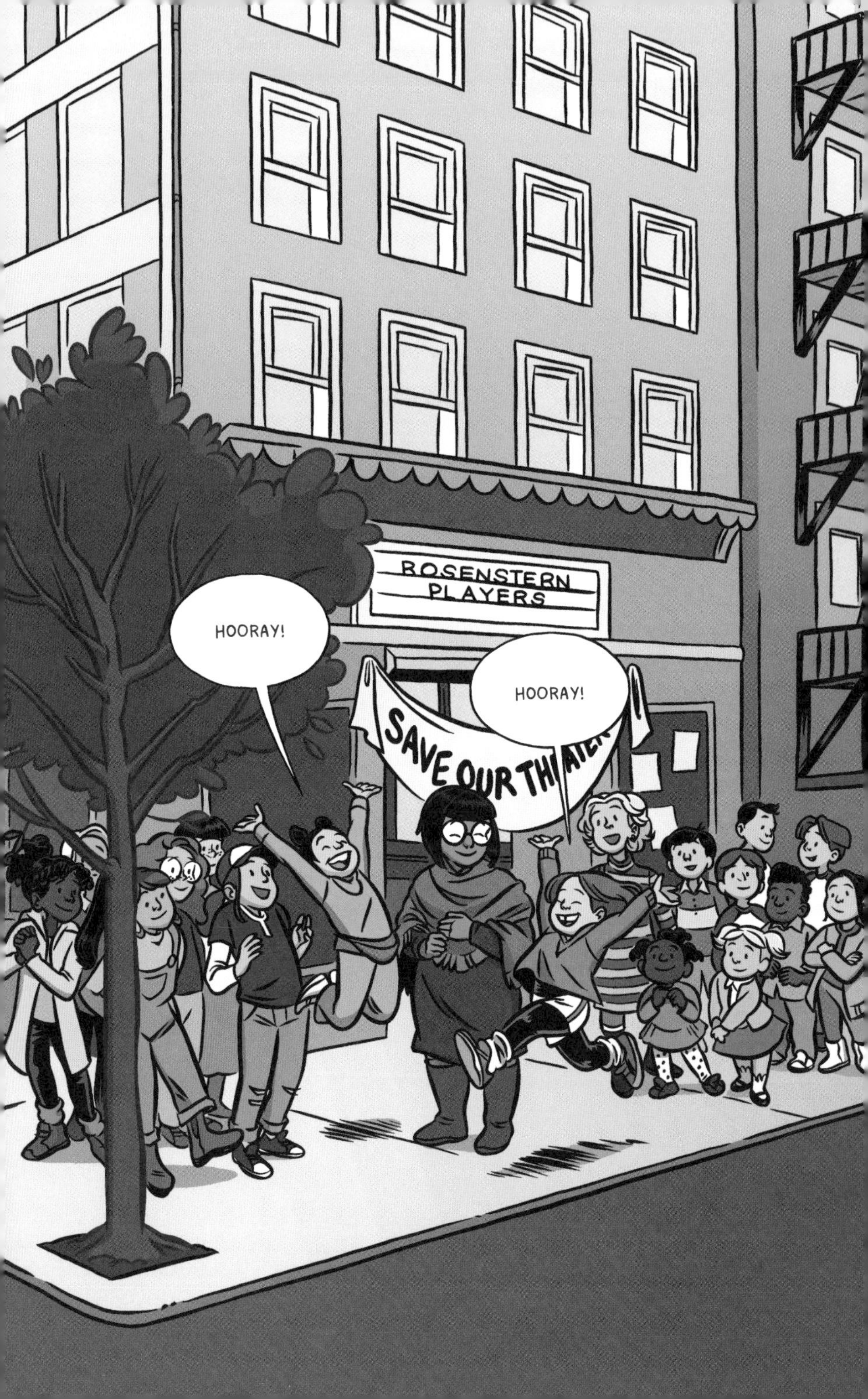
ROSENSTERN PLAYERS
HOORAY!
SAVE OUR THEATER
HOORAY!

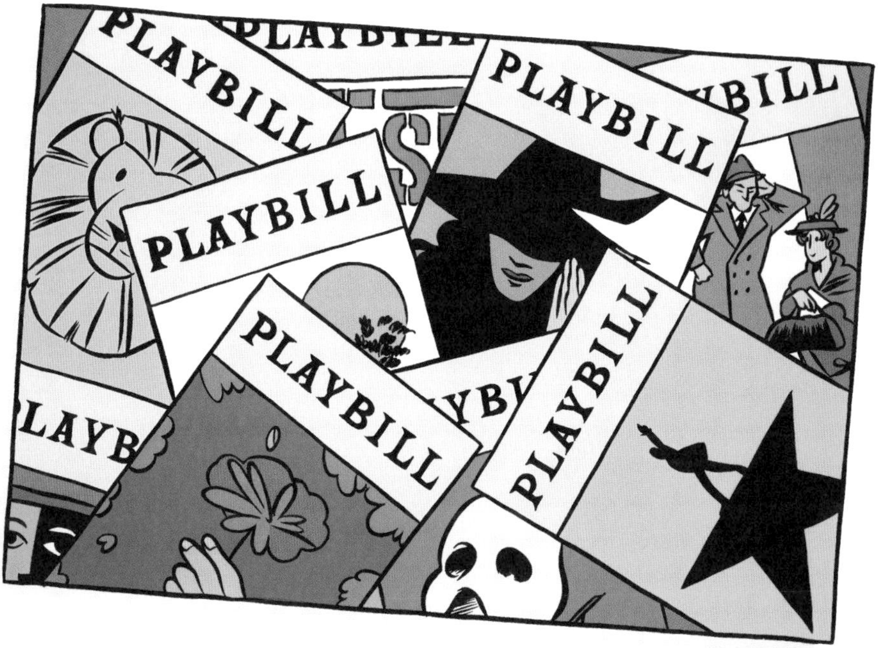
PLAYBILL
PLAYBILL
PLAYBILL
PLAYBILL
PLAYBILL

Dear Logan,

You will not believe what we did last night. We had the most glamorous, exciting Saturday night in the history of the universe. We went to a Broadway play. We sat right in the middle of the theater, up close. And we ate dinner out - just the seven of us, plus Stacey's friend Laine. And we RODE IN A LIMO. (Limo is short for limousine.) I'll tell you the rest when we get back.

Love,
Mary Anne

Logan Bruno

689 Burnt Hill Rd.

Stoneybrook, CT 06800

CHAPTER 11

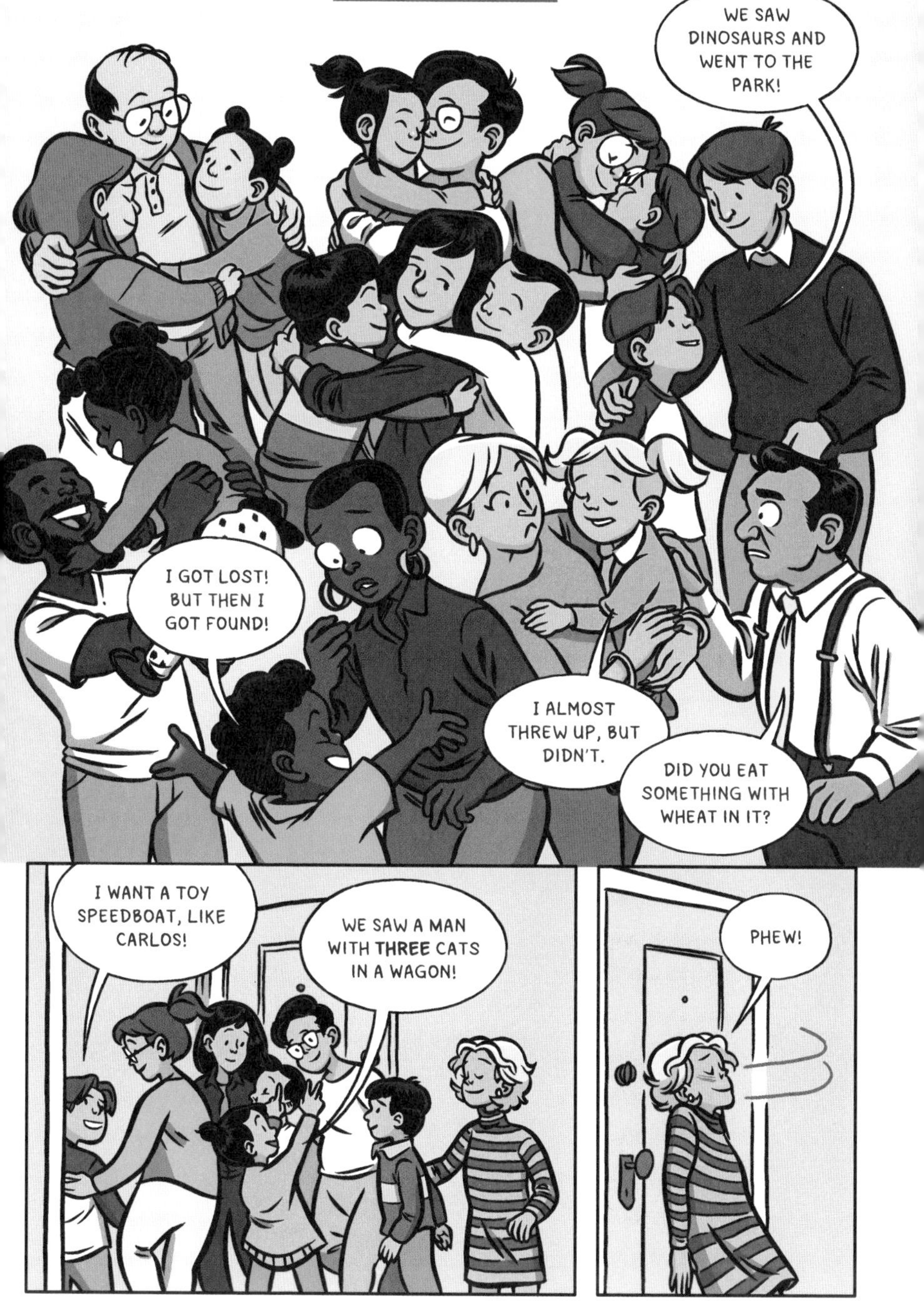
WE SAW DINOSAURS AND WENT TO THE PARK!
I GOT LOST! BUT THEN I GOT FOUND!
I ALMOST THREW UP, BUT DIDN'T.
DID YOU EAT SOMETHING WITH WHEAT IN IT?
I WANT A TOY SPEEDBOAT, LIKE CARLOS!
WE SAW A MAN WITH **THREE** CATS IN A WAGON!
PHEW!

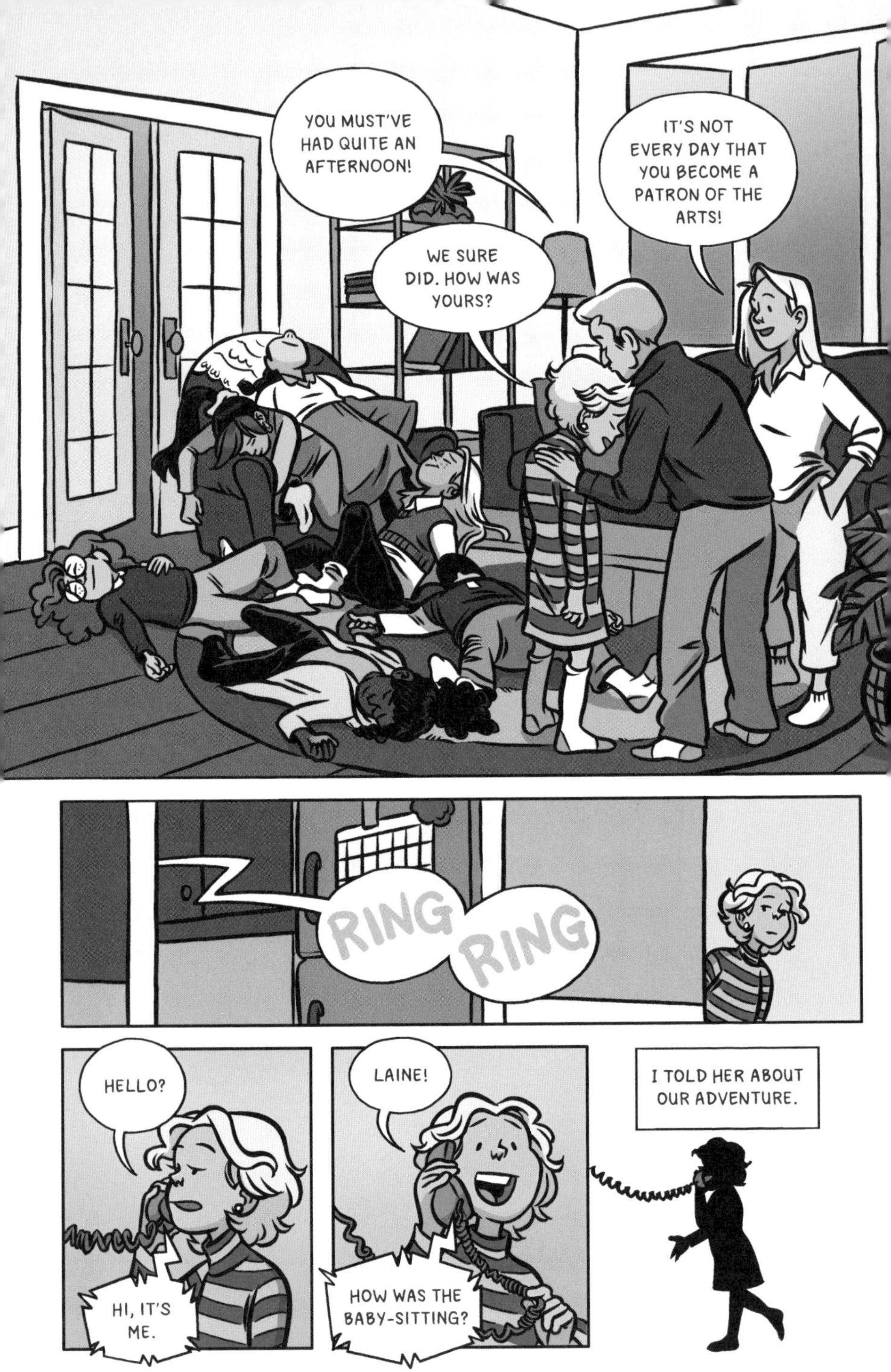
YOU MUST'VE HAD QUITE AN AFTERNOON!
IT'S NOT EVERY DAY THAT YOU BECOME A PATRON OF THE ARTS!
WE SURE DID. HOW WAS YOURS?
RING
RING
HELLO?
HI, IT'S ME.
LAINE!
HOW WAS THE BABY-SITTING?
I TOLD HER ABOUT OUR ADVENTURE.

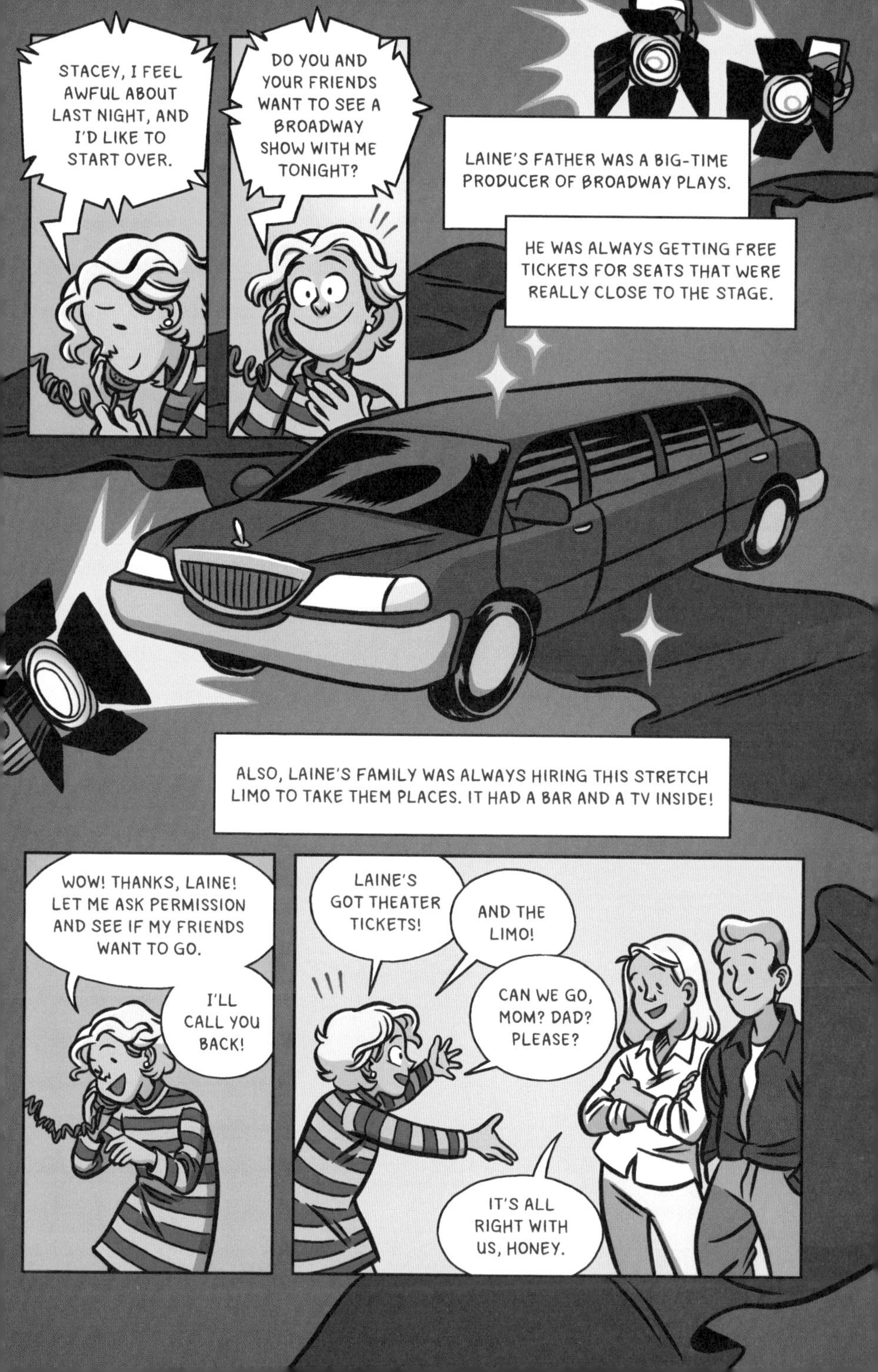
STACEY, I FEEL AWFUL ABOUT LAST NIGHT, AND I'D LIKE TO START OVER.
DO YOU AND YOUR FRIENDS WANT TO SEE A BROADWAY SHOW WITH ME TONIGHT?
LAINE'S FATHER WAS A BIG-TIME PRODUCER OF BROADWAY PLAYS.
HE WAS ALWAYS GETTING FREE TICKETS FOR SEATS THAT WERE REALLY CLOSE TO THE STAGE.
ALSO, LAINE'S FAMILY WAS ALWAYS HIRING THIS STRETCH LIMO TO TAKE THEM PLACES. IT HAD A BAR AND A TV INSIDE!
WOW! THANKS, LAINE! LET ME ASK PERMISSION AND SEE IF MY FRIENDS WANT TO GO.
I'LL CALL YOU BACK!
LAINE'S GOT THEATER TICKETS!
AND THE LIMO!
CAN WE GO, MOM? DAD? PLEASE?
IT'S ALL RIGHT WITH US, HONEY.

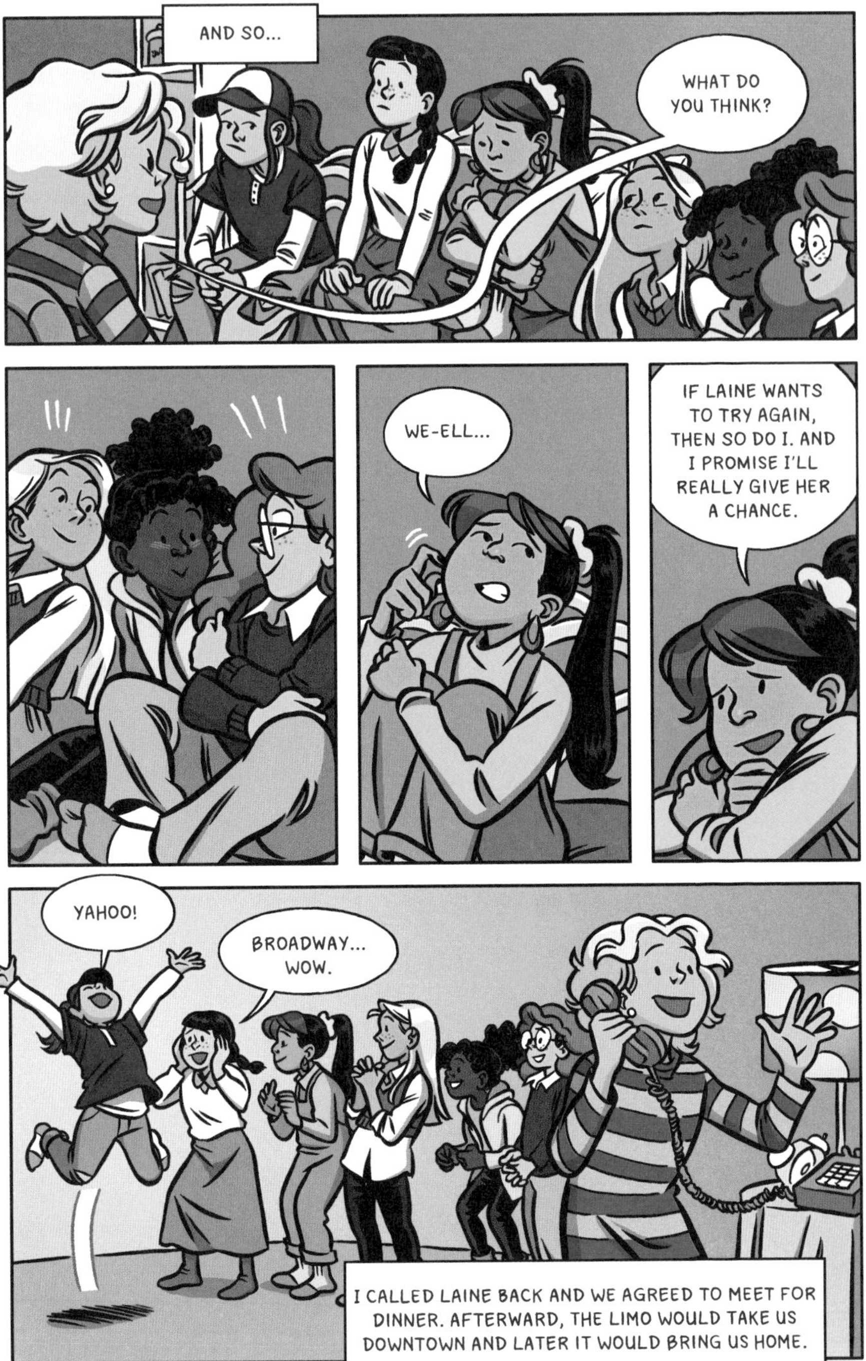
AND SO...
WHAT DO YOU THINK?
WE-ELL...
IF LAINE WANTS TO TRY AGAIN, THEN SO DO I. AND I PROMISE I'LL REALLY GIVE HER A CHANCE.
YAHOO!
BROADWAY... WOW.
I CALLED LAINE BACK AND WE AGREED TO MEET FOR DINNER. AFTERWARD, THE LIMO WOULD TAKE US DOWNTOWN AND LATER IT WOULD BRING US HOME.

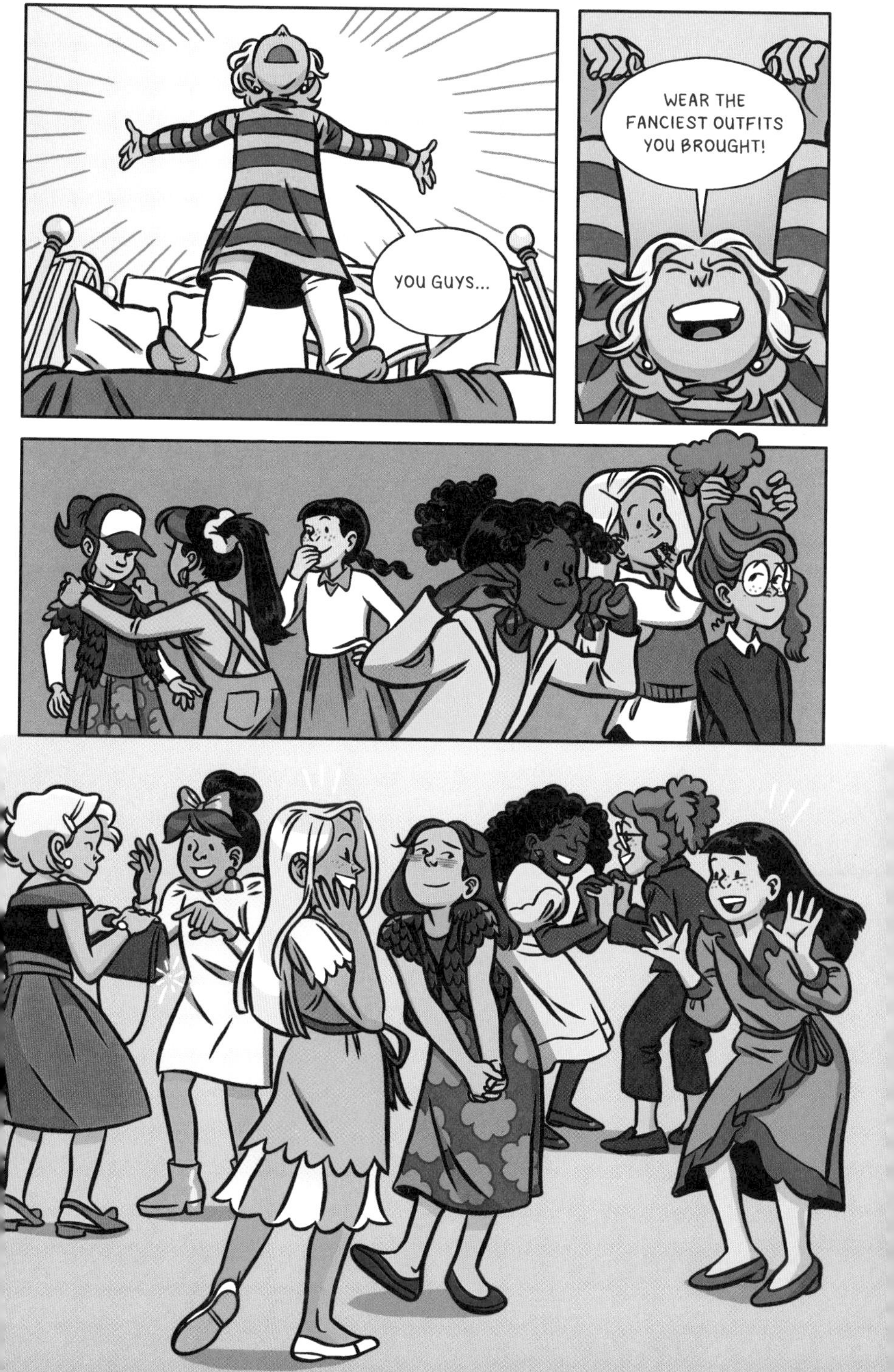
YOU GUYS...
WEAR THE FANCIEST OUTFITS YOU BROUGHT!

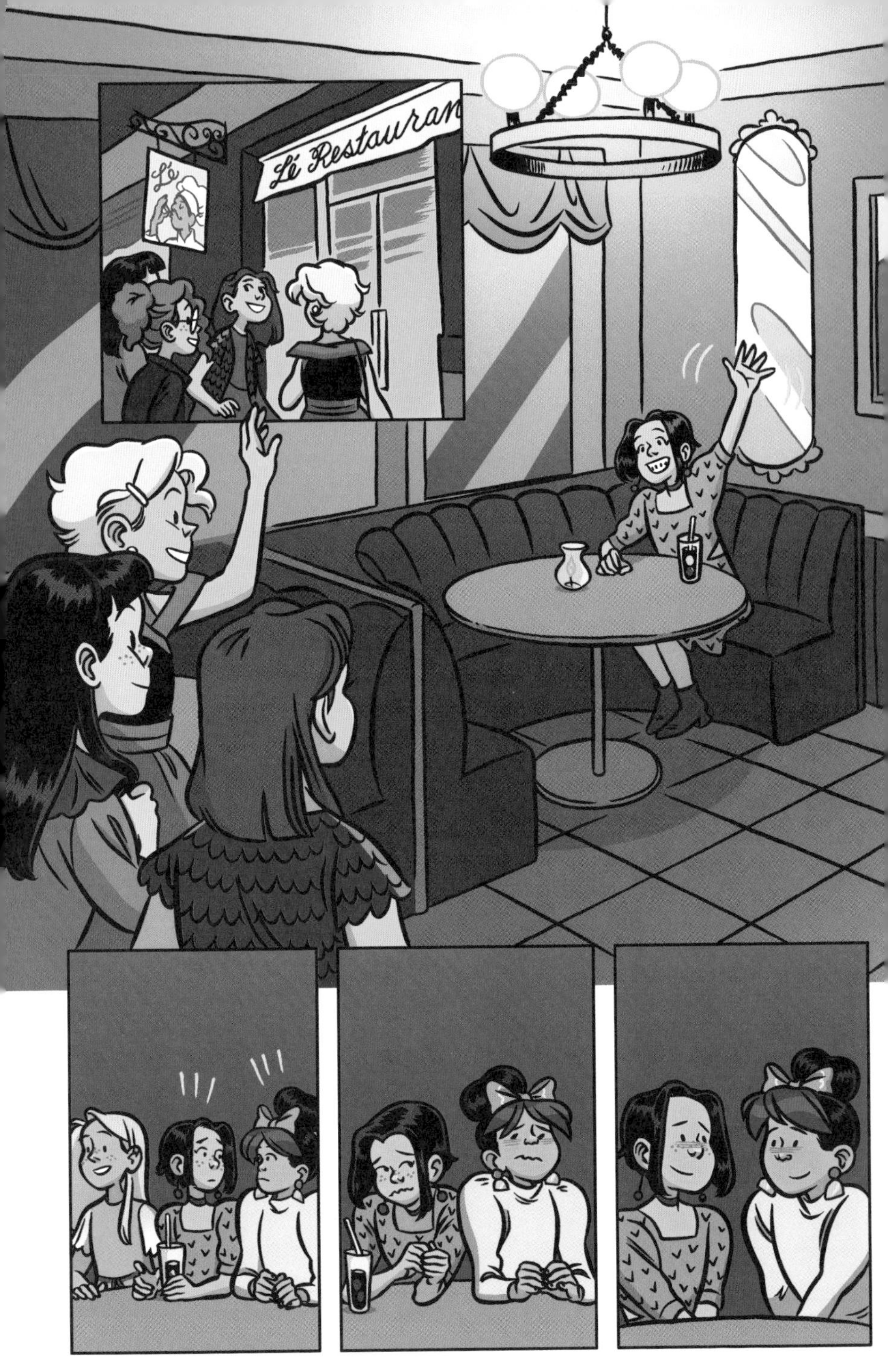
Lé Restauran

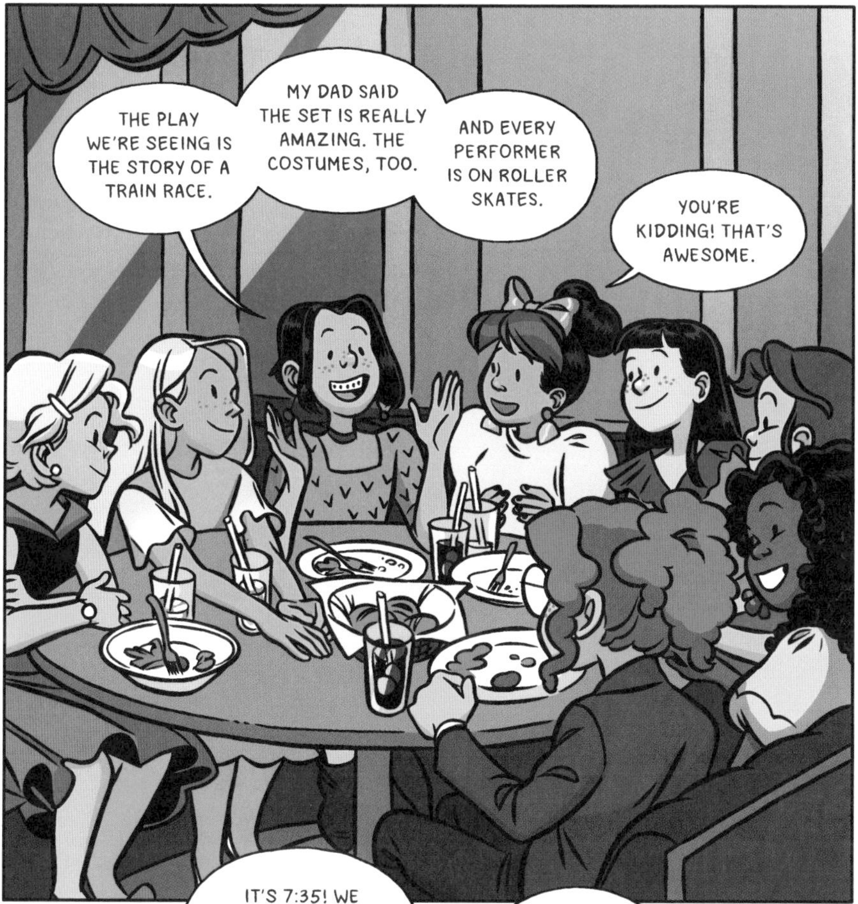
THE PLAY WE'RE SEEING IS THE STORY OF A TRAIN RACE.
MY DAD SAID THE SET IS REALLY AMAZING. THE COSTUMES, TOO.
AND EVERY PERFORMER IS ON ROLLER SKATES.
YOU'RE KIDDING! THAT'S AWESOME.

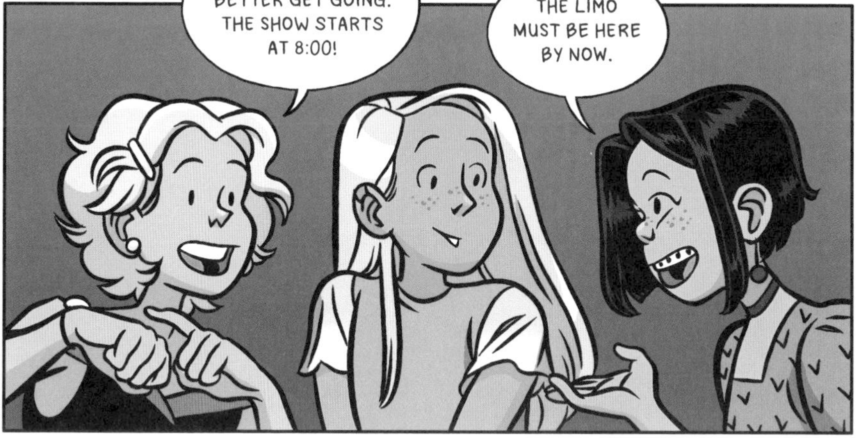
IT'S 7:35! WE BETTER GET GOING. THE SHOW STARTS AT 8:00!
THE LIMO MUST BE HERE BY NOW.

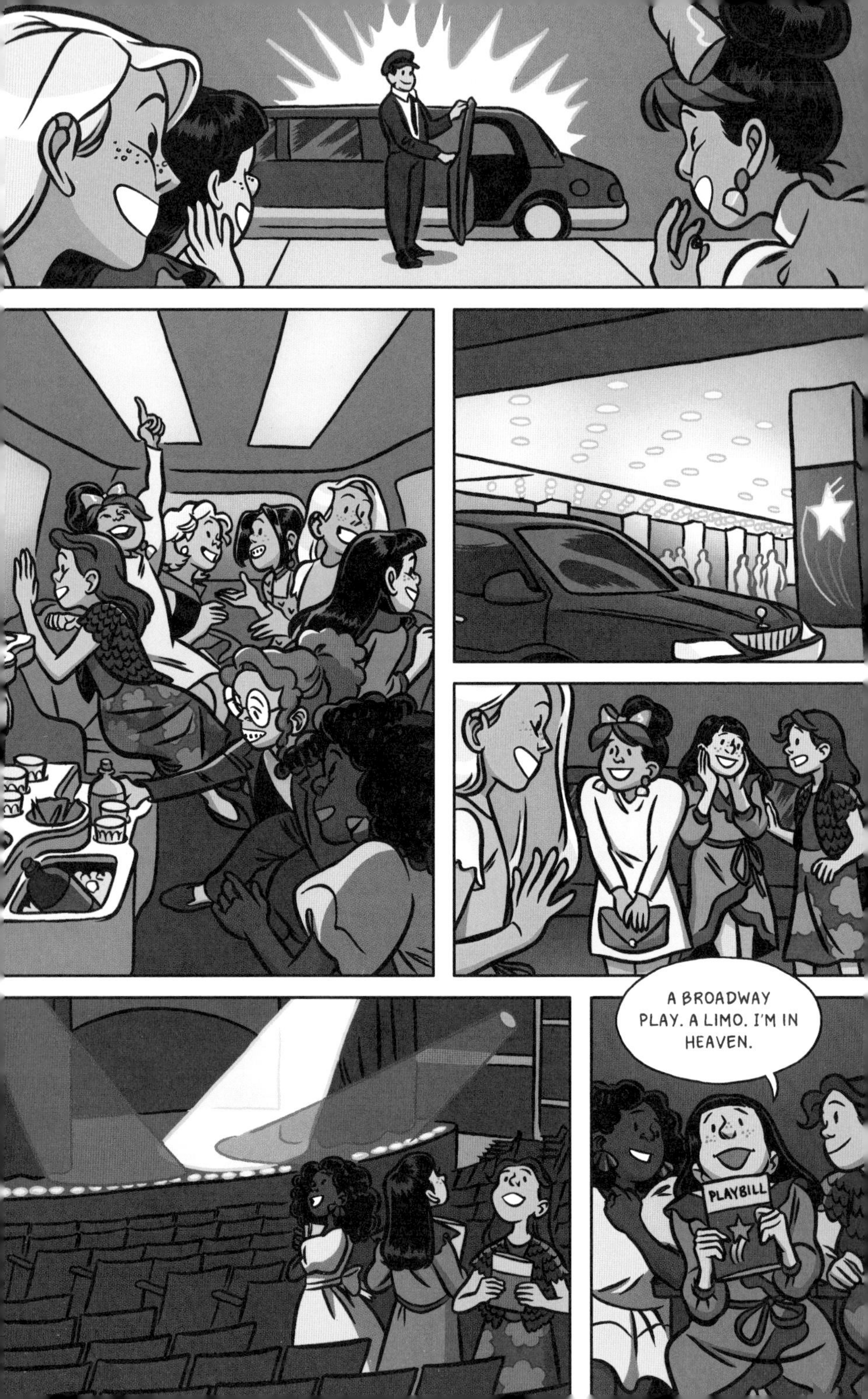
A BROADWAY PLAY. A LIMO. I'M IN HEAVEN.
PLAYBILL

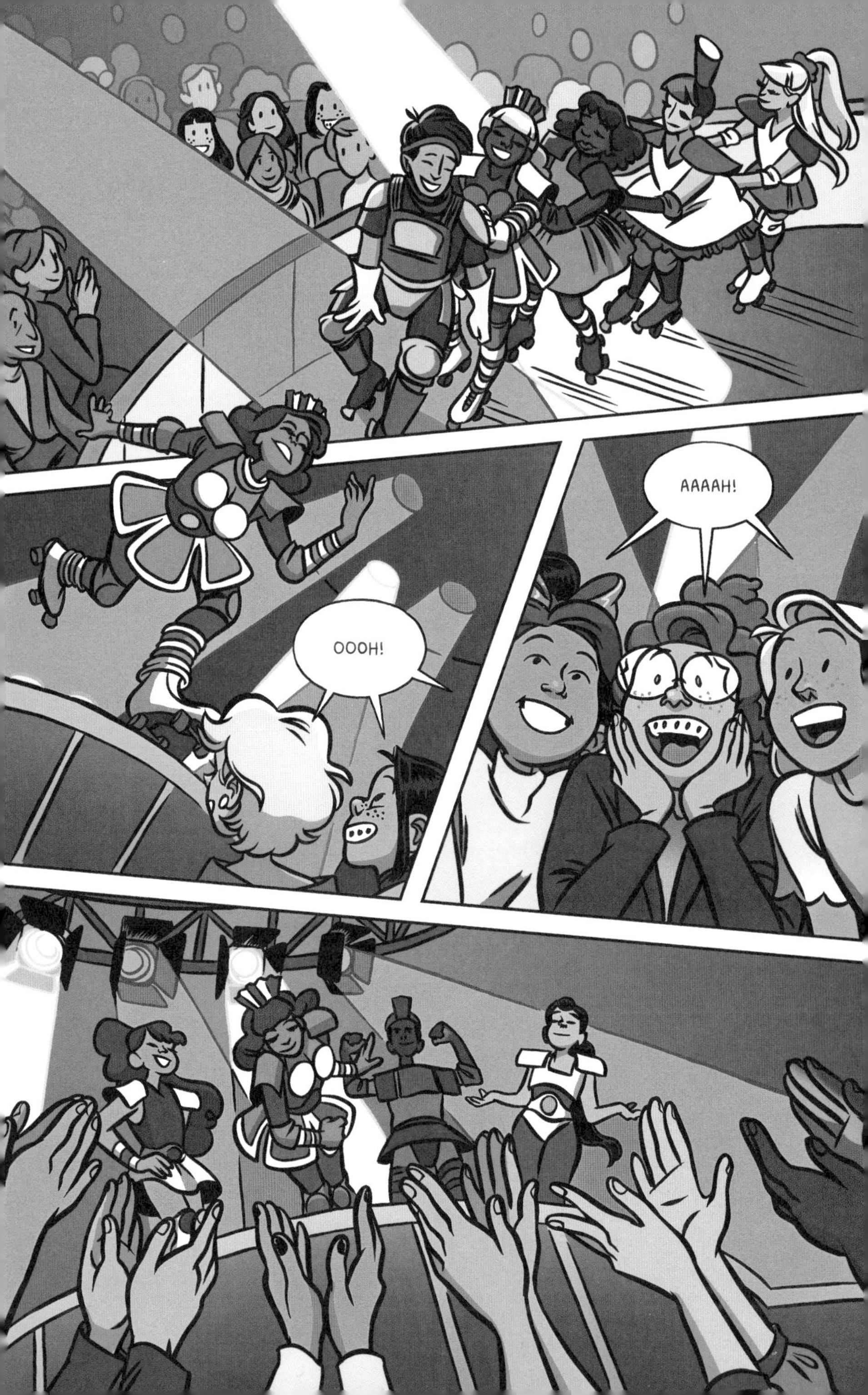
OOOH!
AAAAH!

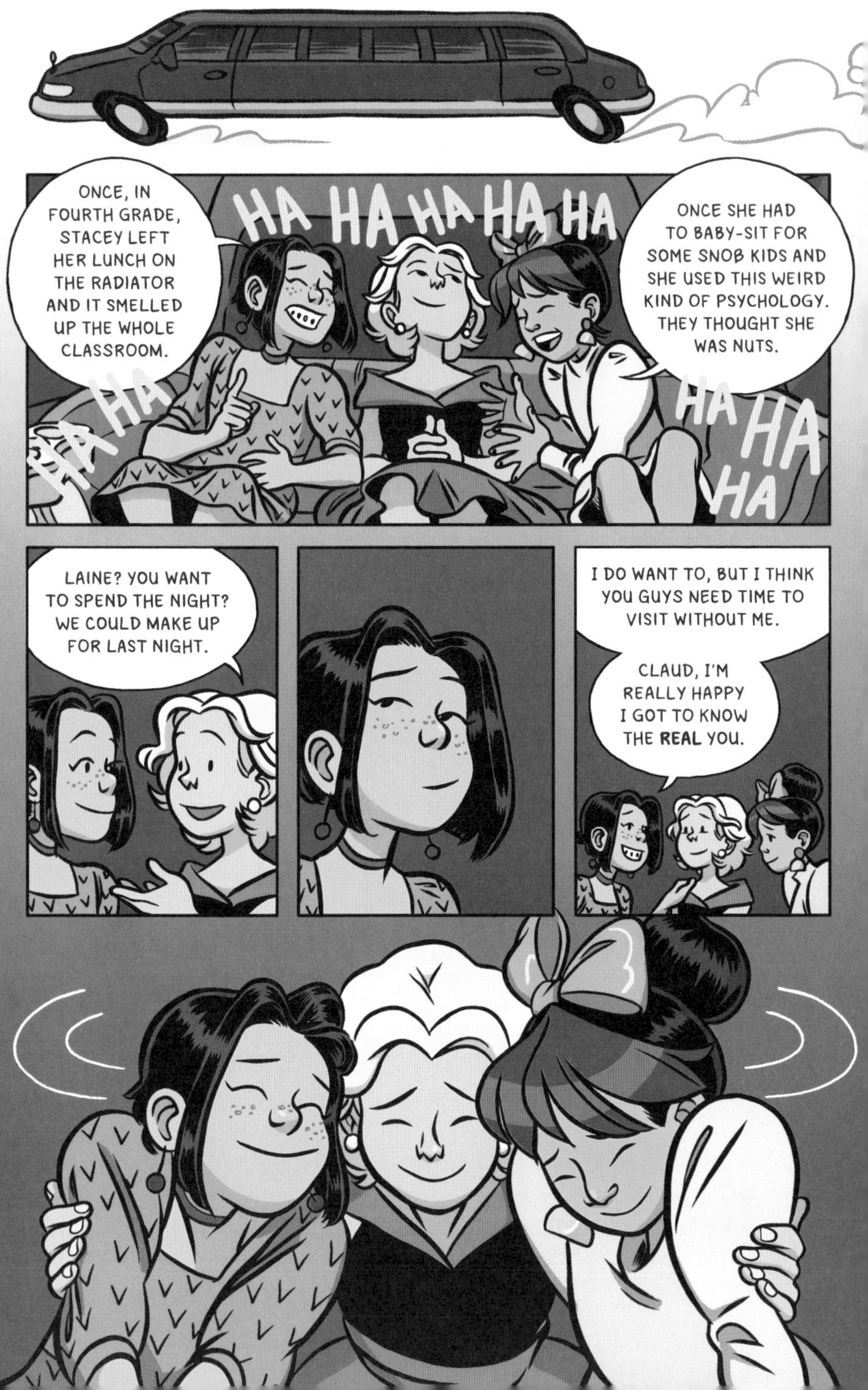
ONCE, IN FOURTH GRADE, STACEY LEFT HER LUNCH ON THE RADIATOR AND IT SMELLED UP THE WHOLE CLASSROOM.
HA HA HA HA HA
ONCE SHE HAD TO BABY-SIT FOR SOME SNOB KIDS AND SHE USED THIS WEIRD KIND OF PSYCHOLOGY. THEY THOUGHT SHE WAS NUTS.
HA HA
HA HA HA
LAINE? YOU WANT TO SPEND THE NIGHT? WE COULD MAKE UP FOR LAST NIGHT.
I DO WANT TO, BUT I THINK YOU GUYS NEED TIME TO VISIT WITHOUT ME.
CLAUD, I'M REALLY HAPPY I GOT TO KNOW THE **REAL** YOU.

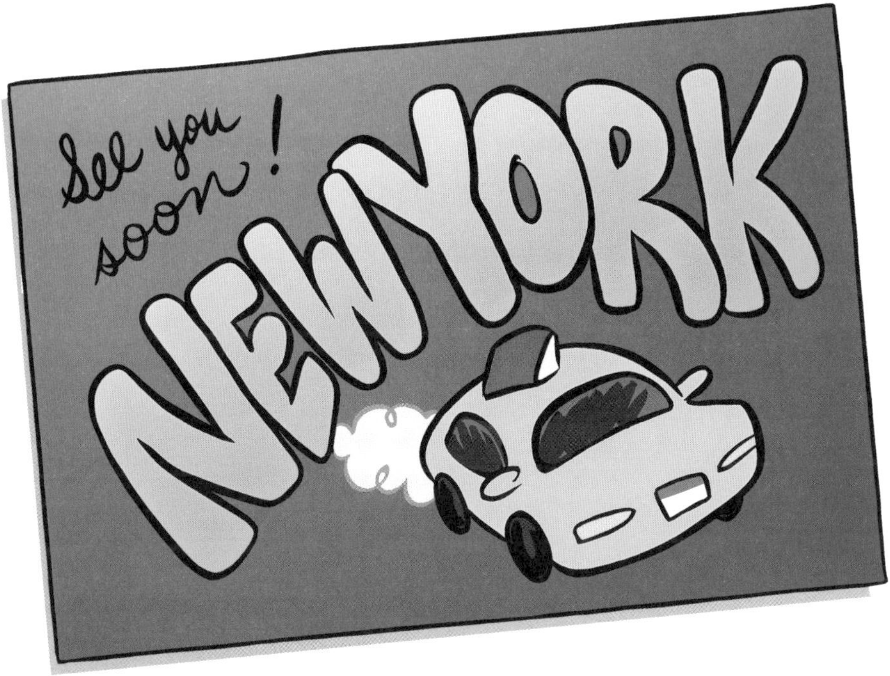
See you soon!
NEW YORK

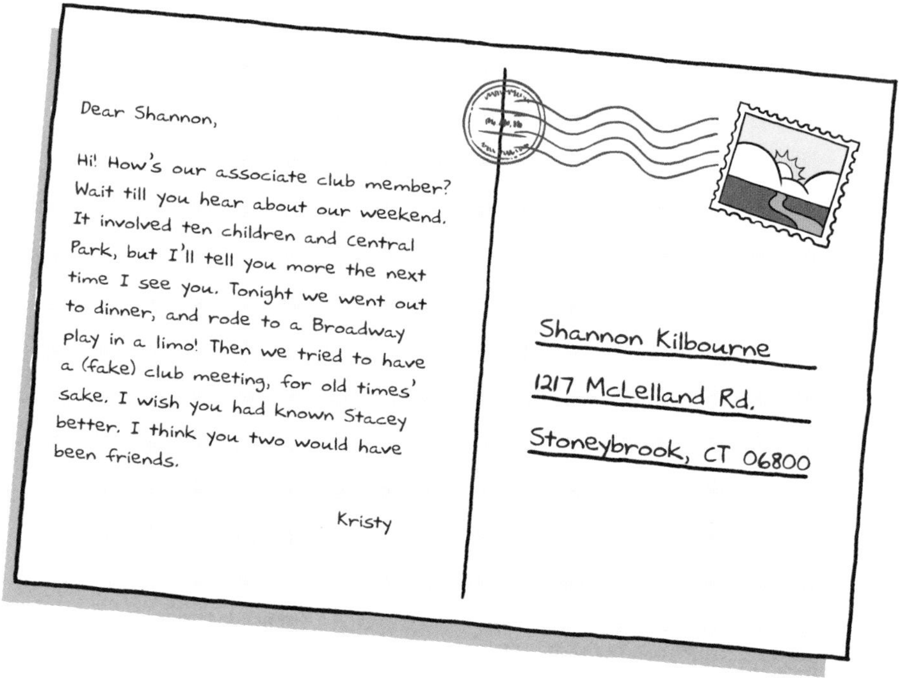

Dear Shannon,

Hi! How's our associate club member? Wait till you hear about our weekend. It involved ten children and Central Park, but I'll tell you more the next time I see you. Tonight we went out to dinner, and rode to a Broadway play in a limo! Then we tried to have a (fake) club meeting, for old times' sake. I wish you had known Stacey better. I think you two would have been friends.

Kristy

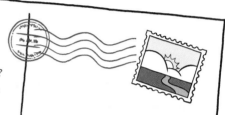

Shannon Kilbourne

1217 McLelland Rd.

Stoneybrook, CT 06800

CHAPTER 12

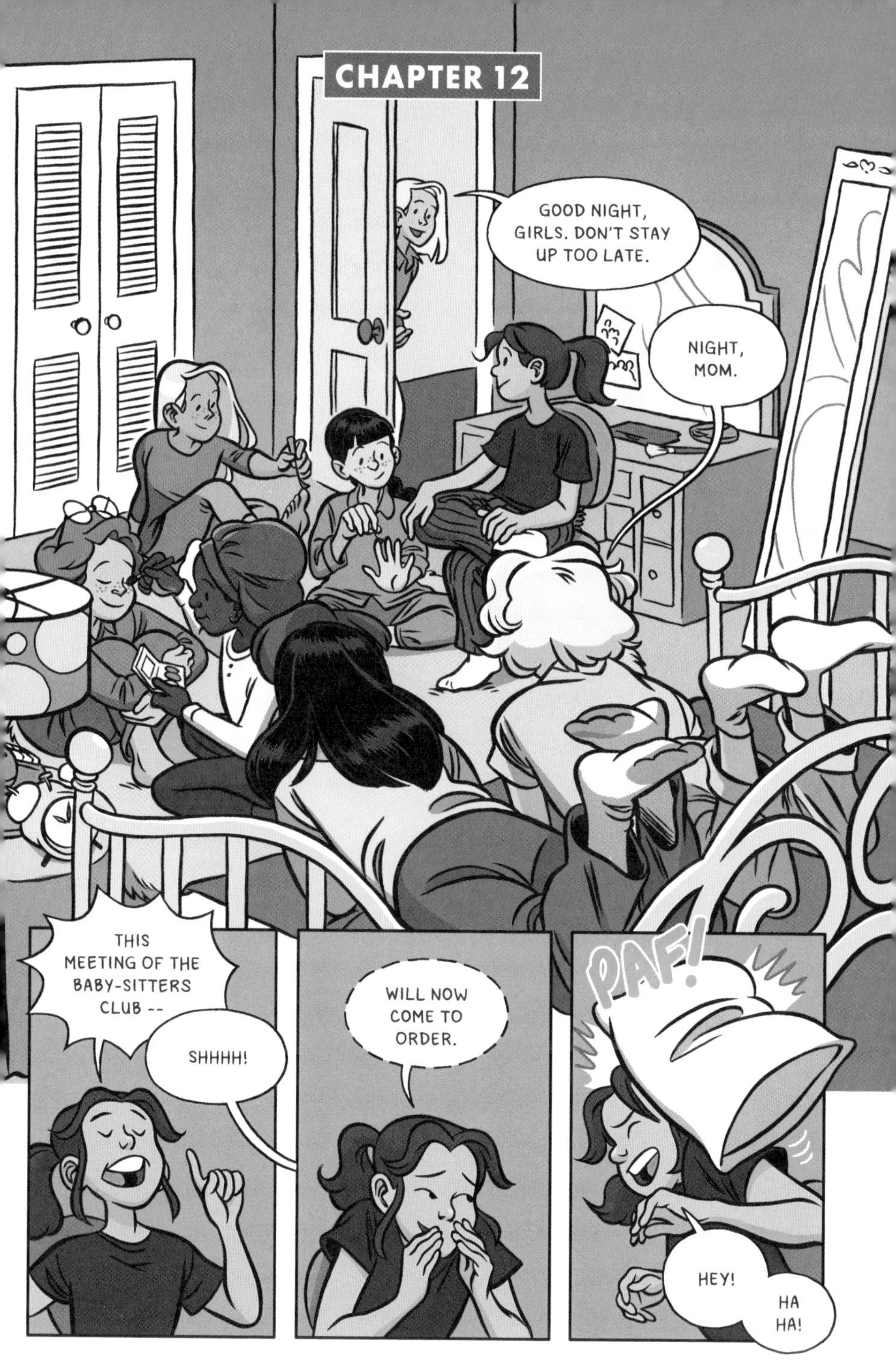
GOOD NIGHT, GIRLS. DON'T STAY UP TOO LATE.
NIGHT, MOM.
THIS MEETING OF THE BABY-SITTERS CLUB --
SHHHH!
WILL NOW COME TO ORDER.
PAF!
HEY!
HA HA!

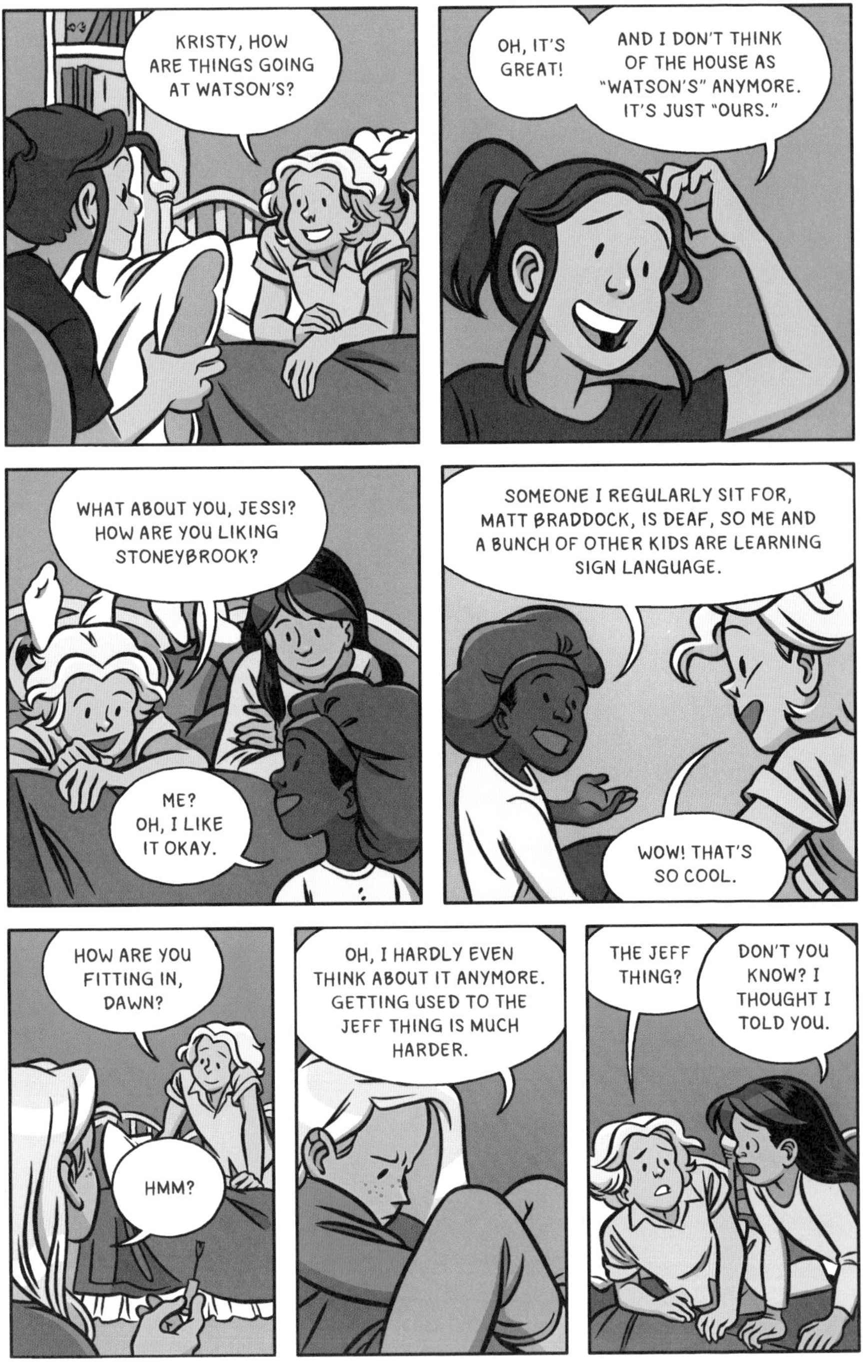
KRISTY, HOW ARE THINGS GOING AT WATSON'S?
OH, IT'S GREAT!
AND I DON'T THINK OF THE HOUSE AS "WATSON'S" ANYMORE. IT'S JUST "OURS."
WHAT ABOUT YOU, JESSI? HOW ARE YOU LIKING STONEYBROOK?
ME? OH, I LIKE IT OKAY.
SOMEONE I REGULARLY SIT FOR, MATT BRADDOCK, IS DEAF, SO ME AND A BUNCH OF OTHER KIDS ARE LEARNING SIGN LANGUAGE.
WOW! THAT'S SO COOL.
HOW ARE YOU FITTING IN, DAWN?
HMM?
OH, I HARDLY EVEN THINK ABOUT IT ANYMORE. GETTING USED TO THE JEFF THING IS MUCH HARDER.
THE JEFF THING?
DON'T YOU KNOW? I THOUGHT I TOLD YOU.

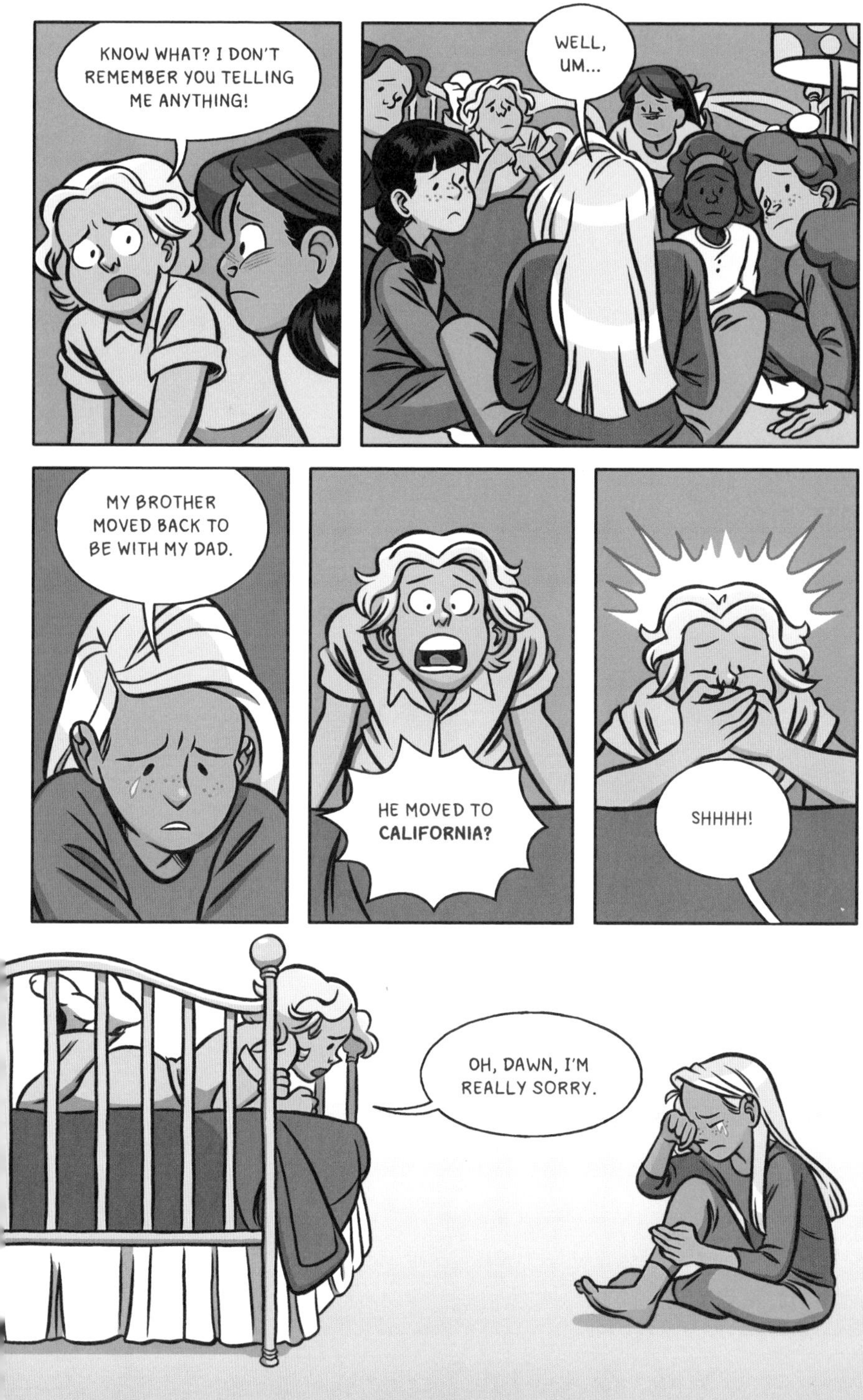
KNOW WHAT? I DON'T REMEMBER YOU TELLING ME ANYTHING!
WELL, UM...
MY BROTHER MOVED BACK TO BE WITH MY DAD.
HE MOVED TO **CALIFORNIA?**
SHHHH!
OH, DAWN, I'M REALLY SORRY.

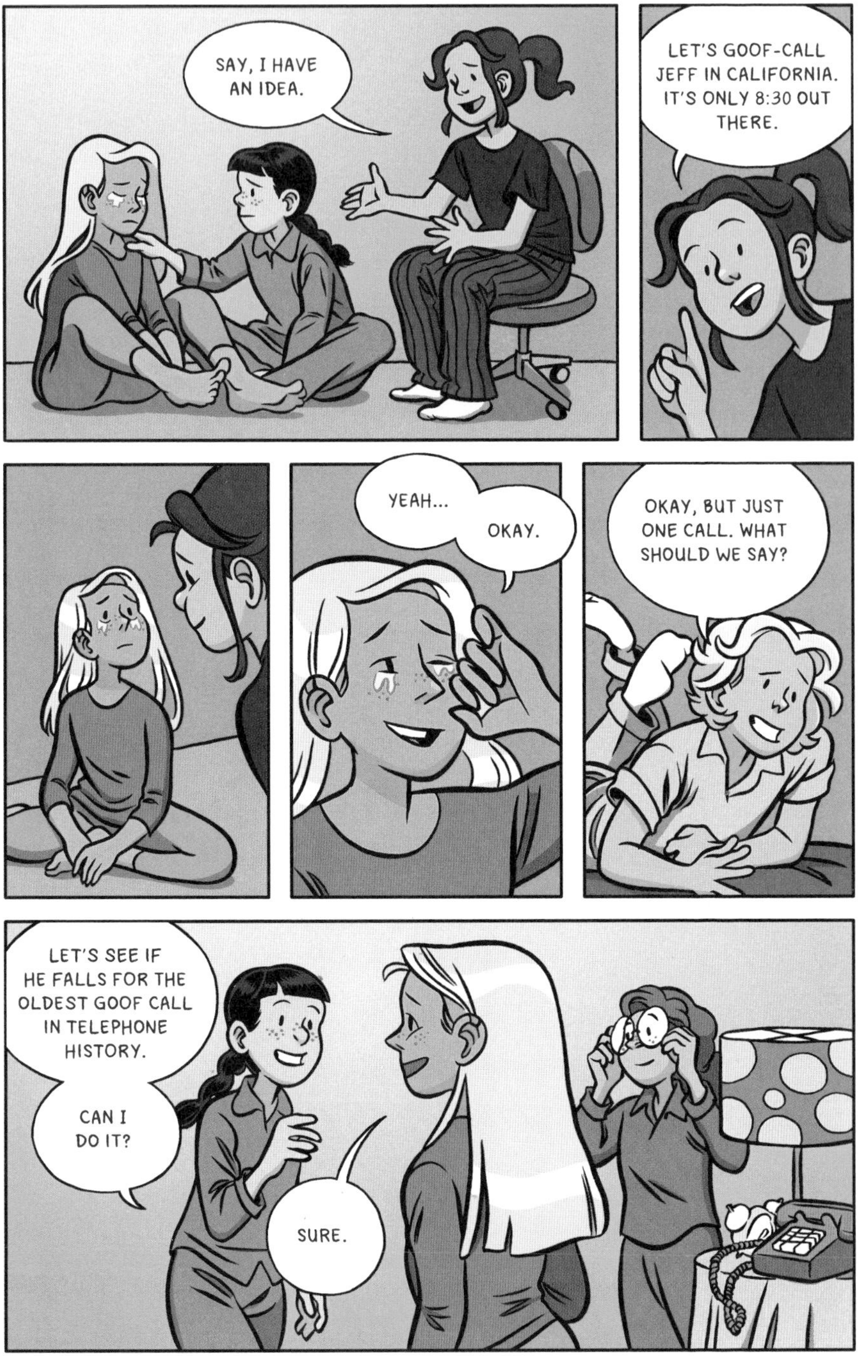
SAY, I HAVE AN IDEA.
LET'S GOOF-CALL JEFF IN CALIFORNIA. IT'S ONLY 8:30 OUT THERE.
YEAH...
OKAY.
OKAY, BUT JUST ONE CALL. WHAT SHOULD WE SAY?
LET'S SEE IF HE FALLS FOR THE OLDEST GOOF CALL IN TELEPHONE HISTORY.
CAN I DO IT?
SURE.

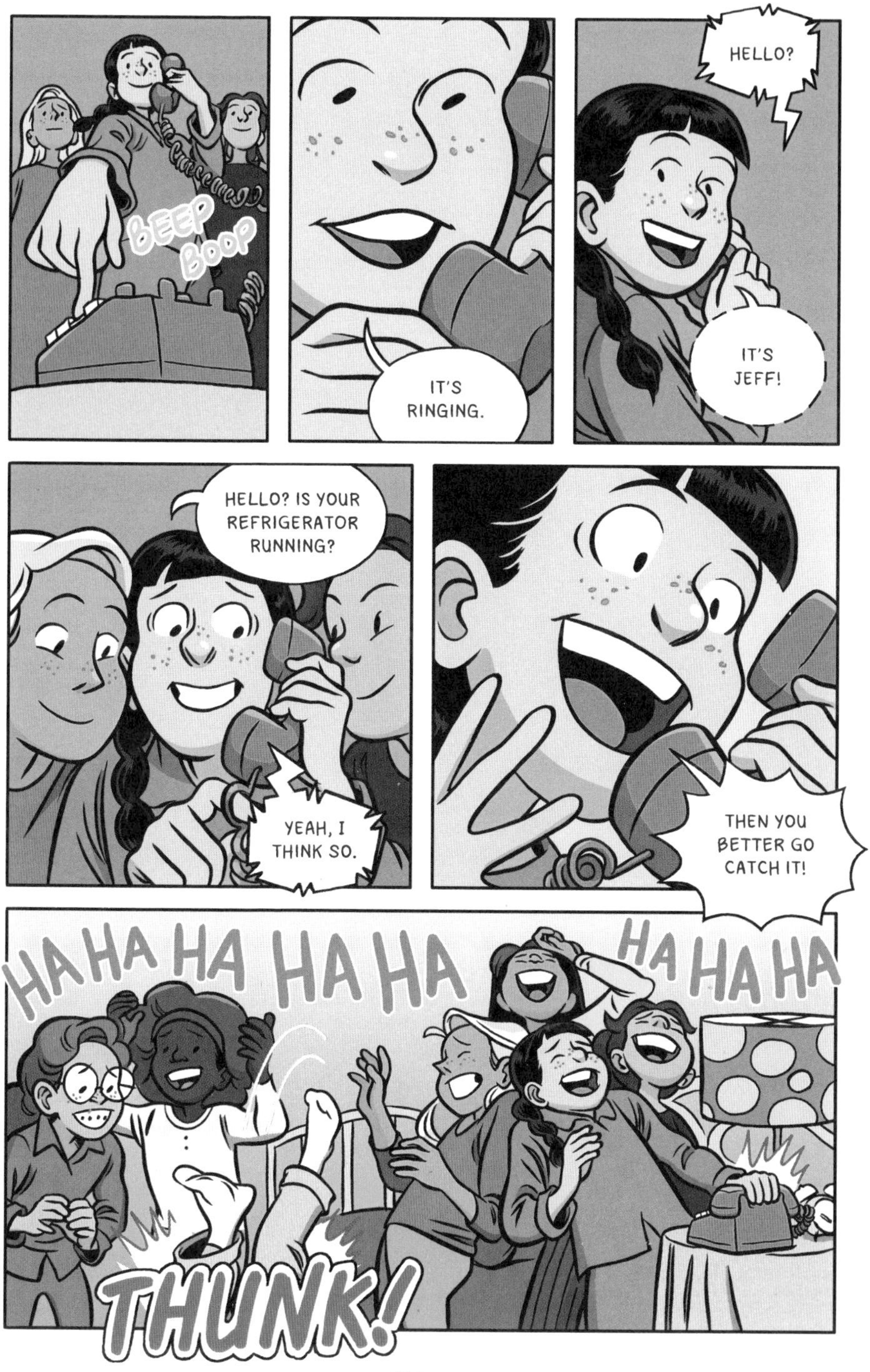
BEEP
BOOP
IT'S RINGING.
HELLO?
IT'S JEFF!
HELLO? IS YOUR REFRIGERATOR RUNNING?
YEAH, I THINK SO.
THEN YOU BETTER GO CATCH IT!
HA HA HA HA HA HA
HA HA HA HA
THUNK!

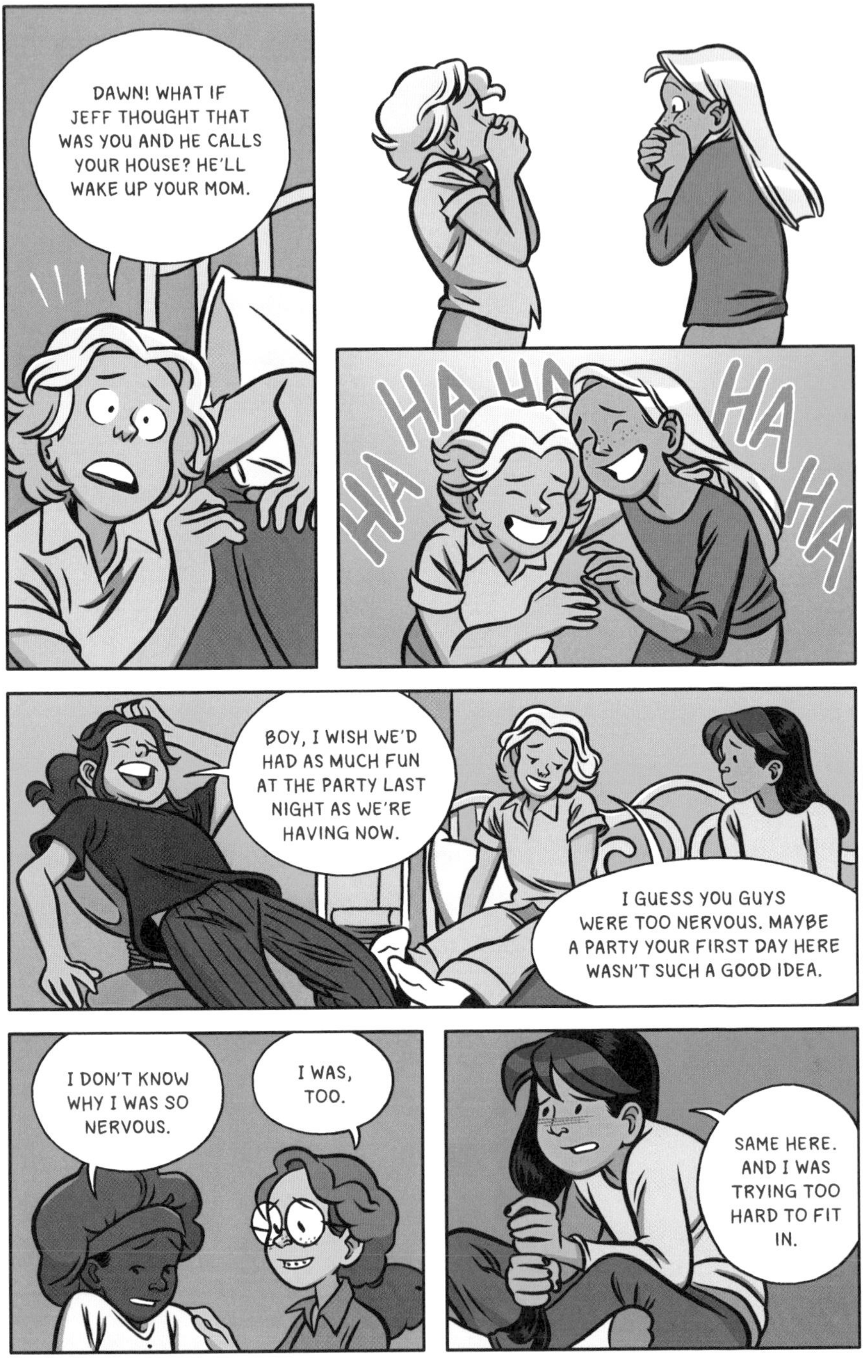
DAWN! WHAT IF JEFF THOUGHT THAT WAS YOU AND HE CALLS YOUR HOUSE? HE'LL WAKE UP YOUR MOM.
HA HA HA HA HA HA HA
BOY, I WISH WE'D HAD AS MUCH FUN AT THE PARTY LAST NIGHT AS WE'RE HAVING NOW.
I GUESS YOU GUYS WERE TOO NERVOUS. MAYBE A PARTY YOUR FIRST DAY HERE WASN'T SUCH A GOOD IDEA.
I DON'T KNOW WHY I WAS SO NERVOUS.
I WAS, TOO.
SAME HERE. AND I WAS TRYING TOO HARD TO FIT IN.

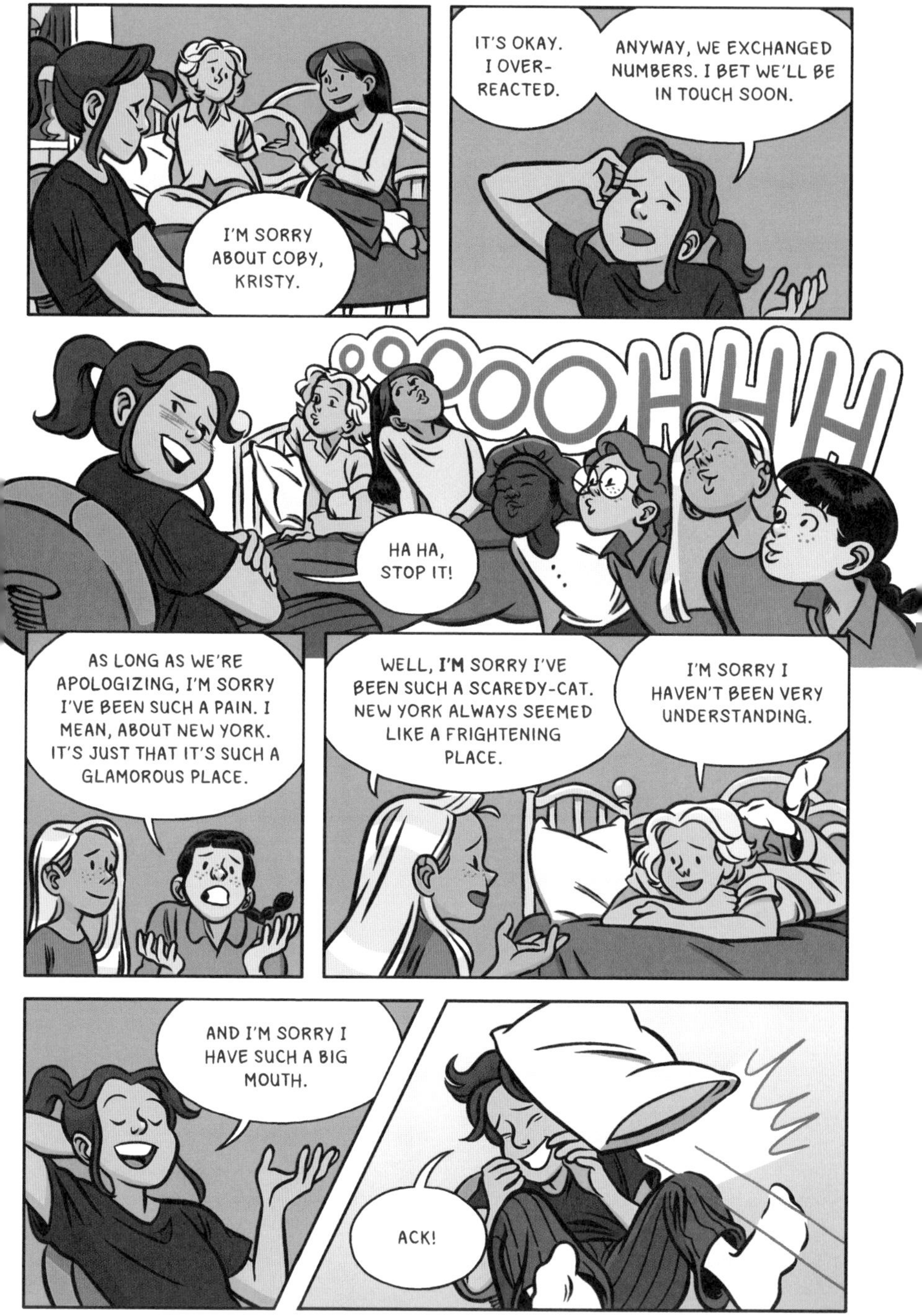
I'M SORRY ABOUT COBY, KRISTY.
IT'S OKAY. I OVER-REACTED.
ANYWAY, WE EXCHANGED NUMBERS. I BET WE'LL BE IN TOUCH SOON.
OOOOOHHHH
HA HA, STOP IT!
AS LONG AS WE'RE APOLOGIZING, I'M SORRY I'VE BEEN SUCH A PAIN. I MEAN, ABOUT NEW YORK. IT'S JUST THAT IT'S SUCH A GLAMOROUS PLACE.
WELL, I'M SORRY I'VE BEEN SUCH A SCAREDY-CAT. NEW YORK ALWAYS SEEMED LIKE A FRIGHTENING PLACE.
I'M SORRY I HAVEN'T BEEN VERY UNDERSTANDING.
AND I'M SORRY I HAVE SUCH A BIG MOUTH.
ACK!

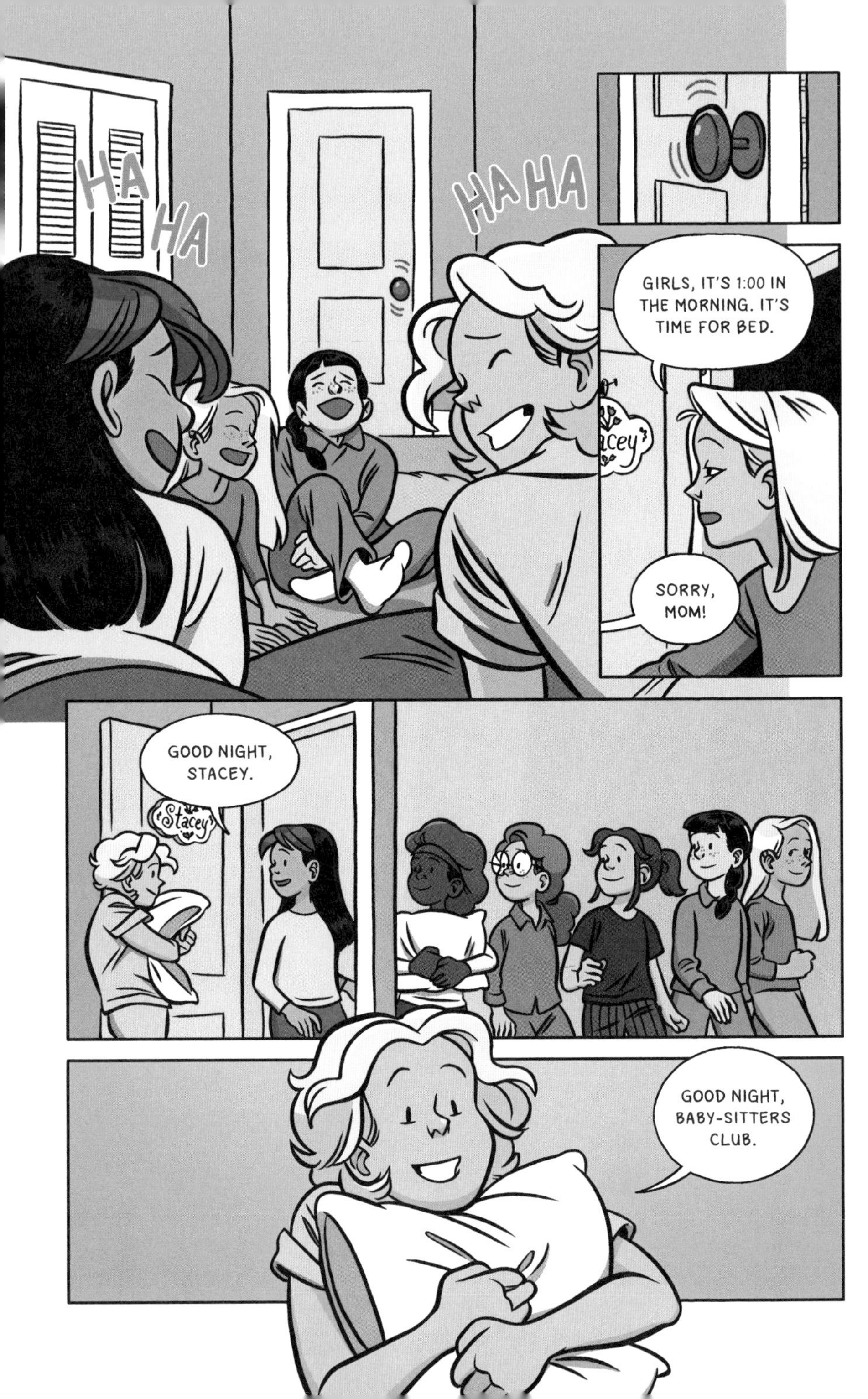
HA HA
HA HA
GIRLS, IT'S 1:00 IN THE MORNING. IT'S TIME FOR BED.
Stacey
SORRY, MOM!
GOOD NIGHT, STACEY.
Stacey
GOOD NIGHT, BABY-SITTERS CLUB.

CHAPTER 13

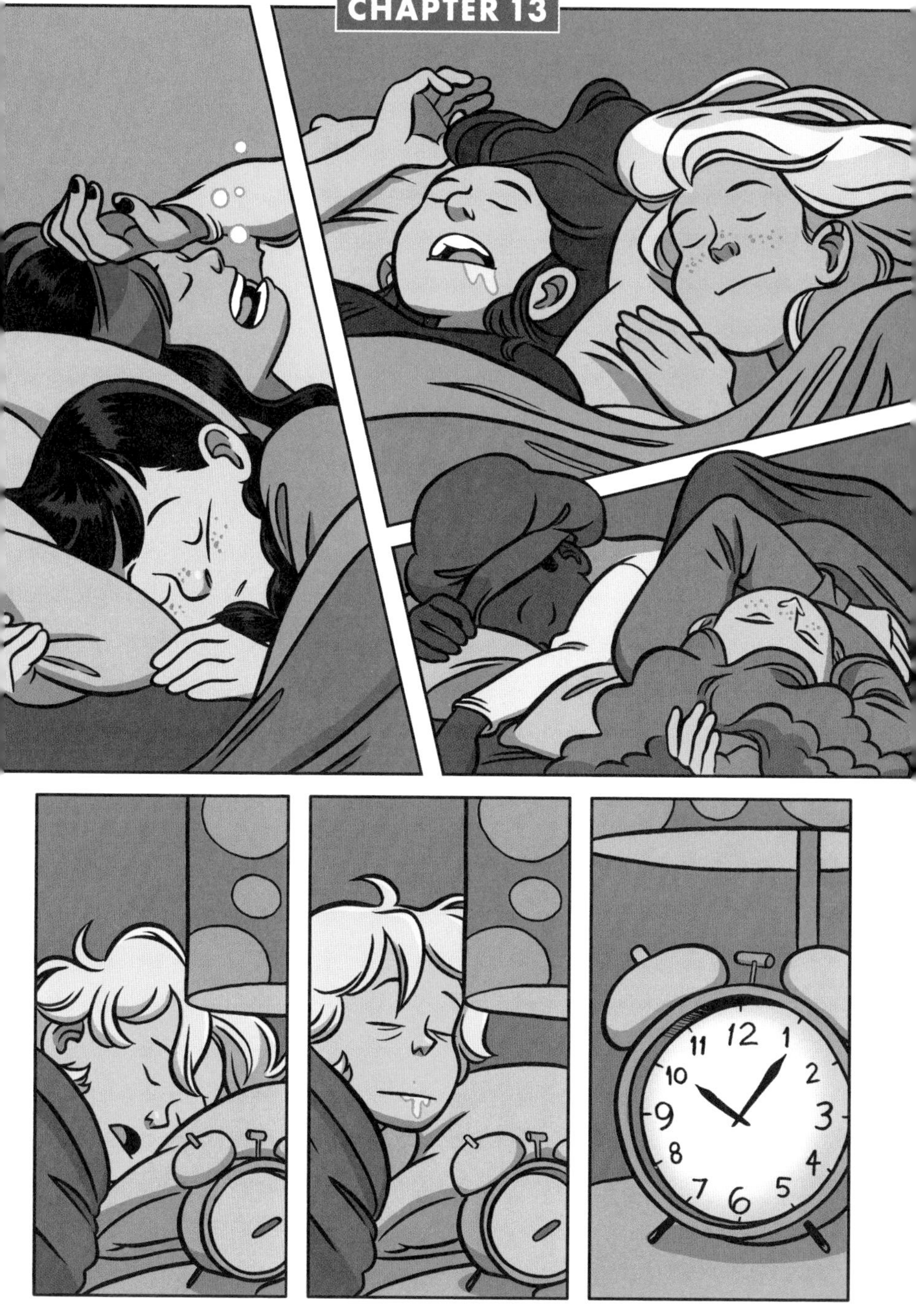

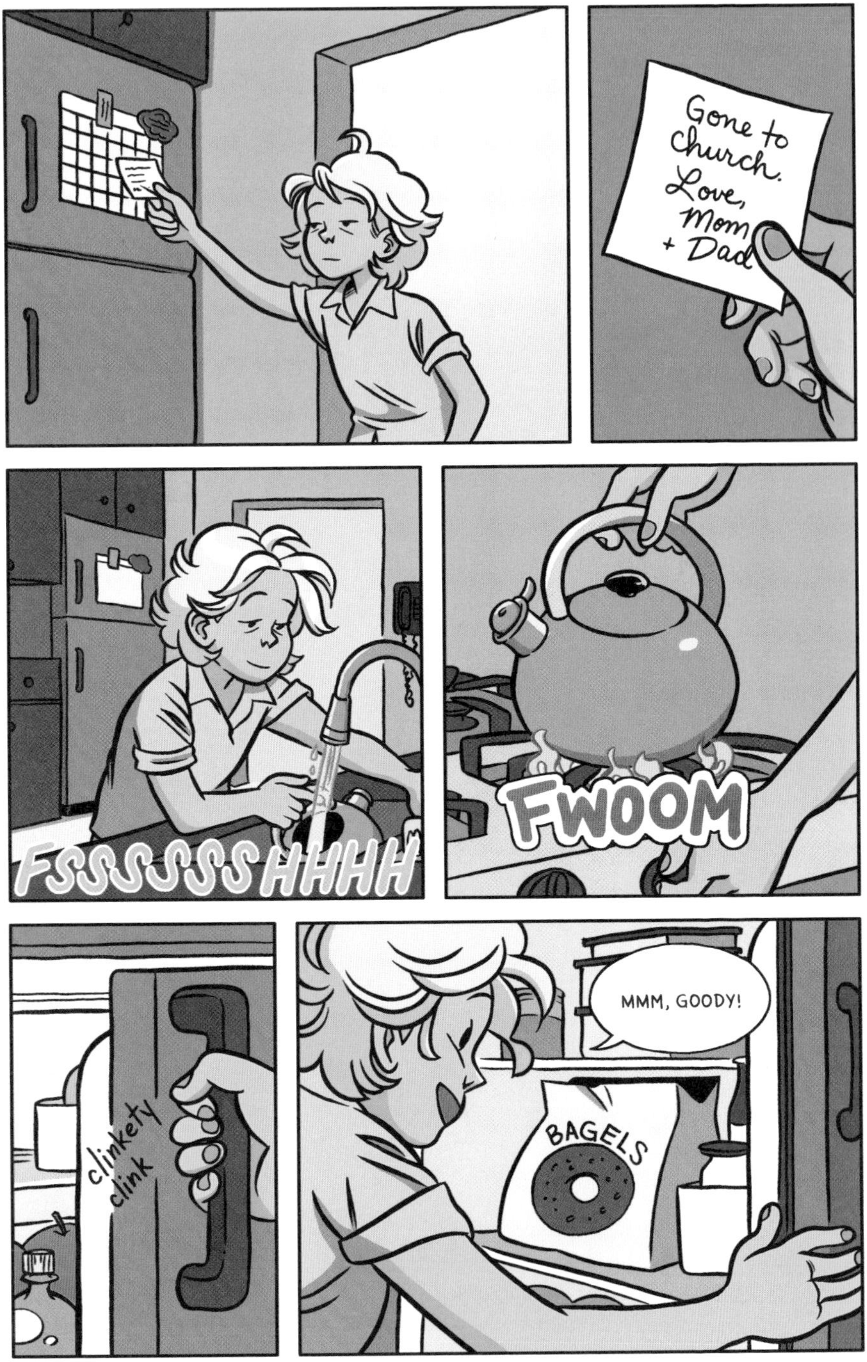
Gone to Church. Love, Mom + Dad
FSSSSSSHHHH
FWOOM
clinkety clink
MMM, GOODY!
BAGELS

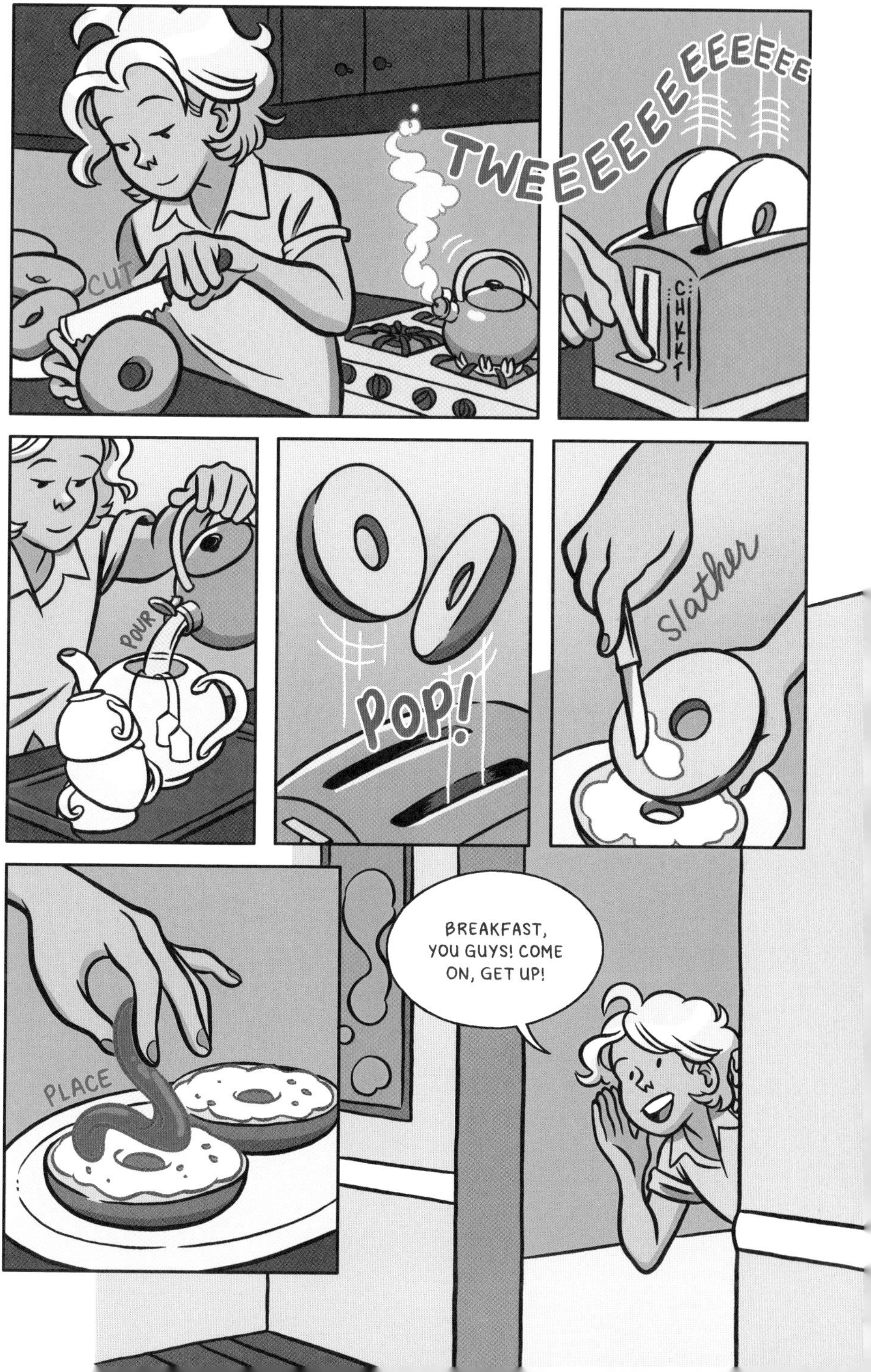
CUT
TWEEEEEEEEEEEEE
CHKKT
POUR
POP!
Slather
PLACE
BREAKFAST, YOU GUYS! COME ON, GET UP!

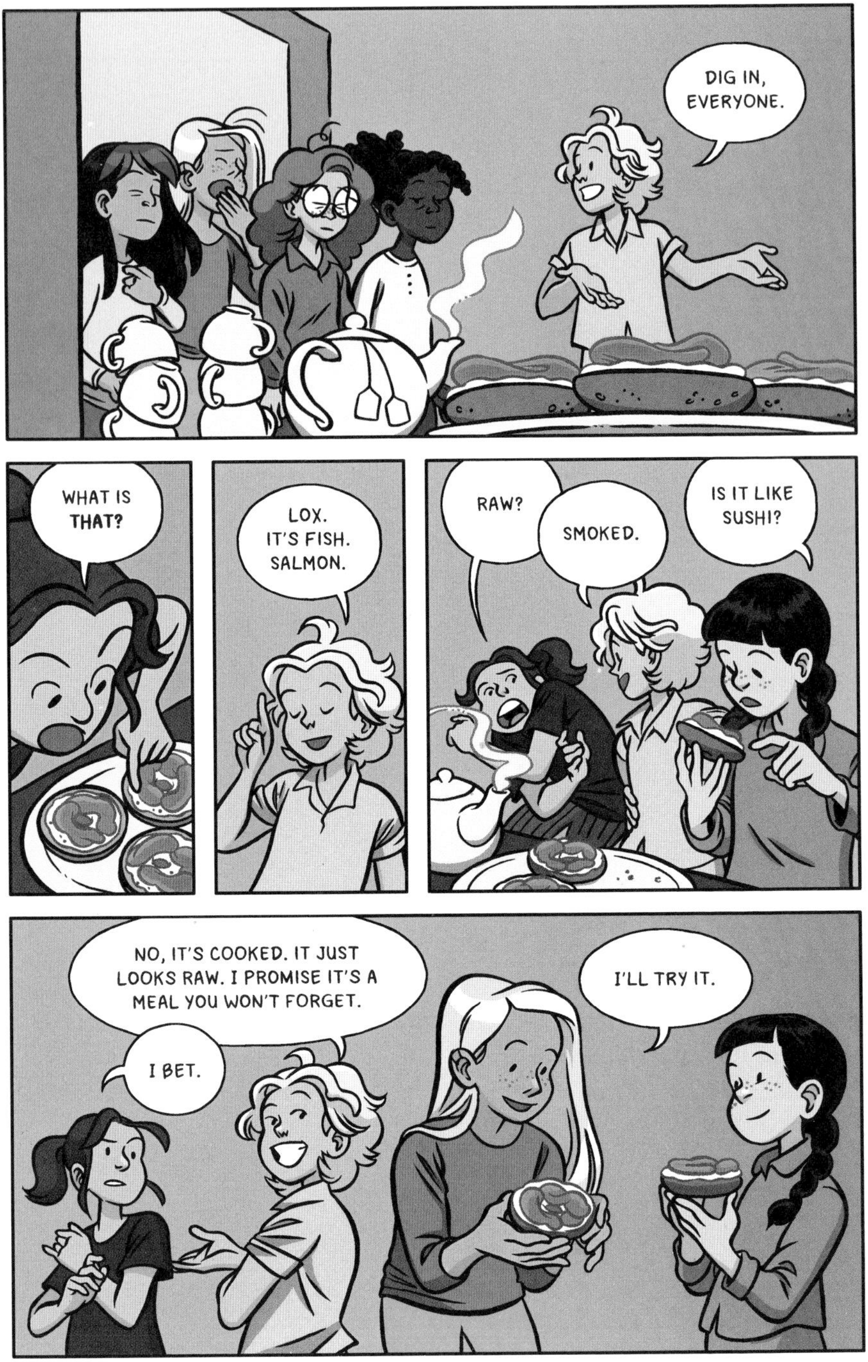
DIG IN, EVERYONE.
WHAT IS THAT?
LOX. IT'S FISH. SALMON.
RAW?
SMOKED.
IS IT LIKE SUSHI?
NO, IT'S COOKED. IT JUST LOOKS RAW. I PROMISE IT'S A MEAL YOU WON'T FORGET.
I BET.
I'LL TRY IT.

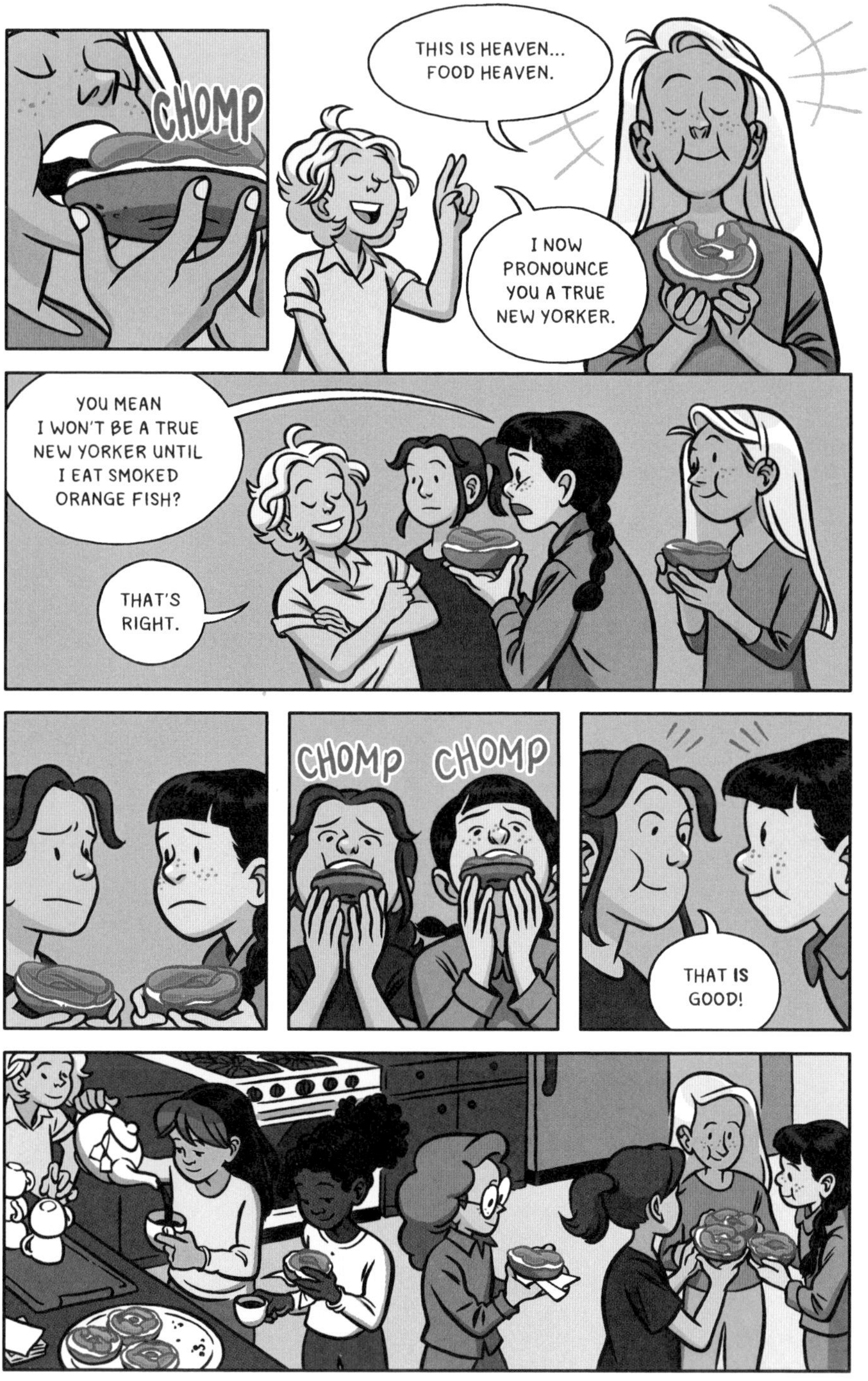
CHOMP
THIS IS HEAVEN... FOOD HEAVEN.
I NOW PRONOUNCE YOU A TRUE NEW YORKER.
YOU MEAN I WON'T BE A TRUE NEW YORKER UNTIL I EAT SMOKED ORANGE FISH?
THAT'S RIGHT.
CHOMP CHOMP
THAT **IS** GOOD!

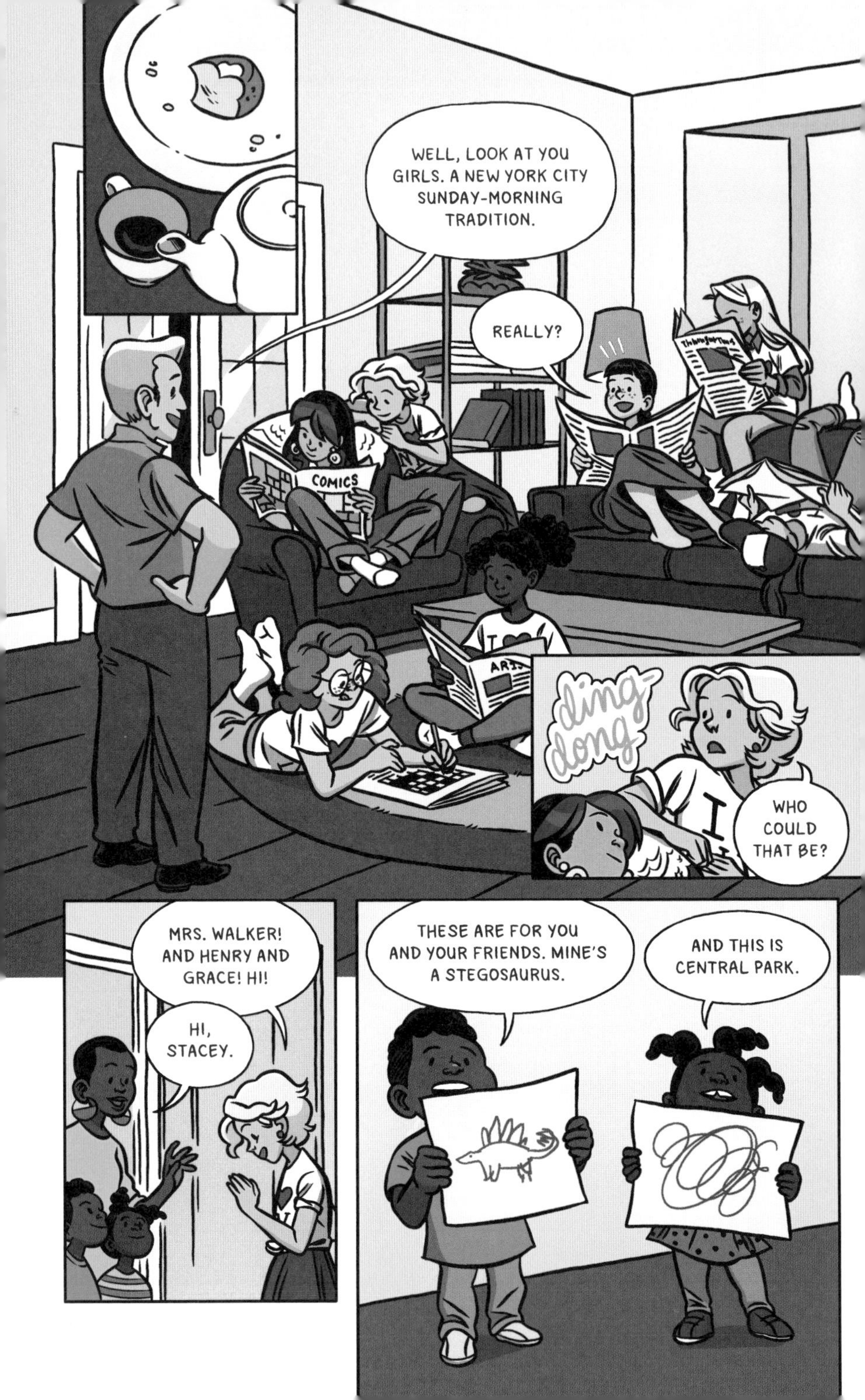
WELL, LOOK AT YOU GIRLS. A NEW YORK CITY SUNDAY-MORNING TRADITION.
REALLY?
COMICS
ding-dong
WHO COULD THAT BE?
MRS. WALKER! AND HENRY AND GRACE! HI!
HI, STACEY.
THESE ARE FOR YOU AND YOUR FRIENDS. MINE'S A STEGOSAURUS.
AND THIS IS CENTRAL PARK.

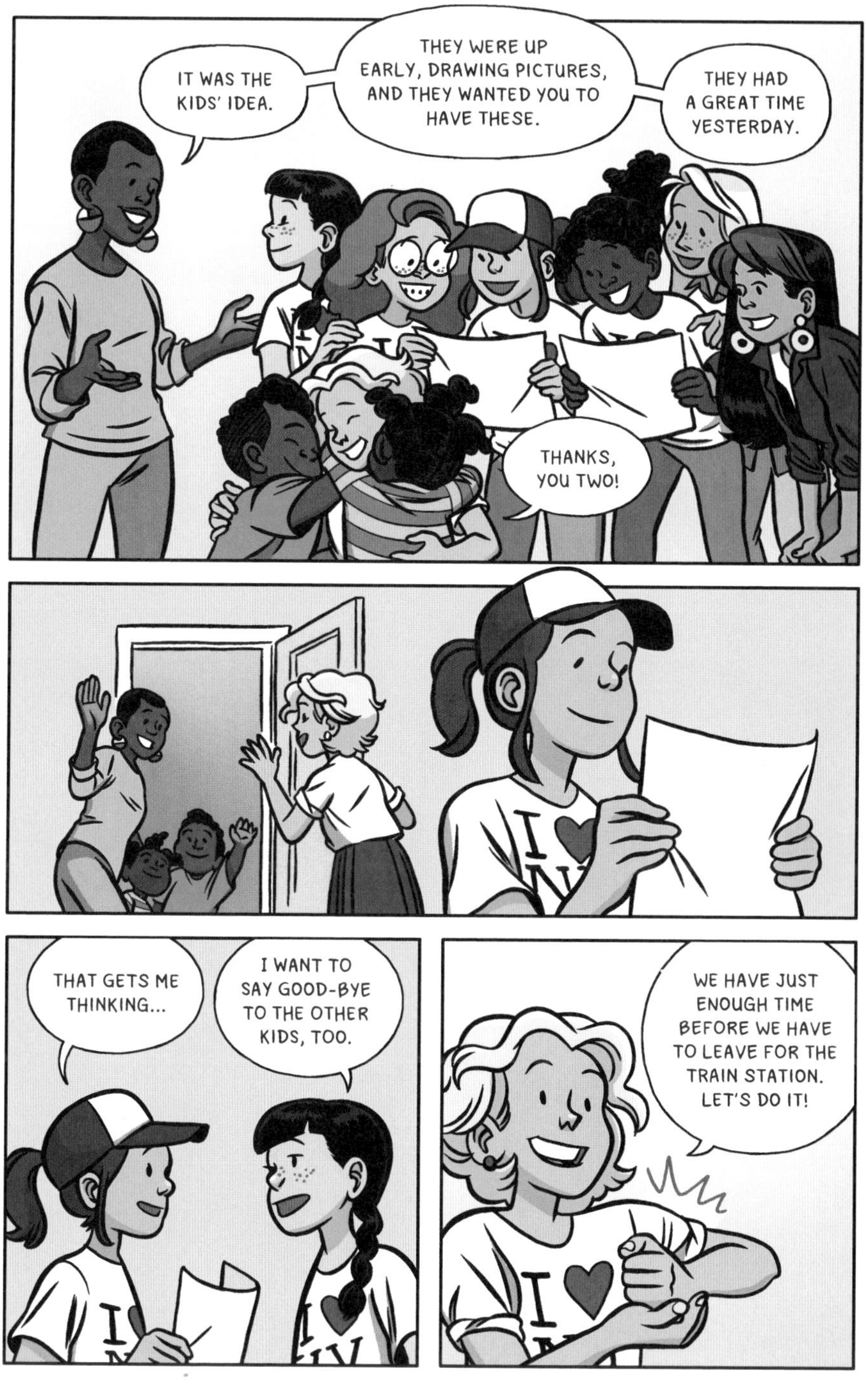
IT WAS THE KIDS' IDEA.
THEY WERE UP EARLY, DRAWING PICTURES, AND THEY WANTED YOU TO HAVE THESE.
THEY HAD A GREAT TIME YESTERDAY.
THANKS, YOU TWO!
THAT GETS ME THINKING...
I WANT TO SAY GOOD-BYE TO THE OTHER KIDS, TOO.
WE HAVE JUST ENOUGH TIME BEFORE WE HAVE TO LEAVE FOR THE TRAIN STATION. LET'S DO IT!

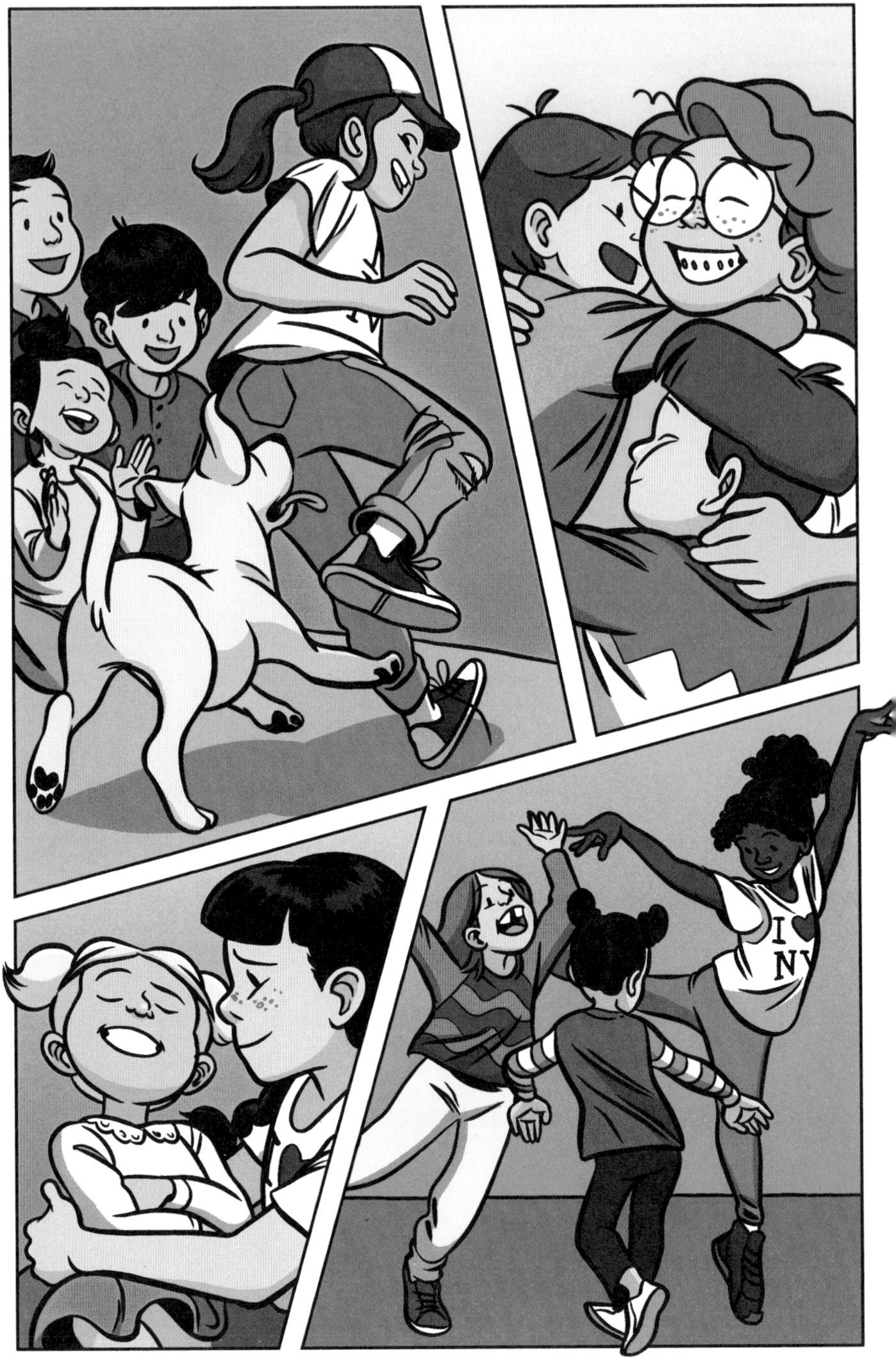
I ♥ NY

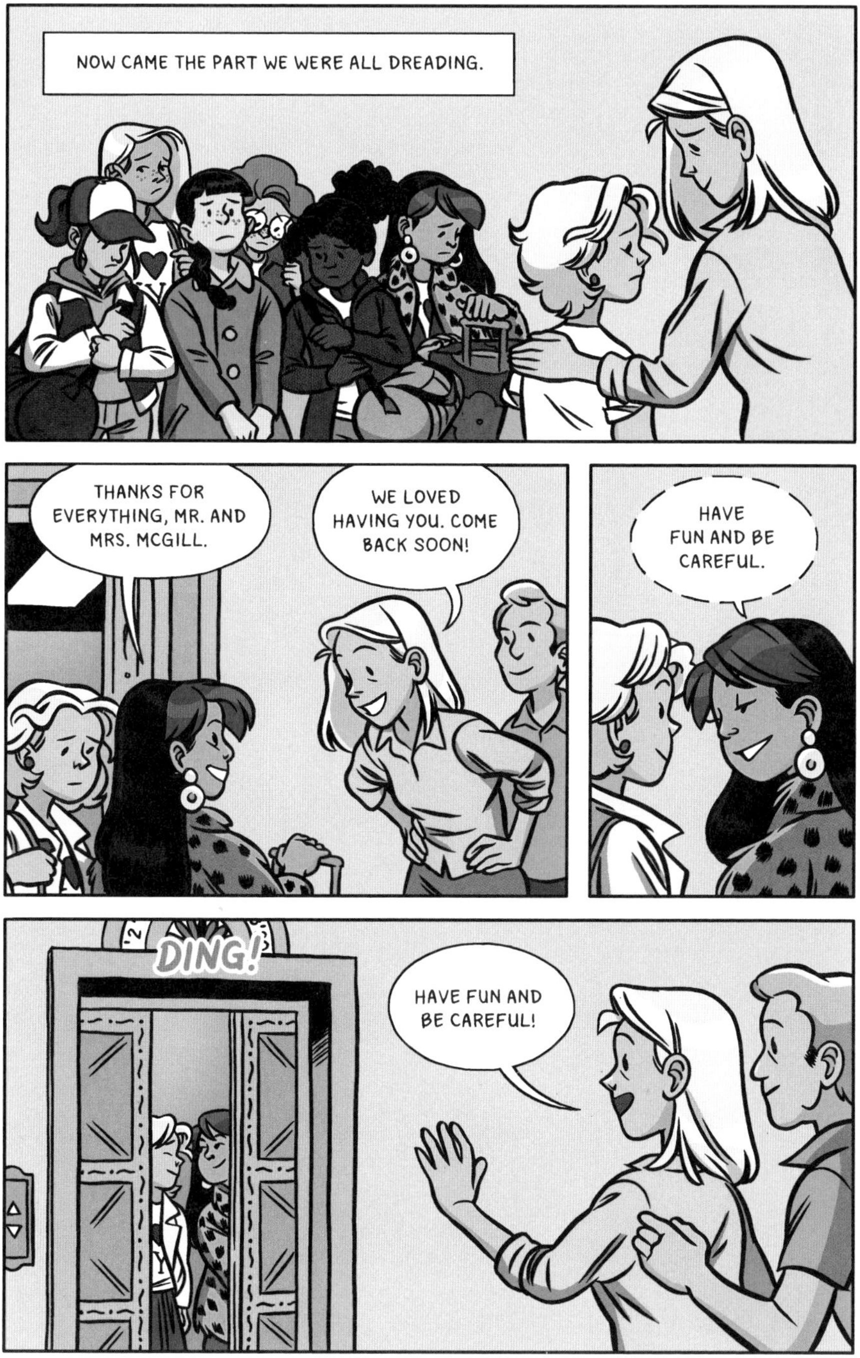
NOW CAME THE PART WE WERE ALL DREADING.
THANKS FOR EVERYTHING, MR. AND MRS. MCGILL.
WE LOVED HAVING YOU. COME BACK SOON!
HAVE FUN AND BE CAREFUL.
DING!
HAVE FUN AND BE CAREFUL!

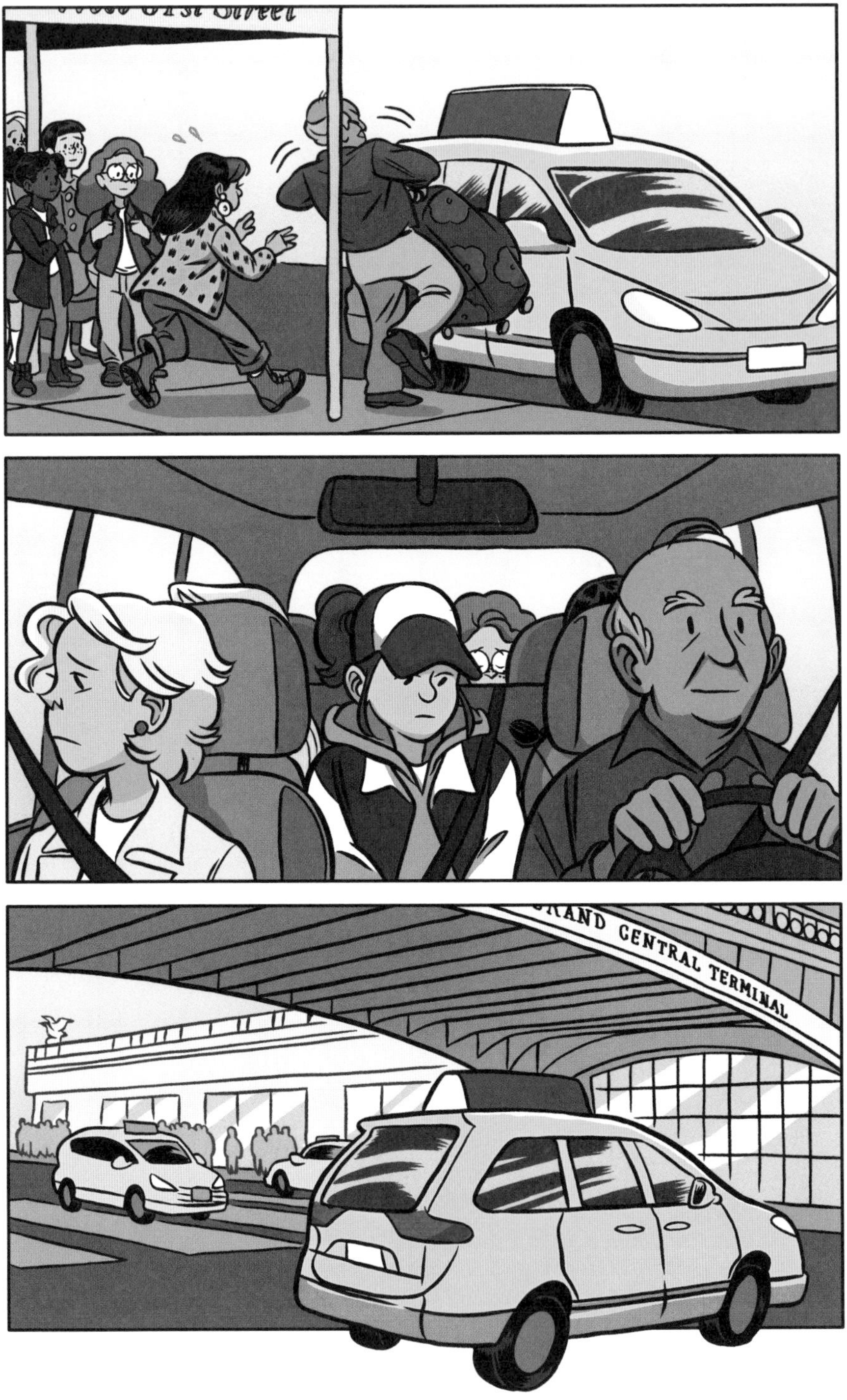
RAND CENTRAL TERMINAL

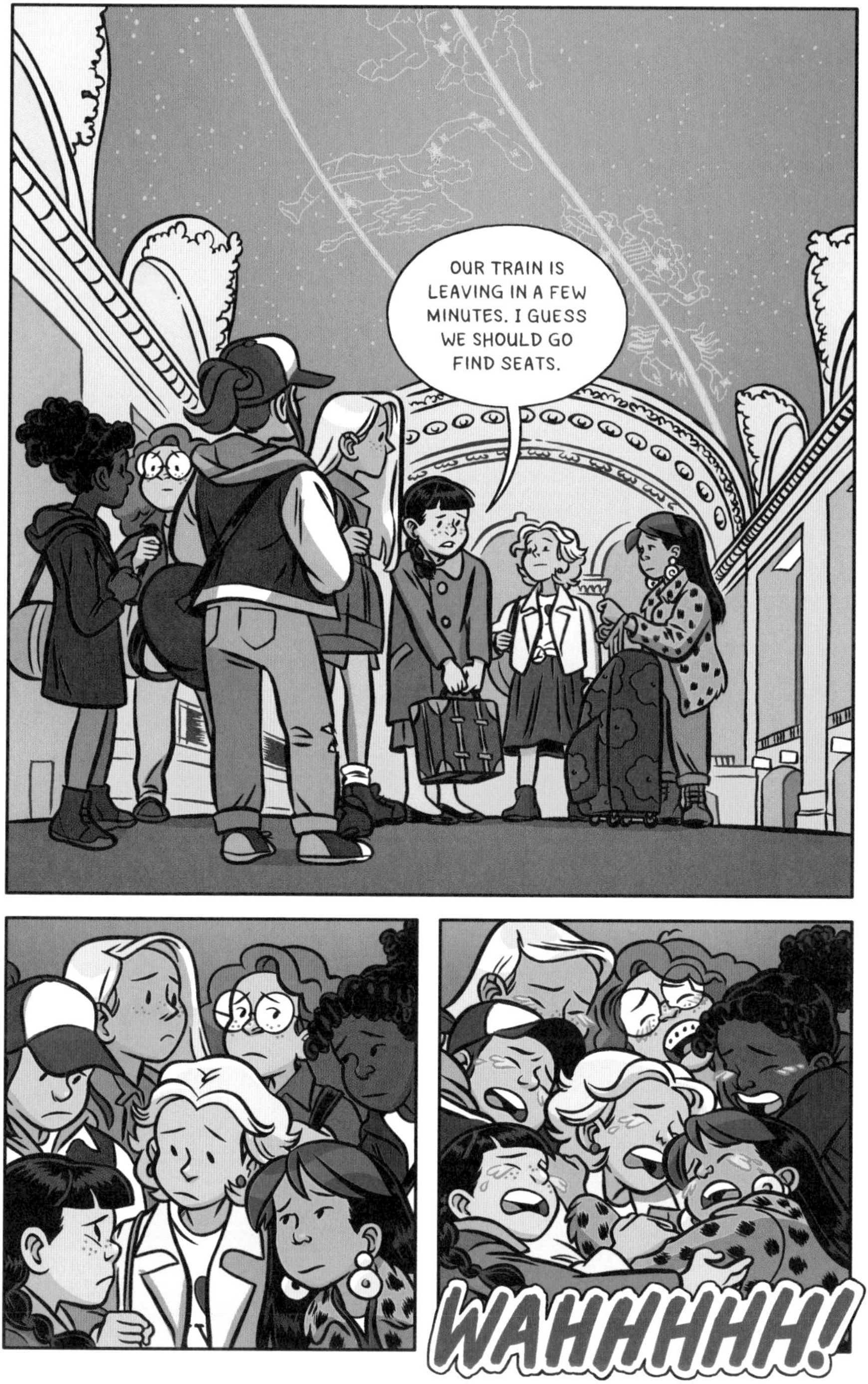
OUR TRAIN IS LEAVING IN A FEW MINUTES. I GUESS WE SHOULD GO FIND SEATS.
WAHHHHH!

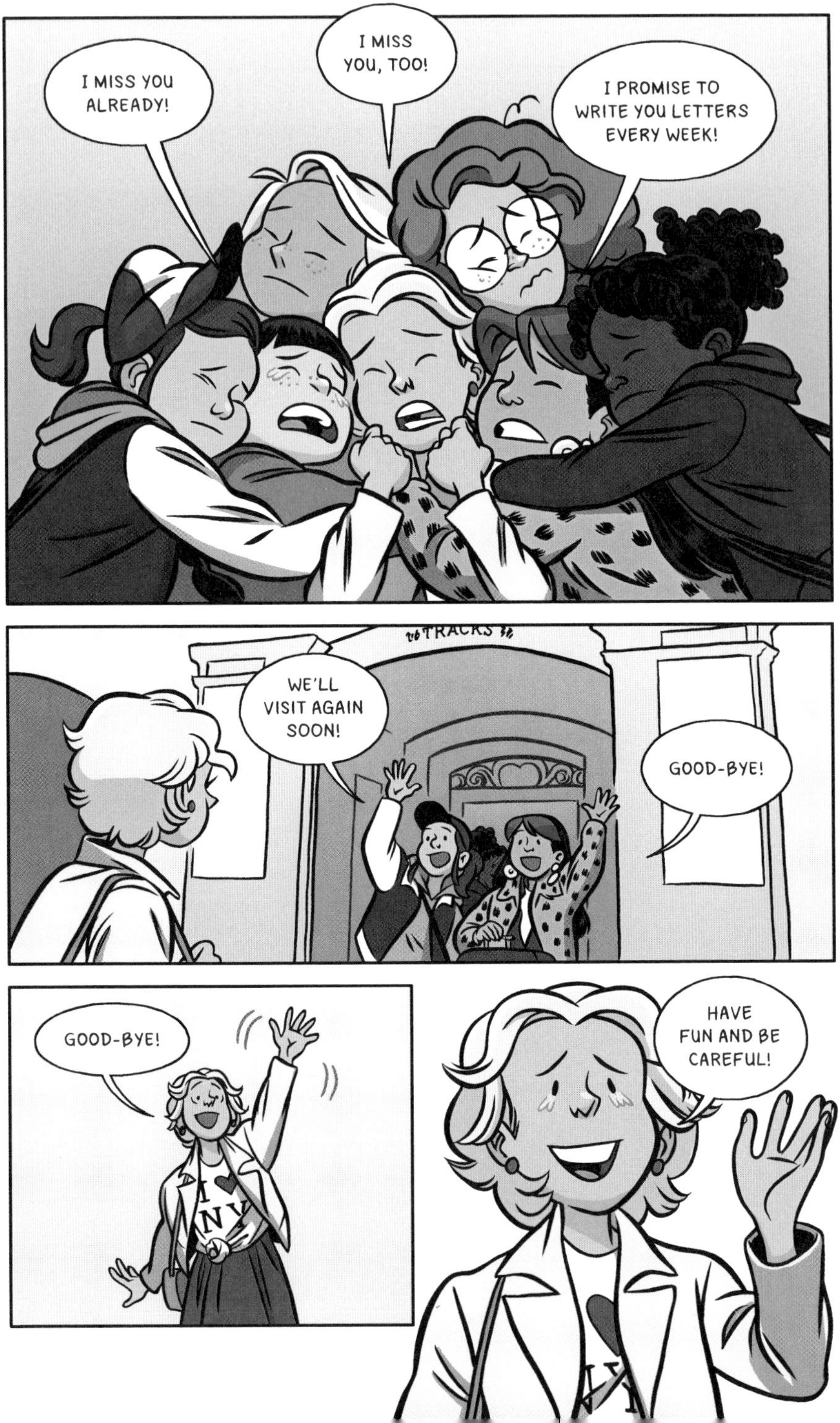
I MISS YOU ALREADY!
I MISS YOU, TOO!
I PROMISE TO WRITE YOU LETTERS EVERY WEEK!
TRACKS
WE'LL VISIT AGAIN SOON!
GOOD-BYE!
GOOD-BYE!
HAVE FUN AND BE CAREFUL!

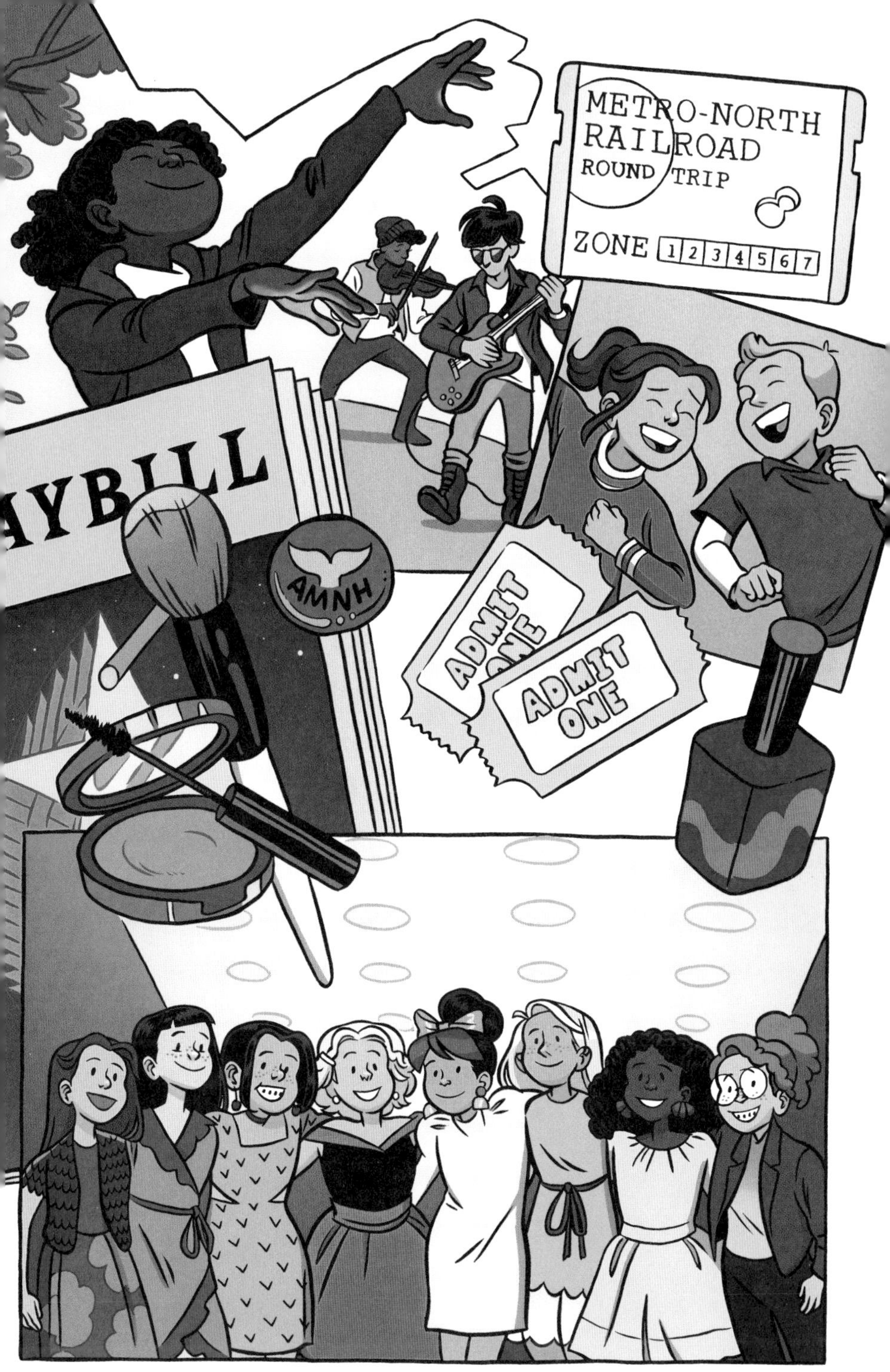
METRO-NORTH
RAILROAD
ROUND TRIP
ZONE 1 2 3 4 5 6 7
AYBILL
AMNH
ADMIT ONE
ADMIT ONE

DON'T MISS THE OTHER BABY-SITTERS CLUB GRAPHIC NOVELS!

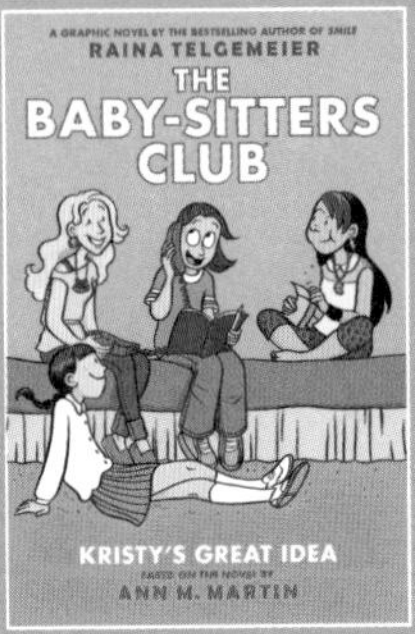
A GRAPHIC NOVEL BY THE BESTSELLING AUTHOR OF SMILE
RAINA TELGEMEIER
THE BABY-SITTERS CLUB
KRISTY'S GREAT IDEA
BASED ON THE NOVEL BY
ANN M. MARTIN

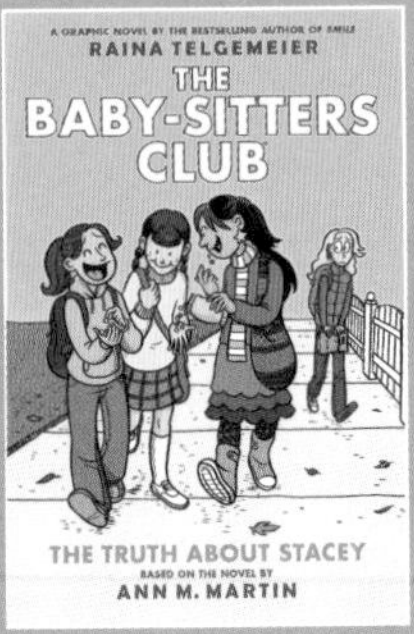
A GRAPHIC NOVEL BY THE BESTSELLING AUTHOR OF SMILE
RAINA TELGEMEIER
THE BABY-SITTERS CLUB
THE TRUTH ABOUT STACEY
BASED ON THE NOVEL BY
ANN M. MARTIN

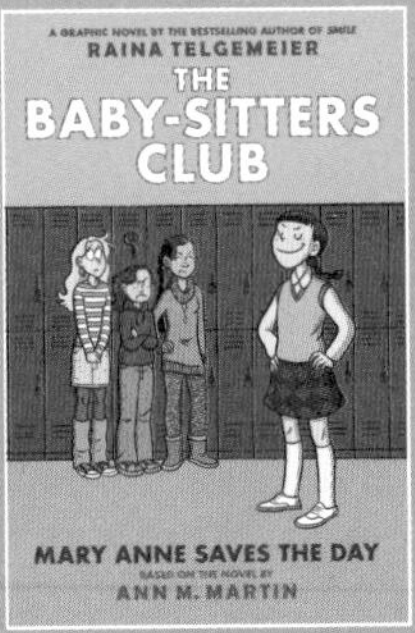
A GRAPHIC NOVEL BY THE BESTSELLING AUTHOR OF SMILE
RAINA TELGEMEIER
THE BABY-SITTERS CLUB
MARY ANNE SAVES THE DAY
BASED ON THE NOVEL BY
ANN M. MARTIN

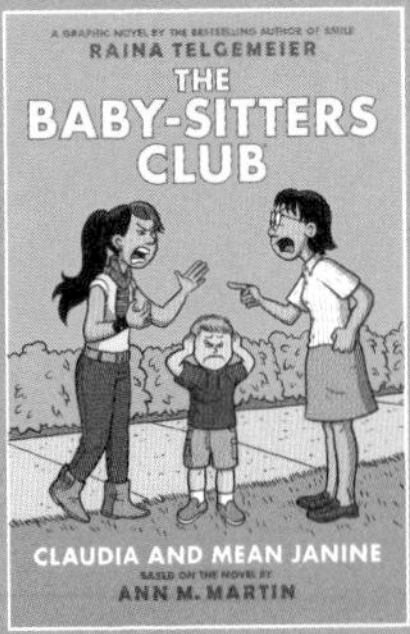
A GRAPHIC NOVEL BY THE BESTSELLING AUTHOR OF SMILE
RAINA TELGEMEIER
THE BABY-SITTERS CLUB
CLAUDIA AND MEAN JANINE
BASED ON THE NOVEL BY
ANN M. MARTIN

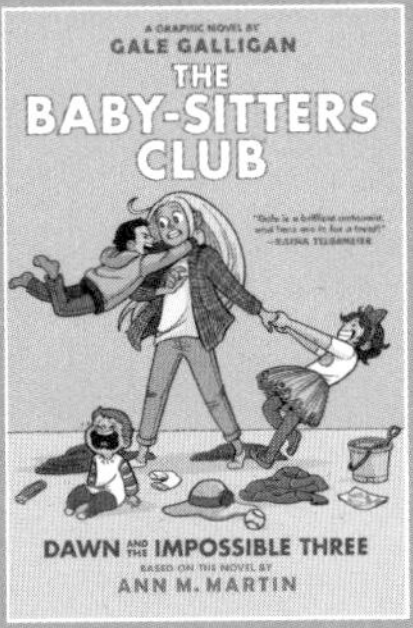
A GRAPHIC NOVEL BY
GALE GALLIGAN
THE BABY-SITTERS CLUB
DAWN AND THE IMPOSSIBLE THREE
BASED ON THE NOVEL BY
ANN M. MARTIN

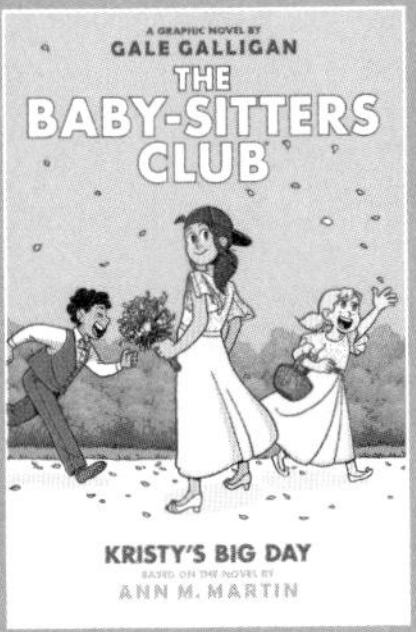
A GRAPHIC NOVEL BY
GALE GALLIGAN
THE BABY-SITTERS CLUB
KRISTY'S BIG DAY
BASED ON THE NOVEL BY
ANN M. MARTIN

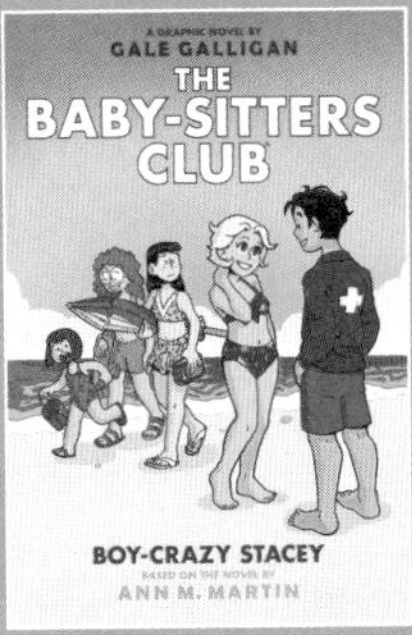
A GRAPHIC NOVEL BY
GALE GALLIGAN
THE BABY-SITTERS CLUB
BOY-CRAZY STACEY
BASED ON THE NOVEL BY
ANN M. MARTIN

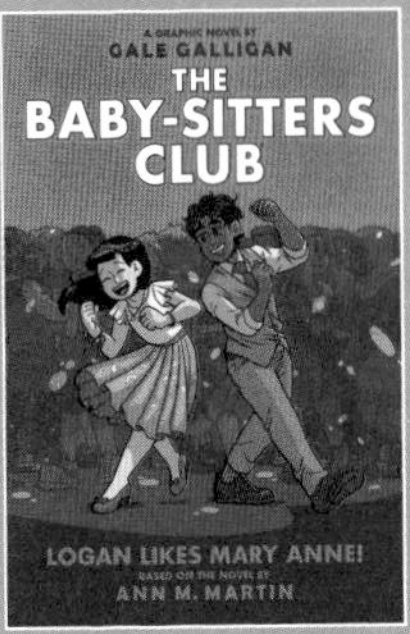
A GRAPHIC NOVEL BY
GALE GALLIGAN
THE BABY-SITTERS CLUB
LOGAN LIKES MARY ANNE!
BASED ON THE NOVEL BY
ANN M. MARTIN

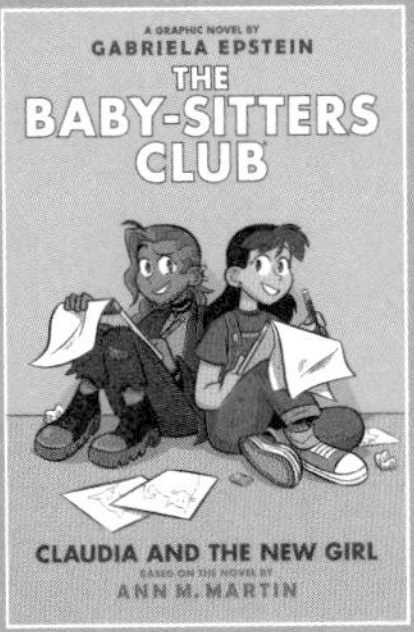
A GRAPHIC NOVEL BY
GABRIELA EPSTEIN
THE BABY-SITTERS CLUB
CLAUDIA AND THE NEW GIRL
BASED ON THE NOVEL BY
ANN M. MARTIN

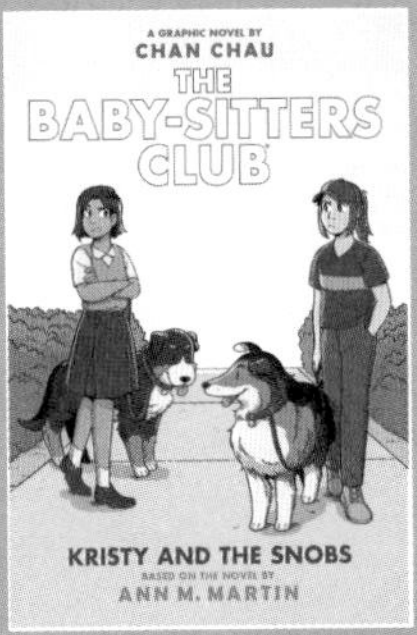
A GRAPHIC NOVEL BY
CHAN CHAU
THE BABY-SITTERS CLUB
KRISTY AND THE SNOBS
BASED ON THE NOVEL BY
ANN M. MARTIN

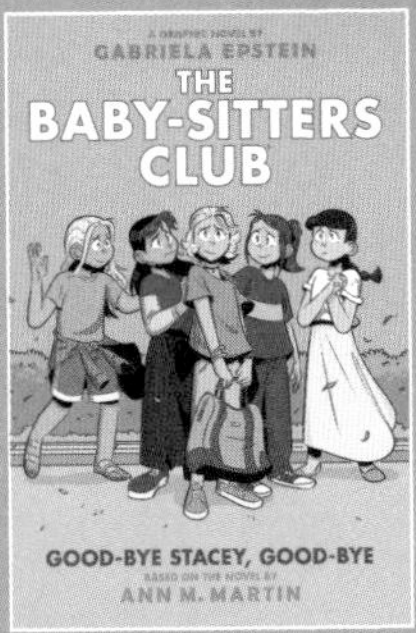
A GRAPHIC NOVEL BY
GABRIELA EPSTEIN
THE BABY-SITTERS CLUB
GOOD-BYE STACEY, GOOD-BYE
BASED ON THE NOVEL BY
ANN M. MARTIN

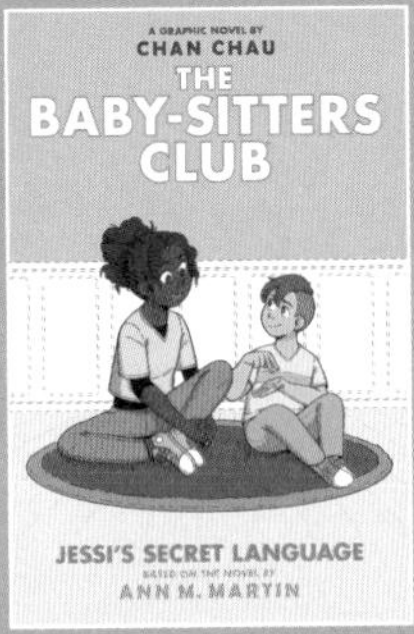
A GRAPHIC NOVEL BY
CHAN CHAU
THE BABY-SITTERS CLUB
JESSI'S SECRET LANGUAGE
BASED ON THE NOVEL BY
ANN M. MARTIN

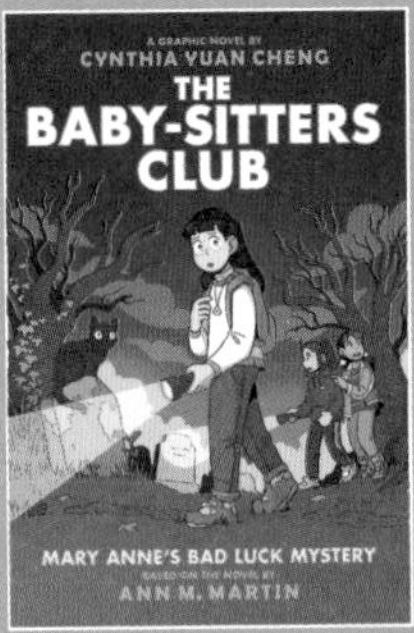
A GRAPHIC NOVEL BY
CYNTHIA YUAN CHENG
THE BABY-SITTERS CLUB
MARY ANNE'S BAD LUCK MYSTERY
BASED ON THE NOVEL BY
ANN M. MARTIN